To:

Brad

———— HILLS ————

Chad Statler

Bloomington, IN  Milton Keynes, UK

AuthorHouse™
1663 Liberty Drive, Suite 200
Bloomington, IN 47403
www.authorhouse.com
Phone: 1-800-839-8640

AuthorHouse™ *UK Ltd.*
500 Avebury Boulevard
Central Milton Keynes, MK9 2BE
www.authorhouse.co.uk
Phone: 08001974150

© 2006 Chad Statler. All rights reserved.

No part of this book may be reproduced, stored in a retrieval system, or transmitted by any means without the written permission of the author.

First published by AuthorHouse 3/10/2006

ISBN: 1-4259-1918-9 (sc)

Printed in the United States of America
Bloomington, Indiana

This book is printed on acid-free paper.

Author photo used with permission by Felix Milfeld.
Cover design by Chad Statler.

In Memory of
Blake Duckworth
May 16, 1990 – April 4, 2005
"Do you prefer ducks or swans?" – Blake

PRAISE FOR "HILLS"

" ... delivers lively action ... along with finely drawn characters. Teen fans who prefer their adventures on an adult level will love this book ... wonderful ..."

– Dorry Catherine Pease
Published fiction, nonfiction author and renowned online editor

"A rare glimpse into the psyche of today's teen. For every young person struggling to understand ... school, life, and the meaning behind it all, this book is a must-read."

– Debbie Wilson
Published Poet and Author
MA English

" ... leaves the reader gripped with suspense at each twist and turn."

– Sharon A. Tricamo
Published Poet and Author
Writer's Society of Jefferson County, Missouri

"... a unique, riveting story that grabs your attention and doesn't let you go."

– John Hudson Tiner
Published Author

_____HILLS_____

1

The intruder breathed heavily as he leaned back against a wall. He cautiously leaned his body around the corner and squinted down the dimly lit hall of the empty school.

Nothing.

Creeping down the hall, he came to an abrupt stop because of a jingle from his belt. Dang keys, he thought. Removing them, he stowed the keys away in his pocket. With them, he could access any room in the school.

He inched down the hall with his back against the wall, being as quiet as possible. He couldn't afford any distractions tonight. His job would take time, so much time in fact, that he had to be careful not to alert anyone. He knew there was a janitor somewhere in the school, so extreme caution was necessary.

Coming to the next corner, he brushed the sweat out of his eyes and strained to see down the darkened hallway. Adrenaline rushed through his veins giving him a feeling he hadn't felt since he was young. The dark sweater hung off his body like a moist towel while the putrid stink of sweat seeped through the black, wool mask that covered his face.

Standing completely still, he listened and waited for any sign of movement. The area was as quiet as a coffin. After a moment or so, he turned the corner and prowled down the hall toward the office.

Silence.

Reaching the office, he jiggled the door handle. Just as he suspected, he'd have to use the small ring of keys now kept soundless in his pocket.

Unlocking the office door, he moved inside and gently shut it. He dashed around the secretary's desk to the Head Staff Hall and passed two offices before reaching the one he was looking for – the principal's office. Rushing through several keys, he found the perfect fit. Pushing inside the office, he twisted around, and accidentally allowed the heavy door to slam shut.

The boom echoed through the office.

The man winced. Frozen in place, his head tilted and listened hoping the janitor had not heard the disturbance.

Nothing.

The intruder slowly let out his breath and turned to find the only computer in the spacious office. Grinning, he walked around the large desk and sat down. The computer held the classified files of students, teachers, income, security and the other things school administrators needed. These files could change a man's life forever.

The computer slept.

Finding the mouse in the darkness, the intruder woke the computer. Opening the file he needed, he began his search and soon pulled up the menu required. The intruder's face relaxed. Maybe this would be easier than he'd expected.

Hank Russell was the janitor on duty that night. He hadn't always worked nights. A few months ago, Hank had worked during the day while the students were in school. Back then, he didn't have many complaints about his job. However, all of that changed when the principal asked if he could work the night shift. Even though Hank didn't want to, he'd accepted the change thinking that it would pay more. With no one to impress, he rarely shaved and even left his frazzled, brown hair intentionally untidy. He simply didn't care anymore.

In spite of this, Hank was proud after finishing his chores. For instance, he had this thing about polished floors. He liked to see his reflection in the floor as he walked across it. He would go around the school and polish a different floor every night.

On this particular night as Hank polished the gym floor, he realized his stomach was queasy. Yawning, he blinked, forced his eyes open and ran his hands over his grumbling belly. He glanced at his watch. It was already past two o' clock. He didn't want to be here tonight. He wanted to be at home in bed sleeping next to his wife.

Maybe, I can just lie down on the bleachers and take a little nap or something, he thought.

A sudden clatter down the hall caused all thoughts of sleep to vanish. It sounded as though a door had slammed. Hank frowned. He was the only janitor working tonight. Who else could have made that noise?

He listened in the darkness, not sure if he'd actually heard a noise. He'd thought he'd heard things before when he worked other nights, but he was never sure. He might have imagined them.

Pulling his flashlight out of his pocket, he headed toward the dark cafeteria. He wasn't supposed to turn on the overhead lights due to budget constraints. Leaving the gym doors open to get what little light he could, he stepped into the hall. He'd probably imagined the noise, just as he had on other nights.

Shining his flashlight around the area, he neither saw nor heard anything. Shrugging his shoulders, he'd turned back toward the gym when his eyes fell on the main office. He knew he would have to clean it soon. He'd been putting it off because he didn't like vacuuming around all the office chairs and desks.

Slouching down the hall, he grabbed a vacuum out of the utility closet and headed back toward the office. Opening the office door, he peered inside and thought he heard a soft fast tapping coming from the Head Staff Hall past the secretary's desk. He slid past the desks and shined his flashlight down the long hall. There … in the principal's office … something caught his eye.

Hank waited for his eyes to adjust to the darkness and then saw a faint light coming from the small crack under the door. He strained his ears for any sound … someone was typing. Hank suddenly realized it wasn't his imagination this time and he wasn't alone.

Turning, he slipped back to the gym where he wouldn't be overheard. Pulling a walkie-talkie from his belt, he gasped, the excitement almost too much for him.

"Uh, this is H – Hank Russell, working the night shift at the high school. We have an, uh, intruder in the school. Repeat, an intruder in the school. Re – uh – requesting immediate backup."

He took a deep breath, now wide-awake. At last, he thought, something interesting around here.

The intruder typed madly as he tried to locate the program he needed. He'd been in the room for nearly ten minutes and still hadn't managed to open it. If he couldn't get to it in another few minutes, he'd have to leave and return another time.

His fingers flew across the keyboard. File after file, program after program. A wicked grin came over his face as the computer finally granted him access. With glee in his eyes, he read the first few lines that faded onto the screen. His scheme was so close to completion. He was going to make it out of the school completely unnoticed and with the information he wanted.

The tingle down his back alerted him before the sound entered his consciousness.

Sirens in the parking lot.

Breaking out in a cold sweat, the hair on the back of his neck stood up and his heart threatened to leap out of his chest.

No, he thought. It can't be.

Removing the small jump drive from his pocket, he shoved it into the port. With some fancy keystrokes and maneuvers, he clicked the Save button but the information was extensive and would take a few moments to save. He heard several different voices outside the office. Breathing in gasps and with his heart pounding, he glanced at the screen, pleading for the computer to finish its task while he formulated his escape.

At last, the computer flashed Download Complete. He snatched the jump drive from the port, closed the files he'd opened and clicked on the Sleep icon. Shoving the jump drive back into his pocket, he stood and put his ear to the door to see if he could hear anything in the office hall.

Nothing.

He cracked open the large door and peered down the hall toward the front of the building looking for movement. Beams of red, white and blue lights blinked and waved off the walls. He saw four officers huddled together, mouths moving and arms gesturing in animated discussion.

Two policemen listened as Hank told them what he'd seen and heard while another two departed from the group and made their way toward the door to the office, flashlights in the air and sidearm holsters unbuckled.

One of the officers approached the office door holding his nightstick almost too tightly in his hands.

"Hey, Crawford," his partner whispered.

"Huh – what?" Crawford nervously replied.

"You okay?"

"Hmm? Yeah, I'm fine."

"You sure? You look kind of shaky."

"Yeah. No, I'm okay."

The truth was that Phillip Crawford was not okay. This was his first call, ever. He'd recently graduated from the academy and joined the Hills West Police Division so Crawford wasn't sure what to expect.

Heart thumping, he advanced toward the office door. The utility belt he wore seemed heavy and uncomfortable. The laces on his boots weren't tight enough. Things just didn't seem right in Crawford's mind. Then again, what did he know? It was his first job.

Crawford pushed his thick rimmed glasses up on his nose and wiped sweat from his brow as he glanced over at his partner, Chris Hendricks, who seemed fine.

Heck, Crawford thought, Hendricks loves this kind of stuff.

The intruder lay in the shadows and watched as the two officers approached the door. If he managed to get out the office door, he might have a chance at getting around the corner. Then he should be able to get down the hall, out the building doors and across the parking lot to his truck.

He thought about the placement of his truck and thumped his forehead. Stupid. He'd parked it at least forty yards away from the doors that morning. What had he been thinking?

If I rush them, I don't have a chance, he thought. If I stay here, I'll be caught for sure. Reaching under his sweater, he withdrew a

9mm from his belt. He hadn't thought he would need it when he had arrived but now he realized that protection was necessary.

The shell racked into the chamber with a loud click. He didn't think he wouldn't have to use it but if he had to, he wouldn't hesitate. He shoved the gun back under his belt where he could easily grab it.

Crawling on all fours, he passed the other offices and printing room door. Underneath the secretary's desk, he paused. For a moment, he listened to his heart as it shook his chest with every beat. His hands twitched on the floor as his wide eyes nervously glanced around the quiet office – he hadn't thought it would come to this. He never imagined he might have to fight his way out of the school. Glancing around the desk, he saw the two officers move closer. Flashlight beams shined through the window as one of them reached for the doorknob.

There's got to be a way out, the intruder thought. There has to be.

His head spun as he looked for an escape. The chair wouldn't help him. The items on the desks were useless. Noticing the water sprinklers on the ceiling, a slight glimmer of hope came to mind. With a quick look at the nearby wall, he found a red fire alarm. The office door creaked slightly as the officers began to enter.

The intruder sprang from under the desk, leapt toward the wall and brought his hand down hard on the fire alarm. A sudden wailing echoed through the empty halls. The police officers jumped at the harsh sound of the alarm and, in that instant, the intruder flew towards the door no longer worried about stealth.

The intruder threw open the door to freedom just as Crawford turned his head. The corner of the door smashed into his face, busting his eyebrow. Whipping backward, Crawford fell to the floor and clutched his bleeding head. Hendricks took a swing with his nightstick but the intruder caught his arm in motion.

He summoned all the strength he could muster and punched the cop square in the face knocking him hard to the ground. Ducking another nightstick coming at him, he turned and sprinted down the hallway.

"Stop right there," one of the officers hollered but the intruder continued to dash down the hall. "Stop or we'll fire!"

At that statement, the intruder yanked his gun from under his belt with his right hand, spun and shot three times at the oncoming officers. Out of instinct, the other two police officers immediately dropped to the floor as Hendricks took cover behind a corner.

"Return fire," Hendricks yelled through a bloody nose as screams of the fire alarm vibrated through the building. Hendricks turned his head to the radio on his shoulder. "Shots fired. I repeat, shots fired!"

Hendricks looked at the two men who had fallen. They didn't seem to be hurt.

"Come on," he yelled, hoisting one of them off the floor. "Let's get him."

The intruder was five feet from the cross-hall on his right when he heard more gunshots fired. Starting to slide on Hank's waxed floor, the intruder realized the sharp turn into the hall was going to be almost impossible to maneuver. Leaping, he twisted in mid-air, landed on his back and slid across the newly polished floor into the next hall.

Bullets hit the nearby wall with a loud burst and drywall exploded in the intruder's face. Jumping up, his head collided with a nearby water fountain. Cursing, he regained his footing and sprinted for the exit door.

As the officers turned the corner and hit the waxed floor, their feet shot out from under them and into the air. They slid across the hall, crashing into the students' lockers and each other.

The intruder turned and fired two more shots in their general direction as he came upon the next corner. One of the officers dropped like a sack of cement at the noise as the other tripped over him and fell hard to the floor.

Flying around the next corner, a bullet sped past the intruder's arm, ricocheted off the floor and shattered the glass exit door. Shards of glass cut into the intruder's head as he plowed through the frame.

Reaching the parking lot, he spun and fired four more times hitting nothing but brick.

Twenty feet from his truck … shots rang out behind him spurring him on even faster. Three bullets rammed into the side of the truck.

Nearly there, another shot then a sudden pain ripped through his left calf like a sharp dagger causing him to trip, fall and roll on the hard cement scratching his face. He landed on his chest ten feet away from his truck – and freedom. Police sprinted toward him, pulling handcuffs from their belts.

Panic flooded his mind. He couldn't be caught. He had to make it. His plan wasn't supposed to end this way. He tried to move his good leg.

As quick as his body allowed, he was up on his left leg, dragging his bloodied right leg toward his truck. He grabbed the truck door, yanked it open, clambered inside and slammed it shut. Quickly shoving the keys into the ignition, he left the officers in a heavy fog and the stink of burned rubber.

From the parking lot, the police fired their remaining rounds at the truck. Sparks flew as bullets hit the cement and bounced off like pebbles on water. One of the bullets blew through the intruder's back window and continued through the front windshield, shattering them both to pieces. Glass rained down on his bleeding leg and lodged into his back and shoulders making it difficult to turn his head without pain. He needed immediate help.

Over the hill in the distance, he saw more flashing lights and his heart sank. He didn't think he had the strength to outrun and out drive the police. However, as lights the emerged over the hill he was relieved to see that it wasn't a squad car but rather two fire trucks speeding down the road toward the school responding to his fire alarm.

He knew the officers would continue the chase. He couldn't afford that, not with a wounded leg. He needed to create something the police wouldn't be able to get past – something like a roadblock.

The intruder's mind raced through the pain. Seeing the broad front of the fire truck, an idea occurred. It might work, he thought with gritted teeth.

Pushing on the gas, he aligned his truck with the first fire truck. The intruder's lips curled as his engine roared over the fire truck's blaring siren. He could see the driver of the fire truck waving his arms frantically for the intruder to move but he did not oblige.

Instead the intruder gripped the wheel tighter as the two vehicles flew towards each other … twenty yards … ten yards … then at the last second the fire truck driver yanked his wheel hard to his left just as the intruder yanked his wheel to his left. The universe stopped as the two vehicles missed each other by inches.

With the sudden jerk of the wheel, the top-heavy weight of the fire truck overturned and smashed on the hard pavement, sparks flying and wheels spinning.

The intruder's truck continued speeding down the road. A glance in his rearview mirror showed the second truck as it slammed into the overturned one with a roaring crunch that shook the ground and boomed into the silence of the night. Taking another quick glance, he saw the firefighters jump out of their overturned vehicles.

Excellent, he thought. The police chasing him shouldn't be a problem with two crashed fire trucks blocking the only road in or out of the school.

Wincing in pain, he clutched his bleeding calf and tried to examine his wound in the darkness. The blood ran down his pant leg and spilled onto the floor of the truck. Speeding down the deserted highway in the middle of the night, he wished he were home – safe and sound.

In his wake, sounds of sirens echoed from what remained of the destruction at Hills West High School.

Three Months Later ...

The bright morning sun rose over the city of Hills West. Autumn was on its way and was not afraid to show it. Leaves had jumped into full autumn colors causing emerald green hills to don coats of oranges, yellows and reds. Grass shook off its morning dew as the sky brightened and birds filled the plate glass sky.

A woman prepared breakfast in her kitchen. Long, brown hair pulled into a bun, her light brown eyes carried that certain twinkle of youth. At thirty-eight, slim and attractive she could still raise the eyebrow of any man.

Glancing out the kitchen window, she watched a hummingbird as it flew from flower to flower going about its daily routine. Hovering over the blossomed honeysuckle, it seemed to glance up at the large white farmhouse before it turned east and zipped away. Olive colored shutters framed the windows that stared out at the large field extending from the backside of the house before reaching the woods that went on for miles.

As she flipped a pancake, a sound came from upstairs. She paused a moment and listened. "Matthew," she called. "I can hear your alarm. It's time to get up!"

The boy stirred in his bed. Reaching over, he smacked his alarm and heard a small crash. He rolled over to see what had made the noise. He wasn't sure if it was his alarm clock or not, his eyes weren't functional yet.

Lying back in bed, he groaned. He hadn't had nearly as much sleep as he'd meant to last night. He blinked his eyes open and glanced at his watch.

Matt had finally made it to sleep last night after two long hours of dread. Today was his first day at a new high school. He'd been a nervous wreck all night. He wouldn't normally be this nervous, except for the fact that he'd been home schooled for most of his life. Now that it was time for high school, his mother wanted him to get some life experience under his belt.

"Matthew."

His mother's voice paused.

"Hey, Matt!"

Matt groaned again. Attempting to put his pillow over his head to block his mother's calls, he only succeeded in knocking it off his bed to join his fallen alarm clock.

"C'mon, Matt, get up before your pancakes get cold."

Oh, that's exactly what I need for the first day of school, Matt thought as he slowly crawled out of bed. No sleep and cold pancakes.

Standing up, he ran his fingers through his long disheveled dark hair, stretched and glanced up at himself in the mirror. Going into my freshman year at five foot nine, he thought. Great, I bet the ladies will be all over me. He turned away, dragged his feet into the hall and began to descend the stairs en route to the kitchen.

Last week, Matt had turned fifteen and had been disappointed not to get the one thing he'd wanted – a dog. He'd asked for a dog every year, but his mother had never bought into the idea. He figured his mom thought it was "just one of those things" that would wear off eventually.

Matt passed the living room and paused. Small piles of parenting self-help books lay on the coffee table in front of the longer couch. He knew his mom worried about raising him alone. She'd bought all of the books feeling she needed the help but he thought she'd done okay. The only problem he found with all those books was the fact that sometimes he had trouble finding the remote control among all the piled books.

Matt yawned again as he sat at the kitchen table where his pancakes waited for him. His mother, Mary, moved to the table holding warm, buttered toast.

"Did you sleep well?"

Matt raised sleepy eyes to his mother. "I get toast, too?"

"Yeah, I think you need a good start, don't you?" She smiled innocently.

Matt's sleepy eyes stared at her with a look of absolutely no expression.

She paused.

Then, breaking the silence, she questioned again, "Did you sleep well?"

"Good enough ... I suppose."

He rubbed his eyes and turned back to his pancakes trying hard not to fall asleep face down in them.

"You know, now that you're a responsible fifteen year old you're going to have to be able to jump out of bed in the morning," she said.

Ever since Matt's birthday, his mother seemed to bring up the words 'responsible' and 'fifteen' all the time. She'd say things like, "You're fifteen now. You should be responsible to take the trash out without me telling you." Or something like, "A responsible fifteen year old would know to do the dishes even if I'm not watching."

Still not awake, Matt finished breakfast, trudged into the bathroom and took a shower. His clothes lay on his dresser. He'd laid them out the evening before at his mother's request.

"Pick out what you want to wear to school now," she'd said, "so you don't have to worry about it in the morning."

Matt had never understood why moms worried about things like that. She probably doesn't have enough to do, he thought.

Once dressed, he packed his school supplies. Grabbing a couple of spiral notebooks, he threw them into his backpack as well as the gym clothes his mom had suggested. Finally, they got into the family's red Suburban and left for school.

"I know you are a little nervous, but it's okay," Mary encouraged as they pulled out onto the long driveway. "There's plenty of kids who have been home schooled and are in the same boat you are."

Matt wanted to say, "Well, I don't like this boat regardless of who's on it," but refrained from doing so.

"This is a walk in the park for you," his mother went on. "I know you'll do fine. Don't be nervous."

"Yeah … right. Nervous? Who's n – nervous?" he stammered in reply.

He tried a weak smile, but the truth was that his heart was pounding as if his chest would split apart. Matt wished he had some friends he could seek out once he arrived at school but friends had never come easy for him. He'd made a few acquaintances with neighbors over the years but he doubted he would get any help from them. He wasn't even at school yet and he felt more lost than he had in a long time.

"You know what?" Mary asked as she pulled onto the highway.

"Wha – uh … What?" he managed.

"I remember my first day of high school. Want to hear about it?"

Matt knew he was about to hear the story whether he wanted to or not so he nodded.

"Well," she began, "the bell rang that first day and students were supposed to go to their first period rooms. My first period was Science so I headed that way – or so I thought. Once I was in the class and seated, I looked around and saw a bunch of upperclassmen. Then I thought to myself, 'This isn't right, I'm supposed to have freshmen in my class,' but I held my seat and when the bell rang my Science teacher came in from the hall."

Mary went on, "He gave us the usual pleasantries. You know 'Welcome. How was your summer?' Yada, yada, yada. Anyway, he began to take attendance calling everyone's name but mine. Then he asked, 'Is there anybody's name I didn't call?' I raised my hand and he looked over my schedule.

"After a few seconds, he told me that I was in the wrong class and escorted me next door to the room where I was supposed to be. I was so embarrassed. It seemed like all the eyes in that class were on me – and they probably were. Then, once I reached my real class all the friends laughed at my stupidity and I laughed too. I sat down with a bunch of my friends and we went on with class.

"The moral of the story is that in the end, after all the embarrassment, everything turned out okay. The embarrassment wore off and nobody remembers things like that. So don't worry."

Oh, great encouragement story Mom, he thought. Before we talk about the cool and exciting things about high school, let's review all the most horrific and embarrassing things that could go wrong.

"Remember," his mom went on, "just walk in, make sure you're in the right room and make it seem like you know what you're doing. Everything will be fine."

Okay, okay, okay. Matt smiled thinly at his mom and tried to regulate his breathing.

Matt saw the enormous school through the thicket of trees. It seemed as if half of him wanted to stay in the car never to come out while the other half wanted to hurry up and get through the year. He didn't know which side to agree with.

Mary pulled into the school's long driveway. Suddenly, Matt's hands went cold. Rubbing them together only seemed to make it worse. The giant brick building loomed closer like an angry monster preparing to make Matt its meal for the year.

"Remember, I'll be here to pick you up after school," Mary said with a sweet smile. She looked at him and noticed the sweat that lined his forehead.

"Honey, are you okay? You look kind of pale."

She slowed the car.

"Yeah. Yeah, Mom, I'm cool. I'm fine. Don't worry," he lied. He was nowhere near 'cool' or 'fine'.

He gaped at the tall school. How was he supposed to find his way around that place?

A thought came to mind. Opening his backpack, he unzipped his binder and grabbed the schedule he'd received in the mail. On the backside of the schedule was a detailed map of the entire school. His classes were printed on the front. He'd kept it safe, enclosed in his binder like a treasure. Glancing out the window, he saw the drop off area. Once again, his heart pounded and his palms went cold.

"Just remember what I told you," his mother said. "Act as if you know what you're doing, and everything will be fine."

Mary stopped the car and Matt stared out the window at the towering school as he waited for blood to flow back into his legs.

"Go on, then," Mary urged. "Go ahead. I'll be right here after school to pick you up, okay? Good luck."

"Yeah – yeah, Mom." Matt wasn't listening. He drifted out of the car and stepped onto the sidewalk. Looking back, he gave a slight wave to his mom as she drove away.

There is no turning back now, he thought.

Other cars pulled up unloading other kids his age. All sorts of students jumped out of the dozens of vehicles that were lined alongside the school. Some looked like walking zombies while others hugged and talked with their hands. Nice even tans adorned their bodies. Matt figured they had just gotten back from the Bahamas or something.

He stepped out of the way when a couple of students on skateboards rolled past the sign that read, NO BICYCLES, ROLLER SKATES, OR SKATEBOARDS ALLOWED ON THE PREMISES.

His eyes blurred at the mass of confusion – bodies moving, backpacks dropping, buses unloading, teachers laughing, boys yelling, cars honking, girls giggling ...

Matt shook his head. How was he supposed to manage all year long? Only a few feet from the door, Matt realized his hands were still frozen.

Stepping inside, Matt's eyes widened when he found himself in a gymnasium-sized cafeteria. He stared at the high ceiling of the cafeteria and could see what looked like two more floors above him. Each floor had a balcony that surrounded the cafeteria. From the ceiling, a black and silver flag hung with a huge picture of what looked to be a pirate. The flag read, HILLS WEST EAGLES. FIGHT, EAGLES, FIGHT!

A dull tone suddenly erupted over the noise of the students and made Matt jump. What is that, he thought. The fire alarm?

It stopped.

"C'mon, people. That's the bell," a voice called. "Keep moving. You've got six minutes now."

Matt looked toward the voice to see a tall man wearing a tight belt that held in his well-fed stomach. Short, brown hair faded into patches of gray and a thick goatee covered his face. The engraved nametag on his chest read, Dr. Richard Pierce, Principal.

Okay I've got six minutes, Matt thought as he pulled out his schedule.

Locker # 4488   Class: History of Man
                                       Hour: 1st

Locker Combination: 1-11-33   Rm. #: 118
                                       Teacher: Mr. Shane Brakeman

Matt began walking as his mother's advice echoed in his head, "Just act like you know what you're doing … Just act like you know what you're doing …"

He walked up a set of stairs to the second floor and noticed the row of two lockers, one on top of the other, lining one side of the hall. Matt wished he had a hundred eyes as he looked in every direction. He found it difficult to read the teachers' names above the doors, look at his map and watch out for students that rushed by jabbering with one another.

Matt managed to squeeze his way through the crowded hall and headed upstairs to find his locker. When he finally found it, he saw it was surrounded by another large group of people.

"Excuse me," he said trying to push his way through. "Sorry. Trying to get to my locker."

Someone elbowed him in the gut and to make things worse when he did get to his locker, it was on the lower row.

Just my luck, he thought as he kneeled, worked the combination and examined the inside. Even though it was a half-body locker, it still had lots of space. He got what he needed out of his backpack, threw it and his other things inside and fought his way back out of the crowd. Pulling the map out of his pocket, Matt located where he was and where he had to go.

Just as he turned the corner, a girl emerged from a small group of friends and caught Matt's attention like no other girl ever had. The noise of the chattering students around Matt slowed to a crawl. All noise and rowdiness ceased. Matt's attention was focused solely on this one person.

Matt wanted to stare and stare some more though he knew he shouldn't. She looked to be slightly shorter than he was. Her long auburn hair flowed to just beneath her shoulders. Her eyes were green sparkling emeralds and it was easy to see from her figure that she was fit and took good care of herself.

While she laughed with her friends, she glanced at Matt. Matt wanted to look away with everything inside him but his eyes weren't responding. He might never see something like her again.

Her laughing slowed to a smile. Was she smiling at him? Maybe?

She walked past him and he watched her go as the chaos of the hall returned with a deafening roar. Matt had never known a girl to have that kind of effect on him.

Forcing himself to turn away, he collided into the biggest human body he'd ever seen. His biceps bulged like dumbbells and his knuckles were molded pieces of metal. His shaved head with signs of sprouting facial hair gave him that skinhead look.

"Hey, punk, watch it."

He grabbed Matt at the elbows making him drop his binder.

"What da' heck is yer problem?"

Matt had no idea what to say in reply.

"Can't a guy walk wid' out hav'n to see a dirty maggot like you gettin' in his way? Get in my way again an' you'll end up worse than y'are now! Get it?"

His giant finger waggled in Matt's face. Matt eyed it making sure it didn't poke his eye out.

"Get it?" the dinosaur snapped. "Or are ya' deaf, too?"

"Uh … y – yeah … umm … yeah," was all Matt managed.

"Yer deaf, huh?"

Matt's vocal chords shut down on him. "Wha – what … no – uh, no! I'm, uh … I mean, yeah! I can hear."

"Then ya' got it?"

"Yeah … uh, yeah. Got it."

"Good. Now git."

Matt quickly scooped his binder off the floor and had started around Big Foot when he stuck a boot in Matt's path. Matt tripped and fell face-first onto the hard floor much to everyone's amusement. The big guy laughed and lumbered off the other way.

"I'm fine. I'm fine," Matt said angrily as he stood again and brushed himself off. "Don't everybody help me up at once. Stay calm. I'm okay."

Shaking his head, he headed for the stairs. He'd gone from seeing the most beautiful person in the world to seeing the biggest person in the world in less than a minute. That must be some kind of record or something, he thought.

Still, he did see that girl. And he was pretty sure that she saw him.

Matt walked down the hall trying to find Mr. Brakeman's room for his class, History of Man. Remembering his mom's anecdote, he checked the door to be sure it was the right room. Once he had double-checked, he entered.

The dark red carpet was the first thing Matt noticed. The room had five rows of desks with five in each row. Some students were already sitting and they didn't seem to be in any particular order.

The man who sat at the podium in the front of the class sported light-colored hair that draped over his ears in a disheveled mass. Matt guessed he visited the gym on a regular basis and maybe ran daily. He looked fit. That must be Mr. Brakeman, Matt thought.

The dull tone rang as it had earlier and Matt reminded himself that this was just the class bell. The remaining students in the hall scattered about in an attempt to reach their first period class before their teachers began roll call. Matt took a seat near the middle of the room just as Mr. Brakeman put his papers away and looked up at the class.

"Sit down, everybody."

After a moment or two, he said, "How y'all doing?"

Mr. Brakeman had a distinct Southern accent that caught Matt's attention. "As y'all may've guessed, I'm Mr. Brakeman."

Some of the students shifted in their seats.

"I'll learn all of your names soon. I assume that y'all had a good summer?"

Mr. Brakeman paused as if he expected someone to say something.

He broke the awkward silence. "All right. If that's it then, let's get started."

He began to take attendance.

"Craig Aster."

"Here."

"Brett Brick."

"Here."

He continued calling names. Matt listened but Mr. Brakeman reached the end of roll call without calling his name.

Matt's mind raced. I double-checked the room number before I came in here, he thought. This isn't right.

Mr. Brakeman looked up from the list. "Now, is there anybody's name I din call?"

Matt looked around to find he was the only person with his hand in the air.

"Ah, a slacker huh?" Mr. Brakeman said with a joking smile. "C'mon up here, boy, and bring your schedule with ya'."

Matt cautiously approached the front of the room and handed him his schedule.

"Do ya' have your ID with ya'?" Mr. Brakeman asked loud enough so the other students could hear.

"My what?" Matt replied quietly.

"Ya' know. Your i – den – tif – i – ca – tion," Mr. Brakeman said as if Matt didn't understand English.

"Uh …" he stammered. "I've got a driver's permit."

Some of the students laughed along with Mr. Brakeman.

"No," he said. "Did ya' get an ID for school? Like this."

Mr. Brakeman showed Matt the ID badge around his neck. It had his picture, name and school logo on it. Matt shook his head.

"Are ya' new?" he asked.

Matt nodded. "I was home-schooled. This is my first year."

"Ah, okay." He handed Matt's schedule back to him. "Then the office people must have not marked ya' down on the roster because it's the beginning of the year."

Matt sighed with relief.

"What's your name?"

Mr. Brakeman bent over his desk and wrote as Matt said, "Matt Cross."

"Okay, Matt. I'll make sure they get ya' on the roster." He handed him a piece of paper. "Ya' need to take this pass and go to the office. Ask if they can give ya' an ID."

Matt turned and walked back to his seat, grabbed his map and left as Mr. Brakeman continued class.

The door to the office was along the wall near the cafeteria. He recalled seeing it as he had entered that morning. Matt reached the office and opened the door. A secretary sat at her desk behind a long counter taking calls on multiple phones.

"Hills West High School, please hold," she said. Then, she clicked another line. "Hills West High School, please hold."

Matt walked up to the counter and contemplated all the papers scattered on it. He wondered how the woman made sense of it all.

"Uh ... excuse me," he said. "I got this pass from –"

The secretary held up a finger. "Please, hold," she said without looking at him.

Matt waited and listened to her as she tried to stay current with all the calls. Becoming impatient, his eyes wandered and he noticed a hallway extending beyond the back of the secretary's desk. A sign nailed to the wall next to the desk read, HEAD STAFF HALL. STAFF ONLY BEYOND THIS POINT.

Must be the principal's office down there, Matt thought.

Waiting a few more minutes, Matt realized that he was never going to get the ID badge if he didn't do something to help himself. Standing, he walked around the secretary's desk and down the hall. The women never looked up from the phones.

Signs above the offices read, MRS. ANNE RASHLY, STUDENT COUNSELOR ... MR. SCOTT FEARS, ASSISTANT PRINCIPAL ... and then DR. RICHARD PIERCE, PRINCIPAL.

Matt stopped and tapped on Dr. Pierce's door. From inside someone called, "Come in."

Matt opened the heavy door and saw a large man sitting at an impressive oak desk with a flat screen computer on top. Surprised at the size of the office, nearly the size of Mr. Brakeman's classroom, he stopped. On the wall behind the desk, an old black and white sports poster boasted of an athlete going up for a jump shot in basketball. A large drawing of a mean looking Eagle wearing a black and silver jersey hung on the wall to his left.

Dr. Pierce sighed and glanced at his watch. "School hasn't been started for, like, five minutes and you've already been sent to the office?"

Matt paused unsure how to reply.

"Well, don't just stand there," Dr. Pierce snapped. "Sit down and tell me what happened and we'll find a suitable punishment. And shut that door."

Matt turned and shut the door. He could still hear the secretary saying, "Hills West High School, please hold" down the hall.

Turning back to face Dr. Pierce, he sat down. "Is it always this hectic around here?"

"Oh no," Dr. Pierce said. "It's the first day of school. It's crazy like this for maybe three or four days and then things start to settle down."

A silence descended.

"So …" Dr. Pierce leaned back in his chair. "What did you do?"

"Oh," Matt exclaimed. "Nothing."

"Typical. Someone else did it, right?"

"What – no, I was just … uh – Mr. Brakeman gave me this pass and he, uh, sent me here, see, to get an ID."

"An ID?"

"Yeah, all the cool kids have 'em. So I want one, too."

Dr. Pierce laughed. "Smart guy."

"I guess." Matt shrugged.

"Okay, let me go get the camera. Don't go running off now, I'll be right back."

He got up and left as Matt waited in the chair. Soon though, he was up and walking around the room, looking at the newspaper articles posted on the walls, *"Eagles Win 53 to 52 Against the Vikings"* and *"Hills West Beats the East"* and *"Eagles Heading to State"*.

Next to one of the football pictures was a small excerpt from an old newspaper. The headline read, *"Retired Science Teacher Leaves His Fortune to Hills West School District."*

Curious, Matt crept around the desk to get a better look at the small print.

> Clarence Williams, 52, died yesterday of a massive heart attack. As a former science teacher at Hills West High School, hundreds of people including faculty members and students attended the funeral service.
>
> Williams taught for over 30 years at Hills West retiring last year. Many of the students and teachers who attended the service reported they thought of him less as a teacher and more as a friend.
>
> "He met his students on a different level ... than any other teacher," former student Phyllis Long recalled. "[He reminded] me of my own family."
>
> His wife, Angelina Williams, 48, heir to the Murraine Estate and fortune announced she will write a check to the school's Science Department for over 1.2 million dollars as specified in Clarence's will.
>
> "He always talked about how he wished Hills West had a better science program," she said, "so the money will be donated specifically to the Science Department of Hills West High School."
>
> Angelina Williams has decided to sell the Murraine Estate and remain on the West Side of Hills. She says she is "trying to get away from the rich life."
>
> She will be ..."

"What are you doing?" Dr. Pierce kindly interrupted as he came in with a camera and other pieces of equipment.
Matt jumped. "Oh, I was just checking out the articles and pictures. This school's got some kind of a success rate, doesn't it?"

Dr. Pierce smiled as he set the equipment on the desk.

"Yes, it sure does. We work hard to keep it that way too."

He walked over to the poster of the basketball player going up for the jump shot. Matt noticed that the lettering under the poster read "EAGLES LOSE BY ONE SHOT".

"See this poster?" Dr. Pierce asked.

"Yeah." Matt stepped up beside him.

"This guy, here, going up to shoot is Ron Harver. He played for North Front."

Dr. Pierce paused.

"Man that was a good game," he went on. "Well, not exactly, because we lost but you know what I mean."

Leaning closer to the picture, he pointed. "Do you see this guy behind him?"

Matt nodded.

"That's me. Ever since I was a little kid, I've loved basketball. I used to play here. I was supposed to be guarding Harver. He was their top scorer but I lost my concentration for maybe two seconds. Suddenly, he had the ball."

He sighed as he recalled the event.

"I tried to stop it, but he'd already shot. The ball went in just as the buzzer went off. We lost by two that night. It was our only defeat of the year."

"Wow …" Matt said quietly.

"Yeah." Dr. Pierce gave a small laugh. "You see that's one of the reasons I became the principal of this school. Now I supervise everything that goes on and make sure that no one in this school ever loses their concentration again. This poster reminds me that the school can always be better, always. No matter how good we think we are, can always get better."

Dr. Pierce dropped his eyes and turned back to his desk. "So, how about that picture?"

As the day progressed, Matt felt better. Things weren't as bad as he'd thought they were going to be but then it was only fourth period. He glanced at his schedule and headed in a new direction. He was supposed to go to Ms. Sarah Ellis's English class in room one-thirty-three.

Matt walked into Ms. Ellis's room and saw twelve desks on one side of the room and twelve on the other. Both sets of desks were facing the middle of the room. This way the teacher had a path she could walk up and down while she taught.

Matt sat down. Voices from the hall caused him to glance up at the door and there was the gorgeous girl he'd seen earlier that morning.

His heart stopped.

Separating from her group of friends, she walked in and took a seat on the opposite side of the room. She tossed her beautiful dark hair out of her face and leaned over to say hello to another girl. Matt found himself staring again and tried to compose himself before she noticed.

The bell sounded and a young woman entered the room. Long straight blonde hair flowed down her back as she strolled in and stood in front of her desk. Her clothes were neatly pressed as if she were an executive. Small diamond earrings caught the florescent glow of the lights on the ceiling. She stopped at the front of the room and waited for the students who hadn't found a seat.

"Hello, everyone," she said. "I am Ms. Ellis, your English teacher. I hope everyone has had a good first day so far."

A few students with their heads down on the desks groaned in response.

"Good," she smiled brightly. "Glad to hear it."

The lecture soon became the same as every other class Matt had attended so far, so he laid his head down on his arms and listened as Ms. Ellis went over the rules and expectations. He noticed other students sleeping at their desks. Matt felt like doing the same.

It became difficult to keep his focus. His head rested on his arm as he tried to stay awake. If only I could be in bed with the covers over me with no worries, he thought. He'd curl up with his pillow, the picture of his father watching him from the nightstand.

In the picture, Matt, his mother and his father stood with arms around one another while on vacation. The sunset behind them was red and gold over the blue of the sea. Taken a few months before the accident, they all looked so happy. Matt wished they could be happy like that again but it just didn't seem possible. His father, Brian, had died when Matt was four and Matt didn't think he'd been truly happy since that time. His mind began to drift as these thoughts poured into his consciousness.

Matt came home from pre-school all those years ago and dashed upstairs to his bedroom. He'd been waiting all day to get home and play with the new video game his dad had given him for his fourth birthday. Busy playing, he almost missed the ring of the phone.

"Hello?"

"Is Mary Cross there, please?" a voice asked that Matt didn't recognize.

"Uh ... hang on. Mommy," he called for his mother who was cooking dinner downstairs.

A few seconds later, he heard his mom pick up the phone from the kitchen. "Hello?"

Matt hung up the phone and gone back to his game when his mom's shouting rose over the sound of the game.

"What?" he heard. "What hospital?"

'What hospital'? Matt thought. Who's hurt?

"Matt, Matt. Hurry," his mother called from downstairs. "We've got to go to the hospital, baby. Get your shoes on."

Matt switched off the game and reached for his Velcro-laced shoes.

What's going on? His mind raced. Whatever it was, he knew the situation was serious by the urgency in his mom's voice. Matt grabbed his jacket and threw it on as his little legs sprinted down the stairs.

"What's wrong, Mommy? Why are we leaving?"

"Daddy's in trouble, sweetheart," she said quickly as she led him out the door.

Matt had never seen his mom this upset. From the passenger seat, Matt could see his mother's chest rising and falling. He was beginning to get scared.

"What's wrong with Daddy?" he asked. "What happened?"

"Apparently, your father was in a car accident," she said. "We're going to see him now at the hospital."

Matt's small mind tried to decipher this new information. He furrowed his brow. "Will he be okay, Mom? He'll be okay, right?"

The look his mom gave him didn't reassure him. "Yeah, sweetheart. Yeah, he'll be fine."

Daddy will be okay, Matt thought. Mommy said so. He repeated this over and over again in his head as they sped down the road.

At least twenty minutes passed before they arrived in the hospital parking lot. Matt and his mother jumped out of their parked vehicle and ran through the automatic sliding doors into the Emergency Room. Matt tried to keep up with Mary as she ran up to the front desk. The receptionist pointed the two of them in the right direction. Mary took Matt's hand and the two of them dashed down the hall. As they'd turned the corner, a white-coated man nearly collided with them.

"Excuse me, ma'am," he said. "This hallway is for family and personnel only. We can't have people running around our halls."

"I am Brian Cross's wife, Mary Cross," she breathed heavily. "And this is his son, Matt."

The doctor glanced down at Matt and back up to Mary. "I'm Dr. Black, Brian's doctor. Follow me please."

"What's wrong with Brian?" Mary asked as she ran along beside the doctor.

"He was in a car accident. I really can't give a full report on how badly he's hurt. My staff is with him now."

The doctor ushered them down the hall and into a room where a few chairs sat and a TV stood in the corner – the waiting room.

"Please stay here until we have finished examining him. It may be a while." Dr. Black turned and hurried out of the room.

Matt and his mother sat on a hard blue couch near a desk that housed numerous out-of-date magazines. For close to forty minutes, Matt's mom had sat, paced and sat again.

Every nurse who passed by the room was asked if she could see Brian and they all gave her the same response, "We will inform you as soon as we know something, ma'am."

Matt turned the television on and watched it while his mother stood in the doorway glancing up and down the hall. Almost an hour later, his mom sat in a chair next to the door and began to pray.

"Oh Jesus, dear God, please don't let any harm come to him. Please, I beg of you …"

Another half hour passed when Matt noticed a doctor heading toward the waiting room. Something told Matt this was the moment of truth. He started to pray as best as he knew how. He'd seen people hold their hands together and bow their heads when they prayed at church so he tried that. Matt prayed silently with his hands folded in his lap as he asked God to save his daddy.

Dr. Black walked into the room. Mary stood and Matt, seeing his mom stand, did so too. The tears in her eyes frightened him and he clung to his mother's hand.

Dr. Black lifted his eyes. "Your can see your husband now."

Mary let out a breath that she'd been holding for over an hour.

"If you'll follow me, please …" Dr. Black turned and led the two of them down the hall.

"I want to prepare you for what you are about to see," he said. "We've tried to clean Brian up as best we could, but he's still bleeding in some areas. He may be bleeding internally."

"What happened?" Matt's mom asked.

Dr. Black glanced at her as he continued to walk. "He was hit head-on by something. We don't know what. Apparently it was a hit and run incident. Unfortunately there were no witnesses at the scene to describe who or what hit him. Whatever it was, he's lucky to have gotten this far."

Dr. Black stopped at the Emergency Room door.

"Because you have your son with you, I must warn you that Brian has many broken bones. We don't know the extent of the damage yet. If he is bleeding internally then we'll have to operate. But right now, we're waiting for more test results and for a specialist to arrive.

"Brian's in and out of consciousness and I don't know if he'll even understand what you're saying. I tried earlier and all he managed was, 'I know him'. He's on heavy pain medication. He doesn't know what he's saying. The good news is that his vital signs are stabilizing and he's breathing on his own. Please, only speak with him for a few minutes. The specialist will be here soon. As soon as I know any more I'll let you know."

"Thank you, doctor," Mary whispered.

"And another thing," Dr. Black paused. "You might want to prepare your son. I don't know if I'd let many children see him."

"All right. Thank you."

The doctor nodded and walked away.

Mary knelt down to Matt's height. "Baby?"

"Yeah, Mommy?"

"Daddy's pretty banged up. He really looks bad. You don't have to see him if you don't want to."

"No, Mommy. I want to."

"Are you sure? He doesn't look like himself."

"I want to see Daddy!"

"All right." She stood and took his hand. "Come on, then."

They walked through the Emergency Room until Mary spotted Brian's name on one of the doors. Opening the door, she walked in first with Matt following behind. He shut the door without any noise as if that would make the difference between life and death for his father.

When Matt looked up to see his dad, his eyes went wide. His mother was right. He hardly recognized him. Mary grabbed Matt and put him on her lap. From this angle, Matt knew that under all the bandages, scratches and odd-looking braces, this was his dad.

Beep … Beep … Beep … Matt's eyes moved to the heart monitor above the bed.

Mary touched Brian's arm. "Hey, sweetheart."

He looked exhausted. Matt thought he was asleep.

"Brian? Baby?" Mary said sweetly.

Brian's swollen eyes had slowly opened and Matt resisted the urge to hug him.

"Oh ... hey," Brian whispered.

"There you are. How are you?" Mary took his hand in hers and gently kissed it. "You've given us quite a scare, you know?"

"Yeah," he took a shallow raspy breath through his trembling lips. "I'm doing as well as ... I c – can be." He coughed a hacking sound. "I guess ..."

Brian smiled but with all the deep cuts on his face, Matt knew it must have hurt. He wanted to cry. Maybe he shouldn't have come ...

"Look who's here," his mom said looking at Matt.

"Hey, champ ... how are ya'?" Brian winced as if a sudden pain had struck him. Slowly, his face cleared.

"I'm good. Are you okay, Daddy? Does it hurt?"

"I'll make it ... How'd ya' ... how'd ya' l – like that new video game I ... I bought ya'?"

"I love it ... Dad."

"What happened?" Mary asked, leaning forward. "The doctor said someone hit you."

"Yeah ..." He took a slow breath, trying to control his trembling. "I was g – going down the road ..."

He took another breath and stopped as if someone had snatched his voice box. Then he began coughing again. Matt wanted to cover his ears and block the sound out but he knew that wouldn't work. He wished with all his might that the coughing and pain would stop. After a few more seconds, the hacking subsided and Brian relaxed again on the soft pillow beneath his frail head.

"The doctor told us you were saying that you knew him," Mary said.

Brian stared at her and a curious look came over his face.

"He said you mumbled something about knowing the driver," she went on.

Brian sighed as he closed his eyes. "I don't remember."

Mary frowned.

"You know …" Brian said suddenly as he drew in another raspy breath. "The car's – eh … the car's totaled. My arm, ribs, ankle and n – neck are broken … I probably shouldn't … shouldn't be alive r – right now."

"Don't talk that way." Mary tightened her grip on his hand. "Just thank God, you are here, right?"

Brian caressed Mary hand with his thumb. "I'm feelin' b – better than … I was earlier."

Matt stared at his dad. The person under the bandages talked like his dad but he sure didn't look like him. The scratches and gashes along his face made him appear disfigured. One jagged gash showed under the bandage right above his right eyebrow. The cuts and the neck brace scared Matt. He had an awful sinking feeling in the pit of his stomach.

"You're going to get out of here," Mary whispered. "We're going to get through this, okay? It's just another bump we have to get over. We can handle this. No matter what happens, be strong for me, for us."

"I will, Mary." His breath quieted and his eyes closed.

Tears welled in Mary's eyes. "You are not going to die here. We're going to have more kids. You're going to be around so we can spoil them. They'll grow up and have grandchildren and we'll spoil them too. We'll both die old in our sleep after we've lived out our lives." Matt heard the desperate tone in his mother's voice. "That's how it's going to be, right? That's what we've always talked about. You have to be strong, Brian. Promise me that you'll be strong."

With eyes still closed, he muttered just above a whisper, "I … promise."

Dr. Black knocked on the door and peeked in the room. "Excuse me, but the specialist has arrived. It's about time you two left."

"All right," Mary said without looking at the doctor. He nodded and left.

Mary sighed as she gazed into her husband's eyes. "That's our cue. You'll be strong, right?"

Brian winced in pain. "Eh – yeah."

"All right." Mary kissed his hand again. "We'll be back in a little bit, okay?"

"I love … you, Mary."

Her loving smile spread across her face and Matt watched her cheeks turn a deep shade of red.

"I love you, too, sweetheart." She gently ran her finger down his cheek. "Give Daddy a kiss, Matt, and tell him we'll see him later."

Mary lingered as Matt kissed his father's hand, then taking Matt's hand she led him to the door.

"Hey … M – Matt."

Turning, he looked at his father. "Yeah?"

Brian met his son's eyes and managed a weak smile.

"I love ya' … son."

"I love you too, Daddy."

Once Matt and Mary knew Brian would be okay for the night, they crossed the hospital to the cafeteria. After their meal, Matt eyed the ice cream machine and asked his mom if he could have an ice cream cone. She agreed and got one for herself too.

"They have good ice cream here," Mary said as she took a bite of her cone. "But I'm not planning on coming back for the ice cream."

Matt smiled through a mouthful of ice cream. He agreed, they had good ice cream here but that wasn't enough of a reason to come back. He would never come back to this place again.

They headed back to the Emergency Room to get an update. Walking down the hall, they heard a commotion coming from the Emergency Room. "Get Cross to surgery – stat," someone had yelled.

Matt's mom gasped and he'd looked up to see her eyes go wide with fear. Instantly, he knew that something bad had happened. Mary rushed down the hall, dragging Matt as he'd stumbled along trying to keep up with her.

"Come on, Matt." Mary urged him along.

One of the nurses tried to stop them. "Ma'am, you aren't allowed down there."

But they'd already turned the corner.

Dr. Black intercepted them in the hall. "Mrs. Cross, please don't run."

Mary's breath was coming fast and hard. "What's wrong with my husband?"

Dr. Black sighed and lowered his eyes for a moment. "He's unconscious and bleeding internally. His vital signs are failing. My staff is doing the best they can to revive him. Please go back to the waiting room. I'll come back shortly with an update."

Mary hadn't moved. She stood there in the hall staring at the doctor. Matt tried to understand what was happening. Finally, she nodded and turned back toward the waiting room, straight as a steel rod. Dr. Black turned and hurried down the hall.

Matt sat beside his mom on the rough blue couch in the dimly lit waiting room. As soon as they sat down, his mom started to pray again.

He interrupted her. "Mommy?"

She stopped praying. "Yeah, babe?"

"What's eternal bleeding?"

"Not eternal bleeding, sweetie. It's internal bleeding. It's when someone is bleeding on the inside of their body."

Her eyes had closed and she went back to her prayer. For at least another hour, Mary's praying never ceased. Matt wanted to turn on the television but thought that he would get in trouble if he interrupted his mother's praying.

Matt glanced at his mother. She was crying. Why is she crying, he wondered. Daddy's all right. He promised he would be all right. Mommy said he would be all right.

Mary rocked back and forth in her chair as she prayed. Matt's eyes had begun to water and he felt a sob form in the depths of his throat. She was making him very nervous.

Matt looked down the hall to see Dr. Black approach. "Mom," he said.

She looked up, took a few short breaths, managed an "Amen" and then stood.

Dr. Black looked into Mary's swollen red eyes and gently shook his head.

"I'm sorry ..."

The doctor's voice stabbed Matt's mind like an iron pitchfork. He began to cry tried to get into his mother's arms. He would be safe there, he knew. But she had already collapsed to the floor.

Her screaming and crying had gone on for days. Matt still heard her screams in his nightmares.

Mary dropped her fork. It clanged on her dinner plate, snapping Matt to attention from his daydream.

"Matt, could you pass the rolls, please?" Mary asked kindly.

It was dinner that night after his first day of school and the two of them had been quiet during the meal. Matt was nearly finished eating his chicken when his mom said, "Matt? We need to talk."

"About what?" He took another bite.

"Your Uncle Bruce called today."

"Uncle Bruce? Dad's brother? We haven't seen him since Dad's funeral."

"I know, babe. Well, he and I talked for a bit. He said that he's good and his business is working out well for him. He also said he had some business near Hills and wondered if it was possible for him to come and stay with us for a while."

A piece of chicken fell from Matt's mouth. "What? We haven't heard from him in eleven years and he wants to come stay with us?"

"See that's what I said but your Uncle Bruce said he was sorry for not being around. He said it was too hard for him to think about Brian. But he wants to be here now."

"Why?" Matt asked. "There's no point. We're getting along fine by ourselves. If he wanted to help us he should have called us eleven years ago."

"Well, it's not that simple, sweetheart."

"Why?"

"I got a call from the bank about a week ago," she said. "Apparently, there's been some confusion with the house payments. After your father died, I thought the money was all okay but the bank tells me it wasn't. Now we owe the bank a lot of money. Money, we just don't have right now."

"So you want to have Uncle Bruce come and help us?" Matt asked. "You mean like charity?"

"No," Mary said sternly. "I don't want charity. However, I do think that Bruce would be an asset to the household. He can help us with the finances. He feels he would be paying off his debt for blowing us off for all those years and if he helps us, maybe we won't lose the house."

"We could lose the house?" Matt was startled.

"Not if we come up with the money."

Matt thought a moment. "Exactly, how much money do we owe the bank?"

"The bank says that if we can't come up with eleven thousand dollars in the next eight months, they'll have to foreclose."

"Eleven thousand dollars?" Matt asked bewildered. How could they come up with that money that fast? "Eleven . . ?"

". . . thousand," Mary finished for him.

"How could you not know about this?" Matt asked in disbelief.

"Your father and our banker were always good friends. He let it go for a long time after your father died but he finally had to draw the line. He gave me a call a few days ago to let me know how serious it had gotten."

Where were they going to get eleven thousand dollars? Matt knew money was tight sometimes, but he'd never thought they were going to lose the house over it. The bank couldn't take the house away. His father had built this house. His spirit was in every stud and nail holding it together.

"I've done the math," his mother went on, "and we simply can't make that kind of money in eight months."

"I could get a job or something," Matt offered.

"No, babe. I appreciate your concern but I've already made arrangements with your uncle."

"What?" Matt felt uneasy. "You've already told him he could come? You never asked me about this."

"I'm sorry but I had to make a difficult decision for the both of us."

Matt threw his chicken leg onto his plate in aggravation. "Well, fine. If you're sure you know what you're doing, then you just go do it then."

Mary nodded. "Good. Bruce said he'd be here tomorrow afternoon."

5

Matt's eyes flew open as his alarm blared in his ear. He moaned as he smacked it and rolled over. He'd barely gotten any rest last night and now he had to get up again. Getting up at this time everyday would be no easy task. Forcing himself out of bed, he prepared to take on the second day of school.

The silence in the car that morning caught Matt's attention. He looked at his mom from the passenger seat as they sat in traffic heading for school. Her elbow was propped on the window ledge and her head leaned on her fist. A look of impatience penetrated her face.

"What's wrong, Mom?"

"Oh, nothing really." A long sigh escaped her lips.

"Are you lying?"

"Well … I don't know. Last night I was looking through one of my old scrapbooks for pictures of Bruce. I found one of him before Brian's funeral and it made me think … I'm beginning to wonder if letting him come and live with us was a good idea."

"Why wouldn't it be?"

"Well … Bruce showed up at your father's funeral and that night he and I talked. I told him a lot of the things that were going on in our lives. Actually, I pretty much poured my soul out to him because he was the first one who had actually sat and listened. He tried to be comforting. I mean, after all, he is your father's brother."

Mary seemed deep in thought as she went on.

"After a while we stopped talking because I had to tend to the other visitors. Bruce headed over to a group of young ladies …"

She paused.

"Those ladies were probably in their early twenties – beautiful, mind you. He began joking around with them. He became so loud and disruptive that people began to whisper about how rude they were getting. After ten minutes or so, I went over and asked them to step outside if they were going to continue. Now, don't get me wrong – I like a good joke every now and then. Any other time would be a great time to joke around, just not then."

She paused a moment again and ran her hand through her hair. Matt could tell the memory was really upsetting.

"I don't know." His mother tightened her grip on the steering wheel in frustration. "The only time I recall talking to him was that night, but he seemed so different with those girls than when he'd been talking to me. I guess I just don't know him."

There was an awkward silence between the two of them until Mary changed the subject. "So, do you think you're going to make some friends today?"

"I don't know." Matt shrugged. "I hope so. I wasn't so successful yesterday."

"Well, I'll be hoping you do." She pulled the car up to the school.

Matt grabbed his backpack and jumped out of the car. "Thanks. Bye, Mom."

He shook his head as she drove away. What if Bruce was obnoxious like he'd been at the funeral, he thought. What would someone like that do to our family?

Matt didn't know, but he certainly wasn't looking forward to finding out.

"Mornin' class," Mr. Brakeman said as he shut the door.

A low sleepy rumble of, "Mornin'" came from the students.

"Before we get started …" He sat at his podium. "I think I should tell y'all about your final project. It's very early in the year to be thinkin' about semester finals, I know. However, for this year I've decided that we won't be takin' written finals."

Some of the students opened their eyes at this news.

"Instead of a written final, I think that y'all would enjoy something else much, much more. I'm thinkin' if every student in my class does fifteen hours of recorded community service a semester, then people all over the city would benefit from it."

Students interested in what Mr. Brakeman had to say a moment ago, dropped their heads back to their desks and drifted off to sleep again.

"So how 'bout it?" Mr. Brakeman asked. "Community service sound good? I think it's a good idea. Anyone have any questions before y'all get your memo thingy?"

Nobody said anything.

"Okay, then. If there aren't any objections, I'll hand out the paper and log sheets."

"As y'all can see on the sheet," Mr. Brakeman said as he passed a handful to each row, "the whole shebang is worth two hundred and fifty points a semester. It's a big part of your grade. I put a long list of ideas that y'all can do for community service on the back. You need to have fifteen hours a semester signed by the adult supervisor and given back to me before it's time for finals."

He looked up. "Cool?"

No response.

"Okay. Cool," he answered himself.

The tedious classes that day seemed to drag on forever.

Matt had pushed his mother's story of his uncle to the back of his mind and found himself slightly anxious to see him again.

Matt thought Gym would be the one class that would go by the fastest. He was, of course, wrong again. They sat and learned the rules of baseball the entire period and were only able to play the game for about ten minutes. Then, it was time for them to change out of their gym clothes and wait for the bell to ring.

It wasn't long before Matt was outside waiting for his mother. She was late. Matt looked at his watch, almost twenty minutes late. Where was she? He'd been waiting for the last bell to ring all day and now he had to wait even longer. Just when he thought she'd forgotten about him, her Suburban pulled around the bend. He got in the car and Mary greeted him with an apologetic smile

Soon, they headed into their driveway and, nearing the house, Matt could see a large green truck parked in the driveway and a man sitting in the old rocker on the porch.

Wiping sweaty hands on his jeans, Matt exited the car as his uncle came down the front steps to greet them. Bruce had the same build as Matt's father — tall with broad shoulders. His clean-shaven face beamed as his short black hair and leather jacket rippled in the breeze.

"Hey," Bruce exclaimed. "Matt, is that you? No way."

He reached out and gently laid his hands on Matt's shoulders. "You've got to be kiddin' me. Last time I saw ya', you were this tall."

He dropped his hand down below his belt to illustrate. "Wow, let me look at ya'."

He sighed as he stared into Matt's eyes.

"Yep, you're my nephew, all right. You're the spitting image of your ol' dad."

Mary approached. "He sure has grown in the last eleven years, hasn't he?"

"Yeah and you're looking more and more beautiful every time I see you."

She blushed. "It's good to see you, Bruce."

He paused and looked the two of them over again.

"Well … I've been sittin' on that porch for about a half hour. Let's take the party inside, shall we?"

Sitting in the living room, Bruce soon revealed what he'd been up to for the last eleven years. He told stories of the different jobs he'd had and the places he'd been. He'd drifted around for five years after the funeral. He'd gone from place to place, looking for work, never staying for more than a month or so. He mentioned he'd been to every continent except Antarctica. "But I've got the plane tickets to go anytime," he laughed.

Then after drifting around, he said he'd settled down in his small apartment and started his own business selling power tools over the internet. He could do that job anywhere and it accommodated his lifestyle.

As Bruce finished his storytelling, Mary went to the freezer and pulled out a few large steaks for dinner.

Bruce jumped up. "Oh no, Mary. You've worked hard all day. Please sit down – let me cook."

That definitely scored some points with Mary. Matt had to give Bruce credit for knowing how to make a good first impression.

After a mouth-watering dinner, Mary gave Bruce the tour of the house and then escorted him to his room upstairs.

Matt went to his room to begin his homework. Just as he wrote his name at the top of his worksheet, he could hear the soft mumble of voices of his mother and uncle across the hall. He laid his pencil on his desk and softly approached the closed door across the hall to listen in on their conversation.

"Would you like me to help you unpack?" Matt heard his mom ask.

"Well sure, if ya' like," Bruce replied. "I can always use the company."

Clothes hangers rattled.

"So Mary?" Bruce said.

"Yeah?"

"How's Matt been doing? I noticed he wasn't very talkative durin' dinner."

"Oh …"

A pause.

"He's just not used to another guy around. That's all. You know how it is. He's trying to getting by – trying to keep good grades. He's been telling me about the girls he's seeing at school. It's kind of cute, you know? Reminds me of when I was a freshman. I was going out with this guy named Scott through most of high school. I thought I would spend the rest of my life with him."

Another slight pause. "Heck … I didn't even meet Brian until my senior year. Then, you know … Matt came along."

"I know … it must be hard sometimes," Bruce replied in a slow drawl.

"Ah, well it's …"

Matt envisioned his mother biting her bottom lip. It was a frequent gesture when she was thinking about what to say.

"It … it's hard all the time," her voice shook.

I shouldn't be listening to this, Matt thought, but his feet remained planted.

"I can imagine," Bruce said quietly.

"You have no idea …" she cried. "I've always wished I had someone to help me parent."

The bed creaked and then creaked again.

She went on, "When Brian was around, he did that. Once he died, I had no idea what to do. I still have no idea."

The catch in her voice hurt Matt. He'd never understood what his mom had gone through raising him by herself.

"Shh, shh, shh …" Matt heard Brain say softly. "Why do ya' think I've come all this way? Now, ya' don't have to try as hard. I'll give ya' a little nudge – whenever ya' need it. I'm here to help."

Matt barely heard Bruce whisper, "Don't you worry."

The silence was deafening.

Matt strained to hear something, anything, but there was nothing.

His mind went crazy.

He couldn't see anything and so leaned in ever so slightly to the crack in the door. Mary faced Bruce, gazing up into his eyes. His hands rested on her shoulders.

Mom, Matt's mind exclaimed, that's Uncle Bruce, not Dad. What the heck are you doing?

Almost as if she'd heard, Mary blinked and snapped back from wherever her mind had been. His mother glanced at the full suitcase of clothes still lying on Bruce's bed. "I think you are nearly finished unpacking, then? Good night, Bruce."

She turned toward the door rubbing tears from her eyes. Matt stumbled back, quickly turned and fled.

"Bruce, how many slices of bacon do you want?" Mary asked the next morning standing over the sizzling pan on the stove.

"Oh … three, I guess," he said over the rim of his coffee cup. He glanced back at the newspaper in his hand.

"Hey, Mary." Bruce sat his mug down.

"Yeah?"

"I think ya' should know something," he said.

"What's that?"

"I got Matt a little gift before I got here yesterday. It's in the barn right now."

"Oh?"

"Yeah, I thought it would warm him up a little. Like ya' said, since he's probably not used to another guy around."

"What is it?"

"Oh, ya' know ... nothing big, just –"

"Well, hello sunshine," Mary exclaimed as Matt trudged down the steps. "I was going to let you sleep a little while longer."

"I ... uh ... woke up when I smelled bacon. You never make bacon anymore."

"Well, have a seat," Bruce said cheerily. "We'll get ya' some bacon straight away."

Matt sat patiently in his Science of Life class. The morning sun shone through the windows and brightened the wide science lab. Several gadgets and tools spread out across the room. There were numerous sinks and Bunsen burners in the back of the room. A television sat in the corner with multiple stacks of videos and discs beside it.

Mrs. Raidner, the seventy-two year old science teacher, flipped through her textbook and dropped her bookmark. When she bent to pick it up, the textbook fell out of her hand and to the floor as well.

"Oh, dear," she muttered.

This was normal. Matt had almost gotten used to the white-haired Mrs. Raidner fumbling through her lessons. Resting his arms on his open textbook, he dropped his head and sighed.

This was going to take a while.

"Class, could ... would everyone turn to page sixty-six, please – uh ... read the pages here?" Mrs. Raidner began. "We'll take notes when you're all ... done – finished."

Much of the class was already on page sixty-six but Matt kept his thoughts to himself. He looked down at his book and read:

Newton's Third Law of Motion
For every action there is an equal and opposite reaction.

Sounds like something written on a fortune cookie. Matt thought with a smile as he read the rest of the page.

After a moment or two, Mrs. Raidner brightly asked, "Finished? Well, then … I'll just turn on this contraption here for our … uh – notes."

She flipped the switch on the projector but nothing happened. "Uh, why isn't it … working?"

The students tried to stifle their laughter as Mrs. Raidner cleared her throat and flipped the switch on and off while the electrical cord swung freely from the projector cart.

Matt glanced at the clock and prepared himself for a long class.

"Well, if the uh … projector won't work …" Mrs. Raidner admitted defeat. "Well, then I guess I'll, um – have to read them to you and you all will have to write as I read."

"No!" the class exclaimed in unison.

It would take Mrs. Raidner at least two days to get through a page of notes at this rate and there was no way the class would sit through that. A student sitting two seats in front of Matt raised his hand. "Um – Mrs. Raidner," he said. "I think I know the problem."

He stood, snatched the plug dangling from the cart and plugged it into the wall. He turned and on his way back to his desk, flipped the switch on the projector. It immediately hummed to life.

"Oh, yes," Mrs. Raidner said. "I knew that was supposed to – uh …" She stopped and smiled at the class. "Very good. What is your name, young sir?"

"Blake Gross," the boy said.

"Well, um – good job, Mr. Gross, at uh – assisting me. I will tally ten extra credit points to your record at the end of class."

Matt rolled his eyes, doubting that Mrs. Raidner would even remember to add ten points to Blake's grade.

"Right, um, okay then. We'll – uh – begin the lesson with … would everyone turn to page sixty – uh – five … I mean six. Sixty-six, please."

Mrs. Raidner noted that everyone already had their books turned to page sixty-six. She blinked. "Uh … right, then. Newton's Third Law of Motion: For every action there is an equal and opposite reaction …"

The bell rang.

Matt jumped out of his seat and scrambled out of the room squeezing himself through the herd of students surrounding his locker.

Squatting down to his low locker, he worked the combination. Gaudy laughter could be heard above the crowd from the center of the hall.

Matt turned on the floor and looked through the forest of legs from the walking students. He could scarcely see the child in the hall. Her face was pale and her eyes wide. Matt stared and then realized that this was not a child. She was a teenager.

Wow, she has to be only about three and a half feet tall, Matt thought.

Matt had never seen anything other than a child her size. Her small hands carried a large math book and notebook looking to drop at any moment. She threw short brown hair out of her face and looked up at the three tall seniors that loomed over her, nasty grins spreading across their faces. Her white fingers clamped around her books as if they would never let go again. Stepping back, she looked from side to side as though pleading for someone to stop the taunting, her cheeks a deep shade of red.

"Hey, midget. Do us a trick," said the biggest one.

Matt recognized him as the giant who'd tripped him on the first day of school.

"Buzz off, creep." She whipped around and headed in the opposite direction.

"Oh," he replied with a tone of sarcastic fright. "Did Mini-me jus' call me a 'creep'? What'll I do? What'll I do?"

His buddies snickered.

The girl looked over her shoulder at the three of them with intense eyes. "I'm serious, you jerk!"

"You know what, Randy?" one of them said to the giant. "I wonder how much she weighs – probably, forty pounds, fifty maybe? Let's see if the janitor will notice her in the trash can …"

"C'mon guys," Randy smirked. "Let's take out the trash," then added, "… where she belongs."

Randy advanced on the small girl.

Matt shook his head and turned away. Don't get involved, he told himself. Just go to class.

Matt gulped down his anxiety and glanced back at the girl again. No, this was too one-sided. Nobody deserved that kind of ridicule. He doubted she'd ever done anything to those guys.

His mind made up, he jumped up and pushed the students surrounding him out of his path. "Move it. Out of my way."

The three had the small girl backed up against the wall now. She had nowhere to go so she slid down it and sat. Randy sneered, his massive hand reached down to grab the girl when Matt, against his better judgment, jumped between the two of them.

He grabbed hold of Randy's wrists and shoved. "Don't touch her!"

Randy looked surprised. "Hey, it's you, again." He poked at Matt's chest. "Didn't I tell ya' not to get in my way again?"

He stepped in front of Matt's face, challenging him.

"Just go," Matt snapped. "Why would you pick on her? Just walk away."

Randy stepped back. "Ya' know what?"

He paused. "I don't think so."

"I mean it," Matt said a little more forcefully. He had no idea what he was doing, but he knew, for sure that he was about to get his face rearranged if no one came to his aide.

"What ya' gonna' do 'bout it if I don't, huh? Fight me?"

Randy suddenly lurched at Matt's shoulders and threw him against the wall. "See what happens when ya' get in my way?" he hissed. "Ya' get fixed."

With his last ounce of courage, Matt defiantly said, "Try it."

To Matt's surprise, Randy dropped his head and stepped back, looking to his buddies with a sigh. A look of regret came over his face as he nodded.

Good, Matt thought as he exhaled and allowed the blood to run back into his face. It's over ...

In the blink of an eye, Randy's massive fist flew through the air and slammed into the side of Matt's face. Matt collapsed to the ground on top of the little girl as hot stinging pain danced across his jaw. He tasted blood.

"What ya' gonna do now, huh?" Randy barked looking down at him. "Got anythin' else you'd like ta say?"

Any students who weren't already paying attention to the argument gathered around the fighters. If a teacher who wanted to break up the tussle would have to squeeze through a jungle of students to get to them.

"Stand up," Randy demanded.

Matt rolled off the girl and she attempted to crawl away from the growing mob of students.

"Shawn! Terry!" Randy shouted to his friends. "Grab the midget."

Shawn and Terry scooped up the little person by her arms, like a rag doll. Her books and purse fell from her grasp, spilling open, allowing her personal feminine items to roll across the floor like marbles. Laughter burst from the students as they pointed at the sight.

The girl's face turned a deeper shade of crimson as she struggled to pick it up, but Shawn and Terry did not loosen their grip on her arm.

"Get up," Randy yelled at Matt.

Matt tenderly touched his face as he got to his hands and knees and looked up at the towering senior. Randy threw another solid fist solid into the side of Matt's face and again Matt dropped to the floor with a hard thud.

"C'mon, you," Randy bellowed in Matt's ear. "Be a man. Get up and fight."

Much of the hall had gone quiet as they watched Randy and Matt. Matt winced but managed to hoist himself onto all fours again, trying to stand.

An enormous leg slammed into his ribs.

Matt cried out in misery just before the wind in his lungs vanished and he collapsed for the third time, gasping and coughing.

He felt so helpless but there was little he could do. Every time he tried to get up, Randy knocked him down. How could he possibly fight?

"Stand up," Randy demanded. "Or have you had enough?"

Matt laid chest-down on the floor. He felt like he'd had enough. He winced in pain. The cold tile felt good on his face. He didn't want to get up.

Randy leaned over to admire his handiwork. "So, that's it, huh? That's all the fuss yer gonna do? You can do better."

He threw his boot into Matt again on the same side of his body. Matt recoiled and sputtered as he tried to curl into a ball.

"Tha' all?" Randy seemed disappointed.

He threw his oversized foot into Matt's side again and Matt's chest heaved.

"Yer pathetic," Randy sneered as his foot repeatedly struck Matt's body.

Matt cried out in pain and struggled for breath as he turned blurry eyes to the onlookers. He stretched a trembling hand toward the other students. That was when his fingers fell upon something – a strap … the small girl's purse strap? He fought back tears as his trembling fingers took hold of it.

Randy shrugged. "Well, that's that."

He grabbed Matt by the shoulders and tried to hoist him to his feet so he could finish him off and declare victory. Eye level with Randy's belt buckle, Matt exerted his last ounce of remaining strength and swung the girl's purse. It came up hard, right between Randy's legs. Randy's eyes shot open as he grabbed his crotch with a wail and dropped.

Matt collapsed to the floor and gasped for air as he tried to crawl away. Randy's eyes flared and his teeth clenched. As his anger intensified, he launched himself through the air and tackled Matt to the floor with both arms whirling.

Matt curled into a ball, his body throbbing with pain. He could feel blood running down the side of his face. He felt it running down his throat in a thick wad as well.

Wasn't anyone going to stop this? Why didn't someone do something? Tears rolled down his cheeks merging with the streams of blood and fell from his face.

Suddenly, the assault stopped. He heard Randy struggling with something.

Cautiously, he removed his arms from over his head and saw another student behind Randy, one arm wrapped around his neck. Whoever this person was, he had clutched Randy's throat with his forearm and was leaning in close to Randy's ear.

"Didn't you hear him, Randy?" he growled. "He said beat it."

"Oh, how's it goin', Andrew . . ?" Randy sarcastically managed through his gasps. "How was … yer summer?"

Randy elbowed Matt's savior in the ribs, causing him to loosen his hold. In an instant, Randy rolled on top of Andrew and started to pummel him with powerful hits and punches.

Matt tried to creep away glancing at the small girl still held by Shawn and Terry who had not budged from where Randy had told them to stay. His gaze fell back to the fight between Andrew and Randy. Andrew couldn't even move with Randy on top of him like that.

Randy's fist slammed against Andrew's cheek and Matt could see blood stain his teeth. Not a second later, a girl with long blonde hair jumped into the fray, onto Randy's back and pulled him to the ground. Randy threw the girl off his back and sent her rolling into the crowd.

Twisting back to Andrew, Randy stood and reared his leg back to kick Andrew just as he had Matt, but the girl reappeared, grabbed Randy's ear and yanked him to the ground with one hand, while punching and smacking him as hard as she could with the other. Andrew recovered his breath and attempted to move his sore body to assist the girl.

"Break it up! Move. Everyone, out of the way," a voice rose from down the hall.

Matt sighed with relief.

Rescued …

The girl stopped smacking Randy, allowing Matt to observe the look of pain that came over Randy's eyes as he struggled to get the girl to let go of his ear. Shawn and Terry exchanged worried looks, released the small girl and sprinted down the hall.

The little girl fell beside Matt to see if he was all right. Matt replied with a painful nod.

Dr. Pierce broke through the ring of onlookers. The blonde girl immediately released Randy's ear and Randy managed to stand, wiping blood from his lip. He grinned at the sight of Dr. Pierce.

"Hey, Mr. P," he said casually. "How's it goin'?"

"It's *Dr. Pierce*, thank you." He pierced Randy with a look of hostility. "And things were going fine until I was informed by my cameraman that you had started a fight with a freshman. Lily – of all people – does not need that kind of attention."

The small girl's dropped her eyes to the floor as Dr. Pierce mentioned her name. Dr. Pierce turned to the swarm of onlookers who still encircled the combatants.

"Hey, fights over," he growled. "Go on, get to class."

As the crowd thinned, he peered at the bleeding students lying and standing around the hall.

"Mr. Stang," he said to Randy. "One might have thought that nine months in juvenile hall would have done you some good."

"Yeah." Randy grinned. "They din' like me a whole lot – so I left."

"Hmm … yes, I'm sure that's how it went." Dr. Pierce's sarcasm flowed.

Pushing Randy out of way, Dr. Pierce grabbed the blonde girl off the floor and reached down to Andrew only to gasp at the sight of their injuries. He looked around, examining the others. The girl who had come to Andrew's aid had hardly a scratch on her. However, Andrew had a bloody nose and a cheek that was beginning to swell. Matt, with a bruised jaw, bruised ribs and a bloody mouth, appeared to be the worst of the lot.

Dr. Pierce spun back to Randy and pointed a sharp finger in his face. "Undoubtedly, you started this mess. Why don't we all go back to my office and look at what the cameras have to show about all this, eh? I'm sure they got every last detail."

He gave Randy a slight shove in the direction of the office.

Andrew helped Matt off the floor and they limped down the hall toward the nurse's office. Lily and the blonde followed.

"Hey," Dr. Pierce called over his shoulder.

The four turned back.

"Where do you think you're going?" he yelled. "You think that you four are going to get away clean? No, you're coming too."

6

Randy winked at the secretary as Dr. Pierce shoved him into his office.

"Marie," Dr. Pierce stopped and said to the secretary.

"Yes, Dr. Pierce?"

"Call Nurse Francis and have her come down here with some Band-Aids and ice packs to patch these kids up."

"Yes, right away."

Dr. Pierce turned toward Matt and the other three. "As for you all, wait over there until the nurse arrives."

He pointed to five chairs sitting in the corner as he continued down the hall toward his office.

"Dr. Pierce," called an African American boy in a wheelchair from down the Head Staff Hall. "I put the footage of the fight in the top drawer of your desk."

"Thank you, Mr. Loveland," Dr. Pierce replied with slight irritation in his voice. "I appreciate it."

Dr. Pierce shoved Randy into his office, slamming his door so hard that it bounced back from the latch leaving it slightly ajar.

There was an awkward silence between the four who sat in the waiting room.

On the walls, posters hung listing different things a person could do instead of getting into trouble. Some of them were downright silly. One read:

"101 THINGS TO DO INSTEAD OF DRUGS".
    1. Watch a flower grow …

At the bottom of the poster someone had written, "DO DRUGS" in permanent marker. Apparently, the secretary hadn't caught it yet.

Matt watched Andrew as he licked blood from his wounded lip and tried to look as if he were feeling all right. Rubbing his hands over his shaved head, Andrew leaned back in his chair and tried to rest. He reached up and wiped blood from the small patch of facial hair on his chin.

Andrew exceeded Matt's height by a few inches and judging by the massive size of his arms was undoubtedly active in sports. Andrew looked to the blonde freshman girl who had leapt into the fray to help him.

"You okay, Abby?"

Abby nodded and leaned back in her seat.

Matt's eyes fell to the little girl sitting next to Andrew. Her small legs dangled several inches from the floor. Her pert nose sniffled as she sat on small, shaking hands not wanting the others to see.

Matt cleared his throat and looked at Andrew and Abby. "I – uh … I want to thank you two."

Andrew and Abby's attention swung to Matt.

"Really," Matt continued in a quiet voice. "I was …" He paused and couldn't think of a word to define exactly what he was. "Well, thanks."

"It's not that big of a deal, really." Abby's voice was weak.

"Yeah," Andrew smiled. "I've wanted to do that to Randy for over a year now."

"And I couldn't let anything happen to Andrew," Abby went on. "I had to at least try to help him. Dad would have hated to make a trip to the hospital."

"I didn't need help, Abby," Andrew spoke matter-of-factly. "I was handling the situation just fine, thank you."

"Sure you were." Abby rolled her eyes. "Right up until you jumped in."

"You two are brother and sister?" Matt interrupted.

"Unfortunately." Andrew sighed.

Matt gave a weak smile in response. He could still see Randy's fist slamming into his face and his boot throwing itself into his ribcage. His body cringed. He tried not to think about it.

A question came to mind. "When I was … well, you know. Why'd you help me?"

Andrew took a deep breath and replied, "Well, I knew if I told Dr. Pierce that Randy was picking on Lily then there was a chance I wouldn't get suspended or anything. Dr. Pierce has a soft spot for …"

He stopped and glanced at Lily, forgetting she was in the room.

"He does not," Lily snapped. "I'm just the same as everyone else. I wear the same clothes as everyone else. I have a family like everyone else. I go to this school like everyone else. How much more like everyone else can I be?"

"Sorry, Lil," Andrew said. "I didn't mean it like that."

"Well, like I said," Matt interrupted. "Thanks again. I owe you guys one."

Andrew nodded.

"My name's Andrew, by the way. Andrew Backer. I'd shake your hand but there's blood on it."

Matt smiled. "I'm Matt."

Andrew looked at Abby. "This is my little sister, Abby."

She gave a weak smile. "Charmed."

"And, of course, you know Lily. You know I —"

A large middle-aged woman approached with ice packs and Band-Aids in hand. "Never fear, Nurse Francis is here," she chirped.

As Nurse Francis began to patch up their injuries, Matt heard harsh voices coming from within Dr. Pierce's office.

"Listen to me, Mr. Stang," Dr. Pierce growled. "The year has just started and I'm about ready to expel you right here and now."

"Why don't ya'?" Randy shot back.

"Don't push me, Mr. Stang. I've sent you to juvenile hall before. Don't think that I am not capable of doing it again."

"Actually," Randy's voice bragged, "ya' know, that place wasn't half bad. The food was good and I learned mo' crap there dan I ever did 'ere. No hard feelin's if ya' send me back, all righ'?"

"No, Mr. Stang," the emphasis landed on the last name. "It's not 'all righ'. It's not that easy. If it were my decision, you'd be out of here right now."

"But ya' can't do it alone, can ya'?" Randy said with what sounded like glee. "You'd 'ave to take it up with my uncle, wouldn't ya'? 'Member him? The assistant principal?"

Dr. Pierce sighed at this remark and collapsed in his chair.

"That's right. Unfortunately, Mr. Fears is your uncle, and your mother is determined that you get an education, not that you care. If I had my way, you would have been gone a long time ago. However, since your mother and uncle are constantly breathing down my neck, it seems to be more trouble than it is worth."

Dr. Pierce sighed and Randy smirked.

"And so, yes Mr. Stang, I would have to take it up with the assistant principal," and then he added, "and your mother."

"Well, then, if yer done …" Randy moved toward the door. "I've got some learnin' to do. Gotta get back to class, ya' know? Don't wanna miss anythin' important."

"Sit down, Mr. Stang," Dr. Pierce barked.

The chair groaned as Randy flopped back into it. "What now?"

Dr. Pierce reached for the walkie-talkie on his hip. "Sixty-five to sixty-six. Do you copy?"

A moment or two later a deep male voice responded, "This is sixty-six. Go ahead."

"Sixty-six, what is your location?" Dr. Pierce asked.

"I'm in gymnasium one. Over."

"Could you come to my office for just a moment, please? I have a situation that requires your assistance."

"I'm on my way."

Less than a minute later, a clean-shaven man with a blunt chin appeared in the doorway to the office. He was a bit shorter than Randy. However, he shared many of the same features as his nephew. His large arms looked as if they were about to bust out of his shirt as his squinty eyes scanned the office.

He glanced at the four sitting obediently in the corner and moved to Dr. Pierce's office. Opening it, he leaned through and said, "Yes, Dr. Pierce, what do you —? Oh."

Mr. Fears sighed, stepped into the office and closed the door behind him.

"What are you accusing my nephew of doing now, Dr. Pierce?"

"Your nephew has been fighting again," he replied.

"Really?" Mr. Fears paced behind Randy.

"Yes, and you can't stop the punishment this time."

Mr. Fears stopped pacing. "Why don't we take a look at the camera footage and see what it has to say about this?"

"With pleasure."

Dr. Pierce opened the top drawer of his desk and pulled out a video. He flashed it in front of Randy's face before inserting it in the VCR.

The screen lit up starting the scene where the bell rang and students poured into the hall. Lily walked against the side of the wall with her books in hand. Randy and his buddies were walking in the opposite direction.

One of Lily's books dropped and as she started to pick it up, Randy stomped his foot on it causing her to jump. Bending over to pick up the book, Randy kept what looked to be a malicious eye on Lily. He gently handed the book to her.

"There ya' go," he said through the jumble of the hall. "I didn't want you to bend down so low to pick yer book up. Ya' might get stuck. Oh, whoops — too late."

Lily held the book tight to her chest as if it was going to jump out of her hands. Through the legs of the other students, the three of them could see Matt sitting at his locker. He had turned toward the commotion.

Lily tried to walk away from Randy's group but the words, "Hey midget. Do us a trick," came through to the viewers. The two men and Randy continued to watch the scene until the fight was broken up and the students were sent scurrying.

Dr. Pierce turned the film off with the click of his remote. "As you can see, Mr. Fears, it was terrible. Your nephew could have sent that freshman boy to the hospital if the other two hadn't jumped in."

"Right you are, Dr. Pierce." Mr. Fears stood a bit straighter. "However, if you were watching the tape, you would have seen that Randy was trying to help the girl pick up her books. Is that a crime?"

"No, but –"

"No, it is not," Mr. Fears went on. "And, if you were watching the footage a bit closer you may have also noticed that the freshman boy pushed Randy first. So therefore, Randy acted in self-defense."

"Self-defense? The freshman was beaten to a –"

"Okay, here's what I'll do," Mr. Fears interrupted again. "Because I know we'll be discussing this for days."

Dr. Pierce paused. "I'm listening."

Mr. Fears glanced down at his nephew and back up to Dr. Pierce. "I will give my nephew one week of an out-of-school suspension."

Randy jumped from his seat. "What? Uncle –!"

Mr. Fears cut him off. "Yes, one week of an out-of-school suspension."

"He could have hospitalized that student," Dr. Pierce exclaimed. "The severity of this incident is grounds for expulsion."

"You shut up," Randy hollered thrusting his finger in Dr. Pierce's face.

"Randall!" Mr. Fears shouted stifling his nephew.

Mr. Fears composed himself and looked back to Dr. Pierce. "Yes, that is very true. He could have been hospitalized. But the year has just started. The out-of-school suspension will act as warning. If anything happens that's remotely related to Randy …"

Randy sighed and his shoulders slumped. "Am I done?"

"Yes." Dr. Pierce leaned to the intercom on his desk. "Marie? Contact Mr. Stang's mother and inform her that he has received one week of an out-of-school suspension. And send in the other students."

"Yes, sir."

Dr. Pierce turned back to Randy. "Now, get out of here."

Matt, Lily, Andrew and Abby limped into Dr. Pierce's office with new bandages and holding ice packs on their faces.

"And the saints come marching in," Dr. Pierce said sarcastically.

Once the four of them had found a seat, he began.

"Well, congratulations on being the first group sent to my office this year for fighting. Unfortunately, I don't have a prize or something for you. Normally, I would bring you in here one by one, however, I'm tired of this day already and I'm sure you are too. Giving out detentions and suspensions is our main priorities today so I'm not going to sit and debate this so don't try. First, we're going to watch the tape of the incident."

He clicked his remote, and the film began. Matt tried to turn his gaze away from the television, but he had to watch. With every kick Randy threw, his ribs throbbed with pain. Within moments, Dr. Pierce arrived on the scene.

"Okay," Dr. Pierce said as he clicked off the screen. "I just want you all to know that I'm on your side. I think Mr. Stang deserves much more punishment than the four of you. However, it is true Mr.... . Cross, isn't it?"

Matt nodded.

"It is true Mr. Cross, that you touched Mr. Stang first."

Dr. Pierce stopped almost as though he expected Matt to defend himself. Matt was quiet so Dr. Pierce went on.

"And, I know you barely got a hit in but that does not excuse you from the rules of this facility. The rules say I should suspend you, but I believe it was Mr. Stang who stepped over the line this time. So instead, I think detentions are in order ... one week."

No one said a word, so Dr. Pierce continued, "As for you Lily, you will not be punished. You didn't do anything to anyone today."

Lily sighed with relief.

"However, you two ..." Dr. Pierce motioned to Andrew and Abby. "You two will join Mr. Cross in one week's worth of afternoon detentions."

The four students nodded. They had to accept the terms. Like Dr. Pierce said, he wasn't about to debate it.

"Your detentions begin next week." Dr. Pierce waved them away. "You are dismissed."

———

That night, before dinner, Matt explained what had happened. Mary wasn't happy about the idea of Matt fighting but she told Matt she'd rather him be in detention than be suspended.

"Actually, I'm thinking of grounding you," she said.

Bruce stepped in. "Listen, I feel the same way about this whole thing as you do, Mary. But I also feel that Matt was right to stand up to old what's-his-face?"

"Randy," Matt said.

"Right, Randy." Bruce continued, "Matt should be rewarded, not punished."

Bruce studied Matt, "In fact, speaking of reward …"

He grinned. "Follow me, Matt."

Matt frowned and looked at his mother who shrugged as Bruce opened the front door and went outside. Bruce led Matt and his mother through the yard to the barn where he opened the large wooden door.

"I was going to give this to ya' yesterday," Bruce said. "But I never really got around to it."

He walked toward a rusty fence near the back of the barn, opened the gate and grabbed an overturned box. "Hey, there ya' are."

He picked up the box and brought it to Matt.

"I heard that you've always wanted a dog, Matt." Bruce winked at Mary and Matt's eyes widened in excitement.

Approaching the box in Bruce's hands, Matt gasped as a small, black Labrador puppy peeked over the box edge with bright beady eyes. His long floppy ears perked and his long tail began to wag uncontrollably at the sight of Matt.

"Oh my gosh," Matt exclaimed with a huge smile. "I don't believe it!"

Matt reached into the box, grabbed the puppy and held it in his arms. The puppy's tail wagged madly as it licked Matt's laughing face.

"His name's Newton," Bruce said with a bright smile. "The guy who sold him to me … well, ya' could say he thought it would be funny if he named all the puppies after great men of history. I had a choice between Einstein, Michelangelo, Caesar, da Vinci, Isaac Newton or Socrates.

"Newton here was the best looking one and I couldn't resist. However, I think Newton is too long of a name for a dog so I've been calling him Newt. He doesn't seem to mind."

"It doesn't look like it." Matt laughed. "Thank you so much!"

Mary stood at the barn door her hand covering her mouth, her eyes fixed on the glow that lit up Matt's face.

"I just thought ya' looked like ya' needed some company around the house." Bruce smiled.

"Thank you so much Bruce," Matt exclaimed. "Oh, thank you, thank you, thank you!"

"But wait," Bruce added. "There's something else."

Matt paused a moment. "What? There's more?"

Bruce smiled. "Yeah. There's more."

He reached into his back pocket and produced a thick leather bound journal.

Matt put Newt on the ground and carefully took the journal in his hands. The leather looked rough from years of use. A brown band held the journal tightly shut. Matt unfastened the band and opened it to see hundreds of journal entries written on the pages throughout the book.

"It was your father's," Bruce explained. "I asked your mother at Brian's funeral if I could keep it. She allowed me to take it but I never read it. I guess I thought it was too painful. I think he would want you to have it."

Matt flipped through the pages in awe. He glanced at the first entry:

December 2, 1983

"December second ..." Matt thought aloud. "That was Dad's birthday."

"Yep," Bruce said. "He started writing in it the day he turned eighteen. I don't think he ever missed a day."

Matt's jaw dropped, and his hands began to tremble as he flipped through the pages. Every day, his father had filled in a page from his journal. He held in his hands the thoughts and memories of his father. There were so many things in this journal to read and discover. He couldn't even begin to express his gratitude.

Matt wiped wetness from his eyes and looked up at his uncle. He lurched out at him and squeezed him. All thoughts of the events that had occurred that day seemed like ancient history.

"Thank you ..." Matt cried in his uncle's arms. "Thank you so much ..."

Bruce blushed "You're welcome."

He looked up at Mary who had a tear running down her cheek. She smiled at him as she covered her mouth and wiped her eyes on her shirt.

Newt ran up alongside Matt and propped his paws up on his leg, his tail still wagging. Matt looked down and smiled. "C'mon, Newt," he said as he dashed out into the yard. "Let's go, you like to play fetch, don't ya'? C'mon."

Mary and Bruce stepped outside and watched as Matt threw a nearby stick. The small dog was a dark blur as he raced across the wide yard barking. Newt tackled the stick and tumbled over it as he tried to stop. He popped back up again and raised his ears at the laughter coming from the three.

Bruce turned to shut the barn door.

"That was really nice of you," Mary said with a smile.

"Well, I know that ya' just want him to be happy." Bruce blushed. "I thought I could help a bit."

Mary stepped in front of him, gently grabbed his shoulders and looked deep into his eyes. "Thank you ... Bruce."

He averted his gaze from the twinkle in her eye. "You're very welcome."

7

The next day, Matt sat in class and pulled his father's journal from his backpack. Looking around, he saw that Mrs. Raidner was sifting through her papers and not watching the class. He quietly opened the journal and read the first page.

December 2, 1983
Dear Journal,

Today was my 18th birthday. I went out for a bite to eat at Fiddles, a little diner on the other side of town with my buds. I had Nick and Kevin go with me. They've been my friends for as long as I can remember.

We had a good time messing around at the diner and throwing the uneaten tomatoes at each other. But when we headed back out to the car, I saw a boy about my age leaning on it. He appeared to be looking in my car for something.

He tried opening the door, but I had it locked.

I was like, "Hey, what are you doing?"

The boy looked at me. He hadn't shaved in days. He smelled like trash. He didn't answer me. He took a couple steps back.

So I took another step toward the boy. "What are you doing?"

The boy turned and ran. Nick, Kevin and I took off after him. We managed to take him down about a hundred feet away. Nick held one arm while Kevin held the other. I held the rest of his body down to the ground.

"What are you doing?" I asked. "What's the matter?"

"You have no idea what it's like," he said.

I looked at my friends as they held him down and they shook their heads in confusion.

"What are you talking about?" I asked.

"I don't have anywhere to go," he said. "I need somewhere to stay. I've been on my own for over a week now. I just wish I had a car to take me somewhere new."

When he said that, I got really angry. "So you were going to steal mine?"

But of course, he denied that. "No! I was only looking."

"It didn't look like looking to me," I said.

"I need somewhere to stay. Please help me. I don't want to be lost anymore. Please..."

I looked at Nick and Kevin for support. "Come on, man," Kevin said. "He's not our problem."

"Yeah," Nick said. "Let's go."

I didn't want to leave the boy there, but I was afraid that if I took him in, then my friends wouldn't look at me the same way. I was afraid of what they would say. This boy was begging me to help him, but I couldn't bring myself to do it.

We let him go.

My choice has been bugging me all night. That's why I'm writing this down. Maybe I can figure out if I did the right thing.

Why couldn't I tell my friends to shove off? I could have helped get that boy on the right track. But he's still out there

*wandering around – lost. I don't know.
Maybe I'm just messed up.
            Brian Cross*

    Matt looked up at the clock to see that class was almost finished so he packed the journal away and thought about his father's choice. He didn't know how he would have handled the situation either.

    As soon as the last bell rang, Matt sprinted out the door onto the parking lot where his mom was already waiting.
    "C'mon, Mom. Let's go, Newt's waiting for me."
    Mary looked at her son as she pulled out of the parking lot. "Uh, we're not going straight home, Matt."
    Matt swung his head to look at his mom. "What? Why?"
    "Remember a couple of days back when you mentioned that you had community service to do for a project or something?"
    "Yeah, Mr. Brakeman's class."
    "Well, my friend, Donna, works at Wind Ridge, you know the assisted living home in town? Anyway Donna stopped by my work today and we were talking. She said that kids your age get their community service done over there. They go in and read to the sick."
    She stopped herself.
    "Well, I shouldn't say sick, really. They just can't live on their own anymore away from help so they live there. They have their own room and everything but they have help just around the corner if they need it."
    Matt looked at her and frowned. "Reading to the sick?"
    "I told you they're not sick. They just can't live by themselves."
    "You're serious?"
    "What do you mean?" his mother went on. "Of course, I'm serious. I think it'd be great. I mean, think about it. You'd meet a lot of people and it's not that hard. You just have to go every now and then. You only need how many hours a semester, ten?"
    "Fifteen," he corrected.
    "Fifteen, see, you can do that in no time."

Matt quickly did the math in his head and sighed when he realized his mother was correct.

"You'd better make up your mind fast because if you decide to do this, I told Donna that you would have your first go at it this evening."

"What?" Matt exclaimed.

He slouched in his seat as his mother turned onto the road leading to Wind Ridge. Newt would have to wait.

Matt and his mother walked to the front desk of Wind Ridge together and Mary asked the receptionist for Donna. As the receptionist went to fetch her, Mary turned to Matt.

"Now listen, Matt," she said. "Some of these people are very old. So if they say funny things or look at you weird, it's okay."

"Mom, I'm fifteen – not five."

"Right. I'll be back to pick you up about an hour or so. Do you have something to read?"

Matt looked around, reached over the counter and grabbed a newspaper. "Yep."

Mary shook her head and smiled as a thin, dark-haired woman with a clipboard approached from down the hall.

"Oh, hi Mary," she said. "I was wondering if you were going to show up."

Mary gave an innocent shrug. "Well, my son thought he should get started on his community service."

Matt restrained himself from saying otherwise.

"So, this is Matthew? Hi, I'm Donna." She extended her hand.

Matt shook it without much enthusiasm.

"Well," Donna began, "if you're all set then we need to find you a buddy. Hmm ... Why don't we start with someone who's easy to talk to?"

"That'll do," he replied.

Matt gave a reluctant wave to his mother as she left. Glancing at her clipboard, Donna led Matt down the hall.

Matt was surprised at how much different this was from a nursing home. He could see inside the thin windows on the doors to the rooms. The floors were carpeted dark blue with the walls papered a baby blue. There was more than enough space to fit a bed, furniture, a TV and a small kitchen with a refrigerator. It was similar to a small apartment.

"Here it is," Donna said, stopping. "Room three thirty-three."

The door was wide open and Matt saw a man inside sitting at a table. His eyes were intently staring at something of interest in front of him. Donna tapped on the doorframe.

"Hey there, Gordon." She walked in and Matt followed behind her.

Framed pictures of exotic landscapes of mountain ranges, jungles and arctic scenes created colorful walls and grabbed Matt's attention. With further examination, Matt noticed the pictures weren't just pictures but rather completed puzzles. Squinting his eyes a bit, he could see the thin lines of the puzzle pieces in a bright picture of a tiger and her cubs in the jungle.

"Gordon," Donna spoke a bit louder as if the man had difficulty hearing. "You have someone who would like to meet you. His name is Matthew Cross, and he's going to be with you for a while. Is that okay?"

He didn't reply.

"Matthew, this is Gordon Parish," she said.

"Hi," Matt said timidly.

"I'll be checking up on the others around the hall if you need me," Donna said as she headed for the door. "Have fun, you two."

Matt moved around the table so he could see Mr. Parish's face. The man didn't look old. His body didn't appear to have any physical problems. In fact, he appeared to be in perfect working condition. His lightly tanned face and graying brown hair matched his thin dark eyes. He continued scanning the puzzle pieces through his thin-rimmed bifocals that sat low upon his long nose.

Mr. Parish was working on another puzzle. The box cover showed this one to be a landscape of a grassy green rolling hill with blossoming sunflowers at the bottom. The landscape was underneath a crystal blue sky with thin clouds wafting through it. The box boasted of containing one thousand pieces. Matt raised his eyebrows in surprise.

All the pieces were blue, green or covered with yellow sunflowers. He knew he could never work a puzzle like that and was amazed to see how far Mr. Parish had gotten. All of the edges of the puzzle were completed and he was well on his way to completing the center. Grabbing another chair from under the table, Matt sat down opposite Mr. Parish.

"Well, hi there ... uh, Mr. Parish. I need some community service hours for school so ... I thought I would come and help around here. I could maybe keep some people company – keep you company."

Matt gave a false chuckle. Mr. Parish said nothing and didn't even look up from the table. Matt furrowed his brow at Mr. Parish's apparent lack of interest.

"Well, I thought I would start out reading the paper to you. So you just, uh, keep ... working there."

Mr. Parish didn't move.

"Yeah ... just like that. Great."

The only movement Matt saw was his eyes darting around at pieces spread over the table.

Matt opened his newspaper. "I'll uh – read some headlines and you can just stop me if you want me to read more, okay?"

Matt made another futile attempt to make eye contact but was again unable to do so.

"Okay, then." He scanned the newspaper. "Uh ... here we go, *'The Found Strike Again at Wilson's Watches.'*"

Matt looked up but Mr. Parish hadn't budged.

"Um – *'Four Car Pileup in Grocery Store Parking Lot', 'Nine-Year Old Nearly Drowns in Swimming Pool', 'Electrical Fire Nearly Burns Down Local Church', 'Up and Coming Juggernut Festival Facing Problems'* –"

Mr. Parish held up a finger and looked at him. Matt stopped.

"Read that one," he said in a voice barely above whisper.

"*'Up and Coming Juggernut Festival Fac'* –?"

"No," he interrupted with a voice that was more audible. "The one before that."

"*'Electrical Fire Nearly Burns Down Local Church'?*"

"Yes. That one."

Matt began:

"New Life Fellowship Church caught fire yesterday, August 31, at about nine o' clock pm. Fortunately, the youth group that meets at that time had left the building to go bowling.

The pastor of the New Life Church, Dr. Chris Fredrickson, stated he was just leaving when the fire broke out. He reported that he had been in his office, when he smelled the smoke. 'I went to the kitchen,' he said, 'and saw it was on fire.'

The local fire station two blocks from the church responded immediately and was able to get to the fire from spreading throughout the church.

Youth pastor, Neil Richardson, said, 'When the youth van pulled up, I saw smoke with [the firemen] putting the fire out. I couldn't believe my eyes. Had we been in our basement ... we might not have been able to get out.'

Fire Chief, Thomas James said that they were still unsure what started the fire. 'We're hoping it was electrical,' he said. 'We would have a serious problem if it was an act of vandalism.'

The youth are planning local fundraising to help offset the costs of the new kitchen. One of the youth group members, Valerie Dickson said, 'Well, we would have a bake sale but I guess we can't do that now, can we?'"

Matt glanced at Mr. Parish who was listening intently.
"That's pretty much it on that one," Matt said. "Do you know the church they're talking about?"
Mr. Parish smiled. "Of course, I know it. I was only the preacher there for forty-five years."

"Really?"

He nodded.

"What made you decide to leave?"

"Well, I didn't just decide to leave," Mr. Parish said. "My wife, Hope, died five years ago. A few weeks later, I had a stroke. The doctors think I may have another but they can't tell when. I don't mind so much, though. I don't fear death. I'm ready to go when the good Lord is ready for me."

"So you had to leave the church because of your health?" Matt asked.

"Well, yes, I suppose, but not really. Hope had passed away and it was coming time for me to retire. I'm getting too old to preach anyway."

Matt put the paper down hoping to talk instead of read. "You're not that old. You've got to be the youngest guy in this place."

Mr. Parish smiled. "Well, that may be true, but I still feel old."

"Yeah, I understand," Matt lied. He had no idea what being old felt like.

There was an awkward pause until Matt broke the silence. "So what do you do all day?"

After he spoke, Matt realized how stupid his question was.

Mr. Parish chuckled as he took off his bifocals. "Well, basically I do all of four — no, five things. I eat, sleep, watch the news, read the Bible and work these puzzles."

"Well, I've got to tell you," Matt commented. "This room is incredible. I've never seen so many puzzles in one place in all my life."

Matt gazed around the room again at the dozens of pictures staggered along the wall. It seemed that the more he looked the more puzzles he saw.

"I mean, you have got to be like the puzzle master or something," Matt commented.

Mr. Parish snorted. "The puzzle master? No, I don't think so. It takes me forever to do these things. Well, not as much anymore. It seems that the more you do the better your eyes see the pieces. Do you see that one right there?"

Mr. Parish pointed to a puzzle on the wall of two dolphins swimming in the sea. "That puzzle took me two days. It's a hundred pieces. Now I do thousand piece puzzles in the time it took me to do hundred piece ones."

"Wow, you've really improved then?" Matt exclaimed.

"Well, kind of. It all depends on how many naps I feel like taking and whether I feel like doing them or not. I might want to watch television or even read. The nurses also come in for a quick chat every now and then."

Matt motioned at the table. "I know that I could never do a puzzle like that."

"Why not?"

"I don't have the patience."

"Ah, horse-honkey! If you want to get something done badly enough, you'll do whatever it takes to do it. Right?"

"Yeah, I guess. But it might depend on what the thing is that I have to do."

"Okay. Do this with me," Mr. Parish said. "Think of something really important to you."

"What?" Matt frowned at this sudden change in conversation.

"Think of something or someone really important to you."

Newt came to Matt's mind. "Okay."

"What are you thinking about?"

"My dog."

"If your dog was lost or hurt, you would have the patience to help it, wouldn't you?" Mr. Parish asked.

Matt had never thought about something like that. Newt brought a whole new joy to his life. He couldn't imagine the pain he would feel if something happened to him.

"Yeah. I would do anything."

"Well, then. Now you see my point. I really cared about my wife. I remember her every time I sit down to do a puzzle."

Mr. Parish paused. His eyes seemed to look far away.

"On occasion, I feel it's as though she's still here with me. Back before she died, we would sometimes do puzzles together. I remember one time we'd worked on a five hundred-piece puzzle late one night. We had put in four hundred and ninety-nine pieces and then there weren't any pieces left.

"Well, Hope was very good about keeping all the pieces in one box so we knew it had to be around somewhere. I tell you we searched every inch of that carpet for that last piece, but we couldn't seem to find it.

"By the end of the night, we were so tired we collapsed at the table where we had been working the puzzle. I stared at the nearly completed puzzle and had an idea. I put my hand on top of the puzzle and rubbed the surface of it. And there it was, lying right on top of the puzzle the whole time. We couldn't see it because the rest of the pieces camouflaged it. I felt pretty stupid but as I sat and thought about it, I realized the incident was a metaphor for my life. I even made a sermon out of it."

His tone became serious as if he were preaching.

"I looked all over the house for that last piece, the only thing I thought could make my puzzle complete. I looked everywhere and couldn't find it. It was only after I had surrendered to the fact that I was never going to find it and collapsed in my chair that I began to realize what I needed to do.

"If I was going to find that last piece, I had to go back to where I had started from – the puzzle. It was then that I realized that only by returning to where I had started from – God – would I ever be complete. It is with God that all spirits find their last puzzle piece. Do you know what that one thing was, the one that changed my heart?" he asked.

"What?" Matt replied.

"The love of Jes –"

"Knock, knock."

Matt looked up to see his mother standing in the doorway.

"Sorry to come back so early, but Bruce called. He said dinner is waiting on us. I guess he likes to eat early. Anyway, we've got to go, Matt. You've still got homework."

"Do we have to leave now, Mom? We were just getting going."

"I'll bring you back soon. Don't worry. Come on, neither of us has eaten yet. I'm starving," she replied.

"All right," Matt sighed as he stood up to leave. "I'll see you later, Mr. Parish."

"Yes, it was nice to meet you, Matthew."

Matt shook Mr. Parish's hand and followed his mother out the door.

"Plus, we don't want to keep Newt waiting, right?" his mom asked as they walked down the hall. "God forbid he pees on the floor."

8

Matt sat in his usual spot in Ms. Ellis' English class working on his assignment. Occasionally, he risked a few glances at the gorgeous girl on the other side of the room. Over the course of a few days, he learned her name was Rose Hudson.

Rose.

What a beautiful name ...

She lightly tapped her pencil on her desk, chewing on her lower lip as she read. Her smooth, tan leg crossed over the other and one of her flip-flops lazily swayed back and forth. She shrugged long auburn hair out of her face and glanced in Matt's direction. Matt shifted his gaze but soon looked back at her.

Rose immediately dropped her pencil and frowned at the paper.

Having trouble? Matt thought. He wanted to help. How easy it would be to meander over there and say something slick and cool like, "Hey baby, you must be the most gorgeous girl I've ever seen. Let me finish that assignment for you and you can repay me by agreeing to go out with me tonight."

He would then crumple up her assignment, throw it in the trashcan without looking and hand Rose the work he'd just finished.

He smiled at the thought. Could he ever be so bold?

Probably not.

Ms. Ellis stood up from her desk, looked at all her hard-working students and said, "Would you excuse me? I'll be right back."

She walked out of the room.

Matt glanced at his notebook, tore off a piece of paper and scrawled something on it. Folding the paper into an airplane, he tossed it in Rose's direction. It glided through the air and gently landed on top of her desk without disrupting anyone.

She took it, unfolded it and read:

Call me sometime.

Rose glanced up at Matt and he winked at her. Rose stood and came toward him, her shining hair flowed behind her. Matt's palms began to sweat and his pulse quickened as Rose moved closer. Stopping at Matt's desk, she bent down and looked at him, her emerald green eyes focused only on him. Matt thought the whole world had vanished, the two of them spotlights in the room. None of the other students had moved.

Rose leaned toward Matt's ear and in a soothing voice whispered, "Why don't you call me?"

She laid a small bit of paper on Matt's desk – her phone number written in a beautiful scroll.

Their faces were close now. And they were getting closer ... closer ... and closer until –

"Matt, wake up. It's time," his mother called from the kitchen, interrupting Matt's dream. "C'mon, sleepyhead!"

Matt blinked as he found himself amongst the sheets of his bed. Squeezing his eyes shut, he attempted to bring the image back but it was gone. With a slight growl, he opened his eyes.

"Are you awake?" he heard his mother call.

"Yeah," he replied, slamming his fists on the mattress. "Unfortunately."

English class wasn't as exciting as Matt's dream. Ms. Ellis talked about "what the characters are feeling" the whole time.

Gawking at Rose wasn't nearly as enjoyable when she was paying attention to the people around her. Matt looked away whenever she happened to glance in his direction.

"This is called personification," Ms. Ellis went on. "Do you see that line at the bottom of page one hundred and thirty-three? Yes, well that is an example of personification. Underline, underline, star, star. People, this important stuff will be on the test as well as on the final. So make sure you mark it in your books. All right?"

She turned slightly and checked the clock on the wall. "Well, I'm done for the day," she said. "We're about out of time."

Dull thuds skipped about the room as everyone shut their textbooks.

"However, I do have one last thing I was supposed to mention. As most of you know, the annual Juggernut Festival is coming up at the end of September. Everyone will find a partner and design a banner for the festival. This banner will be counted as a big part of your grade in this class. Each banner will be judged at the festival and the winning banner will represent the festival for the year. Not to mention," she chimed, "the group who comes up with the winning design will receive two hundred dollars cash.

"The art classes are participating by designing the layout of the place and decorating. So Dr. Pierce asked if the English classes would make the banner. I'm going to make it due Friday – one week before the festival. With that said, we need to pick partners. I have taken the liberty of assigning each of you a partner."

The class groaned and immediately began their protests.

"Oh, really," Ms. Ellis said sharply. "It's really not all that bad. Fate will work itself out."

She waited for the room to go quiet again and grabbed a piece of paper off her desk. "Okay, here we go."

"Matt Cross. You're partnered with Eugene Stone."

Matt looked at Eugene sitting in the corner of the room. Bleached white socks stretched up his white legs and a red plaid shirt was tucked beneath his beige pants just above his belly button. Eugene glanced up from the dictionary he was reading and smiled a large toothy grin.

Matt could have cried.

Ms. Ellis continued to read off the rest of the students and their partners.

"Miranda Gold will be partnered with Jesse Christenson." Matt noticed a long haired boy in the corner of the room who nodded as he briefly smiled at Miranda.

"Rose Hudson …" Ms. Ellis went on. "I've partnered you with Eugene Stone."

Eugene threw his hand in the air. "Excuse me, Ms. Ellis. But I'm partnered with him." He pointed at Matt. "I can't have two partners, can I?"

"Hmm ..." Ms. Ellis stopped to look over her notes. "It seems I've made a mistake."

Matt's legs bounced up and down beneath his desk. Was it possible he'd end up with Rose? What was it that Ms. Ellis had mentioned about fate?

"Right, I see what I did," Ms. Ellis said. "Sorry, I read it wrong. Eugene, you're partnered with Vanessa Valentine and Matt, you're with Rose Hudson."

Matt pinched himself under the desk to make sure he wasn't dreaming again. His heart jumped on the trampoline inside his chest. He gave a soft smile when Rose looked at him but she didn't return it.

With a quick motion, Matt tore off a piece of paper to give to Rose. While he was scribbling his phone number, the bell rang. Rose grabbed her stuff and left with the other students.

Matt jumped up and dashed out the door after her.

"Rose," he called through the crowd.

She increased her pace.

"Rose! Rose, wait a second."

She slowed to a normal speed but didn't turn.

"Hi," he said as he stepped up beside her. "I'm Matt."

"Rose," she said without looking at him.

"Well, hi, Rose. Um – I'm kinda new here so I'm not real familiar with this Juggle-a-Nut thing."

For a moment, he thought he saw smile cross Rose's face. She turned to look at Matt for the first time. "You mean the Jug –"

Matt smiled his calmest smile.

She blushed. "The, uh ... the Juggernut Festival?"

"Right, that's it." Matt paused a moment and cleared his throat waiting for the awkward silence to pass. "So I guess we're working together, huh?"

"I guess so."

"Well, do you know what we have to do?"

Matt walked alongside her as she continued to her locker. "Yeah, my dad works with the school. He and I help with the festival every year, so I'm pretty familiar with what goes on around here."

"Really? What does he do?" Matt asked trying to keep the conversation going. He was amazed the conversation had gone this far.

"He works with the school. He's kind of the school's computer nerd. He makes sure that the printers and computers and stuff are always working."

"Oh, sounds cool. But since we are doing this uh – banner thing, where are we gonna work on it? Are we going to meet somewhere to work or what?"

Rose paused. "Um, I guess we could meet somewhere to start putting it together this weekend, if that's not a problem."

"No," Matt replied eagerly. "No problem at all."

"Oh," Rose went on. "Do you think it might be possible to work on it at your house? My dad's probably going to have to work."

"Yeah. Great – good, fine, yeah, – that'll work, good," he stammered.

"I'll call you and we can arrange it," Rose said. "What's your pho –?"

"Here, take this."

Matt opened her hand and as he did, their eyes met for a moment. Matt put the folded note in her hand.

"I gotta go." He turned and headed in the opposite direction.

"But … wait a sec –" Matt heard Rose's voice but he kept going. He didn't want too much of a good thing.

After his last class, Matt walked into the office to serve his first detention. He wasn't sure what to do. Matt thought students served detention in the classroom but he'd received a note telling him to report to Mr. Fears's office.

Matt approached the secretary.

"Excuse me. Uh – I have detention with Mr. Fears."

"Oh, okay," she replied. "Well, go ahead then. Mr. Fears's office is the second door on your left."

Matt had started in the direction indicated by the secretary when Abby and Andrew walked into the office.

He stopped them. "Hey guys, are detentions normally served in Mr. Fears's office? I thought they were served in classrooms."

"I was thinkin' the same thing." Andrew shrugged.

The three of them walked into the office to find three desks set up opposite Mr. Fears's desk.

Andrew and Abby found a desk and sat down. Matt followed suit. Looking around the room, Matt saw that Mr. Fears's office was much like Dr. Pierce's except there weren't any decorations or posters on the walls. It was very dull.

The bell rang and Mr. Fears walked into the office shutting the door behind him.

"Look what the cat dragged in," Mr. Fears smirked as he leaned on his desk. "I bet you're wondering why you're here, why you aren't with the other students in detention? Well, I was going to let you go with the rest but then decided it would be more … beneficial if you were with me. This way I can keep my eye on you."

He glanced at Matt. "You are a freshman, correct? That means you are probably unfamiliar with the rules of the school. Underclassmen are to respect the seniors, not pick fights with them."

Matt had difficulty keeping his mouth shut. He knew that Mr. Fears had them right where he wanted them and nothing they said or did would make a difference.

"If you three are to be in my office after school for the remainder of the week, then you need to know my rules. I have no tolerance for those who disobey the rules. Understand?"

The three of them said nothing in response.

"Very well. Rule number one – don't talk, period. Don't even try to whisper. That goes for your pathetic chicken scratch notes as well. Writing one *anywhere* in this school will result in me taking it. Don't even try to hide it. I will find out and when I do you will regret it. Believe me, I have quite a collection.

"Rule number two – no food or drinks, period. You cannot even bring an unopened food package in here. You'll have to leave it outside the front door and hope the janitor has eaten."

He smirked at his little joke as he began to pace around them.

"Rule number three – don't work on your homework, period. This is not a study hall. Working on homework will result in me taking it and you will receive no credit for the assignment."

He stopped pacing and cocked his head as if going over the rules in his head.

"Ah, yes. I almost forgot my favorite rule. Rule number four – I make up rules as I go along, period. So don't do anything or I will make a rule against it. Understand?"

None of them moved.

"Good."

Mr. Fears sat down and began his work while the others remained in their seats.

The rest of the week was uneventful.

Every day after school, Matt sat in detention and watched the second hand on the clock. After a while, it was almost hypnotic.

On the last day of detention, as Matt watched the second hand go around and his eyes began to feel heavy. He blinked and glanced at Abby and Andrew to see them staring at the clock with the same lazy expression.

He needed something to keep occupied. A thought popped into his mind. He smiled, reached into his backpack and pulled out his father's journal.

Just as he opened it, Mr. Fears whipped around in his seat and glared at Matt like a cobra waiting for the perfect time to strike.

"Excuse me, Mr. Cross. What do you think you're doing?"

"I just thought that I –"

"You know," Mr. Fears interrupted, "there's your first problem. You 'thought'."

"No, but I –"

"Why don't you bring that book to me, Mr. Cross?"

Matt looked down at his journal and then back at Mr. Fears. He shook his head. He wasn't about to give Fears one of his most precious possessions.

"Excuse me, Mr. Cross," Mr. Fears hissed. "It looked to me like you shook your head at me."

"Yes, I did."

"Do you realize what you're doing, Mr. Cross? I could suspend you right here and now for insubordination."

"You can't do that," Matt yelped.

"I'm the assistant principal. I can do whatever I want. And what I want, Mr. Cross, is that book." He glared at Matt. "Now ... bring it here."

Matt paused and then stowed the journal back inside his backpack. The assistant principal rose from his chair, looking much taller than he actually was.

"I don't think you heard me correctly, Mr. Cross. Give me that book."

"No ... sir," Matt added with the hope that 'sir' would keep Mr. Fears from getting angry.

"You *will* give it to me."

"It's mine ... sir."

Mr. Fears stormed around his desk, stomped toward Matt and scooped his backpack off the floor.

"Stop," Matt yelled. "That's mine!"

He tried to pull the pack out of the man's grasp but Mr. Fears jerked the journal out of the backpack and threw the backpack back into Matt's arms.

"Sit down, Mr. Cross! You're already in way over your head."

Glaring at Mr. Fears, Matt sank back into his chair. He glanced at Abby and Andrew who were frozen to their desks.

Matt's face heated and his heart beat like a hammer. I put the journal away, he thought. Why wasn't that good enough?

"Losing your book might make you think twice before talking back." Mr. Fears said coldly as he glanced over at the clock. "You all are done here except for you, Mr. Cross. I think another three days of detention will help you understand that I am the boss in this office."

Matt clamped down on his tongue to keep from lashing out at the man standing in front of him.

Marching out with the others, Matt turned and watched Mr. Fears as he went across the hall to Dr. Pierce's office. Through the open office door, Matt saw Mr. Fears hand the journal to Dr. Pierce.

His hands gestured wildly and his mouth moved rapidly. He was probably telling Dr. Pierce everything that had just happened. Dr.

Pierce nodded, rose from his desk and stuck the journal on the top of a tall shelf.

Matt swallowed his anger, turned and stormed out of the office.

9

Matt kicked a rock in his frustration as he paced the sidewalk waiting for his mother to arrive. He couldn't believe he'd allowed Fears to take his father's journal. Now he had to go through three more detentions. He would happily serve them if he had his father's journal back. He knew he would never get it back. Fears had said that Matt had lost it. He wasn't about to lose his father's journal, without some kind of fight.

He couldn't go to Dr. Pierce for help. Fears would just argue against him. No one else would be able to do anything about it. That left only him. He would have to do it, but what? Was it possible for him to get the journal back on his own?

Matt sat on the steps listening to the thoughts that jumped in his mind like grasshoppers. Could he get the journal back? How?

He'd seen Dr. Pierce put the journal on top of that high shelf. Would it be possible to get to the shelf without anyone catching him?

Resting his head on his knees, he let his mind wander. Someone would see him if he tried during the day. He would have to get to it when no one was there but, when was the office empty? There were always people in there. There were secretaries, teachers, teacher aides, office aides, janitors, parents, students, not to mention the principals.

Maybe I could pull the fire alarm, he thought. Everyone would run out of the school and he could get the journal.

After a moment, he shook his head. No, that wouldn't work. The principals were always the last ones to leave the building during a fire alarm. They'd probably be in the office somewhere.

How could he make everyone leave? A voice inside his head answered his question.

You don't have to make everyone leave, the voice said. Just wait for everyone to go home.

His head popped up from its resting place on his knees.

That might work.

Yes, he could hide out in the bathroom or something, and then go to the office after dark. He stopped. What about the security cameras? He answered the question. He could hide his face when walking to the bathroom, put on a dark mask and get into the office that way. Yes, that would work.

Then another obstacle came to mind. What about the office doors? Principals locked office doors for the night, didn't they? He nodded to himself, he was sure that they did. There was no way he could open a locked door.

So much for that idea.

He sighed and let his head fall back to his knees. He didn't see how anything would work. He opened his eyes and there around his neck was the photo ID Dr. Pierce had given him.

Matt sat up and glanced over it. He'd heard of people who opened locked doors with their ID or credit cards. Could he do it?

He checked his ID, felt the edges. He'd have to practice. He'd find a locked door and practice on it as soon as he found a spare moment. He would figure it out. Yes, it would work.

He would get his father's journal back.

Matt, Mary and Bruce were silent around the dinner table that night. Matt hadn't stopped thinking about his new plan since he'd figured out what he was going to do. He knew it would work. There was no question about that but he'd be in the school for a good portion of the night. His mother would worry. He needed to come up with an excuse.

Matt broke the silence. "Hey, uh, Mom?"

Mary took a bite of her green beans. "Yeah, babe?"

"Uh … a friend of mine asked if I could, uh, spend the night at his house."

"When?"

"When?" Matt replied. "Thurs – no, I mean Friday."

Mary lifted an eyebrow. "Who is this friend?"

"Oh, just a guy I met at school."

"What's his name?" Mary asked.

"Oh, uh … his name is, uh … Andrew."

Mary looked at Bruce who looked at his plate. Mary's eyes went back to Matt.

"I don't think it's such a good idea," she said.

"Why not, Mom?" Matt protested. "You want me to make friends, don't you?"

"Yeah, but I just –"

"How can I make friends without spending time with anyone? Please, let me go. I want to go. I'll have a great time. That would make you feel better, wouldn't it? You'd know that I was having a good time."

"I don't even know –"

"I think it's a great idea," Bruce spoke.

Matt's face brightened.

"What?" Mary asked.

"Well, think about it," Bruce went on. "The boy's got a point, you know? He's trying to make friends. Give him some space. Let him have his fun. It'll be good for him."

Mary looked in disbelief from Bruce to Matt and back to Bruce. She sighed and shrugged her shoulders as she took another bite of her green beans.

"Okay," she said. "I want you to have fun but make sure you take my cell phone in case you need to get a hold of us."

Matt grinned.

He would definitely have some fun.

Matt's legs anxiously bounced up and down under the table as he waited for the bell to ring. He'd been waiting all week for Friday to arrive. Everything was in order. He'd brought a black duffel bag full of dark clothes and planned to hide in the bathroom for a few hours while he waited for the school to go dark. Once he had his journal, he would walk home and tell his mom that Andrew had dropped him off at his house because his mom had a meeting that morning or something. He'd covered all the bases. His plan had to work.

Matt glanced down at the ID badge hanging from his neck. He had found the time to practice opening the locked doors with it. After a few tries, he'd thought it was a lost cause and that it wasn't possible. Then, just as he'd been about to give up, he'd heard a click and the door unlocked. He simply had to tuck the badge underneath the bolt and pull up.

Matt watched the second hand on the clock crawl toward his release. The dull tone sounded and adrenaline churned inside Matt as exploded from his seat and shot out the door. Racing to the bathroom, he hid his face from the cameras as his insides twisted into knots. He didn't know why. Everything was going to be fine.

Matt reassured himself by taking a deep breath – yes, everything would be just fine.

He stepped into the vacant bathroom, selected a stall and began to undress. He'd worn thick black jeans that covered his dark shoes so all he had to do was change into a short-sleeved T-shirt that he'd stolen from Bruce's closet. He pulled black gloves and a thick black mask from the duffel bag. He would put them on as soon as the alarm on his watch rang.

Once dressed in his dark clothing, Matt stepped up on the toilet seat and sat on top of it with his feet propped on the seat. He leaned back on the wall and sighed attempting to make himself comfortable.

Around five o' clock, the lights dimmed in order to save power. Matt saw the bathroom floor grow dark. With none of the dim lights near the bathroom, it was difficult to see.

For nearly four hours, he'd been as still as possible. It had not been an easy task. Both of his legs had fallen asleep twice and he was about to fall asleep himself. Heaviness started to overtake his eyes. It seemed as if he might be a bit too comfortable. His head had drooped and he'd begun to doze off when the sharp alarm beeped on his watch.

Matt blinked, rubbed his eyes and turned off his watch. In the silence of the school, his watch had blared like a bullhorn. He hoped no one had heard it.

He touched his feet to the floor without a sound and stood up for the first time in hours. He sighed with relief as his joints popped and with another yawn, he stretched in the cramped stall. A smirk came over his face as he unlocked the stall.

Matt looked himself over in the small mirror, took a deep breath and pulled the thick mask over his head. Adrenaline jump-started him. He knew he was ready.

Tiptoeing across the bathroom, Matt peeked around the corner and down the hall. He didn't detect any movement. Glancing back the other way gave the same result. He ran across the hall taking great care to make sure his tennis shoes didn't make any noise. He couldn't afford to attract attention.

Coming to the end of the hall leading into the cafeteria, Matt noticed that the janitors had lined the long tables up against the wall. Matt grinned at his luck. He had to cross to the other side of the cafeteria in order to get to the office and he didn't want to have to wind through a labyrinth of chairs and tables in order to get there.

He glanced up at the balconies to be sure they were empty and then started across the cafeteria. Suddenly, a short crack echoed through the empty halls.

Matt jumped behind the corner. His eyes darted across the balconies as he searched for the source of the sound.

Nothing moved.

Maybe it was nothing. Maybe he was just paranoid.

Another shuffle came from above him. Matt leaned around the corner and looked up at the balcony again. A janitor swung his mop across the floor. If he attempted this approach to the office, the janitor would spot him. Matt realized he couldn't just walk across the cafeteria. He would have to come up with another idea.

He paused in thought.

A white light from the moon shone in through the large windows and reflected off the tile floor. The janitor had just mopped it, which was why he was up on the balconies now.

This presented a problem. Matt's shoes were quiet when walking on dry floor but treading on a wet floor would be much more difficult.

Worried thoughts crept into his mind and he felt himself breathing heavier. Sweat began to seep through his wool mask making it difficult to breath through the small hole for his mouth.

How was he going to get across to the other side without someone seeing him? Maybe he could wait for the janitor to finish mopping and then he could get across the floor without problems.

Matt paused. He'd waited over four hours in the bathroom, what was ten more minutes?

Matt's tossed those thoughts away when he heard footsteps and a mop bucket rolling down the hall on the other side of the cafeteria. If the janitor looked his way, he would definitely see him. He gasped and looked for a place to hide.

Noticing the lunch tables against the wall, he jumped between two of them, leaned back against the wall and held his breath as he thought of what he would do next.

Pushing the mop bucket ahead of him, the janitor strolled past completely unaware of his presence. Matt's dark clothing had saved him. He breathed a sigh of relief as the janitor continued down the hall humming to himself.

Matt focused his attention on how he was to get across the cafeteria. He needed cover from the janitor who was still mopping the floor above him.

He examined the lunch tables that encircled the cafeteria and smiled as an idea came to mind. Lifting his foot, he stepped over the table's wheels to the table beside it and continued to make his way around the cafeteria, hugging the wall and using the tables for cover.

In a small room on the second floor, Officer Phillip Crawford sat alone with his sidearm resting on the table.

"Ladies and gentlemen," he announced as if entertaining a large crowd. "The legendary Phillip Crawford will now attempt to disassemble and reassemble his sidearm in less than six seconds!"

Crawford cupped his hands to his mouth and made the cheering effects for his fictitious onlookers. He cleared a few scattered crumbs from an empty bag of chips that now lay crumpled and tossed on the floor. A triangular tower made out of his twelve-pack of empty soda cans rested near him.

"He will attempt the impossible. Please … he must have total silence for his concentration. Let's watch."

Crawford closed his eyes, took a deep breath and let it out in a slow stream. He stared at his sidearm as though mentally preparing for what he was about to do.

"Just breathe," he muttered.

Inhale.

Exhale.

Inhale.

Exhale.

He depressed the button on his stopwatch and threw it on the desk as he moved to disassemble his sidearm. Crawford had become very proficient at this task. Ever since he'd been assigned to Hills West High School he'd had a lot of time to practice.

He hated his new assignment, walking the halls night after night. It was so boring. Nothing ever happened, at least not since that intruder three months ago.

After he'd been injured the night he'd tried to detain the intruder, Sheriff Stronson had assigned him to the school. However, his dream of becoming a great police officer still lived so he took his present job seriously. Well, at least semi-seriously.

"What?" Crawford exclaimed as he stopped the stopwatch after reassembling his sidearm. "Six point six seconds? Dang it."

"Sorry folks," he told his imaginary audience. "But wait, the legendary Phillip Crawford will attempt to hit a single soda can with fifteen rubber bands from ten feet away!"

Crawford grabbed a soda can off the top of his tower and walked to the shelf. Passing a mirror on the wall, he became distracted. He studied the police hat that hid his short light brown hair. The thick black rimmed glasses he'd worn since he was a child stood out on his face. If he could change one thing about his features, it would be his glasses. He'd always had a problem with his eyes. He could hardly see without them. He didn't want to think about what might happen if he lost them in the field.

Stepping back, he looked at his physique. He'd tried to keep himself physically fit even though he was thinner than most of the other officers at the station. He growled as if to show the mirror how tough he was but then sighed and his shoulders slumped.

"Who am I kidding?" Crawford asked himself. "What am I doing here? I'll never get promoted sitting here. 'Serve and Protect' my foot." He kicked the trashcan in his frustration.

Last week, Sheriff Stronson's had called him into his office. The sheriff's features had always reminded Crawford of a bulldog. He was a large man with short, dark hair. His lower lip jutted out of his pudgy mouth but his eyes had a stare that had earned him his position of authority. None of the officers dared to argue or disobey him.

"Crawford," he'd said. "Sit down."

"Listen, sir," Crawford began as he slowly sat in a hard leather chair. "I know that there have been rumors going around that I've been putting the caffeinated coffee in with the decaf coffee but, rest assured that the rumors are —"

"Shut up and listen," Stronson interrupted and Crawford fell silent.

"Crawford, you are a very ... special officer, in fact you are our most special case."

He flipped through a stack of papers from a file on his desk. "Let's see. It says here that you tried to give a man ticket for changing his tire on the side of the road?"

"Well, you know, uh Sheriff Stronson," Crawford began, as he gave a false chuckle. "It's a funny story really. Sir, that – uh, that man was in a fire zone, see, uh sir. He was also exhibiting very —"

"He was changing a tire, Crawford," Stronson interrupted sternly.

"Yes, well he was ... see, he was a – acting as though he was drunk, uh, sir."

"He's the mayor's son, Crawford," Stronson exclaimed. "He leads the 'No Drugs, No Alcohol' group at the Men's Club in town. He's never touched a drop of alcohol in his life!"

Crawford paused, his mouth hanging open as his mind searched for an excuse.

"Uh ... See that's why it's so funny. Don't you get the irony, sir? Ha! That's a good one, eh?" Crawford gave a hearty laugh and slapped his knee in delight.

Stronson stared at him through blank bulldog eyes. His expression showed no sign of a smile.

Crawford's fictitious laughing diminished into nothing at this sight.

"Sir, uh … you're, uh … you're not laughing …"

Stronson closed the folder. "Because of your incident at the high school and your previous record, I feel the need to give you some kind of … a trial. Yes, that's it. A trial. So I have assigned you to guard Hills West High School for the duration of the year."

Crawford sighed. He wondered if this was a trial or a dead end.

He stepped out into the school's hallway and saw Hank mopping the floor. Crawford saluted him. "You're doing a great job, bud. Keep up the good work."

Hank smiled back and Crawford bit his tongue in frustration. He wished someone would tell him he was doing a great job. Unfortunately, he never got much attention of any kind.

Being a police officer was a profession Crawford felt that he was born to be. Ever since he was a little boy, he'd stayed up at night and dreamed of the day that he would become Captain Phillip Crawford. Maybe one day he could be the sheriff. However, there was no way he would achieve his goal by doing a dopey job like this.

Dropping the soda can on the floor, he crushed it with his boot. If he saw anything out of the ordinary, he was to investigate it. If there was a problem, he was to call t station.

He leaned back against the wall and gazed down the hall. He'd been in that room for nearly an hour, trying to keep himself occupied. It was time he walked around the school a couple times to make sure everything was in order.

He sighed. Everything was always in order. There was nothing for him to do. But he walked down the hall anyway, thinking maybe he would see another janitor.

Approaching the balcony, something below in the cafeteria caught his eye. Someone or something was dressed in black and shuffling from table to table. The hairs on the back of Crawford's neck bristled.

He blinked and shook his head. He'd been cooped up in that room for way too long. He had to be imagining things. He rubbed his eyes with his sweaty palms and opened them again. He scanned the cafeteria again from the balcony.

Nothing moved.

Crawford sighed and allowed his shoulders to relax. He was just tired. That was it. He leaned on the rail and sighed with relief.

Suddenly, a figure appeared from behind the lunch table just feet away from the main office door. Crawford jumped in fright. In a matter of moments, the figure had opened the office door and had disappeared inside.

Crawford grabbed his nightstick from his holster, tightened his belt and adjusted his hat, preparing to take down this intruder himself. Then he would be finished with this dumb job and be given a real assignment.

"Just breathe."

Matt pulled out his ID as he crept down the office hall toward Dr. Pierce's office. His plan had worked perfect so far. All he needed to do was get his journal and get out.

As he reached the principal's office, he jiggled the handle. Locked. He'd expected that. Using his ID, he slid it into the crack between the handle and the doorframe and lifted. Hearing a click, he turned the handle and slipped inside.

Matt grinned. He'd made it into Dr. Pierce's office. It had almost been too easy. He quietly continued toward Dr. Pierce's office and unlocked that door as well. He could see the journal on the top shelf where Dr. Pierce had put it. Matt moved behind the desk and the sleeping computer.

Standing on the tip of his toes, he reached up for the journal only inches away from his fingers. Suddenly, he heard the front door to the office open and close. Open-mouthed, Matt's head spun toward the noise, his eyes wide. Through the window, Matt could see the shine of someone's flashlight. Matt realized that someone must have seen him.

Matt looked back at the journal, jumped up and snatched at it but succeeded only in pushing it further out of reach. His pulse pounded as he heard slow footsteps approach. The light was only feet away from the office door. If whoever it was saw Matt through the window, he was done.

Thoughts raced through his head. Should he hide? Should he jump for his journal one more time? His eyes darted to the window and back to the journal. It was his only opportunity to get his father's deepest thoughts imprinted within those pages.

He jumped for the journal one last time. His fingertips just managed to snatch it before he fell. Dropping to the floor, he bumped the desk just as the light passed over the office.

Underneath the desk, Matt curled himself into a ball. Remaining still, his eyes darted around the room as a faint light appeared above his head. It wasn't the flashlight beam. Matt cursed under his breath. He'd bumped the desk and wakened the computer.

The officer, seeing nothing, turned, and continued down the Head Staff Hall. Matt was relieved to find that the computer faced the opposite wall so the police officer had not spotted the glow from the screen. Moving out from under the desk, he peered over the edge making sure the coast was clear. As Matt began to stand, something caught his eye. Glancing at the screen, he noticed the word *LanCaster* in bold letters. Matt clicked the mouse and the computer slept.

Officer Crawford passed Dr. Pierce's office once again as he headed for the exit. Matt swiftly ducked as the officer passed the window and disappeared around the corner.

Matt relaxed, rose and approached Dr. Pierce's door with the journal in hand. His eyes darted around the office as he crept back into the hall. Reaching the front office door, he looked through the window and into the cafeteria. The officer was nowhere in sight. Matt gently opened the door and slipped behind another lunch table.

Glancing up at the second floor balconies, Matt searched for the man who was mopping the floor but that man had also disappeared.

Matt noticed the cafeteria floor seemed to be much drier than it had been ten minutes ago. He should be able to walk across the floor, continue down the hall and leave through the side door. With one last glimpse around, Matt advanced across the cafeteria moving toward the same hall where he'd first entered.

Crawford refused to give up and swinging around, he approached the cafeteria from a different hall. He paused and looked around, squinting into the darkness. There, he thought he saw the silhouette of someone creeping in the darkness.

"Hey!" he yelled.

Matt spun and saw the police officer sprinting across the cafeteria heading right for him. Whipping around, Matt dashed down the darkened hall throwing all caution aside.

"Stop right there," the officer called.

Charging down the hall with the lockers flying past him, Matt glanced back toward the officer. He could just make out the officer at the other end of the hall coming toward him, full force.

Coming to the bathroom he'd hidden in earlier, Matt bolted inside, opened a stall door and jumped on top of a toilet hoping the officer hadn't seen him. He quieted his breath and listened for the officer to run past. A few seconds later, he heard the thump on the tile floor as the man's boots hurried past the bathroom. Matt released his breath, stepped off the toilet for the second time that night and opened the stall.

Approaching the entrance to the bathroom, Matt knew he had to get out and find another exit or get caught. Sliding along the wall, he listened for the officer trying to be as quiet as he could. The eerie silence sent chills down the hairs on Matt's arm. Stepping toward the door, the automatic hand drier screamed to life and resonated off the quiet halls.

Matt shook his head in disbelief. "Oh, no ..."

Running down the hall, Officer Crawford heard the hand drier howling in the bathroom. He skidded on the floor, spun and headed back eager to make sure the intruder paid dearly for thinking he could mess with Phillip Crawford's territory and get away with it.

Matt jumped out of the bathroom, whirled and saw the officer coming at him with a stern look of determination on his face. Matt bolted back toward the cafeteria.

"Freeze," the officer yelled from behind him. "Stop right there."

Matt continued to sprint down the hall, through the cafeteria and into the next hall. He was beginning to run out of breath. He couldn't run forever. He had to hide somehow. Then, he would get out of the school when the coast was clear.

Turning the corner, Matt dashed down the hall, twisting each doorknob hoping that one might be unlocked. He glanced down the hall for the officer.

Nothing.

Door after door – locked. His legs were heavy, his breathing hard. Sweat dripped through his mask. It appeared that there was no hope. He couldn't outrun the officer. The officer would catch him and Matt would be in even more trouble for attempting to get his journal back.

Chances of escaping seemed smaller and smaller as Matt ran farther and farther into the shadows. With fading hopes, he gripped the doorknob to the furnace room just before the officer rounded the corner. He yanked the knob with all his might. To his relief, the door swung open.

He threw himself inside and shut the door hoping the officer hadn't seen him. A sigh of relief escaped him and a smile crossed his face as the officer's footsteps echoed on down the hall. Leaning up against the door, he slid to the floor exhausted. Matt retrieved his breath, resting for a moment.

As he waited by the door he heard a scuffle from the far side of the room. Matt shot back up again with the realization that he was not alone in this room.

10

Matt waited for his eyes to adjust to the darkness, then took a nervous step forward and almost tripped over a mop bucket.

Something moved in the shadows.

"Who's … who's there?" he stammered.

There was no response.

Matt quietly crept across the room, listening for any sound. With his arms extended, he felt his way around the room. Bumping into something solid, he ran his hands over it. It felt like a stack of crates. Again, he heard a sound.

"Who's there? Where are you?"

With a small click, a white light extended into the darkness. A string swung back and forth from a light bulb on the ceiling. Blinking, Matt examined his new surroundings.

On the floor were pillows, blankets and a box full of small bags of chips. A wooden crate filled with soda cans sat beside a pallet.

Matt could not see who had turned on the light. "Who's there?"

"Don't be afraid," a male voice spoke from the shadows.

Matt saw someone's feet in the corner, the rest of his body was hidden.

Matt took his mask off. "I'm not afraid," Matt said boldly.

"I am." Matt heard the worry in the stranger's voice.

"Why?"

"You found me."

"And that's bad?"

"Yes. Now I have to leave."

Matt squinted at the figure. "Who are you?"

A boy stepped out of the shadow. The light ran from the bottom of his leg, up his chest and made its way to his face. His head hung down almost as if in shame, however, the boy's deep clear blue eyes were still the prominent feature on his face. The warmth and gentleness of his eyes made Matt feel comfortable. The boy's perfectly shaped nose and chin caused Matt a tinge of jealousy. There was no doubt this boy would get attention from ladies. His shoulders were slightly broader than Matt's were. He looked to be about an inch taller than Matt.

The boy glanced up through the locks of ragged light brown hair that hung below his eye. He looked a bit familiar to Matt.

"Do I know you?" Matt asked curiously.

The boy continued to gaze at Matt's feet. "Yeah, we're in English class together."

"What's your name?" Matt asked.

"Jesse."

"What are you doing here?"

Jesse sighed. "This is … uh, where I live."

"Wait …" Matt glanced at Jesse's pallet. "You mean you actually live –?"

Pity overwhelmed Matt but he quickly stifled it. He figured that if he were in Jesse's position, pity would be the last thing he'd want.

"What about you?" Jesse asked quickly to change the conversation.

"What?" Matt replied.

"Who are you?"

"Matt."

"Hmm … and why are you here?" Jesse swung a lock of hair out of his face.

"Because of Fears. He took my dad's journal and wouldn't give it back." Matt showed Jesse the journal. "So I had to take matters into my own hands."

"Oh … right."

"You know what I mean?"

"Yeah."

Matt saw a slight smile cross Jesse's face.

Matt grinned and started to walk around the room checking out the small nook in the large furnace room. "So you really live here?"

"Well I try to," Jesse replied as he began to pick up his belongings. "The hard part is making sure no one sees me."

Matt watched Jesse put his belongings in a backpack.

"What are you doing?"

"I have to leave," Jesse answered. "They'll find me if I don't."

Matt noticed a crate full of Jesse's belongings as well a baseball and a Swiss Army knife. Picking up the baseball, he tossed it in the air a couple of times. "So, ah, where are you going to go?"

"I don't really know yet. God has a way of letting me know where to sleep every night."

Matt tossed the ball into the air again. "Oh, God. Right."

As Jesse continued to pick up his things, Matt changed the subject. "You know, I sort of got that officer's attention."

Jesse reached over and snatched his baseball out of the air. "Yeah, I figured that." He stuffed the ball into his backpack.

"Well, I'm sure he's looking for me out there."

"Wrong. He's looking for us now. If he sees me, he'll think that I'm you. So we have to get out of here together."

"Do you know –?"

A disturbance on the opposite side of the room silenced both of them. Someone jiggled the locked door handle.

"I know you're in there," the officer called through the thick door. "Open up or I'll kick the door down!"

Matt jumped at the noise. His heart rate skyrocketed. Jesse spun and stuffed a pair of jeans into his backpack.

"Open the door," the voice yelled.

Looking around, Matt saw that the only way in or out was the door. Jesse approached the wall with his backpack in hand.

"Jesse," Matt whispered. "What are we going to do?"

"Come on. Quick," Jesse answered in a hushed voice. "We've got to get out of here."

"Gee, ya' think, professor?" Matt retorted. "How?"

Dropping his backpack, Jesse unzipped one of the pockets and pulled out the screwdriver from his Swiss Army knife.

"What are you going to do with that?" Matt asked wide-eyed.

The beating on the door grew louder. Jesse moved aside a stack of crates revealing a ventilation shaft.

"This is how I get in and out without being noticed by the janitors or that cop." He began to unscrew the vent from the wall.

"Are you serious?" Matt exclaimed as quiet as possible. "You're crazy!"

"I've done it before."

"But you've never done it with two people before I bet, have you? Do you even know if that thing can hold both of us?"

Jesse clenched his teeth as the beatings grew louder. "If you have another idea, please be my guest. Right now this is the best plan we've got."

Jesse unscrewed the last screw and faced Matt. "I mean there's always the obvious way out."

He motioned toward the door.

Matt looked toward the entrance and paused.

The pounding had stopped. "I'm coming in," the voice called.

A large thump hit the door.

"I agree. Now would be a fine time to leave." Matt turned back toward Jesse.

"Well, get in then." Jesse stepped aside. "I'll move the stack of crates to block the opening."

Matt tucked his journal beneath his shirt and crawled into the vent. It was big enough for him to crawl on all fours without getting stuck. Jesse would have to crawl behind him.

Another thump hit the door harder than the first. It wouldn't be long before the officer managed to kick the door down.

"Keep going," Jesse called as he ventured back out to the center of the room.

"What are you doing?" Matt hissed.

"Giving us cover," came the reply. The room suddenly turned to darkness but Matt could see Jesse come back with the light bulb that had once illuminated the room, in hand. He shoved the bulb in his pocket and peered up the shaft.

Matt crawled a bit further down the shaft and sneezed because of all the dust.

"Are you okay?" Jesse asked as he started into the vent.

"Oh, peachy," Matt grumbled. "Thanks for asking."

"Keep going until you —"

The door flung open at the officer's third kick.

Matt and Jesse could hear him yelling in the darkness. "I know you're in here. Just come out now and it will be easier for all of us."

Matt turned his head and looked at Jesse. He placed his finger to his lips and mouthed, "Don't move."

Matt tried to remain quiet as he heard the officer's footsteps walk across the room. He tried to quiet his breathing and heard Jesse doing the same.

Matt shook his head. What a night this had turned out to be. How had it come to this? He felt so foolish.

Jesse tapped Matt's ankle and Matt looked back at him. "Move slow." Jesse pointed down the vent.

Matt nodded and continued down the dusty shaft as Jesse silently followed.

Crawford shined his flashlight into the corners of the room. Searching for the whereabouts of the intruder, he squinted into the darkness and looked for another way out of the room. Spinning around, he bumped into a small stack of crates. Crawford noticed the bag of chips and the crate of soda cans.

"Someone's definitely been here," he muttered.

Bending over to grab the bag of chips, he noticed the vent cover on the floor. As he flashed his light past the stack of crates and along the wall, it reflected off the exposed ventilation shaft. He blinked and lowered his flashlight. Sitting it on top of the crates, he pushed them aside, squatted and looked down the empty air shaft.

"Hey!" he called. "I know you're up there."

But Matt and Jesse had already gone up the shaft and turned the corner.

Crawford snarled as he stood realizing he would have to crawl into the vent if he were to catch this intruder. He turned to grab his flashlight off the crates and instead bumped into them. They were knocked off balance and quickly fell to the floor. His flashlight rolled and fell off the crates and shattered the bulb to pieces on the cement.

The room was dark.

He looked at the vent biting his lips in apprehension. He could venture after the intruder but it wouldn't be much use. His eyes were bad enough already. If he didn't have a light, he'd practically be blind.

A soft noise came from the hall. Crawford cocked his head, turned toward the hall and looked up at the ceiling. He could hear the intruder shuffling along in the vent. Pulling out his handcuffs and unbuckling his sidearm, Crawford grinned. Whenever the intruder decided to come out, he'd be waiting.

Matt and Jesse suppressed their coughs and sneezes as they made their way down the dusty shaft. Coming to a three-way intersection, Matt looked back to Jesse. "Which way?"

Jesse pointed right.

Matt continued down the shaft with ease. The only difficulty was seeing in the dim light. He had to admit crawling through the ventilation shaft was a good idea. Just then, Jesse grabbed Matt's ankle and shook it.

"What?"

Jesse signaled for silence and pointed below them.

"Are you sure?" Matt whispered.

Jesse nodded. "I heard him," he mouthed.

"What do we do?"

Jesse paused a moment in thought.

Matt had no idea how they were going to get away this time. If the cop was tracking them, he would catch them as soon as they exited the shaft.

"Wait," Jesse whispered. "I've got it."

Pulling his backpack off, he unzipped a pocket and brought out the baseball Matt had been playing with earlier.

Jesse handed Matt the ball. "Roll it down the right shaft," he said. "The cop should follow the ball. We'll wait a little bit and go left."

In moments, they heard footsteps head in the direction of the ball. Turning back to Jesse, Matt gave a thumbs-up.

Jesse nodded. "Good, turn left and let's get out of here."

Crawford followed the noise as it traveled down the vent, turned the corner and stopped above a classroom. After a few moments of silence, Crawford concluded that the intruder was climbing out the vent and into the classroom. Looking down the hall, he noticed Hank waxing the floor.

"Hey, buddy!" he called.

Hank looked up.

"You got the key to this room? Somebody's in the vent."

In moments, Hank had the door opened. Crawford found the shaft, unscrewed the vent and a baseball fell to the floor with a dull thud.

"Hmm …" Hank eyed the baseball. "That sucks."

Matt and Jesse soon found themselves at the end of the shaft, which came out into a long brick alleyway. Matt pushed open the vent cover to take a deep breath of fresh air. In moments, the two of them scrambled out of the shaft and crept down the alley to the parking lot.

Matt peeked around the corner of the brick wall to see if anyone was coming but the night was still, almost an eerie quietness to it. He nodded and motioned to Jesse. The two of them dashed across the parking lot to the cover of the woods.

Matt rested against a tree and smiled.

"Thanks a lot, Jesse. I'm sure I'd have been caught without you."

"No problem, I do it all the time. But that's not my problem now. Right now, I have to find somewhere else to stay for the night. It was good meeting you, Matt. I'll see you at school."

He turned and trekked off through the woods.

Matt watched him go. Looking down at his journal, he saw it was open to the entry he had read earlier. He remembered how his father hadn't helped someone who was in need. Afterward, he'd felt bad about it. Matt realized that if he didn't help Jesse after all Jesse had done for him, he would feel terrible. He wasn't about to make the same mistake his father had.

"Hey, wait," Matt yelled and ran to catch up with Jesse. "Where are you going to go?"

"God has a place for me somewhere," Jesse replied.

Matt rolled his eyes. "I'm sure He does. Instead of having that place be a gutter or something, come and stay with me for a while. I've got an extra room at my house. You could stay until you get your feet back on the ground."

"No, I don't take charity."

Matt grabbed Jesse's arm and stopped him.

"It's not charity," he said. "Consider it a debt that I owe you for getting me out of there."

Jesse sighed. "You really want me to come and live with you?"

"If you want to come, the door is open," Matt replied.

"What about your parents?"

"We'll tell them that your parents went on vacation or something."

Jesse shrugged his backpack. "How far is your house?"

"About eight miles from here."

Jesse stepped aside. "Lead the way."

11

The next morning Matt woke to hear Bruce yelling.

"Hey? What are you doing here? You think you can just stay anywhere. Get out of here! That's right, leave!"

Matt gasped, his eyes jerking toward the door. Shaking off his blankets, he ran out of his room and dashed down the stairs. As he passed the living room, he noticed that Jesse wasn't on the couch where he'd slept last night. Blankets lay strewn on the floor.

"I'm not going to tell you again," Bruce yelled from the kitchen. "Get out of here and don't come back!"

"No, Bruce. It's all right!" Matt turned the corner. "Jesse's —"

Matt stopped. Jesse stood at the stove calmly cracking two eggs on the side of a pan while Bruce shooed several birds from the windows.

"— making breakfast."

"Hey, Matt." Jesse smiled. "Want some eggs?"

"I mean it, you danged birds. Leave!" Bruce yelled out the window again.

Matt sighed, relieved that Bruce wasn't shooing Jesse away.

"Sure, Jesse. I'll have some."

He stood at the table and ran his fingers through his tangled hair. "Where's Mom?" he asked.

"Oh, Mary?" Jesse replied. "She's upstairs making my bed and getting my room ready for me."

Matt stepped closer to Jesse. "What did you tell them?"

104

"My parents left me and I don't know when they'll be back. Bruce suggested that I stay until they get back."

"But they're not really coming back, are they?"

Jesse's eyes met Matt's for a moment as he paused, then turned back to stir his eggs.

"Oh, by the way, Matt," Bruce said as he buttered a piece of toast. "Some girl called for you earlier."

"For me?" Matt asked surprised. "Who was it? What did she want?"

"She wanted you to call her back. Said her name was … oh, what was it? I've got it written down somewhere. Lemme find it. Hang on. Oh, here it is – Rose Hudson. She left her phone number. A girl friend of yours?" Bruce's right eyebrow rose in curiosity.

Matt snorted. "I wish."

"Well, you'd better call her back," Bruce continued as he took a bite of toast. "She called awoun' nine thir'y or sho."

"What time is it?" Matt asked.

Bruce checked his watch. "About eleven."

"Jeez!" Matt jumped. "Where's the phone? What's her number?"

Sitting on his bed with the phone in one hand and Rose's number in the other, Matt wondered what he was going to say once he got the nerve to call her. He let out a long breath and closed his eyes.

She's just another girl, he told himself even though he knew he was lying. He looked at her number again for the tenth time even though he'd already memorized it. He shook his head again.

"Oh, to heck with it." He dialed her number.

He heard the phone ring. His heart rate quickened. After a few moments, a female voice answered.

"Hello," Matt said. "Is, uh, Rose there? Uh, please? Uh … oh, hi Rose. Sorry, didn't recognize your voice. It's Matt Cross. You called me earlier?"

The voice on the other end spoke. Matt's mind raced as he listened. Rose wanted to get together today? What was this about?

Matt's face brightened.

"Oh, right, right, the Juggernut Flag for English. But it's not due for a while yet."

Matt shifted his body weight from one leg to the other. "I guess we could get started on it, uh, that is if you think we should."

He stumbled over his words. As he listened to Rose, his mind searched for the correct response.

Suddenly, he exclaimed, "No, you're absolutely right. We should get started on it now."

A pause.

"Well, yeah. You're right. I guess it is … pretty awkward to work together," Matt continued, "but, I agree we uh, better just get it done and out of the way. Then we won't have to deal with it anymore right?"

Matt listened to her response.

"You want to come over here?" Then enthusiastically, "Yeah, definitely."

Matt changed his tone. He didn't want to sound too anxious.

"I mean, uh, that'd be fine. Get a pencil and I'll give you directions to my house."

Matt hung up the phone and collapsed on his bed. He felt like kissing the phone. He and Rose were actually going to work on this together. He was really going to get to sit with her and talk to her and work with her. It all seemed too good to be true.

Jesse appeared at the door and noticed Matt's smiling face. "What's up?"

Matt sat up in bed. "Rose is coming."

"Here?"

"Yes, here, later this afternoon."

"Well, we've got some things to do then."

"What do you mean?"

Jesse sighed as he stepped into the room.

"First off, you've got to do something with your room. You two are probably going to be spending some time in here, right? So you need to pick it up or something. Anything would be great really."

"Thanks, Mom."

"I'm serious. Do you have the hots for her or not?"

"Yeah."

"Well, you need to make a good impression then. You need to change clothes and do your hair."

Jesse walked across Matt's room and opened the window that overlooked that part of the roof. The early autumn breeze filled the room.

"You need to get some air in this place," he said.

"Tell me, Mr. Clean," Matt said sarcastically. "Is there anything else that needs to be done?"

"Matt, if you want to go out with Rose I can help but you need to listen to my advice. I'm telling you, Matt. This could work. This could really work."

"Well, let's go then. I'll start working on my room. Go and pick up those blankets in the living room."

Jesse grinned. "Now you're thinking."

Over an hour later, Matt and Jesse had finished cleaning the house. Matt was straightening his quilt on his bed when his mother walked in.

"Man, Matt. I should have this girl come over more often if you're going to clean the house."

Matt smiled.

"Are you and this Rose going to work in here?" Mary asked.

"Yeah, probably."

"Well, I'm going to warn you now that I'll be checking periodically on you two to make sure that you're working. No handsy stuff, okay?"

Matt hid his blushing face. He didn't know why his mother thought 'handsy stuff' was a better term for 'physicality'.

"Mom, I hardly know the girl."

"Yeah, right. Whatever you think," she said. "This door stays open."

"But Mom, how –?"

"Don't 'But Mom' me," she interrupted. "Don't think that I haven't been fifteen before. This door stays open."

Matt shook his head and smiled as she left.

Matt was brushing his teeth when he heard someone knock on the bathroom door.

"Come een," he managed through a mouthful of toothpaste. "Ith's unlocked."

Jesse cracked the door open, peeked inside and then opened it the rest of the way. Matt spit in the sink and turned off the faucet. "What's up?"

"I wanted to help you out a bit." Jesse laid a small bottle on the counter.

Matt eyed the bottle. "What's this?"

"Cologne."

"Cologne?"

"You don't have to use it. It's just an idea."

Matt took a whiff of the tip of the bottle. "Where did you get this?"

A wicked grin crossed Jesse's face. "The Lost and Found box."

Matt laughed in disbelief. "At school?"

Jesse shrugged. "Girls love a guy that smells good. What can I say?"

Matt heard another knock at the door as he peered in the mirror to do his hair.

"Come in," Matt called.

Bruce opened the door and stepped inside.

"Listen, Matt," he said. "I've been talking with Jesse, and he tells me that this girl's pretty hot stuff. And she's coming here to see you."

Bruce leaned in close and lowered his voice in Matt's ear.

"So don't not do anything, if you know what I mean. You might give her a few Cross family moves, you know? Your dad and I were quite the guys back in our prime. You're the same blood. You need to leave the door open to keep your mom off your back. But, if your Mom starts coming towards your room, I'll warn you guys somehow. I was fifteen once. I know what it's like to like a girl."

"Thanks," Matt said as Bruce left the bathroom.

He smiled unsure how to deal with the conflicting advice he was hearing.

Chad Statler

Matt had just finished his hair when he heard Newt bark.

"She's here," Mary called. "Matt, are you ready?"

Matt put his toiletries back into his cabinet and looked at himself in the mirror. He'd dressed casual. He didn't want Rose to think he'd dressed up or anything but, he thought he looked good.

He took a deep breath. "Be cool, Matt. You can be cool," he said to the mirror. "Oh, yeah, you can be cool."

He posed in the mirror, attempting to find a good 'cool look' when his mother called, "Matt, where are you? Come on."

Matt strolled out of the bathroom as Newt barked and scratched at the door.

"Shh! Newt, it's okay!"

Matt petted him as Rose approached the door and rang the doorbell.

Newt barked again at the sound. "Newt, hush."

He opened the door. Rose stood there with a plastic bag full of supplies in hand. Newt wiggled away from Matt and dashed out the door towards Rose.

"Don't worry. He won't bite," Matt reassured.

"No, it's okay." Rose bent down to pet him. She scratched behind his ears.

"I love dogs. He's so cute." She cupped Newt's face in her hands. "Yes, you are."

The gentle breeze blew her auburn hair across her white shirt. Matt could see a bit of her tan stomach between her shirt and blue Jean shorts. His eyes followed her thin, tan legs down to her white flip-flops.

Matt opened the door a bit wider. "Would you like to come in?"

"Thank you," she said as she turned and waved to her father who sat in his truck. He gave a slight wave and pulled out of the driveway.

Jesse sat at the dining room table with Bruce drinking coffee.

"Oh, hey, Jesse," Rose said as she set the bag on the table. "I didn't know you were going to be here."

"Yeah, I should be sticking around for a while."

Bruce stood and approached Rose, jutting his large hand toward her.

"Name's Bruce. I guess you're Rose then? We spoke on the phone earlier."

Rose smiled as Bruce went on, "And this lovely lady over here is Matt's mom, Mary."

Mary approached from the kitchen and Rose took her hand as well. "I hope you like pizza," Mary said. "I just thawed one. Just let me know when you guys get hungry."

"Thank you," Rose replied. "We will."

The five of them looked from one person to the next as if waiting for someone to say something. No one spoke and Matt began to feel uncomfortable.

Glancing at Rose, he could tell she was also uncomfortable so he broke the silence. "So, Rose. Let's get started."

"Sure," Rose replied quickly. "I brought some material that we can work with. I didn't know if you –"

"It's fine," Matt said, snatching the bag off the table and heading for the stairs. "Come with me."

Newt followed with his tail wagging.

―――――

Following Matt upstairs to his room, Rose glanced around. "Wow. You have a nice room. Do you always keep it this clean?"

Matt blushed and turned his head away. "No comment."

"I understand. My room's the same way. I don't ever pick it up unless company's coming."

Newt jumped up beside Rose as she sat on Matt's bed. Matt lounged in an oversized chair in the corner.

Rose eyed Matt. When he looked at her, she looked away. She didn't seem to have much to say now that they were alone in his room.

"Hello," he said to break the awkwardness.

"Hi."

They were both quiet for a few more minutes, gazing about the room as if hoping they would find something written on the ceiling for them to discuss. Newt looked from one to the other and then back again waiting for someone to say something.

Matt sighed, stood and then realized he didn't have anywhere to go so he sat back down. "Uh … okay. Rose, I want to be honest with you."

Rose was brought to attention. "About what?"

"I'm sure you're feeling pretty uncomfortable right now. But I want you to know that I'm in the same boat. So how about we just forget that we don't know each other and pretend that we've been friends for a while. Maybe that way, it will relieve some of the stress."

A smile spread over Rose's face. "You're nice." She extended her hand. "Hi, I'm Rose Hudson."

He took her hand in his. "Matt Cross."

Matt looked at the bag of materials. "Well, now that we've got that out of the way, are you ready to make a Hug-a-Nut flag?"

"You mean a Juggernut flag?" Rose smiled again.

"Yeah, that thing," Matt replied. "But you know all this talking is making me tired. What do you say we take a break?"

She laughed and Matt beamed. Things weren't going so bad.

12

Rose rested against the headboard of Matt's bed, a spiral notebook on her lap. The words "Flag Ideas" were scrawled across the top.

The two of them had been laughing and talking about their lives, where they'd come from and what their parents were like. Rose's mother and father had divorced shortly after Rose's first birthday. After the divorce, Rose and her father moved to Hills West and hadn't moved since. She said she had no idea where her mother was.

Matt told Rose about his family and what being home schooled was like. He didn't elaborate on his father. He didn't want her to feel sorry for him.

"Well, Rose, we've been talking for a half hour," he said, "but we haven't done much towards the flag project."

"I know," she replied. "I guess I just don't feel like working right now. I'm having fun talking though."

"Yeah?"

"Yeah," she murmured. "I know it seems weird but when you said to pretend that we've known each other, it really helped. I feel like I could talk to you for hours. And I'm not much of a talker when it comes to guys. Does that seem weird to you?"

He shook his head. "No, it … doesn't seem weird at all."

There was a pause.

Newt opened an eye from where he slept on Matt's bed.

"I feel all cramped in here," Matt said, breaking the silence. "Do you want to go for a walk or something?"

Rose smiled and laid the notebook on the nightstand. "I think that'd be great."

Matt loaned Rose an old pair of tennis shoes and tied his. Within minutes, they were headed for the door passing Mary who was folding clothes in the living room.

"Hold the pizza a little bit longer, Mom," Matt called.

"Hey, wait a sec —" but the door closed before Mary could say anything more.

"Quick, Rose," Matt said as they reached the yard. "Let's go."

"Where are we going?" she asked as Matt took off around the house.

Mary appeared at the door. "Hey, you kids get back here. You've got work to do!"

"Just go!" Matt exclaimed.

The two of them dashed through the green field behind the house as the afternoon sun radiated behind them. Neither of them looked back.

Eventually, they came to a stop in the middle of the field behind the house. Rose had her hands on her knees as she tried to catch her breath. Matt paced in a small circle with his arms over his head as he worked to regain his wind.

Then he felt Rose poke him in the back. "You're it."

Matt spun around as Rose sprinted away. "Oh, you did not!"

The warm breeze blew as they played tag and chased each other around the wide field laughing wherever they went.

Rose tagged him again and Matt dashed after her. She squealed as she turned in the opposite direction but Matt caught up to her and poked her arm. As Matt turned away, he tripped on a stick and fell to the ground. Rose tripped on Matt as he fell and rolled over him. The two of them lay in a heap on the soft ground.

Matt sat up and groaned. He glanced at Rose as he began to brush the dirt off his clothes. He noticed a smile cross Rose's face and she began to giggle.

Matt frowned. "What?"

Rose's giggling soon turned to laughter and then no longer able to contain it, she held her stomach and laughed hysterically. Matt did nothing but watch in confusion. He smiled at Rose's laughter.

"What is it?" he asked. "Why are you laughing?"

"I've never … done that before," she managed. "You know how we ran and played and stuff? That was fun." Her laughter began to subside. "My dad always kept me inside as a kid. I guess he didn't trust many people. I'm not used to that."

Matt sat up in the grass. "It's a good thing we finished the flag," he said sarcastically.

Their laughter echoed in the meadow.

Soon Matt and Rose were in the woods hiking along trails created long before Matt had moved to Hills West. They'd hiked a half of a mile or so when Rose sat on a large rock.

"Hang on, Matt. I think I've got something in my shoe."

"Oh, come on, Rose," Matt smiled. "We're on a schedule here."

He grabbed her arms and tried to pull her onto his back.

"Oh, no Matt," Rose cried. "I couldn't. Really, I'm fine. I'm quite – Matt!"

He easily tossed her onto his back.

"Come on, Rose. Have some fun."

"You can put me down now."

Matt shook his head and hitched her higher up onto his back. "Maybe later."

"Matt!" Rose cried as he took off down the trail. She wrapped her arms around his shoulders and laughed as she bounced on his back. "I've never … done this … before, either."

Matt slowed to a stop, breathing heavily. "Neither have I. But I like it."

He heard the smile in her voice. "Me, too. Can you put me down now?"

"No."

Rose sighed and dropped her head onto his shoulder in defeat. He heard her sniff his neck. "You smell good."

"Yeah?"

"I like that."

Matt grinned as he reminded himself that he would have to thank Jesse later.

A sound in the distance caught his attention. "Do you hear that?"

"What?"

"It sounds like running water."
"I don't hear anything."
"It's further down the trail. Hold on, Rose."

Mary took off her reading glasses, sat up in her chair and looked at Jesse who was sitting on the chair next to her watching television.
"Jesse, do you know where Matt and Rose went?"
"Outside somewhere."
Mary stared at him blankly. "Wow. Thanks for the tip, Jesse."
He didn't respond. His eyes were fixed on the television.
"They've been gone a while," Mary went on. "Could you go and bring them back, please?"
Jesse didn't respond.
"Jesse," Mary said a little louder.
Nothing.
"Jesse!"
Jesse jumped. "What?"
"Could you go and bring them back, please?"
"Oh, all right." He got up.
"Thank you. Be careful."
Mary shook her head as Jesse shut the door.
"Teenagers."

Within minutes, Matt found the end of the trail and the source of the water sound. The trail ended at the peak of a bluff overlooking the waterfall. He wasn't aware that there was a stream on his property but he liked the idea.
Rose rested on a rock and watched as Matt stood at the edge of the waterfall. The stream was about twenty yards wide and the clear water made a loud splash as it met the dark blue water. The setting sun hung lower now and shone through the thicket of trees in the woods. The red and purple of the sky intertwined with the greens and oranges of the trees and all of it accented by the blue of the water.
"It's beautiful, isn't it?" Rose asked.
Matt smiled but didn't respond. He stepped to the edge of the bluff and examined the deep blue water rippling below.

"How high do you think we are from the water?" he asked.

Rose frowned at the change in subject. She joined Matt at the edge of the bluff and looked down. "Oh, about thirty feet or so."

"Want to jump?"

"What?"

Matt leaned against a tree and began to take off his shoes and socks.

"I'm going to jump," he said.

Matt noticed Rose raise her eyebrows as he pulled his shirt off, and then looked away quickly. He hoped she was checking him out.

"It's like seventy degrees out here," she said. "That water's gonna be freezing."

"It's not seventy. It's like seventy-five."

"Oh, big difference." She rolled her eyes. "But seriously, there are … rocks down there. How do you know you won't hit one? You could die. You don't even know how deep it is."

"Look at the water, Rose," he said. "It's a dark blue. It wouldn't be that color if it weren't deep. As for the rocks, I'll take my chances."

"But you —"

"Do you ever get that feeling that you've got to do something even though you can't explain why?" Matt asked. He gazed into the pool as though it were whispering the secrets of time to him. "I've got to jump."

He turned to her. "Jump with me."

Rose shook her head and took a step back. "I can't."

"Look at that view, Rose. Why wouldn't you want to stay? We could stay and play for the rest of the evening. Jump with me. Let's do this."

Rose looked from the pool to Matt and back to the pool. "I'm afraid."

"I'll jump first then," he said.

He edged closer until his toes hung off the edge. The roar of the falls echoed through the thicket and the mist from the water tickled his chest sending chills up his spine.

He looked back at Rose one more time. "Come with me, Rose."

Rose glanced at the waterfall one more time and shook her head.

So Matt turned, kicked away from the ground, fell through the air and plunged into the dark pool.

Rose peered over the edge and into the disturbed pool looking for Matt. Another thirty seconds passed but he didn't resurface.

"Matt," she called.

Nothing.

"Matt!"

She didn't see him. Her eyes went wide. "Oh, no. Matt, Matt!" she screamed. "Oh, my gosh, Matt! Where are you?"

There was no response.

What if he had hit the rocks? What if he couldn't come back up? He might be down there drowning. She had to go in after him whether she was afraid or not.

She sat on the edge and yanked off her shoes and socks.

"I'm coming, Matt! God help me …"

She pushed off from the bluff with a short squeal as she fell through the air, holding her nose as she submerged. Opening her eyes underwater, she looked for Matt.

The water was clear and she could see a good distance even underneath the surface. The bubbles and current from the fall fell on her. Rose quickly resurfaced and swam to the calmer part of the pool.

Matt was nowhere in sight.

"Please, God …" she prayed. "Matt!"

There was nothing but the roar of the fall. She swam out into the water, went under and searched for him again.

"Matt," she yelled as she came back up.

"What?" said a voice from behind her.

She spun in the water to see Matt standing on a rock near the edge of the pool. He must have climbed on it while Rose was beneath the surface looking for him.

Rose pointed a harsh finger in his direction. "You think you're real funny, don't you?" She smacked the water. "I thought you were dead or something."

"Had you worried?" He laughed from the rock.

"You're horrible!"

"I'm not that bad, am I?"

Matt jumped into the pool before Rose could respond and sent water shooting in all directions.

She lurched out from the water and grabbed Matt as he surfaced and pulled him beneath again. Matt came back up and threw water at Rose. She stopped in surprise and then threw water back at him.

They continued to play and wrestle as a red sun lowered behind the trees around them.

Jesse followed the trail that Matt and Rose had made in the field to the trail in the woods. He could hear them playing before he reached the bluff. Finding cover behind a large boulder, Jesse watched Matt and Rose.

Matt and Rose wrestled and flirted in the water for a while longer, then swam to the shallow end of the pool and relaxed for a moment.

"How long have I known you?" Matt asked.

"Mmm … a few hours, I guess."

"Now look at us."

"I know. Isn't this crazy?"

"You're crazy," Matt teased.

"No offense," Rose said, "but I'm not the one who wanted to jump off a cliff."

Matt grabbed her in an attempt to dunk her but she held his arm. As he pushed her down, he went down with her. Water dripped from their faces as they popped back to the surface. It was then that Matt realized just how close their faces were to each other.

Holding her around the hips, Matt felt her warm body pressed close to him.

He glanced at her lips. He longed to kiss her, but he wouldn't. No, that would be too abrupt.

But still … she was right there.

Rose relaxed in his arms. Faces close, they gazed into one another's eyes.

She gently laid her hands on Matt's shoulders and, closing her eyes, leaned into him.

The sound of crunching leaves startled Matt and he spun in the water to see a figure step from behind a large rock.

"Jesse?" he called.

Jesse came from behind the boulder, leaned on his knees and looked down at them. "Hey you two, didn't see you down there," he lied. "It's a good thing I found you, though."

"Why's that?" Matt asked.

"Because your Mom wants you guys to come home now. She says you're not finished with the flag yet."

Rose turned back to Matt and sighed

The moment was lost.

The two of them separated and started to make their way out of the pool. Matt grabbed his clothes from the rock and Jesse stood waiting as Rose clambered up the bluff. Reaching over, Matt smacked Jesse on the side of the head.

"Ow," Jesse cried. "What was that for?"

"You had to show up right then, didn't you?" Matt hissed as he held his fingers an inch apart. "I was this close!"

"I don't know what I'm going to do when we get back to the house," Rose said as she tried to wring her long wet hair out on the trail back to the house. "What am I going to wear?"

"It's okay," Matt chimed. "I'll find something for you."

Arriving back at the house, Matt received a firm talking to by his mother. Luckily, it didn't last very long. He then went, changed and found a change of clothes for Rose. He laid them neatly on the bed and while she changed, Matt put the pizza in the oven.

Rose came out of the bedroom wearing a pair of gray gym shorts and a red hooded sweater. Taking her wet clothes, he put them in the drier. They went back to his room and Rose grabbed the notebook of ideas. She lay on his bed assuming the same position she had earlier and Matt returned to the windowsill.

"Man," she sighed. "That was fun."

He looked at her and smirked. "You're still the crazy one."

"Okay …" Matt paced around Rose who was eating a slice of pizza. "Ms. Ellis says that we have to have a distinct theme for our flag. What have we got so far?"

"We've come up with autumn –"

"Too broad."

"Food –"

"Too much."

"Teachers –"

"Too many."

"Pizza."

Matt stopped pacing. "Where'd that one come from?"

"I don't know. I just wanted to hear what you'd say."

Matt shook his head and smiled. "But seriously, we've been working for a while now and we haven't got any farther than when we started."

Sitting in his chair, he took a bite of pizza. Rose slid off the bed, walked over to the window seat and looked out at the sky.

"I want our flag to win. I mean you really do win cash if you win, right?" he asked. "Rose?"

Matt turned to look at Rose who was gazing at the sun as it disappeared beneath the horizon. In the darkness of the sky, a few stars winked.

"I love it when the sky looks like this," she murmured.

Matt plunged ahead. "We need a theme with some kick, you know?"

"You can't see the stars like this at my house."

Matt didn't hear her. "We need something that separates us from the rest of the group."

"What if we did something with stars?"

Matt continued, "I mean I think we can win this if we think about it."

"What if we did something with stars?" she asked a little louder.

Matt stopped pacing.

"Where'd that come from?"

Rose rolled her eyes. "Where have you been in the last minute?"

Matt sat beside her on the window seat. "Sorry. What now?"

"It was just an idea," she said. "Do you know anything about stars?"

He shrugged. "I know a little."

"Like what?"

Matt stood and pushed the window open farther letting in more of the cool breeze. "Come on."

"Where?"

"To the roof."

"The roof?"

"Yeah." Matt grabbed a couple blankets off his bed. "Let's go. We can watch the stars."

He slipped out the window with Rose close behind him. Carefully, they crawled to the highest point of the roof.

"I used to come up here all the time when I was little," Matt said as he laid a blanket on the roof. "I haven't been up here in ages."

"The stars are really bright." Rose gawked at the sky.

"You can see them really well from here. There aren't any street lights."

Matt lay down on the blanket and motioned for Rose to join him. They became comfortable and gazed up at the darkened sky in awe as the stars gradually began to appear in the sky.

"Wow," Rose whispered. "It's amazing. There're so many."

Rose looked at Matt staring at the numerous stars in the sky. "I think stars would be a nice theme. Don't you?"

Matt smiled. "I'm sure we could come up with something."

Silently, they sat for a few minutes listening to the night. Rose was right. The stars were burning brighter than Matt had seen in a long time. He looked from Rose to the stars and back to Rose.

She let out a long breath. "Show me something."

Matt glanced at her. "What do you mean?"

"You said you knew some stuff about stars, didn't you?"

"Well, I know a little. I'm no astronomer or anything."

"Well, show me something."

"Okay," he replied.

He rolled over toward her. His warm body brushed up against her arm and Rose scooted closer so she could see where he was pointing. Matt pointed into the sky.

"Well for starters ..." he said. "There's the Big Dipper."
"Where?"
"See that line of stars there?"
Rose frowned. "Which line?"
Matt took her hand in his, extended her pointer finger and used it to trace the line of stars in the sky.
"Do you see how the stars form a line from there to there?"
"Oh, right. I see it."
"Over there is Orion."
"Where?"
He used her hand to point to the constellation.
"See it?"
Rose smiled at Matt's warmth. She continued pretending as though she didn't know any constellations. He enjoyed having her hand in his.
"I see it," she said. "I think we've found our theme."
Matt smiled. "Yeah, I definitely think so."
He glanced at her and found her looking at him.
"You do?" Rose asked.
Their faces were only inches away from each other.
"Yeah."
Still holding Rose's hand, Matt brought it down to her chest. Matt leaned toward her until their noses touched.
"Now we just have to make it work."
"We'll make it work," Rose replied softly.
Matt saw Rose lower her beautiful green eyes as his lips gently pressed against hers. The warmth of the kiss sent a small chill down his body.
"Matthew," his mother called. "Matthew!"
The kiss ended at the interruption and Matt sighed.
The moment had died again.
He rolled back toward the window. "What?"
"What are you doing up there?"
"We're working."
"Well, you'd better finish up because Rose's dad just called. He'll be here in a few minutes to pick her up. You need to get her clothes out of the drier and she needs to get ready to go."

"Okay, Mom," he replied.

He rolled back toward Rose but she was already getting on her feet.

"Come on," she said. "Let's go before you get in trouble."

"So …" Matt began as he grabbed Rose's clothes out of the drier. "We're going with stars then?"

Rose nodded. "We'll have to get together again this week. Tomorrow doesn't work for me. I've got church and stuff."

"Church?" He paused. "Really?"

"Yeah, why?"

"I don't know. You just didn't seem to be one of those churchy kinds of people."

"'Churchy kinds of people'?" She looked surprised. "What do you mean?"

"Well, you kind of look like you'd be one of those people who'd treat Sunday like a Saturday. You know, sleep in, relax, and do fun stuff. Not church."

"No, I go to church." Her jaw dropped as she thought of an idea. "You should come with me."

Matt raised his eyebrows in surprise and took a step backward.

"Well, I don't want to seem —"

"What a wonderful idea! My dad and I will be by to pick you up tomorrow morning around eight-thirty. Your family can come too if they'd like."

Matt sighed not wanting to argue with her. "Okay."

"Good, now go away." She nudged him in the direction of the door. "I need to change."

"Rose," Mary called over the car horn. "Your father's here."

Rose came out of the bathroom with her dried clothes on and noticed Matt sitting at the dinner table. She gave him a quick hug, shook Mary's hand and waved good-bye to Bruce and Jesse who were in the living room.

"Thanks for having me," she said to Mary. "I liked the pizza."

Mary smiled. "You can come back anytime."

Rose opened the door and stopped. "Oh, I invited Matt to church tomorrow, if that's okay."

Mary paused.

"Oh, yes. I suppose that would be all right."

"You can come too if you like," Rose offered as her father honked the horn again.

"Uh ... thank you," Mary hesitated. "We'll see."

Matt doubted Mary would go to church. Mary hadn't gone to church since his father's accident. Matt didn't really want to go to church either, but Rose wanted him to, so he would.

"Great," Rose smiled. "Thanks again."

She shut the door behind her and was gone.

Matt turned from the door to see his mother, Bruce and Jesse all grinning at him. "What?"

"You've got it bad, man," Bruce said.

"How do you figure?" Matt asked defensively.

"Well, look at it this way," his mom said. "You go outside and go swimming in some waterfall that's back in the woods. She changes into your clothes. Then, you go up to the roof to 'work.'"

"We did work. We figured out what our theme was."

"That took all of four hours," Bruce said smiling. "You're not in trouble or anything. We're just glad that you've got a girl."

Matt paused.

"A girl? I've got a girl? She's not ... I mean, we're not ..."

"Whatever." Jesse shook his head. "You need to be thinking about going to bed soon. We've got church tomorrow."

"Oh, so you're coming too?" Matt asked.

"I was going to go to church tomorrow anyway. If Rose hadn't invited you, I would have. I go every Sunday. So go to bed."

Matt thought of sleep and yawned. Though it was a bit early, he was tired.

The four of them dispersed throughout the house and Matt headed for the stairs. As he passed the living room, he noticed the television was on. Going in to turn it off, the late night news caught his attention.

"Hardly an hour ago," the news anchor said. "A terrible event took place at Hills West High School. Cindy Underwood has the complete story."

"Thank you, Jan. It appears that someone found a way inside the school. Unfortunately, the intruder was able to escape before the authorities arrived at the scene."

Matt turned and called up the stairs for Jesse.

"What?" Jesse called back.

"You don't want to miss this."

"What is it?" he asked.

"Just hurry up and get down here."

Jesse rumbled down the stairs as the reporter continued, "Just a short while ago, someone broke into Hills West High School. Investigators have reason to believe the intruder's target was an office computer. Sheriff Stronson was at the scene earlier. He told us that there are many valuable programs linked to the school's computer. He quoted programs such as, Education High, Green-Go and LanCaster as only a few. He further reported that they were running checks to see if any of them had been tampered with."

Matt and Jesse watched in disbelief.

"I saw that LanCaster program in Dr. Pierce's office yesterday before I met you in the furnace room," Matt said as Jesse hushed him.

The reporter went on …

"This seems to be the second day that an intruder has found a way into the school. Phillip Crawford, the police officer on duty, recalls seeing someone in the school last night as well. We managed to get an interview with Officer Crawford."

She turned toward an officer with thick-rimmed glasses standing nearby.

"Officer Crawford, can you tell us what you told the police?"

"Sure," Crawford stared into the camera. "I nearly managed to catch the intruder yesterday. He wore a dark outfit with a mask on so I couldn't see his face."

"Oh, my gosh," Matt whispered to himself, "that was me. They think that I'm –"

"Jiminy Christmas," Jesse muttered in response.

Officer Crawford went on describing the incident. "It looked to me like he used some kind of keycard to bypass the locks on the doors. Then he managed to break into the offices from there."

Matt could scarcely believe what he was hearing.

"I was getting my dad's journal," he told the TV set.

The reporter continued, "Sheriff Stronson says he believes that the break-ins over the past two nights are the same person. On both occasions, the intruder seemed to make his or her way into the office. We will have updates on this story as it continues to unfold. Back to you, Jan."

"Thank you, Cindy. We have also received information that there was another break-in nearly three months ago that left two officers hospitalized. One of whom was Phillip Crawford, the guard on duty."

"In other news …"

Jesse turned off the television and looked at Matt who stared at the blank screen.

"Well, I'm off to bed," Jesse said.

Matt spun and looked at Jesse.

"Wait, Jesse. Don't you wanna talk about this?"

Jesse paused in thought. "No not really. Good night." He turned back to the stairs.

Matt stood in disbelief. "Wait a second."

Matt dashed up the stairs and threw open the door of Jesse's room to find Jesse already in bed with the lights off.

"Wait, Jesse, seriously. I was just on the news. The cops think that I'm tampering with the computers."

Jesse rolled over and turned on the light. "So?"

He turned off the light.

"Aren't you worried about this?" Matt exclaimed.

Jesse sat up in bed and clicked the light on again.

"Listen, they're not going to have SWAT teams surrounding your house with helicopters or anything. Attack dogs aren't going to search your property. You broke into the school to get your dad's journal back. No harm done. The only thing we did was crawl through the air vents. And come on, you can't tell me you didn't enjoy making it home free yesterday."

Matt grinned as he recalled the event. However, the feeling vanished as Jesse turned off his light, lay back down and rolled over, his back to Matt.

"But what about the person that broke in tonight?" Matt went on.

Jesse turned his light back on to finish the conversation. "What about him?"

"He wasn't us."

"Very good, Matt. Good night again."

Jesse turned off his light hoping Matt would leave.

"No, not 'good night'."

Matt turned on the light himself. "Who was it if it wasn't us?"

"The Easter Bunny, Matt. Heck, I don't know. It's not our problem. They're not going to arrest you. They don't even know who you are. Now ... good – night." Jesse reached over and clicked the white light off for the final time.

Matt sighed and shut the door.

13

Matt slept soundly that night. He dreamed of playing with Rose in the waterfall behind his house. Her wet hair draped over her body like a moist towel. She gazed deeply into his eyes as he did the same to her.

Suddenly, they were transported to the roof looking up at the stars. She turned to him and kissed him sending the same warmth he'd felt earlier.

The warmth shot off them racing toward the sky, exploding like fireworks, everything was perfect. No interruptions this time. No one could reach them here ...

A pillow collided with Matt's head, shaking the image from his mind.

"Get up," Jesse yelled as he swung the pillow down on Matt again.

"What the –" Matt muttered blocking the next swing. "What's wrong?"

"The cops are here to take you away," Jesse exclaimed.

Matt sat up in bed, eyes wide. "What?"

"Just kidding. We're going to church."

Matt groaned, lay back down and rubbed his eyes.

"Come on lazy bum," Jesse exclaimed again. "Don't go back to sleep. Rose is sitting out in the driveway right now. Get up!"

"What?" Matt opened his eyes. "Are you serious?"

Jesse stopped and grinned. "Nope. Gotcha again. You've got plenty of time. I just wanted to wake you up. You've got a big day today."

Matt dropped the pillow to the floor and yawned. Jesse was right. Any day was a big day if it included Rose.

Within the hour, Rose arrived and Matt and Jesse got in her father's black Chevrolet. Jesse sat beside the man in the driver's seat who wore a black Sunday suit. Matt recognized Rose's green eyes and dark hair on him.

The man turned to face the two of them and extended a large, muscular hand. His large arms and chest intimidated Matt. The only other person Matt had seen who was his size was Mr. Fears.

"So this is the famous Mr. Cross?" he asked. "You know, you've really made an impact on Rose. She can't seem to talk for two minutes without bringing you into the conversation."

Matt smiled and quickly shook his hand. He wanted to say something polite but realized he didn't have much to say.

After a few minutes of riding in silence, Rose looked at him with a pleading expression.

"What?" Matt mouthed.

"Say something," Rose whispered.

Matt rolled his eyes. "What?"

"I don't know. Anything."

"So, Mr. Hudson …" Matt began. He asked the first question that came to mind, "What do you do for a living?"

"Well, Mr. Cross," he glanced at Matt through his rear view mirror. "I am the Executive Administrator of Information Technology for the schools in the area."

"And what exactly is that?"

Mr. Hudson smiled. "I oversee the schools in the area to ensure the computers are functioning correctly. I set up the servers. I keep them online. I do all that stuff."

Matt's interest in Mr. Hudson's job shot sky high. Even Jesse turned to listen.

"So, I guess, you've heard of that intruder that's been breaking into the school and hacking into the computers?"

Mr. Hudson sighed. "Oh, yeah. That guy is making it very difficult for me to do my job. Every time an incident like that comes up, I have to scan the entire system and that takes forever. I'm probably going to be at the school for at least two weeks trying to figure out what happened this last time. I haven't found anything wrong with the system so far."

"What do you think the intruder was after?" Matt asked.

"Personally, I think the intruder was trying to fix some numbers on the LanCaster program."

"The LanCaster program?"

"Yes. The LanCaster program handles all of the money that comes in and out of the school. It makes the shuffle a lot less troublesome. The amount of money received goes into the program and then it automatically tells you tax percentages, graph readouts, names, accounts, and just about anything else you'd like to know. I believe every school in the surrounding five counties has the program."

"So I bet there's all kind of money attached to the program, right?" Matt asked.

"Oh, yeah, loads of money."

"Hey, we're here," Jesse broke into the conversation as he peered out the window. "This is New Life Fellowship Church."

The church was much bigger than Matt had imagined. The large, brick building had thin vines stretching their skinny fingers over the sides like a spider web. The multi-colored stained glass windows with pictures of doves and crosses graced the sides of the church. A tall tower rose from the center of the church and at the top, Matt saw the heavy looking bell that hung below the large wooden cross. The back half of the church was marked off with caution signs. Matt noticed burn marks on the side of the building and remembered the newspaper article he'd read to Mr. Parish.

Rose and Jesse led Matt inside and down the stairs.

"Rose, where are we going?" Matt asked.

"Youth group," she replied.

"Oh … youth group." He rolled his eyes. He expected to have a grand old time with a bunch of teenagers he didn't know.

Matt followed Rose and Jesse down the stairs to the basement unsure of what to expect. Opening the door, they entered a wide room lit with neon and black lights. The walls were made of coarse brick and the youth had taken it upon themselves to write anything and everything on the walls in graffiti-like fashion.

As Jesse plopped down on one of the many leather couches along the wall, Matt looked around to see numerous teenagers talking, laughing, playing pool and video games. It was unlike anything he'd ever seen. He never thought a church would have a pool table, let alone video games.

"Well …" Rose approached the pool table. "This is it. What do you think?"

Matt didn't know how to respond. "I like it. It's very … playful."

She frowned. "Playful?"

"Heads up!" someone shouted.

Looking up, Matt saw a cue ball heading straight for his head. He instantly ducked and heard the ball thud on the wall behind him. Matt angrily jumped back up, ready to tell off the shooter.

A long-haired boy approached Matt with a pool stick in hand and wearing a dark baseball cap over his eyes. He began to search the floor. Through thin pursed lips, he looked for the lost billiard ball. He seemed to pay no mind that the ball had almost collided with Matt's head.

"Hey," Matt spoke forcefully. "Don't you think you should apologize or something? That ball nearly took my head off!"

"Matt," Rose began, "don't mess with him. He doesn't –"

The boy glanced at Matt and moved his hands over his cap. Then, he went back to finding his ball.

"What the heck was that?" Matt asked. "Moving your hands around like that."

"You can talk to him all day, but you'll just get the same answer," said a voice behind him. "He don't talk."

Matt spun around to find another tall long-nosed boy who looked to be like the shooter's twin. The only difference was that the second boy wore his baseball cap backward.

"What do you mean 'he don't talk'?" Matt asked.

"I mean …" The second boy bent over, picked up the cue ball and handed it to his twin brother. "… he doesn't talk."

The shooter moved his hands over his cap again.

"He says he's sorry," the twin translated.

"Why can't he talk?" Matt asked.

"I dunno exactly. I think he can, he just chooses not to. Maybe he's savin' it for a special occasion."

"Ask him."

"Hey, Jake," the boy called.

Jake looked up under the brim of his cap.

"This guy here wants to know if ya' talk. Can ya' talk?"

Jake stood for a moment as if in thought.

He then opened his mouth and unleashed a monstrous belch that drowned out the music playing in the background. The room went silent and all eyes fell on Jake.

He just shrugged and continued to line up his cue ball.

"That should answer your question, shouldn't it?" the twin asked with a smile.

Matt laughed. "So he uses sign language?"

"Yeah, sort of," the twin said. "We've made up our own signs. We don't do the official sign language stuff."

"Oh," Matt responded. "That's kind of … different."

"Yep, that's what we're famous for."

Jake sunk three more billiard balls in the pockets around the table.

"Name's Zeke, by the way," the twin said suddenly.

Zeke reached out his hand but Matt noticed the grease that covered it.

"Don't worry," Zeke said. "My hands are just stained. They're not dirty or anythin'."

"Why are they stained?"

"My dad owns Lovitt's Auto Shop in town. Jake and I work with him there."

Jake snapped his fingers and Zeke looked at him. Jake proceeded to sign using his baseball cap.

"Jake says that he didn't mean to nearly knock yer block off with the pool ball," Zeke said.

Matt shook his head mystified at the way they communicated. "That's really cool."

Zeke shrugged. "We just came up with a way to talk when we were kids. If you hang around enough, you'll start to learn some of it too."

Matt felt Rose tug on his arm. "Come on, Matt," she said. "Let's go find a seat or all the comfy couches will be gone."

Rose sat down on one of the couches with Matt beside her. Zeke found a spot beside Matt giving Rose and Matt an excuse to sit closer.

The room was very wide, big enough to hold a pool table, a big screen television and a stage. The couches surrounded the stage in the front of the room. The games were near the rear of the room.

A tall, thin man in his thirties walked toward Matt's couch. His yellow T-shirt was as bright as the smile on his face.

"Hey, there," the man reached his hand toward Matt. "Who are you?"

"Matt," he replied as he rose to shake the man's hand.

"Well, Matt, I'm glad you're here. We're always glad to get a few newbies every now and then. I'm the youth pastor. My name's Neil. You know, like Neil Armstrong. Only well ... not."

Neil looked down at Rose. "I'll let Matt sit back down so you all can get back to howling and shrieking like you guys do."

Matt sat back down. "Who is that?"

"He's the youth pastor," she replied.

"Like the teacher?"

"Something like that. But I've never had a teacher quite like Neil before."

Matt raised his eyebrows in surprise when he saw Lily walk in and give Neil a hug. Lily gave a short wave to Matt and Rose as she sat down on a couch. Her short legs stuck straight out from the couch. She began making conversation with someone next to her.

Matt leaned over to Rose. "You didn't tell me Lily went to this church too."

"You never asked," she replied.

Neil grabbed a microphone and jumped on the stage. "Hi, gang! What's a goin' on?"

No amplification occurred when he spoke. He tapped the mike. "Am I on?"

Matt looked back to the sound booth where Jake stood up, messed with some dials on the switchboard and proceeded to give Neil a thumbs-up.

"Hello? Hello! That's much better. Hi, gang!"

The room gradually got quieter as Neil began to speak. "Let's get to know each other a bit before we start."

Jake projected the lyrics to the music that was playing up on the wall. Everyone sang the songs of worship together. The music was upbeat and fun to listen to. The lyrics had a good message as well. Matt had never heard music quite like this. He surprised himself when he found himself singing along almost wanting to dance.

After the group sang a couple songs, Neil led the group in a get-to-know-you game. Thus far, this church was turning out much different from what Matt had expected. Soon the talking and laughing subsided as Neil stepped onto the stage and began his lesson.

"For those who don't know me, I'm Neil." He gave a short wave. "I'm a good guy once you get to know me. But a long time ago, I wasn't a good guy. I got mixed up in a lot of weird stuff. I mean, I got fair grades. I had loads of friends. I went out with those friends and had a good time on the weekends but do you know what I did during the weekdays? My friends and I worked.

"This old guy came up to me and my friends and asked if we could help him move these hay bales he had in his barn. We went with him but when we arrived at his barn, we saw at least a dozen other guys the old man had hired to help. I didn't know half of them. They were from the East Side of Hills and they didn't like us right from the start.

"As we worked, they were always 'accidentally' getting in our way and calling us names and stuff. The day was about over when the old man left to get our wages. All of us waited in the barn for him to come back.

"Well, the East Siders continued to get in our faces and pushed us around a bit. So I said to them, 'Listen, if you really want to fight then we'll fight. But let's do it this way. You pick your best man. We'll pick ours.' They agreed. I had no idea what I was getting into especially when my friends picked me to fight."

A silence passed over the room and Neil looked around slowly.

"But nothing – nothing prepared me for what happened next. Their guy was this six-seven, two hundred and eighty pound gorilla guy. He'd been working and grunting all day. Every time I would take one hay bale, this guy took two, you know? He had massive shoulders and his arms were as big as my head."

The group laughed.

"I'm serious! I didn't know what to do. My story is similar to the Scripture I'm going to talk about today – David.

"Now David wasn't the most popular guy in town. In fact, he was a shepherd boy. That would be like a pooper-scooper today or something. It's just not the most ... appealing job in the world if you know what I mean. No offense to those of you who are pooper-scoopers."

Neil smiled and waited for the giggles to subside.

"You see, David went to give his brothers in the army some food. While he was there, he saw this huge guy that was even bigger than the one I faced in the barn. This guy, Goliath, was nine feet tall."

He continued, "You see, there were two armies and they hated each other – the Philistines and the Israelites. The two of them were on opposite hills with this large valley in between them. The Philistines sent this Terminator dude down to the valley. I mean, this guy was nine feet tall with a coat of armor that weighed like one hundred and thirty pounds. Plus, Goliath had over a hundred pounds of other armor all over his body.

"He carried a heavy spear with an iron tip on his back. Not to mention, his huge sword that he had on his hip. Goliath came out and said that he could whip any of the Israelites. Goliath told the Israelites, 'Send out your best man. We'll settle this one on one.'

"No one would even think about fighting him. Just like I couldn't believe that this gorilla wanted to fight me."

Neil hesitantly recalled the event.

"When I saw Shrek appear from that group of guys, I could hear the jaws of my buddies hit the floor. I wanted to run. My buddies almost did. But I knew what I had to do. Somehow, I had to beat this guy or he was going to pound me.

"Now remember, David was a young boy. When he saw Goliath, he knew that no man could possibly stand up to him. He knew what he had to do. God wanted him to fight Goliath.

"Now, if one of you guys came up to me and said, 'Neil, I'm going to go and fight Godzilla by myself'. Do you know what I'd say? I'd probably say, 'May the Force Be with You' or something. I mean you'd be dead – deader than dead. You'd be a put-a-fork-in-you-because-you're-done kind of thing.

"So you can imagine how the other people reacted when David, a little fourteen-year old pooper-scooper, walked into the camp of a bunch of tall muscular captains saying that he wanted to fight Terminator by himself.

"Well, they were like, 'All right, whatever. He'll kill ya' and then it'll be over'.

"They gave David this huge sword that was fit for a warrior. But he was just a kid. He couldn't use it right. But he knew how to use this little sling he kept in his pocket. He went to find a few good stones and he put them in a small pouch on his hip. When David went out to fight, Goliath laughed in his face.

"The gargantuan in that barn laughed in my face too. He said to my buds, 'Huh, he's the best? Give me a challenge or something.'

"You couldn't blame him. I mean look at me. I'm a shrimp. I was even smaller back then.

"Well, David went up to the giant and they bickered back and forth for a bit. Then, Goliath decided to kill David. He came at him with his sword and spear and David reached into his pouch, grabbed one of the stones, put it in the sling and swung it.

"The stone flew from the sling and hit Goliath right in the middle of his forehead. One stone … that's all it took – just one little-bitty-ruddy-old-rock that found its way into God's powerful plan. Goliath was out cold before he hit the ground. The Israelites won the war. Their hero? A fourteen-year old pooper-scooper."

His audience laughed out loud and Neil beamed.

He went on, "I, however, didn't even have a sling to defend myself. Monster Man growled as he stomped toward me. He picked up a pitchfork that was lying nearby and threw it at me. Thank God, he missed. The pitchfork stuck in the ground just inches from my foot. Boy, was I scared. I knew that was just a glimpse of what this guy could do to me.

"The dude rushed at me all mad because he'd missed. I glanced at the pitchfork and tried to pull it up out of the ground but it was stuck. There was nothing I could do. My hand was still on the handle as he got within grabbing distance. Just as he was about to grab my shirt, I extended my arm while holding onto the handle and the butt end of the pitchfork bopped him right on the nose.

"He jumped back holding his nose. It was bleeding pretty well and his eyes began to tear up. It was over. I'd won. To this day, I believe God was with me that day. And if it weren't for Him, I'd probably be sucking Jell-O through a straw."

Matt laughed and prayed with the group afterward knowing he had just heard a valuable lesson, one to remember. He would definitely be coming back again.

14

Rose sat on the bed and watched Matt. "No, no. It goes like this."

"I got it," Matt said defensively.

"Look at what you're doing," Rose replied. "You don't 'got it'."

"I'm okay."

"No, look. I'll show you."

Matt sat back and observed while Rose held the scissors against the fabric and cut out the stars.

"You see," Rose said. "Hold the scissors like this and you won't have to fight it."

Matt cut the fabric as she'd shown him while Rose went about gluing the letters she'd cut out earlier onto the flag.

"Do you think we'll get the flag done today?" Matt asked as he continued to wrestle with the fabric.

"We'd better. It's Wednesday. Ms. Ellis said the flags are due Friday. Plus, it's getting dark and that only leaves one day."

"Do you think we'll win?" Matt asked.

"It's possible."

"It's possible? What's that supposed to mean?"

"Here," she said. "Have some glue."

She wiped a little bit of glue on his arm.

"I don't want your glue," Matt retorted. "You can keep it."

He wiped the glob off his arm with his finger and smeared it back on her arm. Rose's eyes went wide and her jaw dropped as she eyed the glue.

"What?"

"Don't even …"

"Don't even what?" Matt grinned. "Put glue on you?"

He squeezed some more glue onto his fingers and smeared it on her arm.

Rose looked from her arm and then back to Matt with a smirk on her face. "Oh, you're gonna get it now."

Downstairs, Bruce gnawed on his pencil as he relaxed with his feet propped up on the couch, his eyes scanning a crossword puzzle.

He looked at Mary who was curled up on a chair across the room and reading. Her eyes skimmed across the pages as she snacked on popcorn.

"What's a four letter word for 'related to Valentine's Day'?" he asked.

"Love," she said without looking up at him.

Bruce stared at the crossword a moment.

"Yeah, I guess 'love' will work." He scribbled the word down in the newspaper's crossword puzzle.

"How about a seven letter word for 'to hold dear'?"

"Cherish." Mary didn't move.

Bruce held the paper closer to his eyes and peered at the puzzle. "Crud. It fits."

"Told you." Mary tossed a handful of popcorn in her mouth.

"Yeah. I guess you're a pretty resourceful gal, aren't ya'?" He smiled. "And speakin' of pretty …"

Mary looked up from her book, unsuccessfully trying to hide her smile. Bruce tried to stifle his laughter but couldn't. Mary threw a couple kernels of popcorn at him. Snatching the kernels off his chest, he tossed them in his mouth.

"You are …" she paused and eyed his rugged smile. "You're something else, I've got to tell you. You just –"

Mary stopped as a loud squealing noise from upstairs distracted her.

She turned her head and called, "Hey, what are you guys doing up there?"

No response.

Rising from the couch, she started up the stairs with Bruce following close behind. Reaching Matt's room, she found Matt and Rose on the floor. Globs of glue were smeared all over Matt's face and Rose's hands were glued together.

Mary glanced at Bruce, her lips curling at the corners. Looking back at the pair, she remarked, "I'm glad to see you two working so diligently."

Matt looked up at his mother and tried to compose himself.

"Oh – uh, hi mom. Bruce." He attempted to sit up straight. "How's it going?"

Rose reached up from the floor and smeared some more glue across Matt's face.

"Come on, you two," Bruce said. "You guys are gonna get stuck to each other if you're not careful."

In response, Matt and Rose dissolved into hysterical laughter.

Bruce and Mary glanced at one another, turned and left the two to their 'work'.

The next day during lunch, Matt walked around the cafeteria with his tray trying to find a seat. He spotted Jesse sitting with some friends and sat down beside him.

"Oh, hey, Matt," Jesse said. "Meet the guys. You already know Zeke and Jake."

He motioned to the two of them. Zeke gave a small wave and Jake nodded.

"This is Andrew," Jesse went on.

"We've met," Matt said as he recalled his incident with Randy.

Matt scooted his chair up to the table and Andrew nodded. He rubbed his hands over his bald head, rubbed them together and began to devour fish sticks.

"Sho, you guysh goin' to dat Jug'nut Fes'val this veekend?" Zeke asked through a mouthful of fish.

"I think," Jesse replied. "Are we going, Matt?"

Matt shrugged. "I guess. I hadn't really thought about it."

"Are ya' guys bringing a date?" Andrew asked.

"No," Zeke answered. "Well I'm not anyway. I don't like the idea of havin' a date and all."

Matt's eyebrows rose in surprise. "You're supposed to have a date?"

"Well, no," Zeke said. "But if ya' brought a date, the festival would be pretty fun. Oh and speakin' of datin' ..." he continued. "You and Rose looked pretty close at church the other day. You guys a thing or somethin'?"

Matt's face turned red and he gave a slight grin. "Well, I don't think we're exactly a thing –"

"No?" Jesse interrupted. "You guys only watched the stars together alone on the roof."

He rolled his eyes and continued, "Just yesterday, you two got in a glue fight when you said you were working. And don't forget the time both of you swam in the waterfall behind the house."

Zeke choked on his milk as it went down. Jake smacked the table and began signing wildly.

Zeke set his milk down and watched Jake finish. "Yeah, no kidding. You actually swam with Rose? Jake wants to know what she was wearing. I think we'd all like to know."

Matt grinned at the boys' sudden change of interest. "Well, she wasn't in a bikini or anything. She jumped in with her clothes on."

"Oh, never mind." Zeke leaned back in his chair.

Jake gave a few quick motions.

Zeke translated. "What color was her shirt?"

Matt thought a moment.

"Uh ... white, I think."

"Oh, man!" The boys whooped together as smiles lit up their faces, drawing the attention of the surrounding students.

"Jeez! Are you serious?" Andrew laughed.

"What do you care, Andrew?" Jesse smirked. "You've got a girlfriend."

"I'm not dead," Andrew retorted continuing to laugh.

"Man," Zeke said as he took a bite of his peaches. "Rose Hudson. Hang on to her. That one's a keeper."

"Well, then . . ?" Jesse trailed off and looked at Matt.

"What?"

"Are you going to ask Rose to go with you or not?"

"Well, I –"

"I'm sure she'd go with you," Jesse interrupted. "I mean she swam with you and everything."

Huge smiles reappeared on the boys' faces.

"I'm not even sure I'm going yet," Matt remarked.

"Did ya' kiss her?" Zeke asked.

"What?"

"Did ya' kiss her?"

"Well, uh, we –"

"It's a simple question. Did ya' kiss the girl or not?"

"Yes."

"What?" Jesse exclaimed as he dropped his fork. "You didn't tell me that. When?"

"Just because you live with me doesn't mean you have to know everything that goes on all of the time."

"Wait …" Andrew leaned closer to Matt and lowered his voice. "You actually kissed Rose Hudson?"

"Well, yeah."

Andrew shook his head.

"Wow. For a freshman, she's pretty good lookin'. I mean, I wouldn't date her. I'm a senior, but she's still pretty good lookin'. If I had a gold star, I would definitely give it to ya'."

Matt shrugged and downed his milk.

"Well, if ya' kissed her then ya' should ask her," Zeke said.

Matt looked at him.

Zeke shrugged. "It's worth a shot, ya' know?"

Jake moved his hand across his brow and nodded.

"See?" Zeke said. "Jake agrees with me too."

After lunch, Matt strolled down the hall between classes with Jesse still arguing about asking Rose to the festival.

"No," Matt said. "I really don't think it'll work."

"Why not? She wants to go with you."

"How do you know?"

"Well, I don't *know* know, but I'd guess so. She's –"

"Jesse, why do I ask you for help?" Matt muttered squeezing his way through a swarm of bodies. "You're just wasting my time."

"Well, she's obviously interested in you if she let you kiss her."

Matt was silenced and thought about Jesse's point.

"But I've never asked a girl out before."

"You act like you're looking for a wife. You just want someone to hang out with at the festival. That's all."

"That's all?"

"That's all, man."

A group of girls turned the corner. Matt could see Rose talking with her friends in the center of the group. Stopping at their lockers, they began to collect their things for the next class.

Matt stared down the hall.

"Oh, my gosh."

"What?" Jesse asked.

"There she is." Matt tried to hide himself behind Jesse.

"Well, go and ask her."

Jesse stepped beside Matt and gently shoved his arm into Matt's shoulder sending him off course and towards Rose and her friends. Matt attempted to veer back into traffic but was already too close. If he turned back now, it would look like he'd chickened out.

Rose glanced up from her backpack and jumped when she saw him.

"Oh, Matt. Hi."

"Uh – hey, there … Rose."

He peered down the hall for Jesse who had managed to get himself lost in the crowd.

"Listen, um … I was thinkin' … you know, since we were partners and all … cause you know we finished the flag and all … I was thinking that, uh … maybe, uh, we could go to the festival to see if we'd won the contest or something."

"Together?"

"Well, yeah. Sort of. Not really. Not if you don't – it was just a thought. I understand."

He began to walk away from her.

"Matt, wait!" she called.

Matt stopped and turned back toward her.

"You never asked me," she said.

"Asked what?"

She approached him again. "Asked me if I wanted to go with you."

"Well, uh, do you … uh, want to go?"

"To the festival?"

"Yeah."

"With you?"

"Right."

"Well …"

She frowned.

Matt's shoulders slumped. If Rose had to think about her answer then Jesse was wrong. Rose wasn't interested.

"Yeah, I'll go." She smiled.

Matt's eyes widened with shock and he took a step backward. "Are you serious?"

"Yeah, I'd love to go with you. I was just messing with you. Can't you take a joke?"

"Well, yeah. I knew you were just playing. It was me who was playing –"

"Call me tonight and we'll talk about it then," she said as the bell rang. "I gotta go. I'll talk to you later, okay?"

Rose shut her locker and headed in the opposite direction.

Matt watched her go and smiled. He felt as though a tremendous weight had just been lifted from his heart.

15

That evening, Mary was folding laundry in her room when Bruce knocked on the doorframe.

She turned. "Oh, hey Bruce."

He stepped up beside her and began folding clothes.

"Laundry, huh?"

"Yep."

"Sounds like fun," he said.

"Not really."

"Well, how 'bout dinner?"

"I'll get started on it in a little while."

"No," Bruce said. "How about dinner?"

Mary frowned. "What? I don't get it."

"How 'bout if I help ya' with the laundry and then we go find some dinner?"

"That was the plan," Mary said. "What do you want to eat? I've got some chicken thawed out. Or if you'd like some –"

"You do remember that Matt and Jesse are going to the festival tonight, right?"

Bruce laid his folded garment on the growing pile of laundry.

"Oh, right." Mary smiled. "So I guess it's just you and me tonight then?"

"Right, so how 'bout dinner? I heard about this place on the other side of town I'd like to try."

Mary paused and with a slight smile on her face. "Are you asking me out?"

"Well, I was just thinkin' that with, you know, them away I could treat ya' to a nice dinner. It's Friday. You've worked hard. I've worked hard. Let's go and have some fun. What do ya' say?"

She studied Bruce's face. "Okay. But just for the record, this isn't a date. We are just going out to dinner as friends. I don't know what Matt would think if he thought we were dating."

"Oh – right. No way … Gotta think 'bout Matt … Hmm, right."

Bruce turned back to folding clothes. He just realized how difficult it was going be to have a relationship with Mary without Matt's permission.

Later that evening, Mary and Bruce dropped Matt, Jesse and Rose off in the large parking lot behind the high school.

"Here," Mary handed Matt her cell phone. "Take this. Call Bruce when it's over and we'll come pick you up. We're going to go find dinner somewhere."

Matt nodded and waved good-bye as he watched Mary and Bruce pull out of the parking lot.

As the three of them turned the corner of the school and headed to the backfield, their eyes went wide at the sight. The annual Juggernut Festival was in full swing.

The festival illuminated the darkness with candles and lanterns hanging from wire along the pathways and the perimeter of the field. Large square wooden booths lined the field while all sorts of competitive games such as obstacle courses, hot dog eating and root beer drinking contests and many others spread throughout the field. Extravagant prizes hung around the booths enticing people to try to win. Other booths held Asian antiques while magicians and entertainers jumped here and there among the crowd.

At the far end of the field, Matt saw a large stage under a tall yellow tent. He heard a band playing and could see a few students dancing and talking. Matt thought about asking Rose to dance. Maybe later. He hoped she danced.

Pushing these thoughts to the back of his mind, he strolled underneath the tall wooden arch that read, JUGGERNUT FESTIVAL ENTRANCE, $6.60 PER PERSON.

Buying tickets for the three of them, Matt gazed around as they headed into the heart of the festivities. He wanted to do everything, but there seemed to be too much to do. He didn't think he could do it all in a short time. Matt recognized many of the students and teachers that passed by as they moved from booth to booth.

Rose was eying the cotton candy from a nearby booth so Matt bought her some. Tearing off a piece, he held it in front of her lips and as she went to bite it, he pulled it away from her bit by bit. She lightly punched him and grabbed the cotton candy stick from his other hand. Jesse looked bored.

Noticing Zeke and Jake walking with a small group of girls, Jesse yelled, "Hey guys. What's up? I didn't think you were coming."

Zeke replied, "Yeah, neither did we, but Jake said he wanted to see the bonfire and I wanted a hot dog." He held up his half-eaten bun and took a bite. "You vanna 'ang wi' us?"

Behind Jesse's back, Rose motioned for Matt to follow her.

"Sure. Hang on a sec," Jesse said. "Hey, guys. Zeke –"

He turned to see that Matt and Rose had disappeared into the crowd.

Dashing through the large groups of people, Matt and Rose ignored the calls of the other students and teachers.

"Hey, slow down there," a voice called.

"Why are ya' in such a hurry?" asked another.

They ran under the big yellow tent in the center of the festival and plopped down in one of the folding chairs near the back.

"Oh, that was fun," Rose said raising her voice over the band as she tore off another piece of cotton candy.

"Tell me again why we left Jesse like that."

"Because," Rose replied. "We're kind of doing him a favor by not making him the third wheel. He wouldn't want to hang out with us all night."

"Yeah, I guess you're right." He pulled off a piece of the cotton candy.

Matt watched the couples dance on the small dance floor. The guys had their hands on the girls' hips and it seemed as though they almost skipped around one another.

Matt glanced at Rose and then took her hand in his. She looked nervous but he knew she liked holding his hand.

"Want to dance?" he asked as he stood.

"What? No, I can't."

"Sure you can. I'll show you."

"I don't dance."

"Yeah, right, everyone dances."

"No, really, Matt. I couldn't."

"Come on. It's easy."

He grabbed her arms and led her onto the dance floor. The band's song changed to a slow number.

Matt murmured, "This is my kind of music," and pulled Rose closer.

"Wine?"

"You know, Bruce," Mary said. "You don't have to go to all this trouble for me."

"Why, sure I do," he replied as he poured her wine. "I've brought ya' to the nicest sit-down place in town. I just want to show ya' a good time. I mean, come on. I drove, I'm buying dinner and we might go somewhere later."

Mary gave him a curious look.

"For ice cream, of course. Can't have a date without ice cream."

"Is that what this is? A date? I thought we were going out to eat as friends."

Bruce squirmed. "Well, I thought that we were going out to have a good time and so far I like getting to know you again."

"Do you mean it when you say things like that or are you just trying to seduce me?"

"Is it working?"

Mary's eyes twinkled over the brim of her wine glass.

A half an hour later, Matt and Rose found Jesse and stepped up beside him.

"There you guys are," Jesse said. "Where did you two go?"

"Dancing," Rose replied.

"Well, while you guys were having the time of your lives you missed Zeke chug down two two-liter bottles of root beer."

"No, way," Matt eyebrows climbed at Jesse's comment. "That's impossible."

He glanced up at the stage built in the shape of a boxing ring inside the large booth.

"Isn't that Zeke and Jake up there fighting?" he asked. "How can he hold all that root beer and still fight like that?"

"He can't." Jesse laughed. "He got rid of it after the contest. He kind of made a mess on the grass over there."

"Oh, gosh …" Rose gagged and put her hand over her mouth.

Jesse, Matt and Rose stood and watched in amazement as Zeke and Jake bounced around the ring while going at each other with long cushioned staffs. Jake lashed out at Zeke with his staff. Zeke casually blocked it and advanced toward Jake with his own combination of deft movements. The object of the game was to win by hitting your opponent three times with the cushioned staffs.

Zeke feinted a high swing and managed to trip Jake and bop him on the chest to finish him.

"Point!" the ref called.

More onlookers gathered around the ring and gaped while Zeke twirled his staff in Jake's face.

The brothers hadn't fought with the other for nearly a week and when the two brothers decided to fight, it usually went an hour or so before one of them conceded.

Matt noted that goading and taunting one another didn't seem to be against the rules either.

Zeke grinned at Jake who was stretched out on the floor of the ring. "Hey, Jake. Ya' know Dad's favorite socket wrenches ya' lost and got grounded for?"

Jake nodded as he stood and twirled his staff.

"I've got 'em. I took 'em from the garage a couple weeks ago. I still have 'em in fact. Too bad I'll be the hero when we get home because I'll be the one to return them."

Jake snarled and dropped his staff, signing with a purpose.

"Oh, my mom's fat, huh?" Zeke grunted. "Well, guess what? She's your mom too, genius."

Jake snarled as he kicked his staff off the ground and into his hands.

The referee signaled to begin again as Jake parried Zeke's attacks. They twirled around each other, swung, jumped, spun, blocked and attacked as if they were simply putting on a show for the crowd.

"Jeez," Jesse called from outside the ring. "How did you guys get so good? Did you take karate lessons or something?"

"No," Zeke yelled as he ducked beneath a swing. "We just watch a lot of old time kung-fu movies."

Jake caught a swing from Zeke, brought it down to the ground and hit Zeke in the face.

"Point!" the ref called again. He put a mark on the scoreboard.

Some of the girls in the crowd clapped at Jake's point and he rewarded them with a wink.

"Heck, this is nothin'," Zeke said. "Normally, Jake and I use broomsticks at the shop. If one of us gets hit … well, let's just say ya' remember it."

Jake glared at him and advanced.

The fight had just begun again when a cold voice from behind Matt growled, "My tax dollars paid for this?"

Matt turned to see Fears shaking his head. "What a waste of time and energy. I can't believe the Juggernut Festival is allowing this sort of violence."

"Oh, come on, Mr. Fears." Jesse smiled. "It's all good fun."

"Hmm … yes. I'm ecstatic," he said sarcastically. "Simply leaping with joy. Now if you'll excuse me, I must use the facilities."

He stormed off toward the school.

"You know," Matt said. "I have to go too. I'll be right back. Let me know who wins."

Unfortunately, the restrooms were located inside the school so it was quite a trek if one had to go. Once Matt reached the cafeteria area, he headed down the path created by the lunch tables toward the bathroom.

Mr. Fears, a few paces ahead of him, didn't seem to be heading in the direction of the bathroom. Instead, he glanced behind him, saw Matt, paused and then motioned for Matt to go ahead of him.

Opening the door to the bathroom, Matt slipped inside but curiosity was chewing up his insides. Cracking the door just a bit, he peeked out to see if he could spot Fears.

Mr. Fears looked around the cafeteria as if he thought someone might be watching him. Then crawling over one of the desks, he started toward the main office peeking around repeatedly. Matt watched as Mr. Fears slid through the office door.

"'I have to use the facilities …'" Matt said to himself. "Hmm, yeah right."

A sudden thought possessed Matt. Why would Mr. Fears sneak into his own office?

Curiosity flooded him. Pushing open the bathroom door, he slid out and followed Mr. Fears.

16

"Thanks for dinner, Bruce. And for the ice cream. You know, this 'date' is kind of over the top, don't you think?"
"Not at all, Mary. I know I don't look like much but I got it where it counts. This is how ya' treat ladies on the first date."
"Is that so?"
"Well, there's no manual or anythin'. But yeah."
They sat at a picnic bench outside the small ice cream shop. Bruce licked his cone while Mary held a cup of ice cream in front of her.
"So, it's official then?" Mary asked.
"What?"
"This is a date."
"What else would it be?"
"Well, I don't know."
She took another bite and motioned with her spoon as she spoke. "It's just that I haven't dated in … gosh, it's been a long, long time."
"Don't worry, Mary. I'll get ya' back on track in no time."
Holding a napkin, Mary wiped some ice cream off the table. "But you know, Bruce, we are just friends. Strictly friends. Imagine what life would be like if we got together – not to say that we are getting together. I'm just saying 'what if'. Could you imagine what that would do to Matt?"
"Well, I think that –"
"I'm just now getting to know you. But I don't think that Matt knows you very well. It would have to be a long time before we could become a real couple."
"Let's not think –"
"And even then, it would be strange. I mean, Brian dies and I go out with his brother? What does that mean? Is that bad? I just don't

know if it would ever work. Perhaps if we talked to Matt about it. But even then he would be upset."

"Matt will under –"

"I don't think we could break it to him gently. I'm sure it would definitely be difficult for him. It would be difficult for all of us, I think. Not to mention Jesse. I don't know how long he'll be sticking around. Not that I want him gone or anything. I think he's a great kid. But these things come up and I haven't had much time to react –"

"Mary, listen –"

"– to them. I'm glad Matt is having a good time making friends and all. I don't want to ruin it for him. If he thinks that me dating isn't a good idea then I don't know what I'll have to do to convince him otherwise."

"Mary, would –"

"It's all a very delicate situation. I think that maybe if we talked about it together then we will find –"

"Mary –"

"– another solution to this mess. I hope that we can –"

"Mary!"

Mary paused.

"What?"

"Your ice cream is melting."

Mary laughed and blushed. "I'm sorry. I'm thinking too much."

"I wouldn't worry about it, Mary." Bruce munched on his cone. "You know, we can go out and not be 'going out'. You know what I mean? Nobody has to think we're a couple. We're just getting to know each other like ya' said. We're strictly friends."

Mary nodded. "Yes, that's right. Strictly friends."

But in the back of her mind, she wasn't sure if that was the correct term either.

Matt managed to squeeze through the slow-moving door to the office. He ducked beneath the counter and looked around in the darkness for Mr. Fears. The only light Matt saw came from the computer in Dr. Pierce's office.

What is Mr. Fears doing in Dr. Pierce's office?

Matt crept along the wall leading to the Head Staff Hall and then ducked beneath the window to Dr. Pierce's office. Peering over the windowsill, he watched as Mr. Fears clicked on a program.

LanCaster blinked onto the screen. Matt recognized the name. Typing in a username and password, Mr. Fears opened a spreadsheet full of numbers.

Matt squinted in the darkness trying to read what the screen said. He could barely make out the links that appeared. He read *Lunches, Library, Taxes, Sports, Art Department, Music Department,* and *Science Department.*

Mr. Fears clicked on the link labeled *Taxes* and then clicked around some more. Digging deeper into the program, he located a page with a line of about fifteen numbers on it and then clicked Delete.

Matt was concerned. Why would he delete anything from the taxes for the school? He suspected that this was not supposed to happen. Done in the dark and sneaking around is certainly a clue, he thought.

Mr. Fears reached into his pocket and removed his wallet. He produced something that appeared to be the size of a credit card. Matt watched in amazement as Mr. Fears read from the card and typed some numbers into the computer. He then proceeded to increase all of the numbers on the spreadsheet by one hundred dollars.

Why would he do that? Matt thought. He's not even supposed to be in here. He's breaking in and – Matt's eyes went wide with shock.

It was Fears.

Fears was the intruder that had been breaking into the school. He had been changing the numbers on the taxes. He manipulated the numbers and then entered a different number. Was he diverting the money into his own account?

What if he was?

If he increased every number on the sheet by one hundred dollars, he could make thousands of dollars. There was no telling how many times the man had done this.

Matt realized that he was in way over his head. Backing up, he crept away and when he was clear of the window, stood up and dashed for the door not seeing the footstool that rested in his path. He tripped over it and landed with a solid thud, air rushing out of him as he hit the ground. His left leg throbbed.

Fears's chair squeaked as he pushed it back from the desk and rose. Jumping up, Matt headed for the door. Dr. Pierce's door opened and Matt's heart leaped as Fears yelled, "Hey, you!"

Matt sprinted across the cafeteria, leaped over a lunch table in a single bound and kept on going for the door.

"Stop!" Fears called.

Why is someone always chasing me when I'm in the cafeteria? Matt thought as he threw open the back door to the school and ran for the festival grounds. Sprinting back to the boxing booth, he nearly fell over Rose and Jesse.

"Jeez, did you fall in the toilet or some – hey!" Jesse snapped as Matt grabbed his and Rose's arm.

"C'mon, run!" Matt yelped over his shoulder. "Don't ask questions. We've got to get out of here."

"What? Why?" Rose cried as she tried to keep up.

"Just do it. Hurry!"

The three of them dashed from one aisle to the next changing directions whenever they could.

"You kids, don't move!" they heard Fears call.

"Come on," Matt managed. "Back here."

They ducked behind a booth and rested for a moment.

"Why exactly is Mr. Fears chasing us?" Jesse was breathless.

"Hang on … I gotta breathe," Matt said. "I went, uh … to the bathroom and … I saw Fears –"

"Hey, get out from behind my booth," an old woman shouted. "Do you all want detention?"

"No, ma'am," Jesse replied in a polite voice. "We were just leaving,"

The three of them moved out into an aisle between the booths.

Matt continued, "Fears was on the computer and –"

"There they are!" Fears called. "Mrs. Dickson, stop those kids!"

"Let's go," Matt screeched and off they raced running for all their worth.

Fears's voice boomed over the teachers' walkie-talkies. "Attention teachers, we've got three students who have violated school policy. Three freshmen, I believe. Two boys and a girl. They are running down the main aisle towards the large tent. Stop them if you see them."

"Oh, great," Jesse said exasperated.

Matt felt raindrops begin to fall. He glanced around for any oncoming teachers as the drops came down faster and faster.

Suddenly, thunder exploded in the sky and the sound rippled across the area. Immediately afterward, it was pouring.

"Hey, there they are," a teacher in front of them called.

"Wrong way. Turn down this way," Jesse yelped as the three of them made a sharp left and continued to sprint.

They stopped at a four-way intersection and looked around for anyone chasing them.

"We've got to end this," Jesse yelled over another roll of thunder.

Teachers motioned for students to get inside out of the rain and large groups of students began running for the school.

"Mr. Fears, I see them," Matt heard a nearby teacher call. "They're by the barbecue pit."

Fears appeared at the end of the aisle and looked around for them.

"This won't work, either." Jesse sighed. "Let's go!"

The three of them all took off in different directions.

Matt looked over his shoulder and saw that neither Rose nor Jesse were with him. He spun around but they were nowhere in sight.

"Oh, wonderful."

Whipping back around, he peered through the rain in time to see a teacher farther down the aisle with a walkie-talkie. Matt turned and jumped between two booths before the teacher saw him. Squeezing his way through the thin passage, he heard a triumphant voice from the other end.

"No more hiding, I see you."

Matt recognized the voice. Fears stood at the end of the aisle waiting for him to appear. Matt ducked and turned away. He didn't want Fears to see his face. Maybe he hadn't recognized him.

Matt headed back in the direction that he'd come from when Fears's voice stopped him.

"Thank you Randy, for coming to assist me."

Matt glanced up to see Randy draped in a long black trench coat dripping with rain waiting at the other end. Thick boots sank into the mud beneath Randy.

He grinned, eyes flashing like lightning. Fixing his evil gaze in Matt's direction, he was like a dog waiting for its master's command to attack.

Thunder roared and the earth shook. Matt was soaked as the rain poured in thick beads. Just a short time ago, the skies had been so calm. How had the situations changed so quickly? What had he gotten himself into?

"You've got nowhere to go, son," Fears yelled over the storm. "Just come on out."

Jesse sprinted toward the school. A large group of students ran toward the building trying to find shelter from the pouring rain. Merging with the group, he noticed Rose charging along with the mob. Grabbing her arm, he yanked her behind a hanging tarp. She gave a sharp yelp and Jesse threw his hand over her mouth.

"Shh, Rose. It's me," he whispered.

Rose smacked him on the arm. "You idiot! You scared the heck out of me."

"Sorry. Where's Matt?"

"Wasn't he with you?"

"No, I thought he was with –"

"Shh!"

A teacher passed by the tarp. Fears' voice echoed from the walkie-talkie on his belt, "We've found one of the students. We'll call his parents right away. Please continue looking for the other two that were with him. They are probably near the barbeque pit as well. Thank you for your help."

Jesse and Rose listened as the teacher surged on by with the mob.

"What are we going to do?" Rose asked. "Do you even know what Matt did?"

"No idea," Jesse said through clenched teeth. "But it had better be important."

Fears stood at one end of the gap between the two booths. Randy waited at the other end.

Matt was trapped.

"Come on out," Fears's voice boomed as loud as the thunder. "You've got nowhere to go!"

"What's going on here?" Matt heard a second voice yell. He couldn't see the man's face from his position.

"Oh, Dr. Pierce," Fears's voice struck an odd awkwardness. "So nice of you to join us."

"What is the meaning of this?"

"I caught the boy there in the office doing God knows what," Fears cried.

"What proof do you have that it's the same kid?" Dr. Pierce roared as torrents of rain beat down on the earth like a snare drum.

"I didn't think I needed proof."

Matt could barely hear the two of them arguing over the storm. He stole a glance in Randy's direction.

"Yer so totally screwed this time, Cross," Randy hollered as he leaned casually against one of the booths. "Try gettin' yer way out of this one."

Matt blinked dime-sized raindrops out of his eyes and felt his chest get heavy. Randy was right. He was screwed ... big time.

"Hey, there," Dr. Pierce called to Matt.

Matt hid his face from both Dr. Pierce and Fears.

With no response, Dr. Pierce moved to join Randy on the other side of the aisle.

"Hey, kid," he yelled again. "Come on out. You really can't do anything now. I promise it'll be better for you in the long run if you just cooperate."

"What 'better'?" Matt heard Randy holler in Dr. Pierce's ear. "He's mine."

Dr. Pierce raised his eyebrows and stood up to face Randy. The two of them stood only a few inches from each other.

"Excuse me?" Dr. Pierce asked. "He's what?"

Randy shoved a large finger in Dr. Pierce's face. "Don't ya' git in my way. I'm takin' 'im."

"You're not taking anybody," Dr. Pierce roared as lightning streaked through the black sky. "You're on the verge of getting expelled. Do you realize that?"

"Just try it, old man," Randy retorted and spread his arms as if ready to fight.

"Don't be stupid, Mr. Stang. You have no idea how close you are –"

"Try it," Randy roared and thunder rolled as if bowling pins were crashing in on all sides. "Do something. Come on. Do something!"

Dr. Pierce stepped back but Randy pushed up into his face prepared to fight.

"Stop it, Randy," Dr. Pierce bellowed over the howling wind. "That's enough. You're suspended for two weeks. Need I make it more?"

Randy growled and shoved Dr. Pierce with all his might against the corner of the booth. Dr. Pierce lost his footing and fell to the muddy ground, elbows sinking into a large puddle. He looked up to see Randy hovered over him with a look of wild fire in his eyes.

Sharp bolts of lightning behind Randy illuminated the large trench coat that billowed in the storm. Randy's expression was unchanging as Dr. Pierce gritted his teeth and pushed himself up out of the mud trying to maintain his composure.

"Had enough?" Randy taunted.

"That's it," Dr. Pierce hollered. "You're done. I don't ever want to see you set foot in this school again! You are expelled as of now. Your career is over."

"You can't do dat to me!" Randy's voice hesitated. "Do – do ya' know who I am?"

"Yes," Dr. Pierce replied. "You're a delinquent. Now step aside so I can deal with the other boy between the booths."

Randy stepped in Dr. Pierce's path and blocked him. "I don't think so," he sneered. "This is not over."

Matt lost sight and sound of Dr. Pierce and Randy as they'd moved the argument out into the aisle. He looked back at Fears who was still standing there.

"I'm tired of waiting, son," Fears said. "We're getting soaked out here. Let's get inside."

Matt's mind flew through several possible ideas as he stared at Fears through the hair that hid his face. It looked as if there was no hope.

The shadow that materialized behind Fears caught Matt's attention.

Jesse.

Yes, Jesse was creeping up behind Fears with a large tarp in hand. Matt looked back to check on Randy and Dr. Pierce but they were out of sight.

Jesse signaled to Matt with his eyes and lunged at Fears, throwing the tarp over his head. Matt wiggled his way out from the crevice as Jesse held the muddy tarp over the struggling Fears.

"Expulsion, expulsion!" Fears's muffled cries came through as he fought to get free.

Matt squeezed his way out of the alley and took off running toward the school.

"Let's go," he called to Jesse over his shoulder.

Jesse sprinted toward Matt and the two of them dashed across the field in the pouring rain where Rose stood as a lookout. Then, the three of them bolted for the school.

Fears freed himself from the tarp and angrily threw it to the ground. He spun to see who'd thrown it over him but whoever it was had already rounded the corner. He growled under his breath and started to follow. As he did so, he heard voices coming from the other side of the booth. Looking down the aisle between the booths, he saw Randy shove Dr. Pierce.

"Randall," Fears yelled over a clap of thunder.

Randy didn't stop.

"Randall!"

Fears looked back at the school, the kids were getting farther away with each passing second but he had no choice. He couldn't allow the fight between Dr. Pierce and Randy to continue. It had already gone too far. Running his fingers through wet hair, he dashed toward his nephew.

"Randall! Randall, stop!"

"C'mon," Randy yelled at Dr. Pierce. "Do somethin', do somethin'. Why don't ya'? Ya' know ya' want to."

"Randy, stop this." Dr. Pierce struggled to remain calm. "You're in way over your head."

"I don't think so," Randy replied as he raised his fist.

Like an all-star football player, Fears flew in and tackled Randy around the waist from behind and they splattered to the ground.

"What are you doing?" Fears hissed in Randy's ear as he pinned Randy's hands behind his back.

Randy turned his head to identify his tackler. "Uncle? What're ya' doin'?"

"The question is Randall, what are you doing?" Fears insisted. "Assaulting the principal? Do you think I can bail you out of this one?"

Randy gritted his teeth. Dr. Pierce stepped up beside Fears.

"Thank you, Scott," he said. "I appreciate it."

"Yes, well, he went too far this time."

Dr. Pierce nodded. "Bring him inside. We'll call his mother so we can do the paperwork on his expulsion."

"Can we avoid the use of police though?" Fears asked as he hoisted Randy off the ground still holding his arms behind his back.

Dr. Pierce sighed. "We'll see. He's expelled. That's good enough for me, I suppose."

Once inside the school, Matt stopped behind a pillar and called his mom asking her to come and pick them up as soon as possible. Squeezing through crowds of people, Matt, Rose and Jesse soon found Zeke and Jake … arguing.

Jake was signing and Zeke's jaw dropped as he sputtered, "Like heck, ya' won! Our scores were tied and I totally hit yer arm. I won."

Jake signed again.

"Oh, sure. That ref was blind. Whatever. I call a rematch, bud." Zeke turned to the others. "Don't believe a word he says."

"Guys …" Matt gasped as rain dripped off him and onto the floor. "Listen … you've got to … hide us."

Zeke stood taller and looked around. "What's the problem?"

"Just do it," Matt snapped.

"Okay, come on. Hey, Andrew, come here," Zeke called. Matt, Jesse and Rose hid behind a row of trashcans while Zeke, Jake and Andrew guarded it.

Andrew kept up his conversation with Zeke and Jake as though nothing had happened.

"One thing that's kind of ironic though," Andrew said.

"What's that?" Zeke asked.

"That nerdy kid … Eugene Stone, he won the flag contest."

"Did he really?" Rose exclaimed from behind the trashcan. "I was supposed to be partnered with him."

Matt hit her arm. "Shh …" He gestured with his finger to his lips.

A few minutes later, Matt's phone vibrated telling him that Bruce and his mom were waiting outside. Thanking the three that had hid them, Matt, Jesse and Rose made their way out to the parking lot and into the car.

On the way home, Mary and Bruce pressed them on how the festival had gone. Nothing came in return except short, noncommittal answers from the three piled into the back seat.

Matt's mind was working overtime. Rose and Jesse might have their own thoughts on what had happened that night but Matt knew that only he had the truth.

His problem now was what he was going to do with the information. He would have to turn Fears in but how? He needed some kind of proof. But what?

Matt decided then that whatever it took, he would find a way to make sure the whole city of Hills knew about Fears's crime.

After dropping off Rose, Matt was glad to get home and change out of his wet clothes.

Feeling the need to apologize, Matt went across the hall to Jesse's room. "Listen, Jesse. I want to apologize for –"

"No. Stop," Jesse interrupted as he pulled a T-shirt over his head. "Before you begin telling me how sorry you are, I want to know exactly why the entire high school staff was chasing us through the festival and the school."

Matt exhaled, turned and quietly shut the door.

"This is just between you and me, right?"

"Yeah."

"Good. Sit down."

Jesse sat on his bed. "All right."

"You saw me on the news the other night, right?"

"Yeah."

"The cops think that I am the guy they're after."

"Old news."

"Well … I think I've found the real guy."

Jesse raised his eyebrows. "You do?"

"It's Fears."

"Mr. Fears?" Jesse exclaimed.

"What?" Matt asked defensively. "What's wrong with it being Fears?"

"Why … How could he possibly do that?"

"As the assistant principal, he has easy access to all of the school funding. I saw him sneak into Dr. Pierce's office, put in Dr. Pierce's password and change a bunch of numbers on the money page of the LanCaster program. He was taking money out of the tax account. And … he was very careful to make sure no one saw him."

"Okay, I'll bite. But why would he change those numbers? And what's he doing with the money?"

"I'm not sure exactly," Matt replied. "But he took some kind of card out of his wallet and entered a number from it into the program. I thought he might be transferring the funds into his own account. All I know is that Fears is the guy who's been breaking into the school in the middle of the night and causing all the problems. It has to be him."

"Maybe Fears was just working on, you know, principal stuff," Jesse said.

"Well, whatever he was doing, he sure didn't want anybody to see him doing it."

Jesse paused and thought.

"Wait … if Fears is the bad guy then he wouldn't have to break in at all. He's got the key to the school. He's got access to everything."

"Not everything."

"What do you mean?"

"Fears isn't supposed to have Dr. Pierce's password. He was in Dr. Pierce's office. Why would he be in Dr. Pierce's office? If he'd been working on principal stuff, wouldn't he do it from his own computer? Whatever he was doing, he didn't want anyone to find out about it."

Jesse was silent, then, "Okay. Let's say, for argument sake that Fears is the bad guy. What can we do about it?"

"We go to the cops."

"Oh, that was brilliant. 'Go to the cops'," Jesse sighed as they left the police station the following day. "I'm sure that did a lot of good. You watch, they'll be hauling Fears off in cuffs by tomorrow."

"Well, I figured they would at least listen," Matt replied.

"They did listen. Right up to the point where they kicked us out."

"But at least now they know."

"What, Matt? What do they know? Nothing more than what they knew before. They were like, 'We know what we're doing kids. We've got everything under control and you've got nothing to worry about.' They didn't even hear us."

Matt was quiet as they treaded down the sidewalk.

"So now what?"

"I don't know. I think we should just drop it," Jesse suggested.

"Drop it? No way."

Jesse stared at Matt in disbelief. "Jeez. Come on, Matt. It was a long walk here and now we've got a long walk home. Just let it go."

17

December came with a sharp frigid wind. Flurries of snow continued to dance around Hills West. The glistening snow would be inches thick in some areas and barely visible in others. Unfortunately, there were no snow days and the daily routine of school continued just as it always had. The intruder hadn't made a move since the incident at the festival and the police had shelved the investigation due to lack of evidence.

After school, Matt often visited Mr. Parish at the Wind Ridge home. Mr. Parish was always glad to hear from him and they enjoyed each other's company. Lately however, it seemed as if not much talking took place.

Matt sat with Mr. Parish and began a thousand-piece puzzle. The two of them quickly finished most of the outside frame. Actually, Mr. Parish had finished most of the frame. Matt couldn't seem to get any of his pieces to fit. Every time Matt thought he had a match, the piece wouldn't drop into place.

One piece was a hair bigger than the slot so Matt tried to force it in. He pushed on it with aggravation and when that didn't work, he began to pound on it muttering obscenities under his breath. The table shook and Mr. Parish's glass of water wobbled perilously close to the edge of the table.

"Matthew," Mr. Parish commented as he grabbed the teetering glass. "What's the matter? You seem to be a little more … stressed than usual."

Matt threw the piece back to the table and rested the side of his head on his fist.

"Nothing."

"Don't give me that 'nothing' jibber-jabber."

Matt looked at him and then bowed his head again.

"I don't want to talk about it," he muttered.

"Look at it this way, Matthew. Who am I going to tell? My pillow? Your trust will be kept with me. Now, please …" He sipped his water. "Tell me. What is the matter?"

Matt looked up and sighed. "It's my assistant principal."

"What about him?"

"Well, I think, uh … I think he may have done some strange things with the school's money."

"Strange things?" Mr. Parish looked startled. "What sort of strange things?"

"I'm not sure. He hasn't done it lately. It was over a month ago. But I always see him at school and when I see him, I don't see a principal. I see someone with a secret. The other day he gave me detention for 'threatening him with my eyes'."

"What do you think he has done with the money?"

"I saw him changing numbers on the tax sheets on the computer in the office. Then, he took this credit card shaped thing out of his pocket and typed in the account numbers of the card. I'm not sure what he's doing but it can't be good."

"What if he was just working on staff things?"

"That's what my friend, Jesse, said. I don't think he would be so secretive about it if he didn't have something to hide. He was on Dr. Pierce's computer. It had to be dishonest."

"Yes, I see your point. But that doesn't tell me why you feel so bad."

"I just … I just wish that I could prove that he's guilty. He's not a nice guy, you know."

"No?"

"No. He's by far the worst faculty member at the school."

"Did you go to the police?"

"Yeah, they told me to shove it."

"Oh?"

"Yeah."

They were both silent for a moment.

"What if you caught him?" Mr. Parish asked as he put another piece into the puzzle. "What then?"

"Uh, I don't know. He'd go to jail."

"And?"

"He'd feel bad?"

"And?"

"I don't know. I don't get it, what do you mean?"

"How would you feel if he went to jail?"

Matt felt Mr. Parish's eyes focus on his face.

"I don't know. Good, I guess."

He felt comfortable talking with this elderly gentleman, but this conversation was going deep.

"Why would you feel good?"

"Because I caught him – I'd be the hero."

"The hero. Hmm …"

"What? What's wrong with that?"

All of the sudden, Matt didn't feel quite so comfortable.

Mr. Parish exhaled. "You see, Matthew. The heroes in the stories are heroes because of the choices they make. They decide to fight evil because they choose to. You know that something wrong is going on with the school's computer. Right now, you're choosing to try to figure out what you're going to do. But, remember, you have to look at the whole puzzle. Put the pieces together and see where they take you."

Matt thought about this for a moment.

"But how will I prove it? I'm just a freshman. He's the assistant principal of Hills West High School. Who are the police going to believe?"

Mr. Parish was quiet.

Matt held his face in his hands. "I don't know," he said. "I just wish that none of this had happened. Why did it have to happen to me? Why not someone else?"

"Moses was a murderer," Mr. Parish replied. "God called him to stand up against the Pharaoh. David was a shepherd. God called him to be one of the greatest kings of Israel. Peter was a fisherman. God called him to build a church. There's no rhyme or reason as to why God chooses whom he does to be a part of his brilliant plan.

"Perhaps you were meant to look to God to find the answer. If that's so, God will help you to find a way to reach your goal just as He did with Moses, David and Peter."

"Why would God want to use me? I don't even know if I believe in Him."

"Maybe that's why this whole incident occurred. Perhaps, this is your wakeup call."

Matt frowned. "I don't follow."

"If you put your faith and trust in Jesus you will achieve much more than if you just let your instincts lead you."

"But how does God know what to do?"

"He knows. He's God. He'll know if your heart is right. He'll know if this is about fame or reward. He'll know if this is about making right something that is wrong. He knows these things and if you are doing the right thing for the right reasons, he'll make you a great hero … in your heart."

Matt thought a moment but shook his head.

"I don't know. I appreciate the advice but I think I can figure this one out on my own. I don't need God. God never seemed to help me before so I don't know why he'd start now."

"It's all part of His extravagant plan," Mr. Parish voice was quiet.

Matt said nothing in response.

They continued to work on the table puzzle. Several minutes passed before either of them said a word.

Matt's mind began to drift. As thoughts of Fears and the computer buzzed around in his mind, Matt began to fit more and more pieces into the mysterious puzzle.

"Mr. Parish?"

"Yes, Matthew."

"What if I broke into the school and hacked into the computer, then I could prove to the police that Fears is doing something."

"How?"

"I don't know. Maybe somehow I can figure out what he did and show the police or something. It's just a thought."

"Let's go with that thought for a moment," Mr. Parish said. "If you did that then wouldn't you be breaking the rules to stop someone else from breaking the rules?"

"Well, yeah. I guess. But I would be the good guy. The cops would side with me."

"Would they? Or would they see two different people who broke into the school, hacked into the computers and stole information?"

"I already told them that Fears was messing around. They didn't want to listen. So this might make them listen."

Mr. Parish paused and looked to be deep in thought. He stared at Matt's face.

"So, let me get this straight. You're proposing to break into the school, break into the office, hack into the computer, get all your information, get out before the police catch you and then convince them that you're the good guy?"

Matt's thoughts stopped in their tracks. He inhaled deeply and then let the air slowly flow out of his body.

"That's what it sounds like doesn't it?"

Mr. Parish was silent, then …

"You must do what you think is right, of course. You must trust your heart, Matt. And only with Jesus in your heart can you know beyond any doubt that you are making the right decision."

Matt looked down and went back to the puzzle. He knew what Mr. Parish thought but Matt was determined not to let himself fall into that line of thought.

He didn't need God.

Three days before Christmas, Matt stood at Rose's front door with a cherry pie in one hand and a soft brown teddy bear with a ribbon tied to its ear in the other. Christmas break had started and Matt was using every day to his advantage. Rose had invited him to a Christmas dinner with her father and Matt was very anxious to see her.

He rang the doorbell and Rose opened it looking as stunning as ever. She wore a simple white skirt with a long sleeved red top that perfectly matched her long dark hair.

"There you are."

She waved to Matt's mother as she pulled out of the driveway. Her eyes fell on the bear in Matt's hand. "Who's this cute little guy?"

Matt smiled. "Merry Christmas, Rose."

"Merry Christmas to you too, babe," she said and gave him a small kiss. "Thank you. He's adorable."

"Well, come on in," she said. "Don't just stand there. You're letting the heat out. Here, I'll take this." She grabbed the pie.

"Dad," Rose called down the hall as Matt shook his boots off. "Dad. Matt's here."

Mr. Hudson came out of the kitchen wearing a black apron that read *Over 40 and Still Cookin'!* He removed his oven mitts and extended his hand. "It's good to see you again, Mr. Cross."

Matt shook his hand. "And you, too, Mr. Hudson."

"Well, sit down and relax for a bit. I've just pulled the turkey out of the oven."

Rose took Matt's hand and gave him the tour of her large house. It could suit a family of four or five but only accommodated two. Everything was neat, featherbeds made and pillows fluffed. Dusted and shined, the oak cabinets and antiques all stood in their allotted places.

Matt, Rose and Mr. Hudson sat at the large dining room table and began to eat their feast. Delicious sweet potatoes, thick mashed potatoes, rich gravy, sweet corn, warm buttered rolls, tasty dressing and warm greens sat on the table. The mouth-watering turkey, steamed apple cider and Matt's warm cherry pie for dessert made everything perfect. There seemed to be too much food but then again, they had lots of time.

Matt enjoyed his food but he couldn't shrug off thoughts about the school and Mr. Fears.

"Mr. Hudson," he said.

"Yes, Mr. Cross?"

"Remember when we were on our way to church and you were talking about the LanCaster program? You mentioned how it regulates the taxes and handles all the money."

"Mm–hmm."

"Would it be possible to divert those taxes into a different account? Say through a credit card or something?"

Mr. Hudson frowned. "If you put your credit account number into the system, it might be possible if you can get through the security. But it takes so much time to do that. It takes me loads of time and I know just about everything about it. But if you know what you're doing, I guess the possibilities would be endless."

After a moment or two of quiet, Mr. Hudson asked, "If you don't mind me asking, why do you want to know?"

"Oh, well, uh … I was just curious."

"Are you sure?"

Matt glanced at Rose and she shook her head.

"What is it?" Mr. Hudson asked. "You guys know something I don't?"

Matt sighed and told Mr. Hudson the story of Mr. Fears at the festival and his suspicions. After he'd finished, Mr. Hudson sighed. "Well, I suppose that –"

A sharp, beeping noise came from Mr. Hudson's hip. "Excuse me a moment."

He grabbed his beeper, checked the number and punched it into his cell phone.

"Hello, this is Simon." A moment passed and then he sighed. "Okay, I'll be there in a little bit."

Rose dropped her fork and hung her head.

Mr. Hudson closed his phone. "I'm sorry, you guys. But I have to go."

"No," Rose cried. "You always have to work. Please stay for dinner, just this once. We've got company."

"I'm sorry, babe," he replied sorrowfully. "It's out of my hands."

"Where do you have to go?" Matt asked.

"The guys across the river need me. They said the snow shut down the power to Hills East High School. It has come back on but they said the grid isn't responding. I've got to go and figure it out."

He looked at his daughter. "I'm sorry, Rose, but I'll probably be late coming home tonight."

"What else is new?" she shot at him.

Matt saw her eyes glisten as her face turned red.

Mr. Hudson turned to Matt. "You'd better get your boots on, Matt. We'll have to leave in a couple of minutes."

Matt arrived home as the setting sun fell beneath the rolling hills. His mother was in the living room watching television when she heard Matt walk in.

"Matthew, how was dinner with Rose?"

"Fine."

"How did they like the pie?"

"They liked it," he lied. They'd never gotten that far. "Where's Jesse?"

"Upstairs, I think."

He bolted upstairs, threw open Jesse's door and slammed it against the wall protector. Jesse was reading on his bed and jumped at the noise.

"Jeez, Matt, what is your deal?"

"We have to talk."

Jesse dropped his book to the floor as Matt sat down and retold the conversation he and Mr. Hudson had. When he'd finished, Jesse lay motionless on his bed. The quiet lasted for over a minute.

Finally, Jesse said, "So?"

"'So'? What do you mean 'so'? This gives us a boatload of new information on Fears."

Jesse sighed. "I thought we'd dropped this a long time ago."

"Well, I've picked it back up again."

"Matt, what are you doing? You're just digging deeper into nothing. You can't stop him. He's the assistant principal. He could expel us if he wanted to. He could squash us like a bug if he wanted. He can do just about anything if he wanted. Please, don't aggravate him anymore. Let it be. Besides, Fears hasn't screwed around for nearly two months now. He's done. If he hasn't done it before now he probably won't do it again."

"Whatever Jesse." Matt stood and headed for the door. "I don't know why I tell you these things."

He made sure to slam Jesse's door as he left.

Matt lay in his bed with his hands behind his head thinking. Jesse's words stuck in his skull and would not budge. "He's the assistant principal. He could expel us if he wanted … He can do just about anything to us if he wanted … Let it be."

172

He rolled over, shut his eyes and tried to clear his mind as he drifted off to sleep. Just as Matt slid into a dream, his mother's voice called from the living room.

"Matt! Matt, come here quick!"

Matt's eyes were thrown open and he jumped from the bed, dashing down the stairs two at a time.

"What is it, Mom?"

"Watch," she said motioning to the television. "It's happened again."

"… Cindy Underwood is at Hills West High School. Cindy?"

The anchorwoman said, "Thank you, Jan.

"As you can see behind me there are firemen and police officers trying to piece together what happened here."

"Jesse, get down here now," Matt yelled.

In moments, Jesse sped down the stairs. "What?"

"Watch."

The reporter continued, "It appears that the fire sprinklers were turned on inside the school. The fire fighters have managed to shut them down. Unfortunately, the science classrooms on the second floor are completely flooded. One report says the water is over a foot high.

"However, this is no accident. The police believe this is yet another intrusion, possibly the same person who has broken into the school for a total of four times now. They think the sprinklers may have been set as a diversion and between the chaos and commotion of the police cars and fire trucks, the intruder managed to escape. Unfortunately, there were no sightings of the intruder, and he is yet to be unmasked.

"And there is yet another tragedy to add to this strange chain of events, Jan. The late Clarence Williams was the husband of Angelina Williams. The two of them had lived in the wealthy Murraine Estate while Clarence taught at this high school. Before Clarence passed away six years ago, he and his wife agreed to donate over one hundred thousand dollars to the Science Department of Hills West High School.

"With the science department damaged, the widowed Angelina Williams has issued a one hundred thousand-dollar reward for the capture and conviction of the intruder."

One hundred thousand dollars? Matt thought. That would be more than enough to pay off the house.

"The police have also decided that it is necessary for the school to be under constant surveillance from now on. There will be additional police officers patrolling the school throughout the night, and a new security system will be installed in the very near future. The new system will include cameras, digital locks and many other security devices that should prevent any future break-in attempts.

"This is Cindy Underwood at Hills West High School. Back to you, Jan."

Matt stared at the television as the news continued. After a moment of soaking in all this information, he looked at Jesse who stared back at him.

"We need to talk," Matt said.

Jesse's eyes were wide. "Yes. Yes, we do."

18

"Admit it. I was right," Matt exclaimed as the two of them reached the top of the stairs on their way back to Jesse's room.

"What do you mean?" Jesse asked.

"Fears did it again and man, did he ever do it again. He flooded the science hall as a distraction!"

Jesse sat down on his bed and sighed. "Sorry for not taking you seriously."

Matt sat down in the chair in the corner and rested his elbows on his knees. "Don't worry about it. The question is what are we going to do now? The cops don't want to listen, so we can't go to them."

Jesse's face fell into his hands. "We don't even know what it is that Fears is doing."

"I think I do."

"What?"

"Somehow Fears has managed to break into Dr. Pierce's computer, hack into the files and change the tax numbers. Mr. Hudson said that if he could change the numbers, then in theory he could manipulate the money into his own account."

"It seems like a good theory," Jesse said. "But even if we somehow managed to hack into the computer to see what Fears did, we wouldn't know his account number. Plus, we'd get caught during the day."

"We'll do it at night. Just like when I got my journal back."

"Wait," Jesse said. "You're suggesting that we –"

"Yeah, we're going to break into the school. Think about it. If it works, we'd get the money we need to save the house from that lady who posted the reward. How awesome would that be? We'd be heroes and we'd save the house."

Jesse lay back on his bed, pursed his lips and closed his eyes. "This whole thing is going to be a lot more difficult than you think."

"Yeah, we're going to need some help."

Jesse sat up and smiled. "I think I know where we can get it."

"Mo, over here!" Jesse stood and waved his arms as he called across the room from a lunch table in the far corner of the cafeteria. The Christmas and New Year holidays had passed and school had returned with the same daily routine.

Matt leaned over to Jesse from his seat at the lunch table. He had just finished his chicken nuggets. "This guy can help us?" he asked.

Jesse nodded. "Oh, yeah. If you want to know about computers, you talk to Mo. He does it all. Hook ups, wiring, programming ... You name it, he's done it."

"What about hacking?" Matt asked.

The tips of Jesse's lips curled upward slightly as he scanned the area for Mo again.

Matt looked above all the other heads as well. "Where is he?"

Jesse pointed. "That's him."

Mo scooted his wheelchair around people, chairs and tables all the way across the room to where Matt and Jesse sat. Matt was amazed at how proficient Mo was at getting around the people and objects in his wheelchair. Any time he happened to bump into something or someone, he apologized with a calm pair of brown eyes and warm smile. He was a small African-American with short black hair and thin framed glasses, but little seemed to stop him.

"Hey Jesse, how's it going?" He looked at Matt. "I'm Mo."

Matt nodded in response. "Matt."

Matt recognized Mo. He was Dr. Pierce's office aide and had been there when Dr. Pierce had hauled Matt in for fighting.

"Mo," Jesse began. "We really need your help."

Jesse glanced around and then in a quiet voice explained everything that had happened to the two of them at the festival and what Mr. Hudson had said. After Jesse had finished, Mo rested his elbows on the armrests of his wheelchair and wrinkled his brow in thought.

"Man, you guys are really in deep, aren't you?" He took a long breath. "So, what do you need me for?"

Jesse checked the area again and then leaned in close. "What do you know about the LanCaster program?"

"What do you want to do?"

"We're thinking about breaking into the school so we can prove Fears is guilty."

Mo threw his head back and laughed. "No way, it's too late. Maybe if you wanted to do it a week ago, you might have been able to pull it off but they've just installed a new security system. And I've got to say, coming from me, it's one of the most advanced systems I've ever seen."

"I think we can handle it," Matt said.

Mo's eyes went from Matt to Jesse and back to Matt again. "You have no idea what you guys are getting into, do you?"

Matt looked at Jesse and shrugged.

"Okay, let me spell it out for you."

Mo lowered his voice. "You want to break in? Be my guest. I'm not going to stop you. But you need to know what you're up against. There will be two cops positioned at the beginning of the driveway making sure that nobody gets past without permission. Then, there's nearly a quarter mile of driveway with cameras every fifty feet before you even reach the parking lot.

"Once you get that far, there are cops in two cop cars waiting for you. Cops carry guns, mind you – but let's say you get past them. Every entrance to the school is bolted shut and the main entrances now have keycard combination locks in order to get in. And I haven't even mentioned the cameras directly above the doors.

"Once inside the school, state-of-the-art motion sensors and cameras will follow you to the office, which requires a keycard to enter after hours. Once you get to Dr. Pierce's office, you will find yet another keycard lock on his door holding it shut.

"If you manage to unlock the door and get to his computer, you have gain access to Dr. Pierce's files. After that, it's easy. You just hack into an elaborate tax system and save the numbers – the correct numbers that is – to a jump drive for proof. Then there's at least four ticked off cops waiting for you at the door that is if they haven't called for backup."

He paused a moment to let the information sink into their minds.

"If you somehow manage to get away, you've got to convince the police that you're the good guys and give them the jump drive. Then, it's up to them to decide whether you go to jail or not."

Mo leaned back in his wheelchair and spread his hands. "Sounds easy enough, right?"

Jesse looked at Matt who chugged down his entire can of root beer and allowed some to drip onto his tray. Wiping the root beer from his lips with his sleeve as he finished, looked at Jesse and let loose a loud belch. "We're going to need some more people."

"Where are we going, again?" Matt asked, trying to keep up with Jesse as they walked down the highway after school. Matt had called his mother and told her that he and Jesse were going to walk home and would be a little late. But the truth was, he had no idea when he was going to get home.

"You know Zeke and Jake?" Jesse asked.

"Yeah, what about 'em?" Matt asked as another car flew past.

"There's a lot more about them that you don't know."

"Like what?"

"Jake doesn't talk. You know that. It's a good thing he doesn't either. If he talked as much as Zeke then his mouth would probably ruin his hands."

"His hands? What are you talking about?" Matt broke into a trot to keep up with Jesse.

"Let's put it this way. One time, Jake wanted to know what time it was so he snatched my watch off my wrist to check the time. I never knew it was gone. He gave it back to me a few minutes later."

"Oh," Matt said with an impressed look on his face. "So he's like a pickpocket?"

"Yeah, something like that."

"What about Zeke?"

"Zeke? He's a mechanic. Jake's a mechanic too but he's not passionate about it like Zeke. Not only is Zeke an awesome mechanic for being just sixteen, but he's also the best driver I've ever seen."

"The best driver?"

"Yep. For example, one time Zeke ticked a cop off when he'd tried to give him a ticket, Zeke took off. As you know, roads in Hills West aren't very straight and the highest speed limit in the city is thirty-five miles an hour. I believe Zeke said he was going a hundred and five. He managed to evade the cop and get away in no time.

"He's got loads of these situations where he's done crazy things like that. You'll have to ask him about it sometime but, let me tell you, his reputation as a driver is unbeatable."

Matt thought a moment. "Okay, great. But where are we going?"

"To their shop – Lovitt's Auto."

"Why?"

"If we're serious about this, then we're going to need to ask Jake if he can get Fears's wallet so we can write down the account number you saw on that card. Then we can compare it to the one on Dr. Pierce's computer once we make it inside the school."

When Matt and Jesse arrived at the eight-car garage, they could see Jake standing on a stool and leaning over the engine of the truck while Zeke was underneath.

"No, ya' idiot," Zeke yelled. "Yer not doin' it right! Dang it, hang on."

He got up from under the car and jumped up on the stool looking over the engine next to his brother.

"Look. Ya' screw this here like that an' that goes there. Got it?"

Jake signed back.

"No, ya' didn't have it right the first time. Look at what yer doing, Jake."

Jake slammed his fist on the hood of the car and signed again.

"Oh okay, fine," Zeke's voice raised a notch or two. "I'll just let the customer come back a week later an' I'll tell 'em ya' screwed their car up."

Jake signed, his arms flying.

"No, you shut up!" Zeke hollered.

"Hey, guys," Jesse interrupted.

Jake and Zeke spun around and saw Matt and Jesse standing there. Jake took advantage of the momentary distraction and pushed Zeke off the stool plunging him to the ground.

Zeke bounced right back up. "Why you little –"

The last of the threat sputtered out as Jake gave Zeke a hand signal that didn't need translation.

Rolling up his sleeves, Zeke advanced on his brother. "I am going to –"

"Hey!" Jesse hollered again.

The two of them stopped and looked at Jesse again.

"Can you cool it for five minutes?" Jesse pleaded. "We need a favor."

Zeke pulled a rag from beneath his belt and approached the two wiping grease from his hands. Jake followed close behind him.

Jesse sighed. "We need to talk."

"You guys are insane," Zeke exclaimed at lunch the next day.

Matt, Jesse, Mo and Zeke sat around the lunch table together discussing the idea.

"I'm serious," Zeke went on. "You guys are just askin' for trouble. Not only do ya' gotta get through the cops at the front, ya' gotta –"

"We know, Zeke, we know," Matt interrupted. "We've heard it already."

"Okay, whatever," Zeke went on. "But still ya' gotta think 'bout whatcha guys are talkin' about. Do ya' even know how yer gonna to break in?"

Matt looked at Jesse and shrugged. "Well, no, we're still working on that."

"Jeez." Zeke shook his head. "Yer outta yer minds. All of ya', even you." He motioned at Mo. "I mean I done some pretty dangerous stuff in my day, but this? This one takes the cake."

"Hey, here he comes," Mo hissed.

All four heads came up as they watched Jake come across the cafeteria, casually glancing over his shoulder as though someone was following him. He quickly dropped Fears's wallet on the table and took a seat beside Zeke.

Jesse opened up the wallet. "He never ceases to amaze. Thanks Jake, you rock."

Jake smirked.

Matt's eyes widened with shock. "How did you get that?"

"The world'll never know," Zeke replied.

Matt watched as Jesse looked through the wallet and pulled Fears's credit cards and checkbooks from it. Grabbing a small piece of paper, Jesse copied all the account numbers. "All right, I've got them."

"Hey, lemme see that a sec," Zeke grabbed the wallet and pulled out Fears's driver's license. "Hmm … Sixty-six Cradle Drive. I di'n know he lived there."

His eyes moved across the card. "Two hundred and fifty pounds? He don't look two-fifty."

"Give me that." Jesse snatched at it. "We can't go getting into stuff we're not supposed to."

"Pfft … to heck with that," Zeke exclaimed. "As soon as y'uns decided ya' was gonna do this, ya' put yer noses in places they ain't supposed to be. Don't matter what ya' do now."

Matt smiled. "He's got a point, you know."

"I don't care," Jesse replied. "We got what we needed."

He tossed the wallet back to Jake. "Now go work your magic and put it back in Fears's pocket."

Jake grinned and left.

———

"At that point, we could have firecrackers or somethin' explode," Zeke suggested as he toyed with a socket wrench in his garage after school that day.

Matt had called his mom and told her that he and Jesse were walking home again. Mary didn't argue. But Matt and Jesse didn't walk home. Instead, Zeke and Jake gave them a ride to their shop so they could begin strategizing a way to break into the school.

"Why would we need firecrackers to go off?" Matt asked.

"Firecrackers sound like gunshots," Zeke explained. "The cops'll think they're bein' shot at."

"You have to remember the rules," Jesse said suddenly.

"Rules?" Mo looked up. "There are rules?"

"Yes. Don't harm an officer. We'd be arrested on the spot for that. Two – don't harm their cars. And three – don't damage the school. We want everything to be as simple as possible so we can't be convicted of anything serious. Got it?"

Everyone nodded.

Jake started to sign and Zeke watched.

"Oh, yeah, Jake just reminded me. If we're goin' to do firecrackers, I know where we can get 'em for cheap. Andrew's got loads of 'em, his dad sells 'em for the Fourth of July and stuff. Andrew would sell 'em to us pretty cheap, I bet."

Matt looked up. "Where's he live?"

"Not far."

"Can we go find out now?"

"Sure," Zeke replied. "Get in the truck."

───

Within ten minutes, Matt, Jesse and Zeke had arrived at Andrew's house. Jake stayed at the shop with Mo so the two of them hoped to come up with more ideas for the plan.

The bright afternoon sun reflected off Andrew's small white house. The three of them walked past a BEWARE OF DOG sign hanging on the metal gate that fenced off weak patches of grass. Scattered weeds overran the bright flowers and the sidewalk leading up to the house.

Matt rang the doorbell and they heard a monstrous bark and growl on the other side of the door. They saw the door shake as a dog pounded its large body into it trying to get outside.

"Hey, cut it out!" they heard Andrew's voice yell. "Muffin, stop it!"

The door opened and Andrew peeked through the crack as he restrained his dog by the collar.

"Hey, guys. Hang on, I'll be right with you. Come on, you beast!"

The three visitors looked wide eyed at one another as the noises of the quarrel between Andrew and his dog expanded into the next room.

"Move it, you dumb dog! No, you stay here. Don't you look at me like that, Muffin."

Something that sounded like glass breaking struck the floor.

"Now look what you've gone and done, you dumb dog!" Andrew exclaimed.

A few seconds later, Andrew appeared at the door wearing a sleeveless T-shirt and gym shorts with a large, smile on his face as though nothing had happened. "Hey, guys. What's up?"

Jesse spoke first. "We, uh ... we need to talk to you."

"Oh ... well, come on in."

Zeke timidly peeked inside. "Are ya' sure it's safe?"

Andrew laughed. "Yeah, Muffin's fine. He doesn't attack unless he's told to."

Zeke rolled his eyes. "Oh, I feel a whole lot better now that ya' gone and said that."

"Can I get ya' something to drink?" Andrew asked as he escorted the three of them into the living room. "You guys can have a seat if ya' want."

Numerous out-of-date magazines and newspapers scattered over the floor of the room. Matt glanced at one of the magazines and raised his eyebrows. It was from the late eighties. Empty soda and beer cans littered the table. Half-eaten bags of chips rested on a pile of crumbs on the couch. The couch itself had three large brown stains on it. Matt hoped the stains came from the soda and not from Muffin.

Andrew scrambled to scoop up as many soda and beer cans as he could. "I would've picked up a little bit if I'd known you guys were comin'. I feel kind of unprepared."

"Ya' haven't seen nothin' till ya' been to my house," Zeke muttered under his breath.

Andrew came back into the room with three cans of soda in hand.

"Is anyone else home?" Jesse asked as he took one.

"My sister Abby," Andrew replied. "But she's upstairs. She won't be a problem. What's up?"

"We need to buy some firecrackers," Zeke said as he sat down.

"Okay," Andrew replied. "It's kind of early though. In case you haven't noticed, it's the middle of January."

"We're not using them for the Fourth of July," Matt said through a chuckle.

"Well, what do you need 'em for then?"

"We, uh, just need –"

"It's classified," Jesse interrupted.

Andrew turned to Jesse and raised his eyebrows. "Classified?"

"Yes."

"I can't let you buy firecrackers without knowing what you're intending to do with 'em. We wouldn't want you blowing up the school or anything, right?"

He laughed at his own joke, but his laughter decreased to a chuckle and eventually died out when he noticed no one else was laughing with him.

"Okay … that's creepy. What are you guys up to?"

"We can't tell ya'," Zeke said. "Not unless ya' side with us, that is. If ya' wanna participate, we'll let ya' in on it."

Matt looked at Jesse who shrugged at Zeke's bluntness.

"So . . ?" Matt asked Andrew. "Are you with us?"

Andrew looked from one face to the next. The three of them didn't seem to be doing anything juvenile. Whatever they were up to, it had to be important.

"Yeah … yeah," he muttered. "I'm with you."

"Okay, then listen …"

Matt explained everything to Andrew. He told him how he'd broken into the school by himself to get his Dad's journal back. He told him what he'd seen Fears do in Dr. Pierce's office and how they'd been chased during the festival, which was why they had used Andrew's help to hide them.

"All right," Andrew said after Matt wound down. "Here's what I'll do, I'll give you all the firecrackers you need. I'll also help in any way I can. I mean if I'm going to do this, then I'm committed."

He looked to Matt and Jesse. "Tonight you guys figure out exactly how you're going to do it. I'll meet you at Zeke's shop after school tomorrow and you can fill me in there. All right?"

They nodded.

"No, it's not all right," a voice exclaimed from the stairs.

All heads looked toward the stairs as Abby dashed down them. Matt hadn't seen her since they'd served detention together. She wore a white sports top with black shorts and tennis shoes. Her skin glistened with a light sweat from her activities upstairs. Her long, golden hair bounced in a ponytail as she came charging down the stairs.

Jesse straightened his back and threw hair out of his face, gulping at the sight of Abby.

"Andrew," she said harshly. "You're not really going to help them are you? Think about it. There's no possible way you guys can pull this off. Did you hear how many cops would be there? You'll get in so much trouble."

Andrew stood rising to his full height with a stern look in his eyes. His jaw clenched as he retorted, "Thank you Abby, for listening in on my conversation. Now go back to working out or whatever you were doing and I'll do what I want."

"It's too late now," Jesse said.

Andrew turned. "What?"

"She knows. She'll let someone else know. Then we're through. Either she's with us or we forget the whole thing. We can't risk her telling anyone."

Matt shrugged. "He's right, you know."

Zeke nodded as well.

Andrew looked at Abby with a wide-eyed pleading expression. Abby shook her head, sighed and collapsed onto the rugged leather chair. "I can't believe you guys are dragging me into this too. We are all going to get into so much trouble."

19

When Matt, Jesse and Zeke arrived back to the garage, it was already dark. Mo and Jake were working on Mo's laptop when they walked in. The three of them filled Jake and Mo in on what had happened at Andrew's house.

"Uh ... Matt?" Mo said as they finished. "I think we, uh ... I know you probably don't want to hear this ... but I think we're going to need the blueprints of the school if we're to make the plan work. If we're going to use the ventilation shafts like we were talking about, then the blueprints would show us exactly where they lead."

Matt leaned on Zeke's truck and paused.

"Any thoughts Jesse?"

"Don't look at me," Jesse replied. "I don't know where we'll get blueprints of the school."

"Me, neither."

They all sat in silence as the wind shook the closed garage door.

"I think I know where," Mo said suddenly.

All eyes focused on Mo.

"Where?" Matt asked.

"It's going to be tough," he continued.

"Where?"

"Fears's house."

"Mr. Fears's house?" the others exclaimed in disbelief.

Mo went on, "Fears was in charge of purchasing the new security system. He worked closely with the installers. After several weeks of working in his office, I saw him leave with what had to be the blueprints. I assume he took them home. Where else would he take them?"

"What do they look like?" Jesse's asked with a hint of hesitation.

"When I last saw them, they were rolled up in a long, white plastic tube. They're probably in Fears's house somewhere."

"Hold on, lemme think about it … oh wait, never mind cause it's crazy," Zeke exclaimed as he pulled on his hair in his frustration. "We might as well walk up to the police station in handcuffs and jumpsuits. It'll never work."

Jake stomped and signed frantically. Zeke didn't bother to translate.

Jesse sat on a stool, drew his fingers through his long hair and tried to think.

"I don't know," he said. "Maybe we could make it work."

"How?" Zeke expounded as he pulled up a stool and sat next to Jesse.

Realizing he couldn't change their minds with that attitude, Zeke took a long breath and seemed to compose himself. In a slow, clam voice, he said, "Look, man. It's impossible. There's no way to break into Fears' house. We'll be caught for sure. Don't even try it. In fact, don't even think about it."

"Nothing's impossible," Jesse replied. "You just need a little imagination. We read the address on his driver's license at lunch today, what was it?"

"Sixty-six Cradle Drive," Mo answered. "I've seen that house. It's big and I believe Fears has a security system installed. Anytime you open a door or window the system rings. When the system is armed, a loud alarm goes off and it automatically calls the police."

Matt sighed and glanced at his watch. It was already past eight. "Well, we can't do it tonight. My mom's going to kill me if I don't get home. Jesse and I'll figure out what to do tonight and we can talk tomorrow."

From his bed, Jesse suggested, "What if we called Fears and lied about a fire at the school or something? Then he'd leave his house and we could get in."

Newt looked comfortable cuddled up against Jesse and getting his head scratched. Matt sat on a chair resting his arms on the desk.

Matt shook his head. "No, that wouldn't work."

"Why not?"

"Fears would arm the security system before he left."

"Oh, yeah. Good point. Well, what if we –?"

A soft knock sounded at the door and Matt's mother peeked through the crack.

"Matt?"

Newt perked up his ears.

"Uh – yeah, mom?"

"Phone for you," she said. "Tell Rose that she can't call this late anymore. I'm not going to –"

Matt took the phone and shut the door without saying a word.

"Hello? … Hey, babe. Uh – what's up?"

Jesse snapped his fingers and whispered, "Don't tell her anything."

"I know," Matt mouthed.

Matt's brow wrinkled as he listened.

"No, no … there's nothing wrong," he stuttered. "I've just, uh – been, uh … I've been a little stressed out lately. That's all. I'm sorry."

A pause then, "Uh, yeah, I've had loads of homework and I've been helping my mom around the house, you know? I've just had a lot of things on my mind."

Jesse could hear Rose's distressed voice on the other end.

"Babe, there's nothing, really. We did – we *do* have something going. It's just – I mean, I'm a little distracted right now. I'm okay. We're okay. Really."

He waited.

"Really, really, babe." he said. "I just need to get a few things straightened out, but it's nothing about us, honest."

Jesse motioned for him to get off the phone and Matt rolled his eyes.

"Rose, you know I'd love to talk about whatever but tonight just isn't a good night, I've got a lot of things to do and it's already late. I'm sort of, uh – in the middle of something right now and – uh – there's nothing you can do right now, okay?"

He glanced back to Jesse who mouthed, "This is the part where you hang up."

Matt stopped and his eyes seemed to stare into nothingness as an idea came to mind. "Wait, Rose. No – wait. Actually, there is something you can do …"

Jesse groaned and flopped face first on his bed.

The next day after school, Matt had been invited to dinner with Rose's family. Mr. Hudson was sitting in the living room reading the paper while Rose and Matt finished the dishes.

Matt wandered into the room and found a seat on the couch next to Mr. Hudson.

"Excuse me, Mr. Hudson."

Mr. Hudson looked away from his paper. "Yes, Mr. Cross?"

"I'd like to talk to you about something very private."

Mr. Hudson put down the paper. "What's up?"

"Do you swear that you will never speak of this conversation to anyone?"

Mr. Hudson nodded. "I swear."

"What if I knew beyond any doubt who the intruder is and that I could stop him?"

Mr. Hudson gave Matt a hard look. "I think that depends on how you go about catching him."

Matt took a breath.

"I would break into the school, hack into the computer and compare account numbers."

"Account numbers? What are you talking about?"

"Now hear me out before calling me crazy, okay?"

Mr. Hudson nodded.

"I think Mr. Fears is breaking into the school after hours, hacking into Dr. Pierce's computer and diverting tax money into his own account somehow. If I got on the computer, I could compare his account numbers with the number on the screen. If they're the same, I would know that Fears is the intruder."

"My, my, my, you are inquisitive, aren't you? How'd you figure that out?"

"That doesn't really matter much. I know I can catch him. All I'd have to do is break into the school, go to Dr. Pierce's office and get it."

"When?"

"At night."

"I don't think that's a good idea."

"Why not?"

"What if the police catch you? You'll be arrested and the intruder will still be out there."

"I'm willing to take that chance."

"Why?"

"I need the money."

"Money? You're doing all this for money?"

"One hundred thousand dollars is a lot of money, Mr. Hudson. My family needs it."

"It is a lot of money, I'll give you that. But it's not worth risking everything."

Matt closed his eyes and envisioned his father building the roof of his house on the farm. With the bright sky behind him, his dad looks down, smiles and waves. Matt waves back. He was happy then. If they could keep the house, that memory would live on.

"It is to me."

"Mr. Cross, I forbid it," Mr. Hudson continued. "You can't beat the system. Do you even know what the administration has done to the school now? They've got –"

"I know all about the new security system. I can beat the whole thing and not you nor anyone else can persuade me otherwise. I'm going to do it."

"When?"

"A week from Sunday."

Matt and Rose walked through her subdivision. She was holding his arm and Matt was enjoying the distraction from all of the scheming that had been filling his mind. He hadn't realized how much he'd missed Rose's companionship.

The sun was just beginning to drop beneath the treetops and the crisp, cool air blew between them.

Rose zipped her red sweater.

"So what were you and my dad talking about?"

"Oh, nothing," Matt lied.

"No really, what was it? You seemed pretty worked up about it."

"Well … we, uh … we were talking about a project."

"A project?"

"Yes, a project."

"And this project … why did you have to talk with him about it?"

"Well actually, I need to talk to you about it."

"Me?" she asked. "What's up?"

"I need your help."

"Okay."

"You see, Mr. Fears has these blueprints of the school and I need to get them."

"For what?"

"The project, but I know he won't give them to me if I asked for them."

"Why not?"

"Because he's Fears and I'm me. Fears isn't really nice to me. So Jesse and I were going to get them ourselves."

"Wait, what? How?"

"We need the prints, he's got them, and so we're going to take them."

Rose stopped and stared at Matt.

"What exactly is this project you're working on?"

"It involves taxes."

Rose searched Matt's eyes for any sign that he might be lying. She couldn't find anything, but couldn't shake the feeling she wasn't getting the whole truth.

"So what do you want me to do?"

"Tell me again, you want me to do what?" Rose requested as Zeke's truck turned onto Cradle Drive the following evening.

Darkness had fallen.

The thick trees surrounding the drive made the house difficult to see.

Jesse eyed the mailboxes along the side of the road. "Forty-three … Forty-six …"

Matt sat in the passenger seat next to Zeke. Turning around, he faced Rose. "Relax, Rose, you'll be fine. You guys are okay, right?"

Jake, Rose, and Jesse were squeezed together in the back seat. There was hardly enough room to move.

"Tell me again why I let you talk me into this?" Rose asked with a look of frustration.

"Because you like me."

"Oh, you think that you're so –?"

"Sixty-six," Jesse interrupted. "That's it there."

Zeke stopped the truck about twenty yards from the house. The engine idled while the five of them inspected the house.

Extending from the mailbox, a long sidewalk wound through the yard and up six steps to a wide porch. The porch appeared to encircle the entire house. Two rocking chairs sat next to a porch swing as it swayed in the breeze. Light shined through curtains on both floors of the house. They could hear a television playing inside somewhere. As a figure passed by a second floor window, they ducked in the shadows of the truck. Matt could tell that it was Fears by his build. He appeared to be talking on the phone.

"Is Fears married?" Matt asked.

"Divorced, I think," Jesse replied. "I'm not sure."

Matt continued to watch Fears. He noticed a small box about six inches in length sitting on top of each windowsill.

"Do you guys see those boxes?" Matt pointed. "What do you think those are?"

"It's part of the security system," Zeke informed them. "It detects if the door and windows are open or closed."

They watched Fears open the window. The yellow curtains billowed in the chilly breeze.

"I'm going to need at least ten minutes," Matt said. "Mo told us what the school blueprints look like, plus, he said they probably wouldn't be far from his room, maybe in his closet or something."

"So how do we get in?" Rose asked.

A wicked smile grew on Matt's face. "I thought you'd never ask." He grabbed a notebook from his backpack and began to sketch.

"What are you doing?" Jesse asked.

"Watch."

A moment or two of silence passed.

"Are you drawing Fears's house?" Jesse asked.

Matt nodded.

"Why?"

"Because Rose is going to convince Fears that his house is the nicest one on the block and she wants to draw it. She's going to show him this sketch to show how sincere she is about doing it."

"Why me? What makes you think he'll believe me?" Rose exclaimed.

"You're a girl," Matt replied. "And I think he'll respond better to a girl than a guy. All you've got to do is tell Fears how pretty his house is and how bad you want to draw it. You can go on and on about his yard and porch and windows and stuff. Fears will be eating out of your hand.

"You need to get Fears to move away from his door and maybe out around his porch or something so I can get in. You just need to keep him occupied for like five to ten minutes. That should be all the time I'm going to need."

"Ten minutes? You're really serious? That's not going to work."

"Trust me," Matt replied. "It'll work. I'm sure Fears would love someone to feed his ego."

Zeke watched as Matt finished the sketch. "Not bad. I di'n know ya' could draw."

Jake nodded in agreement.

"There. I'm done." Matt handed the picture to Rose. "Come on, let's do this."

The nearby streetlight illuminated Fears's yard as shadows from swaying tree limbs crept across the cold, dark grass portraying fingers ready to entwine any passing thing. A light breeze beckoned curtains to fly away from their opened windows as they whipped and billowed into the darkness. There seemed to be only one object in the area that was still – Rose.

She stood on the front porch, her hand rose as she argued with herself as to whether or not she should knock on the door in front of her. She pulled her hand back.

Turning back to the boys, she hissed, "This is never going to work."

Zeke ignored her and motioned for her to knock on the door. Rose turned back to the door, glanced at Matt's rough sketch, shook her head and gave the door three light knocks.

Near the side of Fears's house, Matt watched from his hiding place behind a tree stump. His breath was unsteady.

"Hang on. Hang on," Fears called from inside. "I'm coming."

Wearing a thin white T-shirt, gym shorts and socks, Fears swung the door open. His hair was messed up as though he'd just woken from a nap. His eyes widened at the sight of her.

"Oh," he exclaimed and straightened a bit. "Good evening, Miss Hudson."

"Good evening."

The two of them eyed each other in awkward silence.

"Can I help you?" Fears asked with a hint of impatience.

"Uh, yes, you can," Rose began. "I was wondering if you might be interested in a … uh a picture, a picture of your house."

"No, thank you."

Fears began to shut the door.

"W – wait!" Rose stuttered. "I'm an artist see and I think you have the most gorgeous house on the block and possibly the best looking house in Hills West …"

Fears held the door.

Rose rushed on, "I really hate to bother you, especially since it's so late, but you have such an astounding house that I was … I was drawn to it. I – I just thought that I would ask your permission to draw it and then I would let you have my work."

She held her a breath waiting for his response.

Fears shook his head and, again, the door started to swing shut.

"Look! You see?" Rose held up Matt's sketch. "I've drawn a rough sketch of your magnificent home so you might know what it'll look like."

Rose offered it to Fears.

He stepped underneath his porch light and examined the picture. The door stayed open.

"This is decent," he admitted. "You say you can do better?"

"Oh, yes," Rose continued. "I made this sketch in just a few minutes. Give me a few hours and you'll have something worth keeping."

"Hmm … you may have some talent, but I don't believe that I –"

"Come with me," Rose interrupted. "I realize that it's late, but let me show you what's so wonderful about your house."

"What are you talking about?"

Rose stepped off the porch and gazed at Fears's house in awe.

"Just look at this house," she continued, gazing up at the house. "The pitch of the roof is just perfect. With the sun shining on it at the right time of day, I believe that I could really make the shadows stand out. Come on, Mr. Fears. Come see what I'm talking about."

Fears complied and followed after Rose in his sock feet. Matt was right. The more Rose complimented Fears's house, the more Fears wanted to hear. He followed her down the stairs to the front yard.

"In fact," Rose hurried on, "I could do different angles, I could come over to the side of the house like this, you see?"

She led Fears away from the front door, pointing out the shape of the side of his house.

"It's quite possible that I could even do all four sides of your house. Could you imagine? You would have all sides of your house up on your wall and above the fireplace and when guests came over, they would see it and …"

Good girl, Rose, Matt thought as he jumped up from behind the stump and bolted for the front door.

Throwing the door open, his nose was filled with the smell of cooking chicken from the oven in the kitchen down the hall. Directly ahead of him, he saw a flight of stairs. To his left, stood a wood-floored living room with a long leather couch in front of a medium-sized television. To his right, the dining room sported a long table fit to serve a dozen people.

Matt had no time to be interested in either of these places. He had to find Fears's room and quick. Rose could only keep Fears occupied for a few minutes. He sprinted up the stairs taking two at a time.

At the top of the stairs, Matt ran down the long hall going from door to door trying to find Fears's room. Matt had found two bedrooms, an office and a bathroom before he opened the door at the end of the hall.

Bright lights shined on the yellow quilted bed. The wallpaper and curtains were yellow as well. The bright colors surprised him. Matt never thought that Fears was much of a yellow kind of guy. A light blue chair in the corner had a cordless phone resting on its arm.

Matt moved to the closet, opened it and began scanning for the long tube that contained the blueprints. He pushed countless shoeboxes aside as he searched. His eyes jumped all over the wide closet but nothing remotely resembled a long tube.

Shaking his head in frustration, he spun back toward the room, his eyes dancing along the walls searching for clues. He could hear Rose and Fears talking outside. It had been nearly two minutes. Rose was doing a good job of keeping him occupied.

Matt's mind raced. Where else could it be? Where else would Fears put blueprints?

The thought exploded in Matt's head. An office. He'd seen what looked to be an office in the hall a moment ago. In seconds, Matt was in front of Fears's office. Throwing open the door, he snapped on the lights.

A computer sat in a far corner with another desk in the middle of the room. Multiple file cabinets lined the wall and a wide closet could be seen in the corner. Opening the closet, Matt rifled through cases of folders and boxes. The blueprints had to be in there, Matt didn't know where else to look.

Reaching above his head, he moved a small box unaware that it supported three other boxes. The boxes slipped from the shelf and he couldn't even begin to try to catch them. As they tumbled down, he covered his head with his hands. With a huge crash, the boxes hit the floor and endless amounts of papers littered the area.

"And as you can see, that window over there would easily accent the marvelous —"

A loud crash stopped Rose.

Fears spun. "Did you hear —?"

Rose kept talking, pretending as though she hadn't heard him. "It would definitely accent your garden here and what a beautiful garden it is."

However, Fears was no longer listening. He began to walk back toward the front door.

"No, wait … just a moment," Rose exclaimed. "I haven't even showed you the backyard yet. Wait until you see it."

"I've seen it," Fears's said coldly.

"No, but I think that if –"

"Listen," Fears cut her off. "Thank you for your compliments but I think you should take your business elsewhere."

Rose heart thumped within the depths of her chest. Her face grew hot in the cold of the night.

"I'm not running a business, Mr. Fears," she said quickly. "In fact, it's free."

Fears ignored Rose as he opened the front door to his house and walked in.

"Did you hear me, Mr. Fears?" she asked following him into the foyer. "My service is free. No charge whatsoever."

"Not interested."

Rose stared at the staircase wondering what on earth Matt could be doing that would take this much time. With all hope fading, Rose decided to play the last card she had.

"Mr. Fears …"

He looked back at her. "What?"

"Have I ever mentioned how incredibly handsome you are?"

Matt stopped collecting the papers that were scattered about as he listened to the conversation coming from the bottom of the stairs.

"You're so tall and strong. Any girl would love to have a man like you to hold and protect her."

Matt smacked his forehead. "Rose … why would you –?"

This had gone too far. Rose was downstairs trying to steal Fears's heart while Matt was upstairs trying to steal his blueprints.

Rose was doing everything she could to buy Matt more time. The problem was, there wasn't any more time to be bought.

Matt continued putting everything back into the closet. He didn't care if it was neat, just out of sight. Grabbing the random papers and folders from the floor, he crammed them into boxes and then shoved the boxes into the closet. With hands still shoving, he began to think.

Rose had done all she could with her artist act so how was he supposed to get out of the house without Rose distracting Fears?

"I think you are the most intelligent principal Hills West has had in a long time." Rose went on, "You're definitely more sophisticated than Dr. Pierce."

Fears looked at Rose. "Is that right?"

Rose nonchalantly pulled at her shirt a bit lower to show a bit more of her chest.

"You should be principal, Mr. Fears. I've always thought that the name Dr. Fears had a nice ring to it, don't you?"

His eyes fixated on her. She stepped closer and then closer again. Fears' eyes glanced toward her chest and back to her face.

Rose continued the act. "I really like you, Mr. Fears," she said in a soft lazy voice. "There's something … mysterious about you. I don't know what it is. But maybe we could find out."

A loud thump came from upstairs and Fears blinked.

He cleared his throat. "No … I'm sorry. Not tonight."

"But Mr. Fears, I –"

"No, it's time for you to leave, Miss Hudson."

"I really think you should –"

"You need to go. I will see you at school."

"But sir, if you would just stop a –"

"Miss Hudson!" he snapped silencing her. "Get out of my house and off my property or I will be obligated to call the police. It would be awful to see a nice young lady such as yourself in that kind of trouble. I suggest you leave now."

Rose paused looking uncertain and concerned.

"All right, then, if you're sure."

"I'm sure. Good night, dear."

Rose forced a smile and stepped off his porch. "Well … uh, good night, Mr. Fears."

He stopped in the doorway. "You can call me Scott off school grounds."

"Oh, okay, Scott. Good night."

She turned and headed for Zeke's truck as thoughts ricocheted off the crevices of her brain. *I hope he doesn't think I was serious.*

Fears cleared his throat, stood straighter and turned back toward the house as though nothing had happened, shutting the door behind him.

Matt had almost finished picking up the mess when Fears's footsteps sounded on the stairs. Turning off the lights, he dove beneath the desk and had just pulled his feet in when Fears opened the door.

There was no sound. Fears stood there, breathing.

Matt took a deep silent breath and held it deep inside him. Matt heard his heartbeat echo in his ears. Looking down, he noticed his right hand beginning to quiver. Tucking it beneath his shirt, he continued to hold his breath.

Air threatened to crawl up from the pit of his stomach to the tip of his throat. He needed to open his mouth and breathe, but he couldn't. He had to force himself to keep it down or pass out.

Rose was gone. He was on his own now. He had to do what he had to do. He had to find a way out of the house.

Matt didn't care about the stupid blueprints anymore. He just didn't want to get arrested. His artist idea might have worked if he had known where to look for the blueprints.

He could hear Fears sniff multiple times like a bloodhound searching for prey as he held the door open.

The office remained silent.

Fears exhaled and the door shut as he left.

Matt threw his mouth open gasping and coughing. He leaned over on all fours and took another deep breath, discovering a new appreciation for air.

Crawling out from under the desk, he sat up pushing oxygen back into his system. As he rested his hands on top of his head, his eyes roamed the room and then stopped when he noticed the closet door.

It was ajar.

He stood and opened the door inspecting the disorganization. He sighed and allowed his head to tilt toward the ceiling. There, even in the darkness, he could see it, a long white tube pushed back against the wall on the highest shelf.

The papers and folders had been stacked in front of it and it was out of reach without a chair or stool. Matt started to reach for a chair when he heard Fears's footsteps in the hall. He jumped behind the closet door hoping that Fears would keep going. Luckily, he did.

As soon as the footsteps were out of earshot, Matt grabbed the swivel chair. It twisted and spun as Matt pushed it as far into the closet as he could. He glanced around for a safer chair but the swivel chair was the only one in the room.

Matt shook his head. He would have to be careful not to lose his balance.

Climbing onto the chair, Matt extended his arm up toward the case. The chair dipped and Matt threw his arms out for balance. Looking back up at the case, he stretched his arm upward until his fingertips brushed the end of the tube. Using the closet door for support, he pulled himself onto the tips of his toes.

The chair began to swivel again but Matt disregarded it as he continued to reach, his heels rising into the air. With the chair tilting farther and farther over, Matt ignored his precarious position, held onto the door, grabbed the tube and pulled it to him. As his heels touched the chair cushion, his weight shifted, the chair tipped and Matt was thrown from it landing with a loud thud.

Matt imagined Fears's ears perking up at the noise. He was sure Fears had heard it. Groaning quietly, he rose and pushed the chair to its original position and shut the closet door. He could hear Fears coming back up the stairs, undoubtedly coming to check on the noise. He had to get out of the office.

Opening the office door, he jumped across the hall, grabbed the other door, stepped inside and shut the door behind him. Feeling around the area with his hands, Matt discovered he was in the bathroom.

Matt heard Fears open the door to the office across the hall as he felt around the dark bathroom for the shower curtain. The only source of light came from the crack under the door. Glancing at the crack, Matt was startled to see Fears's shadow fall over it. He was right outside the door.

Fears calmly opened the door and turned on the lights. He yawned and stretched as he stepped up to the toilet.

Matt held his breath again.

The shower curtain was the only thing that separated Matt from Fears. Fears cleared his throat.

Matt heard running water and his jaw dropped when he realized Fears was relieving himself just inches from where he was standing. Fears was completely oblivious to Matt's presence within the shower as he took a deep breath in through his nose and scratched something.

Fears chuckled to himself. "Rose Hudson ... sweet girl. Rose – yes, very sweet. She likes me? She looks pretty good herself."

He laughed again and sighed. "'Dr. Fears' . . ?"

Fears washed his hands, turned the light off and Matt listened as his footsteps moved down the stairs.

Opening the case to make sure that the blueprints were inside, Matt sighed with relief. They were rolled neatly inside the tube. He put the cap back on and took another deep breath as he began to formulate how he was going to get out of Fears's house without being seen.

Rose walked back to the truck with her shoulders slumped. Matt was in Fears's house alone and there was nothing more she could do for him.

She'd failed.

"What are ya' doin'?" Zeke demanded.

Jesse and Jake nodded in agreement behind him.

Zeke went on, "Get back in there and get Matt out of there."

"Fears threatened to call the police if I went back," Rose hissed back.

Zeke threw his hands into the air. "What're we apposed to do? Just sit here and think, 'Golly gee, I hope Matt makes it out okay'?"

"Got any other bright ideas?" Rose retorted as she crumpled up Matt's sketch and threw it in Zeke's face.

"Yeah, I do, Miss Smarty Pants," Zeke replied. "Jake, gimme yer cell phone."

"Why does Jake have a cell phone?" Jesse frowned from the backseat. "He doesn't talk."

"Yeah, but ya' wouldn't believe our text messagin' bill."

Matt peered down the stairs to see Fears watching television in his house robe. He glanced at the door at the foot of the stairs. Maybe he could just run down the stairs, throw open the door and run across the yard to the truck before Fears saw him. Matt shook his head. He was fast but he wasn't that fast.

His best plan was to sneak down the stairs and wait for Fears to go in the kitchen. Then, he would leave through the front door. Yes, he could do that. He would wait.

He looked at the back of Fears's head. If Matt made a sound, Fears would catch him. If Fears turned around, there was no place for Matt to hide. He'd be completely exposed on the stairs, but he had to get out of here.

He braced himself on the rail and placed his foot on the first step.

The phone suddenly screeched as though it had been waiting for the perfect time and Matt jumped back into the shadows.

Fears groaned and went into the kitchen to answer it.

"Hello?"

"Yes, is this Mr. Scott Fears of Sixty-six Cradle Drive?"

"Yes."

"I am with your heating and air provider. We would like to ask you a few short questions and then we'll be out of your hair. Is that all right, sir?"

"Just get on with it."

"Yes, right away, sir. Do you have a heating or air device installed in your home?"

"Yes, I do."

"Do you have a furnace?"

"Yes."

"Where is this furnace located in your house, sir?"

"It's in the basement."

"Well, sir, if it's not too much trouble, could you please go to your basement so I can ask you a few more questions?"

"Yes, I do mind."

"Excuse me, sir?"

"You heard me," Fears said. "It's nine forty-five at night and you're calling me to ask about my furnace."

"I'm sorry, sir. I'm just doing my job as a –"

"Do you really think I care? It's nine forty-five."

Matt had managed to get to the base of the stairs when he heard Fears coming back from the kitchen, heading right toward him.

He dashed in front of the couch but Fears walked past the stairs and into the living room. Matt crawled around the couch as Fears stopped in front of it. The couch groaned as Fears sat down.

"You need what?" Fears spoke into the phone. "… I clearly said that I wasn't going to go to my basement … Yes, I know what you do. Wh – no, I … Oh, fine, but you realize I am going to file a complaint against your company, correct?"

Matt smiled as Fears sighed and got up from the couch. Matt crawled back around to the front, keeping the couch between himself and Fears. Fears started down the basement stairs, the phone still cradled against his ear.

Jumping up, Matt dashed for the door and grabbed the door handle. The piercing alarm that sounded caused his arm to jerk away from the door as if he had received an electrical shock.

Did I set off an alarm? Matt thought quickly. I didn't even open the door.

Matt heard Fears curse from the basement.

"My chicken," Fears hollered into the phone as he rushed back up the stairs. "My chicken is burned, you idiot!"

Fears cut off whoever was on the other end. "Shut up."

Slamming the phone down, he ran into the kitchen where smoke poured from the oven.

Fears cursed again. The smell of burned chicken filled Matt's nostrils and he felt like gagging. He put his hand over his mouth and tried to breathe.

The security machine next to the front door began to cry, "Smoke! Alert! Smoke!"

"Yes, I know, you stupid machine!" Fears yelled over the piercing cry of the alarm.

He stormed back toward the front door.

Matt spun, dashed up the stairs and turned the corner again just as Fears reached the front door.

Leaning against the upstairs wall, Matt sighed. Am I ever going to get out of this house, he thought. Creeping back to Fears's room blueprints in hand, he noticed the curtain whipping in the breeze. Matt felt ten times lighter – the window.

Parting the curtains, he stuck one leg over the windowsill, put his head through and came out the other side. He found himself standing on Fears's roof overlooking the front yard.

"Look, there he is," Jesse yelled from the truck. "And he's got the prints!"

Matt crouched down and hung from the roof, then let go and dropped the few feet to the ground. He jumped up and sprinted for the truck.

Tossing Jesse the blueprints, Matt jumped in the seat and managed, "Come on, guys. Let's get the heck outta here."

"What's the matter, Matt?" Jesse asked excitedly. "You made it out. Look at yourself! You look perfectly fine to me."

"Yeah, man," Zeke said, "we di'n know when ya' was comin' out. We was thinkin' about leaving ya' and lettin' ya' stay all night. That is, if that heatin' and air questionnaire thing di'n work."

Matt tried to hide his grin. "I hate you guys."

Zeke started his truck and drove up the road. As the truck turned the corner, down the street a dark car started up and pulled onto the road following Zeke. Streetlights brightened the inside of the vehicle revealing the white of teeth of the evil face behind the steering wheel.

20

Surprisingly, Matt and Jesse didn't get into too much trouble for arriving home so late on a school night.

Mary was upset at first. "I've been worried sick about you two. I was about to call the police."

After Jesse told her they were spending "quality time" with the assistant principal, she lightened up some. The boys downed their dinner and went upstairs.

Matt spread the blueprints of the school out on Jesse's dresser. Newt lay on the bed and watched. His ears and face twitched with a curious expression. A dim light from a tarnished lamp was the only illumination in the room.

"We're going to need a car," Jesse said after he finished examining the blueprints. "How are we supposed to get away without one?"

"A car means we'll probably be chased," Matt replied. "Do we want to be chased?"

"Only if we get away."

That silenced the two of them.

Newt became bored and rested his head on Matt's lap as he sat on the bed.

"Jesse, come here and look at this. What about here?"

He pointed to an area labeled SHOP ROOM.

Jesse stood, disrupted Newt and examined the print. "What about it?"

"That's another access point. Look at the prints. There are two two-car garages on the far side of the school."

"Hmm ... that room is big enough to hold a car."

"Big enough to hold two cars at least."

"But look again …" Jesse pointed. "There's a problem with that idea."

"What?"

"We would need someone inside the school to open the garage door for us. That means we need to find another way for that person to get inside the school. Get it?"

"Yeah, I get it." Matt sighed. "Well, apart from the main entrances where would be a good place to get into the school?"

Jesse scanned the blueprints again. "When I lived there, I always came through this vent, you know, the one we hid in?"

Matt grinned. "How could I forget?"

He studied the blueprint and saw that the vent the two of them had crawled in came out in a long dark alleyway before extending into the parking lot and the surrounding woods.

Jesse began, "These vents turn into the classrooms. If someone knew where they were going, they could go straight to the shop room from that access point in the alley. We'd need to make sure that whoever goes will be able to get to the shop room as quick as possible and get the garage doors opened."

"Someone small could do it fast."

"Someone very small could do even faster," Jesse added.

"Someone like . . ?"

They looked at each other and nodded.

"She could make it work." Matt grinned. "She'd be perfect."

"I'll call her up," Jesse opened his notebook. "I've got her number here somewhere."

―――――

The next morning, Mary, Bruce, Matt and Jesse sat at the table and ate their breakfast in peace.

"You know," Mary began. "I was thinking … When's your birthday, Jesse?"

"Hmm? Oh, it passed about a month ago."

"It passed a month ago?" Mary exasperated. "And you never told us?"

"I'd never really celebrated it before. Never thought I needed to. I'm just a year older. Happy, happy, joy, joy …"

"Well … do you want to do something?"

Jesse stopped eating and looked up. "'Do something'?"

"Yeah, invite some friends over or something? Bruce and I could make some barbecue. Everyone could come over for a bit and hang out. It'd be fun. What do you say?"

He shrugged. "I've never had an actual party before. So it's really not that big of –".

"How about a week from today, after school?"

Jesse sighed, realizing that Mary wasn't going to back down. "Okay."

"What's today?" Mary asked herself. "Friday? Next Friday, it is then."

Matt and Jesse met up with the others at Zeke and Jake's shop. All eight of them, Matt, Jesse, Zeke, Jake, Mo, Andrew, Abby and the newcomer, Lily, sat facing one another in a circle.

Andrew spun his chair around and rested his arms on the back while Zeke had one leg draping over the other. Abby was sitting straight up her chair looking nervous while Mo resided in his wheelchair with his laptop ready. Matt and Jesse were sitting opposite each other, completing the circle.

"All right everyone," Matt began. "Before we spill the beans, I'd like everyone to know that you are all invited to come over to my house after school on Friday for Jesse's birthday. We're going to have some barbecue and it'll be fun. So see if you all can come. Consider it our last get-together as innocent civilians."

He took a breath. "All right, it's official. Jesse and I have spent hours on this and we've devised a way to break into the school and bypass the cameras and cops and stuff. To accomplish this, we're going to need Lily who has recently agreed to join us."

Lily smiled and gave a short wave to the group as all the eyes in the room turned in her direction.

Matt started again. "Mo and I will run through the logistics in a second but before we do, I have a few things to say. If we all do our part and do it right, the plan should work. I have no doubt about that.

"I think it's key to remember why were doing this. Fears has already flooded the science labs and, I think, we can agree that each of us hates the man in our own way. But I think we would all hate him more if he got away with thousands of dollars of the school money – our money. He's taking the money that goes to making our school great. Without it, we wouldn't have things like the sports and festivals and nice facilities. It's time to take action."

He paused and soaked in the moment.

"I'll be honest," he went on. "This will be dangerous. We are risking a lot. Plus, there is always the possibility that if something major goes wrong, we could get arrested or worse. If anyone thinks they don't want to be a part of this, now is the time to leave. No hard feelings."

Matt checked the circle. Abby was the only one who looked as if she was arguing with herself, but she didn't say a word. No one else moved.

"Okay, then." Matt shrugged. "Here's the basics."

He glanced around at each of them. "The news said that Angelina Williams will pay one hundred thousand dollars for Fears's conviction. Divide that by eight and that's how much each of us will receive. Then, you guys can do whatever you want with the money."

Zeke, Jake and Andrew had looks of anticipation on their faces while Abby and Lily seemed apprehensive.

"This is how it's going to go down," Matt said. "We're going to need two identical cars that are cheap and maneuverable …"

Matt and Zeke had parked on the outskirts of a deserted convenience store parking lot near the edge of town. There were at least four hundred square yards of parking lot, which was more than enough room for Zeke.

Zeke and Jake had found a decent looking 1980 Nissan 280ZX in their junkyard and with a bit of effort found another one just like it that was in need of repair in order to get it running. Jake stayed behind at the garage to do what he could with the cars while Zeke and Matt left for Zeke's training.

Two rows of traffic cones spread on the deserted parking lot, each row about twenty feet apart. Matt stood in between the two rows and began explaining the exercise to Zeke.

"Where I'm standing is the first garage to the shop room. As you know, the first garage is straight around the corner of the high school. Your objective is to drive the car down the side of the school and spin around the corner so you are able to pull right into the garage. Understand?"

Zeke nodded. "So you're wantin' me to make an E-Brake slide going at least forty right?"

"Just make sure you can do it."

"Heck, if I'd a known I was pullin' this kind of a stunt, I'd have brought a different car. Or at least have put different wheels on."

"The two cars have to look exactly alike," Matt said. "If you want to put different wheels on one of them then you've got to put the same wheels on the other one. Plus, you need to get used to this car's maneuverability."

"Yeah, I guess yer right."

The two of them got in the car and tightened their seatbelts.

"Oh, and by the way," Matt said, "don't hit any of the cones."

Zeke grinned as he started the car. "Right."

He revved the car and stomped on the gas sending the car lurching forward down the long line of cones. Matt was short of breath as the car picked up speed, but he knew Zeke was in control. That control was what gave him hope this plan would succeed.

Matt checked the speedometer. Zeke had taken the car to thirty-five miles an hour in just a couple of seconds. The orange cones flashed by the window and Matt's forehead began to sweat.

Everything's going to be fine, Matt thought as he was held to his seat. *Everything's going to be fine … Everything's going to be fine.*

At least he hoped he would be fine …

What if they weren't going to be all right? Matt thought quickly. What if they were at the school and Zeke couldn't pull it off? What would happen to them?

He pushed those thoughts to the back of his mind. He wouldn't allow himself to think about that.

Everything's going to be fine …

Nearing the end of the row, Zeke's palms tightened on the wheel.

"Ready?" he asked. Without waiting for an answer, he hollered, "Hang on!"

The tires screamed as Zeke jerked upward on the E-brake swinging the car around the end of the row.

Matt grabbed the door hold above his head as he felt the momentum of the car swing off balance almost pulling the right side of the car off the pavement.

As they slid, Zeke shifted and pulled right into the imaginary garage and brought the car to an abrupt stop.

Matt coughed as the smoke from the burned rubber cleared from the air. Releasing his white fingers from the door hold, his chest heaved.

"Wow," Zeke breathed. "That was great."

Matt smiled back. "Yeah, it was."

Opening his door, Matt stepped out only to notice that three of the cones were flattened and stuck under the car.

"Hey, uh … Zeke? You might want come take a look at this."

Zeke stepped out and walked around to see what was wrong.

"Hmm …" Zeke mused. "Guess we'll just have to do it again."

"Andrew, you're in charge of the train," Jesse began as the others bustled about the shop. "I've already drawn out a rough sketch of what it needs to look like. You and Abby will be able to work on it together at home."

"I dunno if that's such a good idea, Jesse," Andrew protested. "She's isn't too good at followin' orders."

"How about doing it for twelve thousand dollars?"

Andrew grinned. "I think she'd cooperate for twelve grand."

Andrew laughed and left reading Jesse's sketch. Abby walked up behind him and tapped on Jesse's shoulder.

Jesse turned. "Oh, hey there."

Abby was fiddling with her hands. "I bet you can tell I'm a little nervous."

Jesse tried to hide his smile and glanced at the floor. "That thought might have crossed my mind a couple of times. Why?"

"Well, I just think this is really dangerous."

"You're right. It is."

"Well, I'm just worried about –"

"Don't worry, Abby," Jesse interrupted. "You have the easiest job of the whole plan. You just flip a switch. That's all."

"That's all?"

"Yep. Over twelve grand for flipping one switch. I'd say that's a good deal."

She smiled. "I see your point. I'll do whatever I can."

Trust shone in her blue eyes as she smiled and she threw her blonde hair back over her shoulders. The sun caught the strands under its light.

"Thank you," Jesse said, trying to not stare. "Andrew needs your help. He's working on the train."

Abby headed off in Andrew's direction as Jesse watched her before turning back to his work.

Heading out, he found Jake who was working on the second Nissan making it look just like the first. Jake lay on his back underneath it.

"Hey, Jake," he called. "Do you need any –?"

"Jesse," Mo called from across the garage. "Come take a look at this."

Mo and Lily were working on his laptop in the far corner of the garage.

"I've managed to get a uniform for Andrew," Mo said as Jesse approached. "It looks just like the ones that real technicians wear. It's totally believable."

"Yeah, you should have seen it," Lily exclaimed beside him. "He's been hacking through all these security pages to get what we need. He really knows his stuff."

"Right now, I'm trying to order a U-Haul truck big enough for what we need," Mo continued. "After I get that, I'm going to see if I can get Andrew some credentials as a technician through the Internet. So that way, if Dr. Pierce doesn't believe that Andrew is who he says he is and checks his records, it's all there."

"That's a great idea, Mo. I hadn't thought of that."

Mo shrugged. "You got to look at every angle. And speaking of every angle …" He held up a small clip the size of Jesse's pinky finger.

"What's that?" Jesse asked.

"This is how I'm going to see what you guys are up to," he said. "It's a transmitter. I'll give it to Andrew and he'll clip it to the master recording wire when he leaves for the setup, which will transfer the footage on the cameras to my laptop."

Jesse raised his eyebrows and examined the small clip. "Are you serious? This is like real spy stuff. That's awesome, Mo. You're the man."

He turned to leave, but Mo stopped him. "Wait, Jesse. Look at this too."

Jesse watched as Mo opened a small wooden box. Inside the box were eight small earplugs and a control switch.

"What's this?"

"They're earpiece walkie-talkies," Mo replied. "I bought them off the net."

He picked one up and put it in his ear to demonstrate.

"You see, you put it in your ear and press it like this when you want to talk. There are eight different channels. I can talk to each person from here. Here, have one."

He handed Jesse one and flipped the switch.

"How far do they go?" Jesse stuck the piece in his ear.

"Twenty miles," Mo replied as he pushed on his earpiece. "Can you hear me?"

Jesse's jaw dropped when Mo's voice sounded in his ear. "How much was all this?"

Mo grinned. "You'd kill me if I told you. It's coming out of my part of the reward money when we catch Fears."

The red sun was setting.

Jesse and Jake were making progress with the car at the garage. Small dents and scratches on it disappeared and the car was beginning to look just like the one Zeke was using. It would take more time to complete, but Jake didn't seem to mind and Jesse seemed more than willing to help.

Andrew and Abby arrived from the hardware store with the train supplies as Matt and Zeke arrived with big smiles on their faces.

"We did it," Zeke declared.

Jesse looked up. "You pulled off the stunt?"

Zeke paused.

"Well, sort of."

"He did it once," Matt said.

"Well … keep practicing," Jesse said. "That's the only way you're going to get it."

Jake smirked as he signed from behind the car.

"Yes, I know how to drive, you idiot," Zeke exclaimed in response. "It's harder than it sounds. What have you done the past couple of hours, huh?"

Zeke went to the car arguing with his brother.

Jesse approached Matt. "Are you sure he'll be able to do it by Sunday?"

"Yeah, he'll get it. How are we doing here?"

Jesse turned back toward the garage.

"Great. Andrew and Abby just got back with supplies. Mo's got uniforms and a U-Haul scheduled to arrive and he's working to get Andrew's real credentials."

"Wow. You guys have been busy, huh?"

"Yeah, but I want to talk to you about the next phase, getting the keys and digital combinations."

"Yeah? What about it?"

"Jake's going to handle that right?"

Matt shook his head. "No, I don't think so. There's no way he could pickpocket those cards off Hank's belt, especially with that ring of keys attached to it. I've got a better idea. Where's Abby?"

The next day, after school Abby changed in the locker room and went to the school's weight room to work out. There she found Hank sweeping the floor.

Abby wore a tight pink shirt with white gym shorts that fitted tightly onto her thin legs. Hank's eyes widened. Averting his eyes, he looked down at the floor.

A key ring with multicolored keys sat on the table in the corner of the room. The keycards were attached to another ring, which sat next to the first.

Abby pretended to ignore it.

She turned her back, bent over, touched the floor and stretched her legs. Hank stole a glance in her general direction. His breath seemed to get shorter as he drew out his handkerchief and wiped his brow. Abby turned to face him giving him a little smile as she pulled her blonde hair back into a ponytail.

"Hi," she said with a sweet smile. "Sorry if I'm disturbing you, but I'm trying out for cheerleading next season and I've heard this is the best way to prepare. I'm not interrupting you, am I?"

Hank flashed a smile but didn't respond. His eyes watched Abby as she shrugged and inched her way to the floor laying her stomach down on it. Then with slow, graceful movements, she began her push-ups.

Hank turned away and stared at the broom while vigorously sweeping the floor. When he looked up, there she was again in the mirror along the back wall. She sat on her rear with her legs in a butterfly fashion, leaned over and, with an effortless movement, touched her head to the floor. Air seemed to catch in Hank's throat. He coughed as if clearing his throat.

Abby glanced up and smiled.

She rose and bounced to the table where the keys lay.

"Are these yours?" she asked innocently.

Hank turned and forced himself to speak. "Uh … I'm sorry. Did you say something?"

"I don't think I've ever seen so many keys. How can you possibly know where all of them go?"

"Uh – well, I, um … it's my job to know, uh, that stuff."

"Oh, really?"

She picked up the ring of keys and let them dangle from her fingers. Hank watched as she looked through them. She looked at the keycards on the ring and counted six of them.

"What are these?" she asked as she moved next to him.

Hank squared his shoulders. "Those cards are the keys to the office. With the new … um, security system you need a digital combination in order to get in. I just swipe this card and walk on in. But I shouldn't really be saying anything about –"

"I know you shouldn't tell me …" She winked. "But how else will I know how smart you really are?"

"Well, it is a big job keeping it all straight," Hank admitted, blushing slightly.

"Oh, I bet." She looked over the keycards and noticed small numbers imprinted on the back.

"What do these numbers mean?"

Hank hesitated.

"Oh, come on. Who am I going to tell?" Abby asked kindly. She winked at him again with a cute smile.

Hank chuckled. "Well, you see, there's, uh, a row of twelve numbers on each, um, card. This – I mean, the last six digits of the card is the, um … the, uh … the combination."

Abby's face flushed as she continued to act.

"Wow, that's amazing. So you can go anywhere in this school with these keys?"

"Well, sure I can."

"Oh, my. You must be the most important man in this school. I thought Dr. Pierce was the only one who could do that."

"Well, he is. I mean except for me. I'm the only other one who has total access."

Abby continued to toy with the keys. "Look at all of these colors. There's red keys, blue keys and even some green keys. My goodness, what are they all for?"

"Well, the colors are for the floors. The blue ones are for the first floor. The reds are for the second and the greens are for the third. Then, each colored key has the last two digits of the room number on it. So that way, I'm not really memorizing keys but room numbers."

"Man, you really seem to know your stuff." She handed him back the keys.

He chuckled again.

"I'm going to quiz you," Abby teased.

He laughed. "You're going to prove that I know which key is which?"

"Yep. So tell me, where's the key to Ms. Ellis's English classroom?"

He searched and showed it to her.

"What about Mrs. Raidner's Science Lab?"

Again, he found it.

"Hmm … what about Mr. Burns's Shop Class?"

Hank smiled as he showed it to her. The key was blue. Abby read the number on it – sixty-six.

"Okay. Here's a tough one. What about the building outside the school with the circuit breaker and stuff?"

He held up the only brass key in the bunch.

"You really do know what you're talking about, don't you?"

Hank blushed and clipped the keys to his belt.

"Oh, my gosh," Abby gaped as she glanced at the nearby clock. "I'm almost late for early morning tutoring. I enjoyed talking to you, though. Sorry, I have to go."

Abby waved on her way out of the weight room.

In the crowded hall the next day, Abby collided into Zeke.

"Excuse me, sorry," Abby said as she slipped a small piece of paper into his hand.

"Sorry," Zeke replied as he subtly put it in his pocket and walked on as if nothing had happened. In his next class before the other students had arrived, Zeke pulled the note out of his pocket.

1) A Blue one, #66
2) The only brass one.
3) And the last five digits from the back of every keycard.

Later that afternoon, Abby found Hank sweeping the hallway. She strolled by and then, pretending she'd just found him, she slipped back into her role of the curious, beautiful girl.

"We just keep bumping into each other, don't we, Mr. Janitor?"

"You can call me Hank."

"Okay, Hank." She quickly thought of a question to ask in order to keep the conversation going. "So when do you work?"

"Well, I work the night shift most of the time. But occasionally, I'll work during the day."

"The night shift?"

"Yeah, I clean through the night with two other janitors. We each take a floor."

"It's not just any man who can work through the day and on through the night. You must have a lot of endurance."

"Well, sometimes it gets –"

Just then, Zeke came running down the hall.

"Excuse me, but Dr. Pierce needs yer keys. He must've forgotten his or something. He told me to come get ya'. He says it's an emergency. Quick!"

Hank quickly grabbed his keys off his belt and tossed them to Zeke.

"I'll be right back." Zeke turned and was gone.

Zeke quickly walked down the hall and grinned as he opened the door to the bathroom. Finding the right stall, he went in and bolted the door shut. There he found the two keys Abby had specified in her note.

"There you are."

He grinned as he took a small, aluminum box out of his pocket. Inside was a flat piece of clay he'd taken from the Art Department. He imprinted two keys into the clay and shut the box.

As he put the box in his pocket, he pulled a small piece of paper out of his other pocket and copied the last six digits from each card. He left the bathroom and calmly walked back the hall where Abby was keeping the janitor occupied.

Zeke tossed the keys back to Hank. "Dr. Pierce says, 'Thanks'."

21

It was Friday morning, two days before the heist as well as the day of Jesse's party. Matt sat in Ms. Ellis's English class pretending to be working on his assignment. He glanced up at Rose who was working. He'd been spending so much time with Jesse organizing and strategizing that he hadn't been spending much time with Rose. He knew it was unfair to her but he thought it was necessary.

Suddenly, a surprising thought came to mind. I can't believe I haven't invited Rose to the party yet.

Pulling out a piece of paper, he scribbled:

> Rose,
> Jesse is having a birthday party tonight at my house. Zeke, Jake, Lily and others are coming. Jesse invited you too. Heck, your dad can come too if you want. We're having barbecued hamburgers. I'd like you to come. You can ride with me to my house if you like.
> Love,
> Matt

Matt broke the lead on his pencil, stood up and walked over to the pencil sharpener. On his way back, he casually tossed the note in Rose's direction.

She snatched it off her desk, read it and nodded when Matt glanced at her from his desk.

A few minutes later, just as everyone began to finish the assignment, the intercom on the ceiling clicked to life.

"Ms. Ellis?"

"Yes?"

"Would you please send Miss Rose Hudson to the office?"

"She's on her way."

"Thank you."

Rose frowned as she put her things away. Matt wondered why she had been called to the office. Matt cocked his head at her and she shrugged.

When she arrived in the office, the secretary pointed her in the direction of Mr. Fears' office. She stepped inside to see her father and Fears talking.

"Ah, there you are, sweetie." Mr. Hudson said.

"What's going on?" Rose asked.

"Well, I was here working when I got a call from Hills East. They're having major problems with their grids. I talked to them for a while and from what I can gather, I won't be able to make it home for dinner tonight. I came to tell Mr. Fears that I won't be available."

"Okay," Rose replied.

"Actually, Miss Hudson," Fears said. "It's a little more complicated than that. From what your father tells me, Hills East is having quite a few problems with their computers. In order for your father to fix them, he will be gone for a couple days."

"What?" Rose asked. "Dad, Jesse's birthday party is tonight at Matt's house. He invited us."

"I'm sorry, honey, I'm going to have to miss it."

"Why?" she asked. "Can't someone else fix the computers for once? Tell them you're busy."

"I'm really sorry, babe. I should be home Sunday night."

Rose ran to her father and hugged him. "Don't go, Dad. You don't have to go. You can come with me to Matt's house instead. It'll be fun. You know it will."

"Just have Matt's mother give you a ride home, okay? You'll be fine. I'll call you tonight and check on you."

Mr. Hudson pried her arms off his shoulders and went to the door, looking back at his daughter. "I am sorry, sweetheart. I love you."

Rose remained silent.

Mr. Hudson sighed and left.

Plopping down on one of the chairs in Fears's office, Rose wiped tears from her eyes. She should be used to this by now, but she didn't think she ever would. Out of the multiple times her father had to leave, he'd never been gone for so long.

"I understand how upset you must be," Fears said.

Rose looked up startled. She'd almost forgotten that Fears was in the room.

Going to the door, Fears locked it and pulled the blinds down over the windows. Turning back to Rose, he said, "I know what it's like to be without a father."

He stepped behind her chair, placed his hands on her shoulders and began to massage them.

Rose didn't mind. She sighed as Fears's hands continued to rub her neck and shoulders. She hadn't realized how tight the muscles in her shoulders were. She allowed his strong hands to squeeze and press.

"You know," Fears remarked, "since you came to my house the other night, I can't stop thinking about what you said."

Rose's eyes shot open. It dawned on her then who was rubbing her shoulders. Her heart began to pound harder and harder with each beat.

What was he doing?

Rose needed to get out of the office and as far away from Fears as possible but her body remained still as if she would never move again.

"Do you know how beautiful you are?" he asked gently running his fingers through her auburn hair before resting them on her shoulders again.

"You can trust me," he said in her ear.

His hands began to move slowly down her body. Rose's mind shook with fear. For the first time in her life, she was truly petrified.

After school, Jesse sat at a picnic table outside Matt's house and listened as his guests sang "Happy Birthday". Sitting before him on the table was a hamburger with fifteen lit candles. He closed his eyes and blew them out.

Mary had made barbecued hamburgers, baked beans and garlic bread for all the guests. Corn on the cob and potato salad made their way around the table as well.

Newt's front paws up were propped on Matt's thigh as he eyed the burgers. When Matt shooed him away, Newt moved over to Jesse and did the same thing. He continued to beg until everyone's plates were clean.

Zeke leaned back in his lawn chair and rubbed his belly. "Thank ya' for dinner, Mrs. Cross. I loved it."

"Mmm … yeth. Me thoo," Andrew agreed through a mouthful of burger.

"Hey, Zeke," Jesse called. "Catch!"

A Frisbee thumped Zeke's chest. "Hey!"

Zeke stood up and threw the Frisbee back to Jesse. Before long, Newt was barking and jumping as he joined in their game.

Matt downed his root beer and glanced up at the house seeing Rose slouch inside. He watched for another few moments waiting for her to come back outside, but she never did.

He frowned. She hadn't said much today, perhaps she wasn't feeling well. Matt moved from the table and went inside to find her.

"Rose?"

No answer.

He walked into the living room but there was no sign of her there either. He heard sniffling coming from upstairs.

"Rose? Are you up there?"

Jumping up the stairs, Matt pushed the door to his room open to find Rose sobbing on his bed.

"Rose? Are you all right?"

Rose rolled away from Matt and faced the opposite wall. Gulping large breaths of air, she seemed to try and compose herself.

Quickly wiping her tears away, she sniffed. "Y – yes, I … I'm fine. I'm just not … I – I'm not feeling well. That's all."

"Are you sure?" Matt stepped closer. "Maybe I can help. You could lie here for a while if you like."

He touched her shoulder. She jumped away and shrieked, "Don't touch me! Don't even think about touching me!"

"Hey ... okay." Matt lifted his hands in the air and took a step back. "Would you like to maybe –?"

"Just go away! Leave me alone." She turned away from Matt, dropped off the bed and sat on the floor.

"Rose," Matt argued. "You're the one who always wants to talk. You always said that we could talk about anything."

He sat down on the bed and looked at Rose on the floor.

"Now, please, tell me what's wrong."

She sat up and leaned against the wall. Tears streamed down her face causing her makeup to smear. Her hair was tangled and stuck out at all ends. Matt had never seen her in such bad shape before.

Rose shook her head and sniffed again with her eyes focused on the floor.

"I ... I can't."

"Rose, look at me," Matt said.

She covered her face and peeked up at him through her fingers.

"You know me," he said. "You know you can trust me."

Rose burst into uncontrollable sobs hiding her face in her arms.

"What is it, Rose? What happened?"

"I – I don't ... don't think I c – can tell you," she managed to say through her cries of sadness. "Mr. Fears made me p – promise."

"Fears? Promise what?"

"He said that if I ever told anyone ... he'd fire my dad."

"Tell anyone what?"

Rose shook her head and looked away. Matt sat on the floor beside her and looked directly into her puffy eyes as if searching the window to her soul.

"It's okay, Rose. Please, tell me what happened."

Rose sat up and wiped her nose again.

"He ..."

She stopped.

"Go on," he urged.

"He t – touched me."

"He what?"

"He touched me, okay!" she screamed in his face. "When I went to his office today, he was ... he was kissing me and feeling me all over."

She began to wail again and pulled her knees to her chest.

Matt was motionless.

Fears touched Rose? How could he – he couldn't.

"You're serious?"

"Do I look like I'm kidding?" she sobbed.

"I ... You –?"

He couldn't continue.

He felt sick.

He wanted to gag.

He tried to stand but his legs no longer functioned and he collapsed back onto his bed. His stomach twisted and turned inside him.

His head swam with one sentence that echoed inside his head. Fears touched Rose ... Fears touched Rose.

"I can't ... I don't ..."

This couldn't be happening. Rose was too good of a person.

He'd heard of this type of thing happening but he'd never thought he'd actually be involved with it. It became difficult to breathe so he spread his arms out on the bed to take bigger breaths.

His eyes filled with tears. This just couldn't be happening, not to Rose ... not to them.

He rolled over to face her. "He didn't ... you know?"

He glanced in between her legs.

She shivered but shook her head.

"What ... what did he, uh, do?"

"He was r – rubbing my shoulders and telling me how p – pretty I was. Then his hands moved down to my chest and –"

"Matt," Mary called from the foot of the stairs. "What are you doing up there?"

Matt sighed. This was not the best time for his mother to cut in.

"Nothing, Mom."

"Well, quit doing that and get down here! Do you have any idea how rude it is to leave your guests? You're not being a very good host, you know."

"They're not my guests. They're Jesse's!"

"Same difference. Just get back down here. Do you want to be grounded?"

At that point, he didn't care if his mother grounded him for eternity. He just wanted to sit here with Rose.

He looked at her, feeling torn.

"Just ... go," she said.

"But Rose, I –"

"Just go."

Matt sighed again and looked back to the door. "All right, fine, Mom. I'm coming."

He looked to Rose. "I'm really sorry, babe. I –"

"Go ..."

"What do you want me to do? I want to help."

"You can h – help by leaving," she said. "I want to be ... I want to be alone r – right now."

Matt managed to stand and make his way out the door and down the hall. From the foot of the stairs, the sounds of Rose's sobs upstairs pierced his heart.

The sky had turned dark.

Thick clouds began to roll in and lightning lit the distant sky. The winds had picked up making it difficult to continue their game of Frisbee but everyone continued playing, telling themselves the storm was far away.

"Guys, we really should get inside," Mary cautioned as she cleared off the picnic table. "It's going to storm. Come on in. There's ice cream waiting for you."

They agreed and all ran inside the house. Everyone had ice cream and most of them had seconds. Before long, Jesse and Andrew were smearing ice cream on Abby's face while Zeke, Jake and Lily were throwing chocolate chips at each other.

Everyone's face was full of laughter and fun ... That is, everyone except Matt.

He hadn't said a word since he'd come back downstairs. He couldn't believe what Rose had told him. He'd never thought Fears would ever do anything like that, but then again, Fears was willing to flood the school. He blamed himself for underestimating how terrible this man was.

As the thoughts began to sink in, Matt realized he wasn't sick because of what Rose told him. He was sick with hatred.

This nasty new fire burned inside him, flamed in the middle of his heart. The next time he looked at Fears, he would do something to him. Catch him, string him up, beat him, torture him, Fears deserved it all. He would punch him, strangle him, kick him … Nothing less than pain would suffice.

Fears should feel pain. He deserved to live in shame for the rest of his life and Matt could do it to him.

Oh, what a joy it would be for him to be the one who put Fears behind bars.

Right now, Rose was upstairs sobbing because of the pain Fears had afflicted on her. Matt knew his pain was nowhere near the pain she was feeling. He couldn't even imagine what it was like for her.

The wind picked up outside and knocked the trashcans over sending trash everywhere. The large barn doors swung open slamming against the barn.

"Oh, Matt," Mary called. "You'd better go out there and get that trash. It'll be all over the yard in a minute. And close that barn door too, please. Have someone go with you."

Matt glared at his mother from under his brow. He didn't feel like taking orders from anyone right now, especially not his mother. Jake stood and motioned that he would help.

Matt gripped the edge of the table as he stood and followed.

Jake and Matt ran about the yard picking up the stray trash. Jake went to close the barn door as Matt managed to put the lids back on the trashcans.

Suddenly, Jake was at Matt's shoulder, signing with wild gestures and frantic eyes.

"What, Jake?"

Jake's hands continued to move around his body.

"I don't understand, Jake. Come on. Have Zeke translate. Let's go."

Matt began to walk up to the house. Jake took off running, so Matt picked up speed fighting the harsh wind.

Throwing open the door, Jake flew in, found Zeke and continued to sign.

"Zeke," Matt gasped as he ran through the door. "What's Jake sayin'?"

"Wh – what?" Zeke dropped his spoon with a clatter. "Oh, no …" and bolted out the door.

"What?" Matt cried. "What is it?"

Matt and the others chased behind Zeke with Mary and Bruce following as well. Arriving at the barn, Zeke threw open the door.

Matt raced in to have his heart torn apart.

Inside, lying on a pile of hay was Newt, motionless, blood pouring from his head. Matt stumbled over a shovel and fell to his knees when he saw him.

He was dead.

"Oh, no …" Matt cried. "Newt …"

Abby gave a short scream and covered her mouth when she saw Newt's lifeless body. Lily jumped back and Mary ran up beside Matt, dropped to her knees and held him as she stifled her own tears.

"Newt!" Matt screamed as if hoping Newt would stir. Tears rolled down his cheeks and fell onto Newt's still body. He turned and sobbed in his mother's arms.

Jesse fell to his knees, his hand on the shovel. It was covered in blood.

"Oh, no …" Bruce sighed as he arrived. He too knelt near the shovel.

"A shovel." Jesse held the shovel up as his eyes began to well with tears. "Someone killed him with a shovel."

The twins took their hats off and lowered their eyes. Andrew did the same.

Matt stared at Newt as tears streamed down his face. Just a short while ago, Newt had been enjoying a game of Frisbee. Sobs shook his body again as Matt knew that was the last game Newt would ever play.

"Why?" Matt wailed uncontrollably. "Why, why, why, why?"

Mary looked up at Jesse's guests with pleading eyes. "Maybe you all should go home."

The group turned, walked back to the house and quietly called their parents.

Mary, Matt, Bruce and Jesse stayed behind. Mary tried to convince Matt to go back to the house with the rest.

"I can't go," he hollered at them. "Newt's dead. He was my dog. My dog! Now, he's gone."

Mary and Bruce held him as he sobbed. A few minutes later, Jesse could take no more. He made his way back to the house wiping away his tears.

It was some time later when Mary and Bruce managed to persuade Matt to go back to the house with them. Matt sat in the living room and grieved, holding his face in hands.

The phone's shrill ring echoed throughout the house. Mary quickly answered it.

"No, he can't … No, he's busy at the moment … Why? … He's just – … Well, be quick about it."

She went to Matt and gave him the phone. "He insisted to talk to you. It must be important. I'm sorry."

"Who is it?" he asked.

She shrugged. "Caller ID was blocked."

"Hello?" Matt muttered into the phone.

"Did you find my little gift for you in the barn, Mr. Cross?"

Matt sat up, adrenaline shooting in all directions through his body.

"Who is this?"

"Don't be stupid, Mr. Cross."

Matt's eyes went wide. "Fears?"

There was a pause. Hatred filled his heart and Matt's eyes opened with new fire for revenge. He went to the window and peered between two blinds searching the yard as though Fears could see him.

"Fears?" he said again.

No answer.

"Talk to me, you son of a –!"

"Now there's no need for that kind of talk, Mr. Cross. That will land you another detention. You've already had plenty. Don't try setting any records before school's out."

"Why … You – how could you –?"

"I did it because I don't believe you realize what I'm capable of, Mr. Cross. I know you're after me. You want to try and catch me do you? Well, you can't. I'm smarter than you are and I always will be."

"How would you …" Matt didn't know how Fears knew he was after him. But it didn't matter. "I'll … I'll call the cops," he stammered.

"Calling them will result with you looking worse than your friend. You would be wise to stop trying."

The phone went dead.

Matt looked at Jesse's face, blotchy and stained with tears. Jesse shook his head and dashed up the stairs.

The wind threw leaves and sticks against the windows. Lightning flashed outside and thunder shook the house.

A storm was brewing.

Within twenty minutes, everyone had gone. Bruce offered to take Rose home but she refused to go with him so Mary ended up driving her.

Matt was sitting on the couch in the living room again, hatred continuing to build inside him as he focused on one thought – getting revenge. All he cared about was getting back at Fears. His only wish was to extinguish this one person from his life.

Nothing else mattered.

Grabbing a pillow lying nearby, Matt pulled at it and yanked at it. He heard the threads begin to tear. He continued pulling until the fabric ripped.

He stopped himself. No, he thought. He'd not deal with his anger this way. Ripping the pillow to shreds would not satisfy his anger.

Jumping up from the couch, he stormed upstairs to Jesse's room. Throwing open the door, he saw Jesse lying on his bed with his hands behind his head, expressionless.

"Are you just going to lie there?" Matt yelled.

Jesse sat up. "What would you like me to do?"

"Now is the time for revenge. We've got Fears for three things now. Breaking into the school, killing Newt, and …"

Matt stopped as his thoughts turned to Rose.

"What? What's the third?" Jesse questioned.

"Never mind."

"No, really. What's the third?" Jesse stood up. "Tell me."

Matt sighed. "It's ... Rose."

"He –?" Jesse stopped himself. "He didn't ... do anything to her. Did he?"

Matt lowered his eyes and turned away.

"Oh, I don't believe this!"

Jesse grabbed a pillow and slammed it back down on his bed in frustration.

"That's it," he exclaimed. "We're done. No more plans. Don't you realize what we're doing? If we go through with this, someone else will get hurt. We've already caused enough trouble by putting our noses where they don't belong. Rose and Newt didn't have to get hurt but they did. And it's our fault. More people will get hurt if we go on."

Matt spun to face Jesse with a look of hatred on his face. His eyes tore Jesse apart.

"Oh, so we're back to that are we? I thought we'd decided that catching Fears was worth the risk. What about the money? The house?"

"Forget the money. Is it worth our lives?"

"You don't get it do you? You just don't understand!" Matt cried. "You haven't grown up watching the only father you ever knew spend every extra moment of his day building his dream house. I need that money or I'll never be able to set foot in this house again."

"Is it worth the risk?" Jesse shot back.

"It's worth my life!" Matt cried. "His memory is my life! He's all I have left!"

"Listen to yourself," Jesse retorted. "You've become so involved with the plan and the money that you can't see reality. Newt is dead out in that barn right now. Rose may never be the same. All of this is our fault. Fears might not have hurt Rose if we hadn't taken her to Fears's house. If we had minded our own business, Newt would still be alive and Rose would be fine."

"No ..." Matt shook his head. "No ... I – I don't believe that."

"Fears murdered Newt. He killed him in cold blood, Matt. He took advantage of Rose knowing full well what he was doing. That was his decision. We didn't do anything. You are the one who doesn't understand. We can't do it, Matt. The heist is off."

"You … you … coward!" Matt hollered each word burning with hatred. "This gives us even more reason why we have to do it."

"All you care about is the money. You couldn't care less about Rose or your dog out there."

With that comment, Matt's rage fixated on Jesse. He stepped into his face, shoving his chest against Jesse's chest.

"It's not about the freaking money right now! I want to see that man behind bars for everything he's done to us."

"And then what? What will happen if we succeed, huh?" Jesse spat back in Matt's face. "Do you think it will bring Newt back? Will it make Rose forget? Catching Fears won't fix a thing."

"He has to be stopped!"

Jesse stepped back and pointed his finger at his own chest.

"Well, I'm not helping you. I'm through. One dog's death and another girl's heart are more than enough reasons for me to back off."

"Fine, then leave!" Matt shoved Jesse out the door knocking him to the floor. "Get outta here! I can't believe I ever thought of you as a friend. Go on, get outta here, you coward!"

"Fine. I'm gone," Jesse cried. "I'm never coming back here again!"

He turned and stomped down the stairs.

Mary was doing the dishes from the party when she saw Jesse storming for the door. "No, wait. Jesse. Where are you –?"

The door slammed shut.

Mary ran to the door and opened it only to have the wind nearly blow it off its hinges. She leaned out and called for Jesse but he was already gone. She saw him running in the direction of the woods. Mary called him again. Lightning flashed above her and the earth shook as thunder exploded in the sky like fireworks.

The storm raged.

Matt slammed the door to his room and leaned against it. How did things get this way? He hadn't meant for any of this to happen. It all had to be a terrible dream. He wanted to scream in frustration, lash out in anger and weep for Newt and Rose but all he could do was slide down the door, curl into a ball and cry.

Darkness had overtaken the area.

Thick trees rushed past Jesse as he flew down the trail. His only light source was the frequent lightning that illuminated the sky.

Another roll of thunder caused Jesse to cringe and he tripped over a branch. Bracing himself with his hands, he fell on a pile of sharp rocks. His hands dug into the jagged edges, causing him to cry out in pain.

He held his hands in front of his face and could see the blood run down past his wrists. Cradling his hands in the lower half of his shirt, he stood and continued to run.

He could never go back. He would never go back. Matt's mind was too deluded to see the truth. All he cared about was revenge. He didn't care about the innocent people that might get hurt.

As Jesse looked for a way through, he saw only the spiny fingers of trees warning him not to go any farther. The lightning flashed and the hairs on the back of Jesse's neck bristled.

He tried to think of a place to go and remembered the waterfall where he'd seen Matt and Rose swim. He could go there and hide under a rock or something. He would be safe there.

The lightning seemed to multiply as streaks of electricity cracked and whipped over the treetops.

Matt had it all wrong, Jesse thought as he ran. He doesn't know what to do anymore.

Jesse snarled as he jumped over an oversized rock. A branch flew through the air whipping Jesse in the back, the thorns digging into his flesh like sharpened knives.

He fell to the ground and felt his shirt soak with blood from the multiple gashes on his back. When he hit the ground, his head thudded against a large rock. As he rolled, the rock slashed across his forehead creating a long, thick gash.

The burning pain sensations grew to be almost unbearable. With every heartbeat another sharp stinging pain shot through his head. His bleeding hands clutched it and he wailed.

But it was no use. No one could hear him over the storm.

Jesse needed help. He knew that. But he would not allow himself to go back. He fought dizziness and willed himself to stand and, in doing so, he felt his shirt tear at the gashes the thorns had made on his back.

His agony intensified as he tried to take a step. He gritted his teeth and forced himself to walk, which was growing increasingly difficult as wind and darkness overwhelmed him.

Jesse fought harder than he ever had. He was a survivor, always had been. He'd lived on the streets before, he knew what it was like. He was used to difficult situations but nothing had prepared him for the mess he was in this time.

"Why, God?" Jesse screamed above the storm. "What do you want from me?"

This was all Matt's fault. Matt couldn't see the truth so why was he safe and sound? He was probably in his room working on the next part of the heist.

Salty tears stung his cuts and flowed down his face as he ran. His hands stung with pains he had never felt before. His knees were bruised and swollen from the falls he'd taken. His back bled through his shirt.

He blinked away thick beads of blood as they dripped down into his eyes from the gushing crown on his forehead.

The thunder and lightning danced in the sky as if showing off how loud and bright they could make the world. It crackled and flashed above Jesse. The earth shook like an earthquake.

The silhouette of trees jumped and flashed as streaks of light reigned in the sky. Now, directly above Jesse the sky dropped lower to the ground as if to tease him. His long hair blew in his face. Brushing it away, he looked up to see a thick branch fly through the air like an arrow straight for him. It slammed into his head throwing him to the ground, dazing him.

The sharp rain turned to hail, starting in small pieces then grew and grew until it pounded Jesse's body like pieces of broken glass. Jesse cried out as the hail repeatedly struck his head and back.

He needed to find shelter – fast. But he was too far from anywhere. The house and waterfall were both too far.

He rolled over and heaved upward with a determined wail. Fighting the incredible wind, Jesse tried to regain his balance.

Finding his footing, he centered his weight on a pile of rocks. Suddenly, the rocks slipped out from under him like marbles and he fell to his knees. Bolts of lightning flashed at the tips of the trees and thunder boomed as if Jesse lay next to a cannon.

God had always been there for him. Anytime Jesse had called on Jesus, He had helped. Where was He? Why wasn't He doing anything to help? Jesse had never felt so fearful and disconnected from God in his life.

Why had God left him?

From his knees, Jesse spread his arms and faced the flashing heavens. "God! What do you want from me?"

A lighting bolt as sharp as nails exploded from the clouds and struck a tree just over Jesse's head. The middle portion of the tree exploded into a thousand splinters.

Jesse fell back, shielding his face and a sharp rock pierced his side as he hit the ground.

He rolled over and opened his eyes. In the sudden flash of lightning Jesse saw the severed top half of the tree as it dropped toward earth directly for him.

―――――――

Matt stared out his window at the storm. His thoughts raced from one subject to the next. Fears hurt Rose. What should he do? Should he call her? Help her? If he told the authorities, Fears would fire Mr. Hudson.

Matt yanked on his hair in his frustration. His eyes ached from crying so much.

Newt was dead. Fears must have killed him while Matt was with Rose or maybe when everyone was inside. Why hadn't he noticed that he was missing?

Thoughts raced inside his mind as if his brain was too small to make sense of them all.

He couldn't believe Jesse left the way he did. Matt would have to find a replacement for him. That coward didn't want to be part of the plan anyway. He'd gone off and ran away. He wasn't –

A thunderous boom outside Matt's window shook the house and his thoughts stopped dead. The lights went out and everything turned to black.

Matt jumped up and looked out the window to see sparks and splinters exploding above the treetops.

"Oh, no …"

Jesse's out there. He really didn't like Jesse right now but he didn't want him in danger either. Putting all other thoughts aside, Matt threw on his coat and grabbed a flashlight as he ran downstairs.

"Matt. Stop," Mary called as she lit a candle. "Where did Jesse go? Where are you going?"

"I'm going to get him. Jesse's going to get hurt out there."

"You can't go out there. Don't you know what would happen if –?"

Matt was already out the door.

Dashing through the field, Matt entered the woods. Even with the flashlight, he couldn't see much. He could just make out the trail.

He grabbed tree trunk after tree trunk as he fought the harsh wind shielding his face as leaves threatened to strip the flesh from his bones.

"Jesse," he cried. "Where are you?"

Thunder boomed above him.

Moving from one tree to the next, Matt clutched them as if they were his only means of protection.

"Jesse," he called again. "Where are you?"

A silhouette of the splintered tree appeared in the scattered lightning. Smoking burn marks across the top of the trunk showed where it had split. Matt approached and could see that the severed half of the tree had fallen through the middle of another Y-shaped tree holding it about half a foot off the ground.

Matt stepped forward and tripped. Glancing down at the object, he saw a human hand. Jumping back, he gave a short cry and realized that Jesse was pinned to the ground by the tree. The Y-shaped tree had saved his life.

"Jesse," Matt yelled over the thunder. "Jesse, can you hear me?"

Jesse's unconscious body was covered in blood. Matt felt his bloody neck for a pulse. Finding one, he jumped up and sprinted toward his house.

The storm was beginning to calm when Matt arrived home. He threw open the door just as the lights kicked back to life.

"Bruce," he called. "Bruce. Come quick!"

Bruce burst into the kitchen with a flashlight in hand. "Jeez, Matt. Thank God you're not hurt. Where's Jesse?"

"Come on. He's hurt. Bad."

Within minutes, Mary had called Nine-One-One and Bruce was tying his boots.

Mary hung up. "They're sending a helicopter."

"In a storm?" Bruce asked.

"The operator said the storm barely hit the hospital. It came over the woods and then lost most of its steam so they are on their way."

Matt raced back to the woods while Bruce waited for the helicopter.

Kneeling beside Jesse, Matt realized how stupid he had been to kick Jesse out into a storm. No, he couldn't blame himself. This was Fears's fault. None of this would have happened if Fears hadn't done what he did.

An eternity later, the helicopter sounded in the distance. Matt ran to the edge of the woods and watched as the pilot landed in the open field.

Grabbing a stretcher, the medics followed Matt into the woods. With flashlights and with the storm gone, there was little trouble locating Jesse's still pinned to the ground. Matt and Bruce helped the medics dig the dirt out from underneath Jesse's bloody body so they could slide him out and onto the body board.

Jesse didn't look good. He was fortunate to be alive at all.

Within fifteen minutes, Jesse was loaded in the helicopter. Matt asked the medics which hospital they were taking him. Their answer made him jump.

Jesse would be in the same hospital in which his father had died.

22

During the early hours of Saturday, Matt, Mary and Bruce dashed through the automatic doors to the hospital. Mary knew the way. She had never forgotten.

They arrived at the front desk and asked for Jesse's whereabouts.

"He's in the ICU," the receptionist said. "Room thirty-three."

Reaching the ICU desk, a tall, middle-aged doctor spoke to the three.

"Excuse me," he said. "Who are you?"

"We're with Jesse," Mary said. "We're his family."

The doctor's face lightened. "I'm Dr. White, Jesse's doctor. I, uh – I think you'd better sit down."

Matt's eyes filled with tears as he took a seat next to his mother and Bruce. The terror of knowing whether Jesse would live or die was almost too great to handle.

What if he died? No, he wasn't going to die. He couldn't die.

"How is he?" Matt needed to know.

"Jesse is, um – a very special case," Dr. White began as he sat. "There is good news and bad news."

"Bad news first," Mary's words rushed out of her mouth.

"Okay," Dr. White began, "um – unfortunately, Jesse has fallen into a coma."

At least he's still alive, Matt thought. There's a chance he'll make it.

"Jesse's in his room right now," the doctor continued. "My staff is with him now and we are running numerous tests."

"Why?" Bruce asked. "What's wrong with him?"

"Nothing. That's the thing. Jesse's body is healing at an unbelievable rapid rate. In just a half hour, his body had stopped bleeding and he'd already begun repairing tissue. It is expected that, at this rate, he'll recover fully within a couple of days."

"What was wrong with him when he showed up?" Matt asked.

"Well ..." Dr. White lifted a few sheets on his clipboard and examined the report. "Jesse arrived unconscious with a severe concussion, multiple gashes on his forehead and face, severely bruised ribs, a sprained wrist and multiple gashes in his side. His back had numerous cuts and his knees appeared to be dislocated.

"Within an hour of our examination, his wrists had healed and his knees were fine. The gashes on his head seemed to pull together before we had time to stitch them. Compared to the sever concussion when he'd first arrived, he's now showing signs of a mild concussion. His back is healing and he's breathing fine. My staff and I have been amazed at his progress."

"Will he be all right?" Mary asked.

Dr. White took a long breath.

"If you want my take on the situation, I think Jesse is in a coma because his body is doing everything it can to heal itself. At this rate, I think he'll back to normal in a week or so. This is why we're running tests on him. We're trying to record his healing rate. Jesse could make medical case books."

"What should we do?" Bruce asked.

"At this point, my staff would rather not be disturbed during their tests. You can stay here awhile if you like. Jesse should be finished soon and you should be able to see him then."

An hour or so later, Matt was asleep, spread out on the couch in the waiting room. So much had happened in the last twenty-four hours, his mind needed to rest.

The same person that had murdered Newt had abused Matt's first girlfriend. Matt had gone from hating Jesse to running into the woods trying to save him. Jesse was nearly killed out in the storm. But apparently, he's a miracle.

None of this seemed real.

Bruce watched Mary walk down the hall toward the vending machine.

Mary put her money in the machine and pushed the button. She heard the money clink and the soda fall but it never appeared at the bottom. She pushed the change button.

When that failed, she shook the machine.

Nothing.

She kicked the bottom and punched the front.

Nothing.

All of the stress that she had built up in the last few hours fixated on the machine.

Crying out, she shook the machine with strength unknown. Tears streamed as she kicked it, sending a sharp pain through her leg. Over and over she kicked and flailed. Members of the hospital staff hearing the commotion looked down the hall.

Bruce flew down the hall, grabbed Mary from behind and held her close.

"Shh …" he whispered in her ear. "Shh … it's all right. Everything's going to be all right."

Mary went silent.

She turned toward him, her eyes were pink from crying. Tears stained her blotchy cheeks and her hair looked as if she'd been up for days. She sobbed against his chest.

"It's okay," he said. "Everyone … everything's going to be okay."

"I just hate being here again," she whispered. "Jesse's been nothing but good. He's got so much going for him. If anything happens to him …"

"Hey …" He stroked her back. "The doctors say he'll be fine. We won't lose Jesse like we lost …" He stopped himself. He didn't want to mention Brian.

Mary began to quiet down and Bruce released her.

Mary eyed the vending machine and a dreamy look came over her face. Moving to the machine, she pushed it from the side. It tilted and her soda dropped into the slot. She sniffled.

"Thank you, Brian." She sniffled as she opened the can and took a sip.

"What?" Bruce watched her. "Did you say something?"

"I miss Brian so much," she said. "Sometimes I don't know what to do. I wish I had someone who could do what Brian did for me."

Bruce's eyes were sad.

Running her fingers through her disheveled hair, she looked up at Bruce. She didn't know if it was the light in the hall or because her eyes were full of tears but, for just a moment, she saw Brian comforting her.

She managed a smile.

Bruce smiled back. "What?"

"Nothing …" She sniffed and looked away. "It's nothing."

"What?" Bruce asked again. "What is it?"

Mary looked up at Bruce, looked deep into his calming, confident eyes.

"I see in you what I saw in him," she whispered.

Her eyes glanced at Bruce's lips and back up to his eyes. She leaned in closer –

"Mrs. Cross," Dr. White called from down the hall. "You can see Jesse now."

Matt stirred at the sound of his mother's voice. He sighed with relief. Was it all just a horrible dream?

Could it be?

Opening his eyes, he looked around to find himself still on the couch in the waiting room. Groaning, he sat up and rubbed his eyes. His mother stood in the doorway.

"Come on, Matt," she said. "The doctor says we can see Jesse."

Matt followed her down the hall, through the ICU and into Jesse's room. The doctor pulled the curtain back to reveal Jesse lying on the hospital bed.

Matt noticed the gashes on the side of Jesse's pale face. One started above his eyebrow and traveled down over his eye to end at the top of his cheekbone. Another cut was at the corner of his mouth dividing the outline of his lips into two separate parts. A third cut stretched the length of his forehead. The edges of the gashes had already turned pink beginning the early stages of a scar.

Mary approached Jesse's bed with tears in her eyes and took his hand.

"Oh, look at him," she said softly. "Oh, Jesse …"

"He looks like he's going to be okay," Bruce said putting a hand on Mary's shoulder.

Matt made his way around to the other side of Jesse's bed and looked down at him. He looked so peaceful. Matt's chin began to tremble.

Was this his doing? Was Jesse lying here because of him?

He pushed those thoughts aside. No, this wasn't his fault. Jesse was a victim of a terrible crime. It was Fears that had caused this to happen. Matt turned and wiped the tears that formed in his eyes. This wasn't his doing. Fears was behind it all.

As the night went on, the doctors decided to move Jesse out of the ICU. This was not normal but Jesse's rapid healing rate argued otherwise. Matt stayed next to Jesse the rest of the night not sleeping until late Saturday afternoon. Matt's eyes gradually turned dark and deep bags appeared beneath them while Mary and Bruce fell asleep and woke again multiple times.

Finally, Mary suggested that he get some lunch from the hospital cafeteria. The thought of food made Matt sick but he needed to stretch his legs. Heading toward the cafeteria, he saw Zeke and Jake coming down the hail.

Zeke approached. "Hey there ya' are, Matt. How's Jesse?"

Matt shrugged.

"He looks like Jesse. He's healing, which is good. He's not awake right now and the doctors say there's no way to tell when he'll wake up."

"Can we see him?"

"Yeah, follow me."

Zeke and Jake followed Matt down the hall towards Jesse's room. "So, uh, how's everything else?" Zeke asked. "I mean, ya' know, with the plan?"

Matt dropped his head, hiding his eyes. "I don't know."

"What do ya' mean ya' don't know? We gotta get back at Fears. Ya' don't need me to remind ya' what he did."

"I know." Matt teeth clenched. That's all he'd been thinking about for nearly twelve hours.

"Things are just a bit confusing right now. As of now, the plan's off."

Zeke sighed with frustration. "So that's it then?"

"Yes. Tell the rest of them the plan is off."

Once Zeke and Jake saw Jesse and left, Matt settled back in his chair. Mary excused herself to go to the bathroom and Bruce tried to nap in a chair in the corner. Matt attempted to do the same.

Just as his mind began to drift, there was a knock at the door. Matt looked up to see Fears in a nice looking suit standing at the doorway. Matt couldn't believe it. He jumped out of his chair, all weariness pushed aside.

Seeing Fears's face ignited a terrible fire of hatred. Nothing but pure will power held him back from running and jumping on Fears in front of Bruce.

Bruce stood and shook Fears's hand. "Oh … uh, good morning. I'm Bruce Cross."

"Scott Fears. I'm Matt's assistant principal. I heard what happened to Jesse on the news this morning. I thought I'd come and see how he is doing."

"Well, please, please," Bruce said. "Come on in."

Fears glanced at Matt. "Mr. Cross."

Matt's face turned red while his fists shook at his side.

Fears hadn't come to visit Jesse. Fears wanted to taunt Matt. Fears knew Matt wouldn't do or say anything with his uncle in the room.

Fears glanced at Jesse. "Oh, my …"

"He's lookin' better, though," Bruce said. "We've been with him through most of the night and he's makin' progress."

"This tragedy must have been terribly difficult for you all," Fears said quietly.

"Yeah, it has," Bruce replied. "Maybe not as bad as Matt's got it. He lost one of his best friends already and almost lost another. Just before Jesse's accident, we found out that his dog had been killed."

"Really? Oh, that's terrible news," Fears gawked. "This is all very unfortunate, isn't it?"

Fears's eyes fell on Matt and stayed there. Matt held his gaze. His fist was so tight his fingernails tore into the palm of his hand.

"Well, then," Fears said as he turned toward the door. "I must be on my way."

"Are ya' sure?" Bruce asked. "Ya' just got here."

"No, I really must go. I have an appointment."

"Well, thank you for stopping by anyway," Bruce said.

Fears stopped in his tracks and turned to Bruce. "Good day." He looked at Matt. "And you, Mr. Cross, be sure to get some rest. You don't look so good either."

Matt's anger threatened to explode out of him. Storming out of the room, he found a payphone and dialed Zeke's number.

He heard Zeke pick up the phone.

"Zeke, come back to the hospital and get me," Matt said. "Call Mo and have him call everyone else. We'll meet up at your place in an hour."

"What – okay. Why'd ya' change yer mind?"

"We were waiting for a time to act. Our time is now."

23

Zeke drove down the highway toward his shop. Matt sat silent in the passenger seat. His face cold with determination that would not be broken. He would do this or face the consequences for trying.

"Do ya' know what we're gonna do now?" Zeke asked.

"What do you mean?"

"I mean without Jesse and all?"

"We'll have to find someone else I guess."

"Who? I mean we been –"

"Turn the truck around," Matt interrupted.

"What?"

"We're on the wrong road," he said. "Turn around."

Zeke pulled onto the shoulder of the road and within seconds they'd headed back the way they'd come.

"Do ya' know where we're goin'?" Zeke asked.

"I've got to talk to someone."

"How are you, Rose?"

She sighed. "I'm doing better. I slept through most of the storm last night. There's some good news. It seems that all there is around here is bad news."

Matt and Rose sat together on the couch. She looked much better than she had yesterday. Her hair was styled and her makeup looked great. The stress she struggled with was unnoticeable.

"What are you going to do?"

"There's nothing I can do," she said. "I'll just be sure to never go around that creep ever again."

"You could file a report against him."

"I've thought about it but I don't think he was lying when he said he'd fire my dad."

"But, your dad is always working. You'd like it if he didn't work so much."

"Yeah, but then he wouldn't have a job."

"Hmm … good point."

Matt glanced back toward the kitchen checking to make sure that Mr. Hudson couldn't hear them and then remembered that Mr. Hudson was away until Sunday. It was just Rose and him in the house.

"Zeke told me about Jesse," Rose said. "Is he going to be okay?"

Matt nodded. "Yeah, he's going to be fine with some time. In fact, that's why I'm here."

He paused and took breath expecting the words to spill out of him but nothing came.

"What?" Rose's concern showed.

Matt sighed.

"Listen, I have to tell you something. What I'm about to tell you is very confidential so before I tell you I need to know that you trust me."

"You know I do."

"Okay. Then listen carefully. Fears is stealing tax money from the school. He's the one who's been breaking into the school at night. I found out at the Juggernut Festival. That's why he was chasing us. He goes in, hacks into Dr. Pierce's computer, pulls up the tax money and transfers it into his own account."

"How do you know all this?"

"Just trust me. Before Jesse got into the accident, he and I had come up with a plan to break the school's security system and get to the office. Then we could prove that Fears is the bad guy by comparing the account number on the computer and Fears's account numbers. If there's a match, we've got our guy. We give the cops the evidence and he goes to jail but since yesterday, everything's changed."

"What happened yesterday?"

"Fears violated you and killed Newt. Then Jesse ran away and got hurt. So now we are even more motivated to get Fears."

"Who's 'we'?"

"The original team included eight members. Everyone at Jesse's party yesterday is part of the team."

Rose asked more questions as more thoughts came.

"Why are you telling me all this?"

"Jesse is hurt. We need someone to take his place."

"And you want me to do it?"

Matt squirmed in his seat. "Well ... yes."

"You want me to help you break into the school to catch Fears?"

"I figured that if anyone wanted to put Fears behind bars, it would be you."

She clenched her fists. "Boy, you're right about that."

"Good. Then, you have to come with me." Matt looked at his watch. "We've got a meeting at Zeke's place in a half hour."

"Why? What's the big hurry?"

"We're doing it tomorrow night."

Her eyes went wide with shock. "Tomorrow . . ?"

"Night."

The team sat in their circle in the middle of Zeke's garage as they had before with Rose in Jesse's place.

"Guys," Matt said. "First off, I'm really sorry for leaving you hanging like that when I said that the plan was off. I know you've all worked really hard to make this work and I'm sorry."

No one seemed to object so Matt went on, "Okay, down to business. Rose has agreed to replace Jesse. Everything else will go according to plan. Andrew? Abby? How's the train coming along?"

"It's just about finished," Andrew replied. "We need to get the audio and we're done."

"Okay." Matt nodded. "You and I will get that today."

Matt looked to Jake. "How's the car coming?"

Jake made a quick gesture. Zeke translated, "It'll be ready."

Matt looked to Mo. "You got the stuff?"

Mo pointed to a box sitting on a table on the other side of the garage. "Inside that box is Andrew's uniform and ID. The U-Haul truck can be here tonight if we need it."

"Great. Zeke? You got the keys we need from the janitor?"

Zeke held up an envelope. "Got everythin' right here."

"How's the stunt training?"

"I've done it four times without hittin' a cone."

"Awesome." Matt continued, "Today we put the finishing touches on whatever we've got to do. Andrew and I will get the audio for the train. Zeke, you need to keep practicing your stunt. Rose, can go with you to keep you company. You can explain the plan her then. I'm sure Rose is probably clueless right now."

She smirked. "Just a little bit."

Matt winked at her and turned to Jake.

"Add the finishing touches on the car. Abby can help. When we get back, we'll help, too. Mo, you need to show Lily the ventilation system on the blueprints so she knows where she's supposed to turn and stuff."

Mo nodded.

"This is it," Matt said, standing up. "We're really going to do it. Let's polish things up. Tomorrow night is the night. Let's go Andrew."

Andrew sat behind the wheel of his red '98 Chevy at the train tracks with Matt beside him. For a Saturday, the area was relatively deserted.

"What are you thinking about?" Matt asked, trying to start a conversation.

"When the train's gonna show up," Andrew replied.

"Really? Nothing else going through your mind?"

"I'm a little worried 'bout how things are gonna go tomorrow night."

"You've just got to play your part."

"That's what I'm worried about."

"What do you mean?"

"Well, I don't think I'll have any trouble turnin' off the cameras and stuff but I'm worried Dr. Pierce will recognize me. What if he decides to stay with me in the camera room?"

"He'll leave," Matt reassured. "Don't worry about that."

"How do you know?"

"The high school is hosting the basketball banquet tomorrow and Dr. Pierce is a major fan. All his basketball buddies will be there. I bet it'll kill him to leave for even a few minutes."

"Okay, but I'm still nervous."

They were quiet.

Andrew checked his watch. "The train's late."

"Oh." Matt pulled a laminated tag out of his pocket. "Here. You're going to need this. It's your alias for tomorrow night."

Andrew read over his fake name and picture. "Swinston Electronics. Edward Dinkle. Wait, hold on a second. Edward Dinkle? That's my name? What am I, an elf? You can't tell me that Mo couldn't come up with somethin' better than that."

Matt laughed. "I think it fits pretty good …" Then he added, "Edward."

"Shut up, man." Andrew smiled, putting the tag in his pocket. "Your name's not Dinkle."

Matt laughed. "Okay, okay. Really, what are you going to do? You've got to have some kind of character. A story, you know?"

"What do ya' mean?"

"Everyone's got their own personality. You've got to make Edward seem real. For example, you could say Edward Dinkle's got three kids – two boys and a girl. And he's got a wife who's an attorney. He lives on the East Side in a big house. He went to college at Florida State and ended up as a security system guy."

"You just made all that up?" Andrew asked.

"Yep."

"I'm supposed to do that?"

"That's right. Give your character some depth or history. A phony accent would be nice too."

"A phony accent? You're nuts. I think you're blowing this way out –"

"Do you want it to work or not?" Matt interrupted.

"Yeah, but I –"

"Then put a little more Southern drawl into it."

Andrew sighed. "All right. All right."

He took a breath and stopped. "This is stupid. I'm not going to –"

HILLS

"Just do it. Go ahead. Talk backwoods like."

"Fine … Hi. M' name's Eddie Dinkle. What seems ta be da problem 'ere?"

"See? That wasn't so hard, now was it?"

Andrew smiled. "It's not all dat hard. Der ain't nutton to it."

"Okay, you can stop now."

"Crud, I kinda like it," Andrew went on with his country drawl. "It gives m' character a bit o' whatchamacallit? History. Tha's it. History. I dun took History. Got m'self a C minus. Pa says tha's pretty good for a buck ridin', boot wearin', spit shootin' feller like me."

"Okay Andrew," Matt said. "That's real good. You can come back to reality now."

"Aww, come on, Pa. Us kids are havin' ourselves so much fun shootin' our bb's at the squirrel. We 'bout shot his tail plum off."

"No, seriously Andrew." Matt said suddenly. "The train's coming!"

"Oh, dang it," Andrew cried as he threw the car door open.

"Get the tape ready," Matt said hurriedly.

They jumped out of the truck and approached the tracks. Smoke erupted over the tops of the trees. They could hear the train approaching from around the bend about fifty yards away.

"You see that bend there?" Matt pointed.

"Yeah."

"That's where you need to set up. You'll need to be far enough around the corner that the cops can't see you from here."

"Okay," Andrew said. "I'm startin' to record."

He pushed the button.

Down the tracks the train came, its horn blasting. Matt gave the conductor a small wave. The old looking man casually waved back as the train sped past. Matt and Andrew watched while the dozens of train cars passed by them.

"I got it," Andrew yelled as the caboose roared past.

"Good. Let's go."

Andrew and Matt rolled across the tracks and drove to the deserted parking lot to see how Zeke was doing on his stunt.

"He's doing a lot better," Rose said. "He's really getting it."

Matt and Andrew stood on the edge of the parking lot and watched as Zeke ran over four cones before he even attempted to spin. Zeke yelled, beat the wheel and honked the horn in his frustration.

Andrew raised his eyebrows. "Sure looks like he's getting it. Boy, let me tell ya' …"

Matt jogged over to the car and opened the door. "What's wrong, Zeke?"

"I dunno," Zeke hollered. "Maybe I'm tired. I don't think … ah!" He punched the wheel again. "I dunno."

Zeke got out of the car and walked toward Andrew and Rose. "Just gimme a second."

"Tomorrow night we won't have a second, Zeke," Matt called.

Zeke spun around and irritably said, "You do realize that if I screw up not only does the plan not work, but we could get arrested or even die."

Matt paused and thought about Zeke's point. "Right … uh – take all the time you need."

Zeke plopped down on the curb beside Rose and Andrew.

"I know I can do it," he said. "I think I'm just nervous. That's all."

"It's okay to be nervous," Rose replied. "We're all nervous."

"Yeah," Zeke reassured himself. "It's just nerves. I should be fine tomorrow. Ya' know, with the adrenaline and everythin'. Yeah, I should be fine."

"Do you want to try it again?" Andrew asked.

"Yeah. Jus' hang on a minute."

He fell back onto the grass and lay there for a moment. "I'm okay. I'll be fine."

"Hey Andrew," Matt called as he approached from the car. "We need to call the high school and let them know that you're coming tomorrow. There's a pay phone over there. Follow me."

Andrew sighed as he stood up. "Okay, okay."

Rose got up as well and followed Andrew to the pay phone.

"And remember – history," Matt whispered.

Andrew nodded as the answering machine picked it up.

"Hi," Andrew began, "M' name's Eddie Dinkle with Swinston Electronics. I've been informed that Swinston Electronics installed a new security system for ya' a while back. Well, it's my job ta make sure that everythin' is workin' right. I'm s'posed to check the system ev'ry two months on the dot for bugs, viruses an' da like. I'm goin' to come in Sunday evening 'round six o' clock. I know Sundays may not be good for ya', but if I don't come in on Sunday then ya' run da risk of the system failing on ya'. Neither of us want that now, do we? So I'll see ya' on Sunday. Remember, m' name's Eddie Dinkle. Have a wonderful day."

Andrew hung up the phone and wiped the sweat from his forehead. "We're all terrible, horrible people."

That night, Matt lay in his bed watching his ceiling fan spin. All he could think about was the heist. He checked his alarm clock – two forty-two am. He should be sleeping. He'd already counted to a thousand twice, closed his eyes and held them there for an hour until he drifted off to sleep only to wake again ten minutes later.

He'd heard Bruce and Mary come home from the hospital. They'd arrived around one o'clock and Matt's thoughts turned to Jesse. Matt was, after all, doing all this to avenge Jesse. He was also avenging Newt … and Rose … and he needed the money but, the true reason was that Fears had made it personal.

Matt imagined how Jesse would react when he woke. He would be so full of questions about the heist. Matt imagined the smile on Jesse's face as he went on about how Fears was behind bars and how he'd saved their house.

What a story. The team would be all over the news. Matt could see it in the papers now. The headline would read, *"Teens Foil Assistant Principal's Tax Scam"*.

It brought a smile to Matt's face as he fought his way back into sleep.

After church the next morning, Zeke picked up Matt and Rose and brought them to his shop. Zeke began to help Jake polish the two identical cars. Normally, they would be arguing about something, but not now. Both were silent, getting mentally prepared for what lie ahead of them.

Matt had told his mother that he was going to be studying at Zeke's place and that he'd be home later that night. Mary and Bruce would probably be at the hospital well into the night anyway. They would never know he lied.

Setting his bag down, Matt waited for the rest of the team. Andrew arrived a bit later with Abby, Lily and Mo. A wooden structure lay in the bed of his truck covered with a large, gray tarp. It would have its uses later.

Andrew opened the door to his truck and out leaped his monstrous dog, Muffin.

"Andrew," Matt called.

Andrew stepped out of his truck and shrugged his backpack. "Yeah?"

"What the heck did you bring Muffin for?"

"I didn't want him to come. Honest," he said.

"Okay, so … why is he here?"

"Muffin wanted to come. He'd already gotten in my truck and he wouldn't move. He just stood there and looked at me like I was speaking a foreign language or something."

"Well, I doubt Muffin speaks fluent English, Andrew."

"Yeah, that's true. Muffin has like a four-word vocabulary. 'Sit', 'food', 'poop' and 'attack'. That's pretty much it."

"We can't have him interfering with anything," Matt said.

"Don't worry. Abby said she'd look after him when I'm gone. And Muffin will be with me when I'm setting up the train."

"Well, just keep an eye on him, okay?"

Andrew nodded.

Matt returned to the group. "Okay, then guys, let's sit down before we start."

Once in their circle, Matt asked, "Does everyone have an excuse not to be home tonight?"

They all nodded.

Matt looked to Mo. "Even you, Mo?"

Mo nodded. "I told my mom there was an Honor Society lock-in at the school."

"And she bought it?" Matt asked. "It's Sunday."

"I told her it wasn't my idea to have a lock-in on a school night."

"Okay, then" Matt said. "Everyone relax. Just chill for a couple hours. Andrew, Lily, Zeke and Jake will leave at about five forty-five for the school. The basketball banquet starts at six. We'll all go back to the school together a little before midnight. Everybody got it?"

Heads all around nodded and no one said a word. Matt rubbed his hands together. "This is where the fun begins."

24

Dr. Pierce looked at his watch – six o' clock. The technician hadn't arrived yet. He looked back at the school where the players and parents were talking with the coaches. Shifting from one foot to the other, he ran his fingers over his hair, patted it down and then ran his fingers through it once more.

A truck pulled into the parking lot. The driver parked in a visitor's parking space and a young man jumped down from the driver's seat. He was tall with a big build and sported a thick red mustache that radiated with his huge smile. Stitched into the left side of his blue suit was the name 'Eddie'. A large blue cap flopped down over his ears covering most of his face. Behind him, he pulled what looked like a bag of luggage on wheels.

Andrew sure looked the part. He glanced down at his tag and uniform. His fake mustache tickled his upper lip. He hoped it would stay on his face. Spotting Dr. Pierce, he took a big breath and exhaled.

Just keep breathing, he told himself. You'll be fine.

Approaching Dr. Pierce, Andrew grabbed his hand and shook it.

"Hi! Ya' must be Mr. Pierce. M' name's Eddie."

"Yes, I'm *Dr.* Pierce. Follow me, please. I am due somewhere else and am in a bit of a hurry."

"Oh, no problem." Andrew pulled the oversized bag behind him.

Dr. Pierce led Andrew to the camera room and motioned to the monitor screens. Andrew could hear a soft hum coming from the system.

"As you can see," Dr. Pierce said, "this is where the video feeds go."

HILLS

"Yeah, all righ'." Andrew grinned. "Are ya' gunna stick aroun' cuz I'm prob'ly gonna be awhile. I'm gunna check da system. Maybe reboot it. Ya' know how it is."

Dr. Pierce looked out into the hall. "Ah, yes. That's great – listen, how about you bill the school and I'll sign everything then? Would that be a problem?"

"Works for me."

"All right. Well, then if you –"

Dr. Pierce stopped and eyed Andrew curiously. "Do I know you?"

"Uh, no," Andrew jerked away and started rummaging through his bag. "I don't think so. Uh – where'd you go to college?"

"Oklahoma."

"Oh, yeah! Oklahoma. Now it all makes sense."

"Did you go to Oklahoma?" Dr. Pierce asked eagerly.

"No, not really. I'm just joshin' ya'. I went to college in Florida. Ha! Ain't dat somethin'?"

"Oh, right. Well then, I'll leave you be."

"Thank ya', kindly, sir. I'll be outta 'ere in a jiffy."

Dr. Pierce nodded and hurried down the hall toward the banquet.

Andrew peered down the hallway making sure Dr. Pierce was gone. Seeing no one, he shut the door, pulled an earpiece from his pocket and clipped it to his ear.

"Mo? Mo, can you hear me?"

"Yeah," Mo replied. "I'm here."

"All right, I'm in the camera room. Tell me how to turn the cameras off."

"Okay, listen. On the back side of the control board there's a big, red switch. It will shut down every camera in school. Do you see it?"

Andrew unzipped his bag and pulled out a small flashlight. Shining the light behind the control board, he saw the switch.

"Okay," he said. "I see it."

"Switch it off."

Andrew flipped the switch and heard the system's hum slow to a stop.

"Okay," he said.

"Got it?"

"Yeah, the cameras are off."

"Okay, I'll let Zeke and Jake know."

"Zeke. Andrew's set. Go."

Parked in two different vehicles at a gas station a half a mile away, Zeke started up the 280ZX Nissan while Jake started Zeke's truck.

Zeke touched his ear. "Copy that, Mo. We'll be there in a sec."

He looked out of his window at Jake and nodded.

Jake nodded back.

The two boys put their vehicles into Drive, pulled out of the gas station and headed for the school.

"Okay," Mo said to Andrew. "Zeke and Jake are on their way. Let Lily go."

Andrew knelt and unzipped the large luggage bag.

"Come on, Lily," Andrew muttered. "It's your time to shine."

Lily uncurled, flopped out of the bag and gasped through the sweaty locks of hair that dangled in her face.

"You have … no idea … how hot it is in there," she managed through short gasps.

"Zeke and Jake are on their way," Andrew said. "You've got to hurry and get to the shop room."

"Okay." She started for the door.

"And Lily?"

She turned. "Yeah?"

"Remember – this is the easy part."

Lily rolled her eyes. "Yeah, right."

Leaving the camera room, Lily turned down the other hall.

She pressed on her earpiece. "Mo? Can you hear me?"

"Yeah," he replied. "Where are you?"

"I'm on my way to the shop room."

"You're right on schedule."

Lily put her hand in her pocket and felt the shop room key they'd copied from the janitor. Lily didn't know why her heart was throbbing or why her breathing was unsteady. If this was the easy part, why did she feel so nervous?

Approaching the door, she removed the key, reached up and opened it. She took a quick glance down the hall to ensure no one had seen her and heard distant voices. Probably from the banquet, she thought. Jumping inside the shop room, Lily closed the door behind her.

"Mo. I'm in."

"Great," he replied. "You're looking at two two-car garages correct?"

She could see both garage doors in the wide room.

"Yeah."

"Open the one on the right. There should be two buttons on the wall. Press the one closest to the door you just unlocked to open it. Hurry, Zeke and Jake are almost there."

She pushed the button just as Mo instructed and the garage door began to rise. She cleared a path for Zeke's car while she waited, moving a few boxes and chairs off to the side.

Before long, Zeke pulled the car up next to the garage, his arm hanging out his window. Jake was following close behind.

"Hey, beautiful," Zeke said. "Stand clear. I'm gonna back it up."

She stepped back and watched as Zeke backed the Nissan into the garage.

"Jake," Zeke called once he'd parked the car. "Get the firecrackers."

Jake parked Zeke's truck near the open garage and jumped out with dozens of firecrackers in hand.

"Come on, Lily," Zeke called. "We need to string these firecrackers around the outside of the garage. We've got to make sure the wick is at the edge of the woods so Rose can light it when it's time."

In the camera room, Andrew leaned back in his chair. His job now was to wait for Lily to get back. When she returned she was to get back in the bag again. He'd flip the red switch and restart the system, then he'd and Lily pull out of there.

He sighed and leaned back in his chair. Playing Eddie Dinkle wasn't nearly as hard as he'd thought. Matt was right. Dr. Pierce hadn't even wanted to talk to him. He was too interested with the banquet. After all, he'd –

Andrew's ears picked up the sound of jingling outside the door. His eyes snapped toward the door. He heard a man humming to himself on the other side. He was about to enter.

Andrew threw his bag shut and dropped to the floor pretending to work.

The man opened the door, stepped inside and saw Andrew under the desk.

"Hey!" His flashlight waved in Andrew's face. "What do you think you're doing?"

Andrew squinted past the light to see a thin police officer with thick-rimmed glasses.

"I'm just, uh …" He cleared his throat as he remembered his character. "Oh, me? I'm justa tryin' to fix this 'ere camera system. Tha's all."

"Who are you?" the officer snapped.

Andrew jumped up and stuck out his hand.

"Eddie Dinkle at yer service. I'm a technician, see, for Swinston Electronics. Dr. Pierce thought tha' I should come in 'ere an' check things out a bit. Ya' know how there've been a few break-ins this year? He jus' wanted everythin' to be workin' properly, tha's all."

"He called you?" the officer asked.

"Yeah, well it's customary tha' we call him to 'range the appointment. Gotta do a checkup on 'ese things e'ery two months on the dot. Or else they get all broken and stuff, see?"

"Hmm …" The officer continued to shine the light in Andrew's face as if searching for any sign of a lie.

"If ya' don't mind," Andrew motioned for the officer to lower the flashlight. "My wife complains 'nough 'bout my eyes as it is."

"Right," the officer said as he put it away. "Sorry."

"Now, Officer …" Andrew glanced at the man's badge. "Crawford. If you'll 'scuse me, I gotta do some work on this 'ere thingamawidja."

"How long are you going to be?"

"Oh, not too long. Ten minutes at most."

"Well, then …" Crawford sat down. "You won't mind if I have a seat and stick around a bit, would ya'?"

Andrew swallowed his fear.

Lily, Zeke and Jake finished stringing up the firecrackers. Together, they had managed to do a good job hiding the string in the grass.

"Okay," Zeke said, "that should do it."

He went back to the garage and tossed the keys in the front seat of the car.

"Come on, Jake. Our work here is done. You should be headin' back, Lily. Jake and I will see ya' at the shop in a few minutes."

Lily nodded as she pushed the button, closing the garage door.

Her hand went to her ear. "Mo, the firecrackers are set. The Nissan is in place and I'm heading back to the camera room."

Andrew gasped and his eyes popped as Lily's shadow appeared under the door. She couldn't come into the room. The officer would see her and Andrew would have to come up with a very big excuse as to why a very small girl was in the camera room.

"Ya' know, officer," he raised his voice. "I'll bet tha' not just any ol' Joe can come in 'ere to work these 'ere cameras. Heck, I work wit 'em e'ery day an' I'm still findin' new stuff 'bout 'em. What do ya' think?"

"Well," Officer Crawford leaned back in his chair. "I know just about everything there is to know about this school. I know just about everything about these cameras too. In fact, I could probably do what you're doing right now. They don't need you."

"No offense or anythin', Mr. Officer," Andrew said, "but I got this habit, see. I like to eat e'ery day and I gotta have some money ta put food on da table. Gotta feed da kids, ya' know what I mean?"

Andrew's pulse settled when he saw Lily's shadow back off and then vanish.

Crawford smiled. "Yeah, I guess you're right."

Andrew paused. He had to find some way to get the officer out of the room so he could get Lily back into the bag.

"Aww, shoot!" he exclaimed.

Crawford jumped. "What?"

"I can't believe I forgot m' Phillips. Do ya' think ya' could go get me one? I'm sure they got one in da janitor's closet or somethin'."

"Sure." The officer stood up. "I'll be right back."

"No need to hurry or anythin'," Andrew called as the officer shut the door.

Waiting a few seconds, Andrew jumped to the door and cracked it open.

"Lily," he hissed. "Lily, where are you?"

Lily's head poked out from around the corner.

"Come on," Andrew said through a forced whisper. "Get in here."

Lily stepped around the corner and dashed for the camera room. Once Lily was in, Andrew shut the door, locked it and looked down at her.

"What was all that about?" she asked.

"Nothing."

"Yeah, right! I just saved both our butts. It's not my fault you couldn't get that guy outta here."

"I know," Andrew said. "Just hurry up and get in the bag. He'll be back before long."

Lily shook her head, muttered something about how uncomfortable the bag was and jumped inside, pulling the flap over herself.

"Okay, Mo," Andrew said as he zipped the bag. "We had a little fumble, but we're okay now."

"All right. Do you see a thick, yellow wire behind the desk?" Mo asked. "That's the master recording wire. You need to cut into the outside of the wire, but don't cut the wire. When you clip the transmitter to the wire I'll be able to watch you guys on the cameras."

Suddenly Andrew's hands went cold and were slightly shaky. Oh this is easy, he thought sarcastically. Cut the outside of the wire, without cutting through the wire. Sure no problem.

Andrew pulled out his pocketknife and held his breath as he gently cut into the wire. Pulling the small transmitter from his pocket, he quickly clipped it to the wire.

"Got it."

"All right. Now flip that red switch that you found earlier."

Andrew reached behind the desk and heard the system hum back to life. "Okay. The cameras are on again. Can you see what's on 'em?"

"Hang on … yeah, I can see the hallway. Come out of the camera room."

Andrew grabbed the bag with Lily inside, opened the door and headed back out into the hall.

"Ha!" Mo exclaimed. "I see you! Wave or something."

"I'm not waving. I'll look ridiculous," Andrew replied as he glanced down the hall, the officer was nowhere in sight.

Pulling Lily in the bag behind him, he headed for the front door when he heard someone call, "Wait, wait!"

Andrew turned to see Officer Crawford jogging toward him with a screwdriver in hand. "Here's your Phillips," he said.

"Well, thank ya' for everythin'," Andrew said. "But ya' know wha'?" He gave a fictitious laugh. "It's kinda funny really. I jus' so happened ta find m' Phillips the second ya' left. Is'n nat funny?"

The officer frowned and looked at the screwdriver in his hand.

Andrew opened the door before the officer could say anything. "Well, see ya' later. Gotta be headin' out, ya' know? It's gettin' late. Wife 'ill have m' hide when I get home."

25

Andrew and Lily arrived back at Zeke's shop a few minutes later. Matt was the first one to congratulate them. He was then joined by the others who had been waiting at the garage listening in on the action.

They all patted themselves on the back for a few minutes and talked about the kink Officer Crawford had almost put in the plan. But it wasn't long before they remembered that Andrew and Lily had only completed the setup. The real heist was next and it would be a lot more difficult than what they'd just managed to pull.

Matt looked around. "All right, guys. This is it. We've been waiting for this for a long time now. There's no turning back anymore. We've got to play it smart. Keep an eye out for each other and remember – you are more important than the money. Don't do anything stupid. Okay?"

They nodded in agreement.

"All right. Good luck. Let's go."

The group headed in different directions.

"Wait," Abby suddenly exclaimed. "Shouldn't we pray or something first?"

The others looked at each other and shrugged.

"It couldn't hurt," Zeke said.

Everyone joined hands, but there was one person missing.

"Where's Andrew?" Matt asked.

"I'm here," he called from behind his truck. "Hang on, guys. I'm coming."

The others waited a moment but when he still hadn't emerged, Matt left the group and went to find Andrew. The tall wooden structure Andrew had made sat in the bed of his truck under the tarp. His dog, Muffin, sniffled around the garage while Andrew fiddled with something on the back hitch of his truck.

"What's the hold-up?" Matt asked.

"No hold-up," Andrew replied.

"What are you doing?" Matt looked at the hitch. Andrew had tied an angel ornament to the back of his truck. "What's that for?"

"Luck."

Matt frowned as he watched the angel dangle from the hitch.

"I hope we all have angels working with us tonight," Andrew said loud enough for the others to hear as well. "I'm just trying to keep mine close."

"Oh, okay," Matt shrugged. "Whatever. Just come on. We're going to pray."

Andrew followed Matt back to the group and each of them joined hands.

Abby began, "Dear God, please watch over us as we attempt to break into the school and run from the cops."

Matt glanced up to see everyone trying to suppress his or her laughter.

Abby continued, "We know that you have a plan for each of us. Please keep your protective hand on us as we carry out that plan. Please help us to not get hurt or caught. Help each of us to keep an eye out for each other and come out of this successfully. In Jesus name, we pray. Amen."

"Amen," Matt said as he lifted his head. "It's time to go. Mo, make the call."

Matt and Zeke got in the second Nissan. Andrew, Rose, Lily and Abby squeezed together in Andrew's truck. Jake climbed into the newly arrived U-Haul and revved it up just as Mo grabbed his cell phone from his pocket. Dialing a few extra digits so his number wouldn't appear on the operator's caller ID, he dialed Nine-One-One.

The operator picked up. "Nine-One-One. What is your emergency?"

"Hi, there is a diesel truck stuck in a ditch on Highway Sixty-six," Mo lied while the rest of the team pulled out of the garage. "You know the one that runs through the West Side of Hills?"

"And where exactly is this truck?"

"It's on the other side of the train tracks. After the train tracks, you've got about three miles before you reach it. It's close to Fate's Crossing into Hills East."

"And what is your name, sir?"

"Uh, m – my name?" Mo stuttered. "Uh, John. John …" He tried to come up with a last name. "Dinkle. John Dinkle."

"Thank you, Mr. Dinkle. We'll send someone out there immediately."

"Thank you."

Mo grinned as he put the cell phone back in his pocket.

"Suckers."

Zeke, Jake and Andrew parked their three vehicles at the gas station where Zeke and Jake had been earlier. Getting out of the Nissan, Matt strolled to the pay phone and dialed Nine-One-One.

The operator responded. "Nine-One-One. What is your emergency?"

"Yes, a diesel truck is stuck in the ditch on Highway Sixty-six. It looks really bad."

"Thank you, sir," the operator said. "We've just received another call reporting this. We're sending two units down that way now."

Matt smiled when he heard this. His plan was working perfectly.

"All right," he continued. "You need to hurry. It's holding up traffic and everything."

"The officers are on their way. What is your name?"

"Brian …" Matt responded almost too quickly. "Brian … Parish. Brian Parish."

"Thank you, Mr. Parish. The officers will be there shortly."

As Matt headed back to the Nissan, he laughed to himself. "Suckers."

The driveway to the school was on the other side of the street and about a quarter of a mile down the road from the gas station. Matt and Zeke eyed the two officers at the school's entrance.

Suddenly, the officers looked at each other, exchanged a few words and got into their cars. Pulling out of the driveway, they headed down the road, racing to the fake truck on Highway Sixty-six.

"Okay," Matt said. "That's our cue. Let's go."

Zeke didn't move.

"Come on, Zeke," Matt ushered. "The cops at the front gate are gone. What are you waiting for?"

Zeke hands fidgeted. "I'm about to dive head first into one of the most dangerous chases that I've ever been in. I have a right to be a little nervous."

Matt waited a moment. "Okay. Be nervous. But we do need to get a move on. Once those officers realize that there's no wreck, they're going to head back to the school. Then we're screwed. So if we could move the show along …"

Zeke acted as though he hadn't heard him. He reached into his pocket and produced a large package of gum. "Want some?"

Matt shook his head.

Zeke shrugged and popped a piece into his mouth.

"What's with the gum?" Matt asked.

"Nerves."

"Well, get a hold of yourself. You can do this. I know you can."

"I know. I know, I know, I know, I know." He tapped the wheel nervously with his thumbs as he gnawed on his gum.

"Can we go now?" Matt asked.

Zeke took a deep breath and started his car.

"Okay. Here we go."

A dark car sat in the parking lot across the street. Its windows watched as the cars pulled out of the gas station and started up the road. The car's engine hummed as it pulled out behind the boys. Its brake lights disappeared down the road and into the darkness after them.

Driving the truck, Andrew followed Zeke's Nissan onto the highway with the covered wooden structure wobbling around in the bed.

"Be careful Andrew," Rose said from the passenger side. "You don't want the train to tip, do you? We'd all be up a creek if it did."

"It's not gonna tip," he assured. "Don't worry."

Muffin huddled against the door. His tongue flopped out of his mouth and his breath fogged up a spot on the window.

Abby recoiled in disgust. "Why did you have to bring him again?"

"He wanted to come along," Andrew said. "I wasn't about to refuse that face. I mean, just look at it."

Muffin glanced at them as a string of drool fell from his mouth to the floorboard.

"It's not exactly that 'puppy-dog face' everyone's always talking about," Abby remarked with a look of annoyance.

Zeke turned onto the school's driveway and Andrew slowed his truck to a stop on the shoulder of the highway. Jake waved as he drove past Andrew in the U-Haul.

"This is your stop," Andrew said to the three girls. "I'll see you on the other side. Be careful."

The girls pushed Muffin aside and jumped out of the car heading for the woods on the edge of the school's driveway.

"Hey, Abby," Andrew called.

Abby turned.

"I mean it. Be careful. I don't want to have to explain to Dad why you got arrested."

Abby smiled. "Don't jinx it."

Andrew shook his head and continued down the highway toward the railroad tracks.

The dark car with its tinted windows watched from the distance as the three girls jumped out of the truck and dashed off into the woods. It watched as Andrew drove away down the road.

The driver side door opened and a man exited carrying what looked to be a baseball bat. Keeping his distance, he followed the girls into the woods.

HILLS

Officer Crawford watched a Nissan drive past the school's entrance and continue down the driveway. He grabbed his radio and punched a couple of buttons.

Officers Dave Hutchins and Frank Borkins sat in one of the two squad cars that were parked on opposite sides of the parking lot. About thirty pounds overweight, the two had been partners for over a year and never had had a dull moment in their conversation.

"I'd like to lose like twenty to twenty-five pounds." Dave sipped his coffee.

"Yeah," Frank replied. "Tell me about it."

"Have you tried the Adkins Diet?" Dave asked.

"No. I usually don't set any weight goals for myself. I just go with it. But you know what really chaps my butt? Diet soft drinks. I just want to drink a regular Coke without feeling guilty about it. I've been drinking diet forever."

"I know, man. One time I felt buzzed after drinking a regular Mountain Dew. I felt like I was drunk or some —"

The radio went off and they heard Crawford exclaim, "School to four-sixteen. Do you copy? Over."

Frank grabbed the microphone.

"What, Crawford? Are you bored, again? Over."

"No, I'm not bored! I just thought that you'd like to know there's a Nissan coming up the driveway."

The Nissan appeared in the parking lot.

"We'll take care of it."

Dave flashed his bright lights at the other squad car across the parking lot for help intercepting the Nissan.

Matt and Zeke watched as the two squad cars approached from the now empty parking lot with their lights flashing. They heard the cars let off a short siren blast.

"I think they want us to pull over, Zeke," Matt said.

"Ya' would think that, wouldn't ya'?"

Zeke slowed the Nissan to a stop.

They pulled black masks over their faces but in the darkness of the night, the cops wouldn't be able to see them anyway. An overweight cop emerged from one of the cars with his flashlight waving and walked towards the car.

"You ready?" Matt asked.

Adrenaline rushed through Zeke's veins. He snapped his bubble gum, gripped the wheel and looked at Matt. "Yeah. Yeah, I'm ready."

The officer was within spitting distance when Zeke revved the engine, peeled his tires and tore off between the two squad cars racing through the parking lot.

They could hear the officer yelling, "Hey, come back here!"

Zeke paid him no mind. It was his turn. He had to give Lily time to get back to the garage. Matt looked back to see the officers scramble for their cars. The second car turned on its siren, spun around and took off after Zeke. In a few seconds, the first car did the same.

"Mo," Zeke said into his earpiece. "We're in the parking lot."

"Okay," he heard. "Hang tight."

Lily, Rose and Abby quickly made their way through the woods at the edge of the parking lot. Using the foliage as cover, they avoided the gaze of the outside security cameras.

An eerie silence put the girls on edge. The cold night air pierced their bodies and the night seemed uncommonly dark, even the distant streetlights were dimmer than usual. Small bits of clouds scattered across the sky.

"Lily," Mo said in Lily's ear.

"Yeah?"

"Zeke and Matt are being chased in the parking lot by the squad cars. You need to get down the alley and get to that vent – now!"

"Okay," she cried, running as fast as her legs would carry her. "I can hear the sirens from here."

"Just hurry. Zeke and Matt don't have much time."

"Hey, look out, Zeke," Matt cried spinning in his seat. "They're coming up on both sides!"

"I see 'em, I see 'em," Zeke exclaimed jerking the wheel to avoid a curb.

"Pull over," one of the officers called through his loudspeaker. "You are on private property. Slow your vehicle to a stop."

"Zeke, they want us to stop again," Matt said.

Zeke grinned. "Not a chance."

An idea jumped into Zeke's head and he began to change his mind. Glancing in his rearview mirrors, he saw the two police cars coming up on either side of his car.

"Hold on, Matt!" and he stomped on the brake. The car skidded to a stop and the officers jerked on their wheels to avoid hitting it as they sped past.

"Jeez, that was close. Spin this thing around," Matt yelled. "The cops are turnin' around."

"Yeah, yeah, I know." Zeke shifted into gear. "Hang on!"

Zeke spun the car around a long flowerbed, shifted again and took off down the parking lot.

"We've got a good lead on them," Matt said breathlessly looking back at the squad cars.

"We won't for long …" Zeke glanced in his mirrors. "Not if Lily doesn't get that garage door open!"

26

Lily stopped at the edge of the woods, gasping for breath. She'd never run anywhere before. Her coaches always let her sit out during gym. She wasn't used to all this physical exercise.

"Mo," she gasped. "I can see the school."

"Okay," he said. "You need to go down that long alley. At the end of it, there should be a vent on the right side of the building. It's next to a large fan."

"Yeah," she breathed as she dashed into the alley. "I see it."

"Okay, that's where you need to go. Then follow the route through the vent that we went over earlier."

"The route. Right."

Lily reached the end of the alley, unscrewed the vent from its hinges and began to climb in, but her foot slipped and she fell back onto the hard cement. She gave a short painful cry. She knew she would be feeling that ache for the next week or so.

Groaning, she pushed herself back up and as she did, something at the beginning of the alley caught her eye. She squinted to see a giant figure approach. Scooting away on her backside, she tried to make the figure out in the darkness.

"Well, well …" the malicious voice drawled. "If it ain't the midget."

The figure stepped into a patch of moonlight.

Fear swelled in Lily's soul like a hot-air balloon. Her body shook and as the man neared, the bat he held in his hands rose high above his head.

HILLS

Lily wanted to scream, but no sound came as the heavy bat swung down, straight for her.

From the camera room, Officer Crawford watched as the squad cars attempted to cut off the Nissan. Jerking to the right, it flew past one of the squad cars as he heard the officers talk on the radio.

"Get on his left and we'll trap him against the curb," one of the officers yelled.

"Wait, hold on," the other exclaimed as he attempted to spin his car around.

The Nissan was definitely giving the officers a run for their money. Crawford felt a bit helpless just sitting in the camera room watching. But that was his job — stick to his post. He failed to notice the screen that showed a small girl huddled in an alley as a large man with a baseball bat prepared to beat her into a world of hurt.

"They're trying to block us with the curb," Matt shouted as the officers came at them from both sides again. "Get us out of here, Zeke!"

"I'm trying." Zeke clenched his teeth on his bubble gum.

"We order you to stop your vehicle," blared the squad cars.

Zeke's tires howled as he pulled away, sending the squad cars veering away from each other.

Zeke continued to stomp on the gas as he glanced back at the officers, a large grin on his face.

"Watch out, Zeke!"

Zeke spun in his seat to see himself driving straight for a curb.

"Go, go, go! Turn! Turn!" Matt cried. "Do it now!"

"Hold on to something …" Zeke managed and jerking the wheel to the right he sent the backside of the car fishtailing.

Matt grabbed the dash as the car spun. The tires on the right side of the car lifted off the ground a couple of inches before the car settled down to a stop. The officers jumped out of their squad cars, handcuffs ready.

"Let's go," Matt cried. "We can't stop. They're right there!"

Zeke turned and looked through his back window. "Oh, crap."

"Move," Matt yelled.

"Wait, I've got a better idea."

Zeke stomped on the gas sending the tires squealing as he held the car in place. Burning his tires on the cement, smoke spiraled back onto the officers. Matt watched in amazement as the cops ran from the smoke coughing and holding their noses. Victory, however, was short-lived as an officer appeared at the window spitting smoke.

"You – eh, are under –"

Zeke slammed his foot on the accelerator. "No, we're not!"

The officers dashed back to their cars and set out after them.

"Mo," Zeke yelled into his earpiece. "I'm running out of tricks here. Where's Lily?"

The heavy bat slammed on the pavement next to Lily with a loud crack. She cringed in fright and turned her gaze up to a pair of evil eyes.

"Heh, scare ya'?" Randy asked maliciously. "Good. Ya' ought ta be scared. It was you and yer jerk-off friends tha' got me expelled. Now it's time for a little … payback. By the time this is all over, yer all gonna be expelled."

He raised the bat off the ground and rested it on his shoulder. "What are ya' guys doin' anyway?"

Lily lay motionless on the ground, hurt, unable to speak.

"Looks like yer all makin' a mess out in the parkin' lot," he said. "I've been watching ya' guys for a long time. I can't wait to beat the heck outta ya' and watch the police lock ya' away. I'll be outta here in no time, way before the cops come to find ya'."

Randy tossed the bat in the air and snatched it on its way down. "But enough talkin'. It's time ta play."

Lily turned and tried to crawl away but found herself at the end of the alley, nothing but a brick wall behind her.

"Nowhere to go, midget." He grinned. "You're mine."

Lily prayed that she would live through this. She didn't want to die. She felt so small and insignificant compared to Randy's enormous figure. Cringing, Lily waited for the blow she knew was to come.

Setting her hand down to brace herself, her fingertips brushed up against a large chunk of chipped brick. She grabbed it and a small ounce of hope filled her heart.

This giant came at her with his bat ready. Lily's mind filled with the words of her youth pastor, Neil, when he had spoken of David and the giant he faced. Now, she needed the faith of David. She had to believe that God had His hand on her, that God was in control even when things seemed impossible.

She gripped the chunk of brick.

Randy sneered as he raised the bat to strike. "Wanna play?" he began. "You nasty little –"

Lily reared back and heaved the brick with all her might toward Randy's face.

The brick seared the air. It struck Randy's forehead with enough force to whip his head back. The giant staggered a moment. He tried to utter something as he reached out for the wall.

His knees wobbled and collapsed under him. He fell to the ground in a heap as blood seeped from his forehead.

Lily gazed at what she'd done with wonder. She crawled to him, knelt and with a sigh of relief saw his chest rise, knocked out – not dead. Grabbing the chunk of brick from the ground with a shaking hand, she squeezed it and kissed it.

"Thank you, God," she said and then pocketed it. "Thank you, thank you, thank you …"

She turned her attention back to the vent.

Rose looked from the edge of the woods toward the parking lot and saw Zeke maneuver his way around the police cars and take off again.

"Keep moving, Rose," Abby hissed.

Rose recoiled in sudden anger. "Well, excuse me for making sure my boyfriend is okay."

She stopped and watched as Zeke's car whipped around a curb missing one of the honking squad cars.

"Hey, we have a job to do," Abby continued. "They have theirs. So keep moving."

Abby grabbed Rose and spun her around.

"Let go of me!" Rose yelled as thoughts of people touching her came to mind.

She wasn't normally this angry but, since the incident with Fears she was irritable with everyone – everyone except Matt.

"No, you listen to me," Abby exclaimed over her. "If you want to see your boyfriend safe, then you'd better stick to the plan. We each have to do our part. Matt knew that he would be in this kind of danger when he made the plan."

"I'm going to do what I'm supposed to," Rose lashed back. "What do you have to do that's so important, huh? You just have to flip a switch. Am I right? Oh, big job."

Abby went silent.

"That's right," Rose spat. She turned around and continued toward the backside of the school.

"I have a role to play in all this too, you know," Abby called after her.

"That's not the way I heard it," Rose called back over her shoulder. "I heard that you were too scared and were forced to join the group. You don't care about Matt's cause."

"Yes, I do," Abby shouted. "I've been right there working with the group since the first day. You showed up because Jesse got hurt. You're not a part of the group. You're just … you're just a substitute."

Anger flooded Rose's heart. Her fiery eyes fixated on Abby.

"Say it again! I dare you to say it again! You think you're got it all figured out, don't you? You've got no idea what's happened to me!"

"Do you really want to –?"

"Hey," Abby heard Mo in her ear. "Are you in position?"

Abby stopped and came to her senses. "Yeah, uh, just about."

"You'd better get there quick. Lily's almost to the shop room."

"All right," Abby replied.

She picked up her bag and looked at Rose. "We both have a job to do. I'm going to do my part. You go do whatever you're supposed to do. But I want you to know that you're no teammate of mine. Now get out of my way."

Abby angrily bumped Rose's shoulder with hers as she passed.

Rose wanted to rip Abby's hair out even though she knew she was right. She did have to stay on task. That was the only way the heist would work.

Blue and red lights flashed all around Zeke's car. He'd kept away from them so far but it was becoming increasingly difficult. Speeding down the driveway, he hit the brake and took off in the opposite direction sending the cop cars reeling.

"Stop," the loudspeaker sounded. "Or we'll be forced to open fire."

Zeke looked in his rearview mirror and raised his eyebrows. "Are you serio –?"

Sparks scattered as bullets bounced off the pavement.

"Holy –!"

"Get down," Matt yelled as he ducked beneath the dash.

"We don't have any more time, Mo," Zeke hollered into his earpiece. "I'm headin' for the shop room. If Lily's not there, it's all for nothin'."

"Zeke, she's not in position," he heard Mo say. "The garage door isn't open yet."

"Well, it better be by the time I get there. The cops are freakin' shootin' at us!"

"Lily," Mo exclaimed. "Where are you?"

Lily came to an intersection in the vent.

"Mo," she said. "It's a left at the intersection, right?"

"Right."

"Right?"

"No, left."

"Is it a left or a right?"

"Left."

"Okay, I'm going left."

"Right."

"You're impossible."

"Lily, listen to me. We don't have time for this. Zeke and Matt are getting shot at. They are heading for the garage right now. If you're not there …"

Lily cursed under her breath. Turning left, she scrambled down the filthy shaft. She suddenly felt a rumble in the shaft and a whoosh of air came up from behind her. She coughed again. The air system wasn't helping anything.

Lily grunted as she tripped and fell. She stood and hunched over so not to hit her head and continued down the shaft. Dust flew around her face. Her nose tickled and she sneezed again, almost missing the second intersection.

"Mo," she said. "I passed the next intersection. Now I turn right, right?"

"Right."

"Good. I can see the shop room. I'll be right there."

Lily kicked open the vent from inside the shaft and hopped down to the floor. She ran around the Nissan they'd put in the garage earlier and went to the other garage on the far side of the large room.

"Okay, Mo. I'm in the shop room."

She could hear sirens and engines outside.

"Quick, Lily. Zeke and Matt are coming down the drive. Open the garage door and get out of the way!"

"Okay," Lily cried as she reached up and pushed the button.

Nothing.

She pushed the button again.

Nothing.

Lily's jaw dropped when she saw the tangled chain holding the garage door. The garage door was jammed.

"Oh, no …"

Zeke pulled onto the drive that ran down the side of the school and kept accelerating, palms gripping the wheel tighter than ever while Matt braced himself on the dash with his head down to avoid getting shot.

The brick of the building flew past them in a quick blur as the corner approached.

"You ready, Matt?" Zeke asked anxiously.

"How many times did you attempt this, Zeke?"

"Dozens."

"And how many times did you do it right?"

"Five."

"Oh ..." Matt gulped. "Great."

"Hang on!" Zeke shouted.

Matt closed his eyes and prayed that the door would be open.

Lily pushed the button a third time. The garage door didn't move.

"Oh, dear God ..." she cried as sweat appeared on her brow.

Looking up, Lily saw the red emergency cord dangling from the ceiling. She'd seen a cord like that in her own garage at home. If she pulled it, she'd be able to lift the garage door by hand.

Lily spotted a pile of wooden crates she could climb on in order to reach it. Cursing her small body, she heaved a crate underneath the cord and then one more. She scrambled up the crates and yanked downward on the cord.

Leaping off the crates, she jerked up with all her might on the garage door and it flew open.

She had no time to celebrate with Zeke's Nissan sliding right for her, she screamed in fright and leaped out of the way of the oncoming car.

The tires squealed as Zeke spun the wheel trying to get the car in the garage. The side mirror missed the edge of the garage door by less than an inch as he whipped inside, crashing into Lily's stack of crates that tumbled to the ground.

Matt jumped out of the car before Zeke had brought it to a complete stop, grabbed the garage door and slammed it shut just as the officers sped around the corner of the school.

Matt gasped for air. His whole body was quivering with fear. He looked at Lily and quavered, "Are – are you all right, Lil?"

Dropping to his knees, he noticed she was quivering out of control.

"The button ..." she whimpered. "It – it wouldn't ... I couldn't ... The car was going ..."

"Shh ... shh ..." he said softly.

But she went on, "The button ... Randy was –"

Sounds from outside interrupted her. Tires skidded to a stop on the other side of the garage door. The officers would be trying to get in before long.

"The garage is surrounded," said a voice from the loudspeaker. "Come out with your hands above your head!"

"Zeke," Matt called as he opened the driver side door.

Zeke's hands were frozen to the wheel and a tear ran down his cheek. Just above a whisper, he managed to say, "I did it … I actually did it."

"Heck yeah, you did," Matt replied. "But it's not over yet. We still have loads to do."

"Right." Zeke's voice was weak. "I'm right behind ya'."

27

"Abby, are you in position?" Mo asked.

Abby took the key out of her pocket and unlocked the door to the power building. Stepping inside the small building, she shut the door and turned on her flashlight. "Yeah, I'm set."

"Okay, you should see a large fuse box on the left wall, correct?"

Abby shined her light on the box and opened the small door. "Yeah, I see it."

"Okay, when I give the signal, flip all the switches on the far right column, okay? That will knock the power out of the school for thirty seconds before the backup generator kicks in."

"Okay, I got it."

"Good. Then, just sit tight for a sec."

"Rose, can you hear me?" Mo hissed.

Rose was on the edge of the woods directly behind the shop room garages.

"Yeah," she replied.

"Can you see the garage doors?"

"Yeah, they're right in front of me."

"Have you found the string of firecrackers yet?"

Rose squinted in the darkness as she felt around for the firecrackers that Zeke, Jake and Lily had set earlier. Her hands fell on a string. She grabbed it and held it up in the moonlight. The fuse snaked into the driveway and attached to another line of firecrackers.

"Yeah, I've got them."

"Okay, when Abby hits the power, you have to light them, remember? You got the lighter?"

Rose reached in her pocket. "Got it right here."

"Good. Wait for the signal."

"Matt," Mo said. "Are you and Zeke set?"

Zeke and Lily had settled into the first Nissan that they had parked in the garage earlier, Zeke in the driver's seat and Lily in the passenger's seat.

Matt stood by the garage door with two smoke bombs and a lighter. He turned to Zeke in the car. Looking through the windshield, he saw Zeke put another piece of bubble gum in his mouth.

"Zeke, are you set?" Matt hissed.

Zeke gave thumbs up and threw the gum wrapper in the back seat.

"Yeah, Mo. We're set," Matt said.

"Okay," Mo answered. "As soon as you hear firecrackers, open the garage door so Zeke and Lily can get out of there."

"Gotcha."

"Listen for the firecrackers."

Officer Dave stood outside the first garage and looked at the other officers. "Come on, Frank," he said. "Let's go around the front. We'll intercept them inside."

That's when everything went dark.

Crawford was watching the action on the monitors when the system suddenly shut down, not just the security system, everything. The whole room went black.

Dave looked to his partner. "Frank, what the heck happened to the –"

Loud popping sounds sprung from the edge of the woods. Dave jumped, surprised as flashes of blinding light exploded in the darkness. The officers jumped behind their cars pulling their sidearms from their holsters. Suddenly, sparks flew all around them as the firecrackers beneath their squad cars detonated.

"Someone's shootin' at us!" Frank shouted as he used his arm to shield his face.

Two large funnels of smoke flew out of the garage door ten feet away and landed in the driveway right next to one of the cop cars.

"Smoke," someone yelled over the loud bursts coming from the woods.

The garage door was thrown open and the Nissan's tires squealed as it peeled out of the garage and down the drive.

Dave curled his lips in his frustration. He hadn't expected anything to come out of the other garage.

"There's the car!" Dave yelled as the popping slowed. "Let's go."

The officers jumped in their cars and took off after Zeke. Within seconds, the parking lot was empty and silent.

Thirty seconds later, the monitors blinked to life much to Crawford's relief. However, when he scanned the camera screens, the squad cars were gone.

"What the —? Where . . ?"

Crawford typed in a few keystrokes but nothing happened. He slammed his fist on the table in frustration. Grabbing his hat, he headed for the door. If the cameras wouldn't tell him what was going on then he would go and investigate the area himself.

Matt blinked through his thick mask as he peered down the hall from the shop room before proceeding.

He saw nothing but darkness ahead of him.

Hitching his backpack onto his shoulder, Matt slipped into the hall.

"Matt," Mo said in his ear.

"What?"

"I'd be careful. I just saw another officer in one of the cameras. I don't think all the cops have left the building yet. There may have been another one in the camera room."

Oh, great, Matt thought, like I don't have enough to worry about already.

Approaching the end of the hall, Matt found himself in the cafeteria. He looked at the balconies above him.

"Do you see or hear anything?" Mo asked.

"Nothing."

"Look down toward the camera room. What about there?"

Matt leaned his head around the corner. The camera room was dark and he couldn't hear any noise coming from it.

"It's all quiet."

"Too quiet," Mo added.

Matt smirked. "Shut up."

"Come on, Matt. Get to the office. We can be done with this in no time if you hurry."

"Right. I'm going. I'm going."

Matt had stepped into the cafeteria when the hairs on the back of his neck bristled. Something wasn't right. He glanced around but saw only darkness.

He pushed the warning to the back of his mind. Looking around, he crossed the cafeteria and approached the office. Pulling a small piece of paper from his pocket, he looked at the digital lock on the door handle.

There were four codes listed. He punched the first one in and the digital lock blinked red. That obviously was not the correct one. He read the next code and punched it in. On the third try, the lock blinked green. As the door clicked open, he smiled for the first time in what seemed like ages.

Matt stepped into the vacant office and pushed the door closed. Making his way around the secretary's desk, he approached Dr. Pierce's office. Looking at his cheat sheet, he began to punch in another number but, as he did, he glanced through the window of Dr. Pierce's door.

The computer was gone. His heart skipped a beat. He spun around as if expecting someone to be standing there but there was nothing.

He put his hand to his ear. "Uh ... Mo?"

"What?"

"We have a slight problem."

"What? What's wrong?"

"The computer's gone."

"'Gone'? What do you mean 'gone'?"

"I mean not here, vanished, moved, disappeared, absent, gone!"

"Okay, calm down. It's gotta be there somewhere. Fears can't access the network outside the building. Hang on a second, lemme rewind the camera footage to see if it shows anything."

Someone had to have known they were coming. That was the only logical explanation. There was no other reason why anyone would have taken the computer. Could Fears have known they were coming tonight? No, he couldn't, could he?

He might have. He knew when he could kill Newt. Why wouldn't he be able to figure this out?

Matt pushed these thoughts aside. He couldn't worry about that now. He needed to find the computer and do what he had to do. The cops who left to aid the fake accident would be back soon. He didn't have much time. Matt left the office, walked past the secretary's desk and had reached for the door when he heard, "Hey, Matt, I've got something."

Matt stopped in his tracks. "What? What did you find?"

"I'm watching footage of the basketball banquet after Andrew and Lily left. Someone went into the office and took the computer at … nine nineteen p.m."

"Where?" Matt hissed. "Where'd they computer?"

"Whoever took it, took it to the … furnace room. Ground floor."

Matt knew the furnace room well. It was the same room where he'd found Jesse all those months ago.

"Who took it?" Matt asked. "Can you tell?"

"No, he's got his head down but if I had to guess, I'd say it was Fears."

"All right," Matt said. "I'm on my way."

"Look out!" Lily screamed as Zeke veered into oncoming traffic.

Two cars swerved out of Zeke's way, the drivers screaming at him. Zeke hadn't expected this many cars to be on the road. It was just past midnight. Who on earth would be out at this time on a Sunday?

Zeke jerked on the wheel to avoid another car sending his back end reeling. Lily screamed, as an approaching car had to swerve onto the shoulder to avoid them.

"Would you watch where you're going?" Lily hollered.

"Would you like to drive?" Zeke shouted back glancing in his rearview mirror.

The two squad cars had just pulled out onto the highway. Their sirens and flashing lights were closing in on them. Zeke squeezed the wheel and looked ahead to the four-way intersection. The light was red. He could see a couple cars crossing in the intersection.

"Uh, oh," Zeke muttered.

"What, 'uh, oh'?" Lily peered over the dash. "Uh, oh …"

"This is gonna be a little tricky," Zeke roared as he pushed harder on the gas.

Lily ducked down and put her hands over her head.

"You're crazy!"

Gripping the wheel, Zeke zipped in between the two cars in the intersection. Numerous honks erupted as he did so. Looking in his rearview mirror, Zeke saw two black stripes of smoking rubber on the pavement and drivers waving impolite hand gestures out their windows.

Zeke straightened the car. The police cars flew through the intersection and were soon gaining on him.

Lily opened her eyes and glanced around. "We're alive. I don't believe it!"

She turned and stared at the squad cars.

"Are ya' enjoyin' the view?" Zeke asked irritably. "Why don't ya' take a picture? Get down! They'll see ya'. What do ya' think this is, a joy ride? And get yer seatbelt on!"

Lily sat back in her seat. "It's a little late for that," she said as she pulled her seatbelt over her body.

The buildings and businesses on either side of the road rushed past them in a blurry haze. Zeke glanced out the window to see where they were. He needed to get to the railroad tracks free and clear. Only then would they have a chance of making it. As his car flew down the highway, Zeke rolled down his window and spit his wad of gum out the window.

"What are you doing?" Lily asked.

"Sorry," he replied. "Nerves."

Lily was in disbelief as Zeke passed two more stop signs. Ahead she could see another four-way stop. She knew they needed to make a right turn but Zeke wasn't slowing down.

Lily peered over the dash. "Aren't you supposed to turn right?"

Sweat broke on Zeke's brow. "Yeah."

"Well, don't you think you should slow down a bit?"

"Nope!" Zeke yelled and jerking his weight in his seat, he swerved around the corner only to find himself in the wrong lane. About thirty feet in front of them, a large, red semi truck headed straight for them. The truck's headlights blinded Zeke. The driver honked his horn, his tires howling in an attempt to stop.

"Dear God –!" Lily began as she held the door.

Zeke veered onto the left shoulder and flew past the semi. Lily screamed again as Zeke pulled back into oncoming traffic to get in the correct lane.

Zeke eyed Lily. "Aren't ya' glad ya' got that seatbelt on?"

Lily started to retort something but Zeke didn't hear it through the squad cars that appeared on either side of the car with their sirens blasting.

Zeke knew he would have to get some distance between them in the next mile or so in order to could cross over the train tracks and leave the cops behind him.

The officers yelled through the loudspeaker, "Pull over. I repeat, pull your vehicle over. You are in violation of the law!"

"No joke," Zeke muttered under his breath. "You gotta be kiddin'."

Suddenly, he heard Mo in his ear. "Hey, whatcha guys up to?"

"Who, us?" Zeke answered sarcastically. "Not much really. Lily and I stopped at McDonald's to have a shake. We're sittin' here debatin' politics. What do ya' think is up, ya' idiot? Cops are all over us!"

"Where are you?"

"About a half a mile from the tracks. We're gonna be cuttin' it close."

"Just keep heading down –"

Zeke didn't hear the rest of Mo's response because a squad car smashed into Zeke's backside. Lily cried out in surprise.

As Zeke tried to straighten the wheel, the second squad car collided with the other side.

Zeke overcompensated his turn on the wheel and went into a wild spin. Lily screamed again and grabbed onto anything she could while Zeke braced himself on the wheel. The car completed one and a half spins before stopping in the middle of the highway.

Both Zeke and Lily gasped, sweat pouring down their faces. As Zeke looked out the window, he could see the squad cars stopped and the officers getting out with weapons and handcuffs ready. Zeke turned the key. He could hear the whine of the car, but it didn't start. The car had stalled.

"Oh, no …" Zeke gasped. "This isn't good."

"Wha – what's wrong?" Lily asked.

"The car won't start!"

"It won't what?"

"Mo," Zeke called in his earpiece. "Mo, do ya' read me?"

Andrew was on the train tracks and around the curve just as Matt had instructed when they'd recorded the train sounds. On the tracks sat the large wooden structure that he and Abby had made. This was their fake train.

The train looked like a tall ladder. The difference was that a large spotlight was fastened on the top with a few pieces of wood. There was also an oversized speaker plugged into a stereo with the train sounds they'd recorded earlier.

When Zeke passed over the tracks, Andrew would trip the railroad crossing bar and cause it drop. Then he would turn on the bright spotlight on top of the "train".

Seeing the spotlight and hearing the recorded train sounds, the police would assume it was a real train and would be forced to stop. While they waited for the train to pass, Zeke would be able to get a good lead on them and get away. Of course, this would work only if Zeke timed it just right. He needed to be at least a hundred feet in front of the cops if he was to clear the tracks.

"Andrew," Mo hissed in his ear. "Andrew, do you copy?"

"Yeah. What's up, Mo?"

"The cops have stopped Zeke and Lily. Their car is stalled. They're goners for sure."

"What?"

Andrew grabbed a pair of binoculars off his dash and peered through the woods for Zeke's car. When he finally spotted it, he could see the smoke coming up from under the hood. Cops were storming around with weapons drawn and pointed at the car.

"Oh, man ..." Andrew muttered to himself. "What do ya' want me to do, Mo?"

"I don't know," Mo exclaimed. "Can't you do something? Anything?"

"I'm just not sure what –" Andrew began when Muffin started to lick his face. "Muffin, stop it!"

"What?" Mo asked. "What was that?"

"Nothing. It's just Muffin."

Andrew paused and looked at his dog. Muffin looked at him and opened his mouth allowing his tongue to dangle.

"Wait," Andrew said. "I've got an idea. Move over, Muff!"

Andrew started his truck and took off leaving the fake train on the tracks.

Officer Crawford left his post at the camera room and went to inspect what had happened outside the shop room. The garage door was open and there was a Nissan parked in the shop room.

He frowned. It looked like the same Nissan he'd seen earlier. But if that was the Nissan then where were the drivers and the officers? He pulled his sidearm from its holster and started out into the driveway.

Outside, he stared at a large pile of what seemed to be confetti where the squad cars had been parked. Kneeling, he adjusted his glasses and grabbed a handful of whatever it was. Putting it to his nose, he sniffed. He could immediately tell that the pieces were the remains of firecrackers.

As he stood, he heard a crunch. On the pavement was a small round ball. Crawford recognized it – a smoke bomb.

"Hmm ..."

He pulled out his flashlight and looked across the driveway at the edge of the woods. More firework remains lay in the grass. Approaching the edge of the woods, he heard the crunching of leaves.

Shining his flashlight into the woods, he knew that someone had lit those firecrackers and he believed that that someone was very close.

The truth was that Rose was no more than ten feet away from Officer Crawford. She hoped that her camouflage blended in enough so the officer couldn't see her. She tried to steady her breathing but it was getting more and more difficult with every step the officer took.

Without enough patience to look in the woods for her, switched the safety button off his sidearm and shot one round into the night sky. The boom echoed in the stillness of the night like rolling thunder.

Rose cringed at the noise. If the officer was just trying to scare her, it was working.

"I know you're out here," the officer called into the thick woods. "Just come on out, so you don't get into anymore trouble."

Rose blinked away tears of fright.

The officer shot another round into the sky sending another enormous echo across the area. Rose flinched and gave a short cry. The officer cocked his head at the noise and approached the large tree where Rose was curled in terror. He grinned as he shined his light on the girl.

Too scared to move, all Rose could do was lie still. Maybe if she were perfectly still, the officer wouldn't see her. She held her breath … hoping … praying … he didn't see her.

"Well, well, well," the officer said. "Look what I found."

He grabbed Rose off the ground, looked her over, and then pushed his glasses farther up on his nose.

"You're Mr. Hudson's girl, aren't you? Rose, right? Did I find a little Rose in the bush?" He snickered at his own joke.

Rose stared at the ground.

"Hey," the officer said. He snapped his fingers in front of her face. She didn't move.

He pulled his handcuffs from his belt, yanked her arms behind her back and snapped the cuffs tightly around her wrists. Grabbing her arm, he led her around the building.

"I'm sure your father's going to have a big time trying to clear you of this one," he said. "The firecrackers, the smoke bombs, knocking the cameras out, it was all genius. But I'm afraid you are under arrest and your friends will soon be caught as well."

The officer kept talking but Rose wasn't listening. She looked at the small power building and could see the door ajar. She saw Abby looking at her from the crack. Raising her eyebrows, Rose cocked her head toward the officer with a pleading expression.

Abby shook her head and slowly shrank back into the shadows.

Tears slowly streamed down filled Rose's face. Now she was truly alone.

Unaware of what was happening outside the school, Matt crept along the wall of the deserted hall. Trying to calm himself, he took three deep breaths and counted to ten. It didn't help.

As Matt cautiously crossed the cafeteria, the hairs on the back of his neck bristled again. He didn't know what the warning meant but he made sure to survey everything before moving on down the hall.

As he approached the furnace room, he whispered, "Mo, are you there?"

"Yeah, Matt,"

"I'm almost to the furnace room."

"Okay. I'll tell you how to hack into the computer once you're inside."

Matt grabbed the doorknob and noticed that the door was unlocked. He turned the handle, pulled the door open and peeked inside at a pitch-black room. His only source of light source came from the dim hallway.

He took three steps forward, out of reach of the light and began to feel around in the darkness. He stopped when something shuffled behind him near the door. He spun back toward the door to see it slam shut.

The room filled with darkness.

Matt extended his hands wanting to grab anything that could be of use but there was nothing.

"He – hello?"

Silence.

"Is … is someone in here?" he asked nervously.

He was afraid to find out. He wanted to run. Things had gone too far. It was time to leave but his feet were glued to the floor.

Everything around him was silent.

"Hello?" he asked again.

Someone pulled the string on the light bulb on the ceiling and light flooded the room. Matt squinted. As his eyes adjusted to the light, he saw a gun pointed directly at his chest.

"Congratulations, Mr. Cross," a wicked voice sneered. "You caught me."

28

"That night, the cat slept with me and wouldn't leave me alone all the next day," Bruce went on recounting his travels to Mary who sat on the other side of Jesse's hospital bed.

Mary laughed. "Then how did you get rid of it?"

"Well, that's a whole 'nother story in itself. See my friend –"

Jesse's hand twitched, disturbing the sheets.

"Did you see that?" Bruce asked.

Mary looked at Jesse. "See what?"

Jesse's hand twitched again.

"That."

Both eyed Jesse waiting for something to happen. Suddenly, Jesse gave a short groan.

Mary jumped up and leaned over him. "Jesse ... honey? It's Mary. Can you hear me?"

Jesse groaned again.

"Jesse?" Mary said gently. "Can you open your eyes, sweetheart?"

He moaned and turned his head slightly.

"There you go, sweetie." She motioned for Bruce to come and help her.

"Hey, boy," Bruce said. "Can ya' open your eyes a little for us?"

Jesse raised his eyelids, gave a long sigh and tried to say something but it was only a weak murmur.

"What, babe?" Mary asked. "What did you say?"

"Where's ... Matt?" he mumbled.

"He's at home." Mary checked her watch. "He's probably sleeping right now."

"Are y –" Jesse coughed.

He paused a moment and tried again.

"Are you … sure?"

"Yeah," Bruce said. "He said he was gonna stay home. Why?"

"I don't … I don't think he's … home."

"Where else would he be?" Mary asked.

"With …" Jesse sighed.

Mary frowned. "With who? With Rose?"

Jesse nodded.

Mary looked at Bruce. "Call the house just to be sure."

Bruce nodded, pulled his cell phone from his belt and dialed the house.

No one answered.

He looked to Mary. "Nothing."

"Call Rose's house," she said.

He did. "Nothing."

"He needs …" Jesse sighed. "… he's in trouble."

"Trouble? How do you know?" Mary asked.

"I c –" he gave a short cry. "I … know. Trust me."

"How would you know?"

"How long … how long has it been?" Jesse mumbled.

"Three days," Bruce answered.

Jesse groaned and sputtered, "Matt's … in t - trouble," he said. "He needs … needs you."

"Where is he?" Mary grew anxious. Thoughts of dread crept into her mind. What if Jesse was right and Matt was in trouble?

"Zeke … Zeke's shop," Jesse said. "You'll find him … Zeke."

Mary looked at Bruce.

"Why don't you go check? Just to make sure. I'm sure it won't take long."

Bruce looked at Jesse and back to Mary. He nodded. "Okay."

"Hurry … needs you."

Escorting Rose around the school, Office Crawford led her to his squad car. Rose thought his grip on her arm was much tighter than it needed to be. He was treating her as if she was some kind of criminal. Her mind jumped when a thought occurred to her.

From this point on, she was a criminal.

Opening the door, he put his hand on her head and pushed her into the back seat. He locked the door and shut it.

"I'll be right back," Crawford said through the window. "I've got to get the recordings of you and your buds doing your thing in the parking lot. Stay here. And no funny business."

Rose looked away. She was ashamed of herself for participating in this ludicrous heist. Matt had said the plan would work. He said there was no way it could fail, not if everyone did his or her part. Well, she'd done her part to the best of her ability, hadn't she?

She wished she hadn't lashed out at Abby. Maybe if she hadn't, she wouldn't be in this predicament, sitting here all alone. Now no one could do anything so she would just wait and –

A soft knock sounded on the window.

Startled, she looked up to see Abby standing there. Rose's spirits soared and she smiled. At last – hope.

"Help me get out of here," she said through the window.

"I'll try," Abby replied.

She grabbed the door handle and tried to open it but Crawford had it locked.

"Try opening it from your side," she said and pointed toward the lock.

Rose twisted in her seat and tried to open the door in spite of her handcuffs. That didn't work either. She shook her head.

Abby bit her lip and looked around the car as if there were a secret door she'd overlooked. Then, approaching the driver's side, she took off her shoe and raised it high over her head.

"Wait. You can't do that." Rose shook her head frantically. "Remember the rules?"

She heard Abby mutter, "We're past obeying the rules," but she put her shoe back on, headed for the front of the car and lifted the hood.

"What are you doing?" Rose hissed knowing Abby couldn't hear her.

A few minutes later, Abby had closed the hood and returned to the window with something in her hand.

"What's that?" Rose asked.

"The rotor," Abby said with a grin, putting it in her pocket. "I've learned a few things while working with Jake."

The school's front doors opened and Abby jumped and disappeared behind the car. Officer Crawford walked toward the car with the some discs in his hand. Not wanting Crawford to suspect anything, Rose didn't move or react.

Crawford got into the car and turned. "Miss me?" he asked sarcastically.

Rose looked away without expression.

Crawford shrugged, straightened himself in his seat, hooked his seat belt and attempted to start the car. The car sputtered but didn't start. Crawford cocked his head and turned the key again. Again, the car wheezed and coughed but refused to start.

He looked back at Rose. "You know anything about this?"

Rose was silent.

Crawford shook his head, heaved himself out of the car and lifted the front hood. Rose stared out the windows and hoped that Abby was hiding where Crawford wouldn't find her. She prayed that whatever Abby planned on doing, worked.

"Muffin, stay there." Andrew pushed his dog back into the passenger seat as he drove up to the scene. He could see the cops waving flashlights and yelling for Zeke and Lily to get out of their stalled car.

Andrew pulled his truck onto the shoulder about thirty yards from the scene. As he turned the motor off, one of the officers approached him. Rolling down the window, Muffin leaped into Andrew's lap.

"I'm sorry, sir," the officer kept his distance. "You're assistance is not needed here."

"Oh … yeah, uh, I know," Andrew said. "I've just got to go see a man about a dog."

Andrew chuckled but if the officer got the joke, he didn't show it.

"You see, my dog's gotta pee. I'm sure you know how it is with dogs, especially ones his size. Don't you worry. It'll only take a minute."

"Sir, I highly suggest that you and your dog —"

"Officer, would you want a dog to pee in your car?" Andrew asked as Muffin jumped out.

The officer was silent.

"I didn't think so." Andrew looked down at his dog. "Come on, Muffin. You said you had to go."

Escorting Muffin to the other side of his truck, Andrew took him to an open area where thin patches of grass were scattered over the sandy dirt. The officer returned to the scene while behind the truck, Andrew knelt and gazed into Muffin's clear eyes.

"Muffin, you see those men?" Andrew pointed to the officers. "*Bad* men. They're *real* bad men, Muffin. Get 'em. Go get 'em. Attack!"

Muffin growled and took off toward the officers. One of the officer saw Muffin coming, "Hey, there boy. Stop."

The other two officers, hearing the commotion, glanced up to see Muffin sprinting toward them, teeth bared and barking. A look of hatred glinted in Muffin's eyes as if he planned to tear these men to shreds in an instant.

"Sir," the officer called to Andrew. "Restrain your dog. Now!"

The officers took a few steps back from Zeke's car.

"Oh," Andrew called. "Sorry about that. He only acts that way when he smells bacon."

Andrew choked back laughter. He had to say it. How could he pass up the chance?

Muffin continued to bark, each time a little more fierce. Andrew could see the fear on all of their faces.

The officer's voice was shaky as he switched off the safety on his sidearm and called, "Sir, I'm warning you. Call your dog."

Noticing the gun, Andrew took a step forward. The cop wouldn't shoot Muffin, would he? Wasn't that illegal or something? The officer pointed the gun at Muffin's head. Muffin barked again and growled.

"Sir," the officer called again. "This is your last warning. Restrain your dog."

Andrew began to say something but stopped. He wanted to give Zeke just a little more time to get his car started.

The officer looked from Muffin to Andrew and back at Muffin. As he tightened his finger on the trigger, Muffin leaped. His teeth clamped down on the officer's hand and the gun dropped. Muffin jerked and yanked on the officer's hand as if it were a toy.

Screaming in pain, the officer tried to pull away, hitting Muffin's head with his other hand. Muffin hesitated and then let go, blood dripping from his snout.

As Muffin continued to bark and growl at the officers, Andrew grabbed him by his collar. Pulling against Andrew, Muffin threatened to tear into the officers.

"Sorry, you guys," Andrew said, "I'll get my dog outta here but you'd better keep your distance. He's a beast, I tell ya'. Sometimes he gets loose on me. You never know when he'll —"

Andrew released his hold on Muffin's collar and off Muffin took off after the closest officer. The officers backed up, turned and raced down the street away from the vicious beast.

Running up to Zeke's window, Andrew exclaimed, "Are you guys okay?"

Zeke rolled down the window and Lily nodded. "Yeah, we're fine now."

"Start your car," Andrew said.

"We can't," Zeke replied. "It won't start."

"Try it again," Andrew said.

Zeke turned the key and the engine roared to life.

"Didn't I say something about angels earlier?" Andrew beamed.

Zeke smiled and nodded.

"Muffin," Andrew called. "Muffin, come. You want a snack?"

Muffin immediately halted and dashed back to his master.

"See you at your shop, then?" Andrew asked.

"Yeah, I'll be —"

Zeke stopped.

"What?" Andrew frowned.

Zeke held up a finger. "Listen …"

Andrew paused as a heaving Muffin came to his side. A loud whistle blew in the distance. A train … a *real* train.

Andrew turned and saw the train's headlights through the foliage of the woods. As it passed the three of them, the whistle blew again. About a quarter of a mile down the road, the traffic bars at the railroad crossing began to blink and lower.

"I thought there weren't supposed to be any real trains tonight," Andrew exclaimed.

"Well, apparently there are!" Zeke retorted.

"Come on, come on, Zeke," Lily yelled. "We gotta get outta here!"

Zeke leaned out his window and glanced back at the officers who were sprinting back in their direction.

"Yeah, I'd say it's time to go," Zeke said to Andrew.

"I agree. Come on, Muffin!" Andrew yelled and ran for his truck.

Zeke shifted into gear, his tires squealing as he raced for the crossing. Looking in his rearview mirror, he saw Andrew come up behind him and behind Andrew, flashing lights.

Glancing out his window, Zeke saw the huge train alongside him heading toward the crossing. He threw his arms in the air. "Oh, this is just *fantastic*!"

Bruce threw open the garage door at Zeke and Jake's shop. Mo jerked up from his laptop in shock.

"Who are you?"

"Bruce," he replied as he moved toward him. "Matt Cross's uncle. Remember me?"

"Oh … Uh – yeah, I –"

"Do you know where Matt is?"

Mo closed his laptop and shook his head. "No, I haven't seen him since Friday."

"Bull," Bruce said sternly grabbing the armrests of Mo's wheelchair. Bending down, he looked Mo in the eye. "Tell me where my nephew is."

Mo's tongue felt thick and it became difficult to talk. "Well, he's uh … I'm just here because – uh …"

"Oh, come on! We both know that you know where Matt is. He might be hurt."

"How would you –?"

"Where is he?" Bruce's teeth clenched.

Mo spilled it all, everything that they had been up to for the last couple of months. He told Bruce how Fears was stealing money from the school and how they planned to stop him.

"That's crazy," Bruce exclaimed when Mo finished. "Matt would never do something like that."

"Since Jesse got hurt, he thought it was his duty to avenge him," Mo explained.

"Jesse got hurt in a lightning storm," Bruce retorted. "It had nothing to do with Fears."

Mo continued, "Jesse was in on the plan too but after Newt was killed he didn't want to participate. Jesse was afraid that someone else might get hurt. Then, he got in the accident. It all comes back to Fears, you see."

"Where's Matt now?"

"Hang on," Mo replied. "I'll call him."

He switched channels on the radio. "Matt. Matt, do you read me?"

No response.

Mo looked at Bruce who motioned for him to try again. Again, Mo called, "Matt, it's Mo. Do you read me?"

Nothing.

Then, suddenly, a male voice boomed over a bunch of feedback. "Mr. Cross is unavailable at the moment. In fact, Mr. Cross will be unavailable for a *very* long time. Have a nice day."

The line went dead.

Mo stared at the radio in shock.

"What?" Bruce cried. "Who was that?"

"It's Fears …" Mo said quietly. "It has to be. He must be inside the school. He's got Matt."

"Where?"

Mo pulled the blueprint of the school up on his laptop and pointed to the hall where the storage room was located.

"Last I heard from Matt, he was heading down this way toward the storage room on the first floor."

Mo looked up to see Bruce starting his truck. In seconds, he was gone.

Hands handcuffed to a pipe above his head and feet handcuffed together at the bottom, Matt stood in the darkness of the storage room. The man glared at him with evil eyes that penetrated the black wool mask.

"Well, if it isn't the hero?" the voice taunted.

In spite of the mask and loose clothing, Matt had identified many of Fears's features. The man was tall and muscular and carried himself with a military bearing. Matt wanted to spit in his face but restrained himself, fearing the man would use the gun he held in his large hand.

Walking over to Dr. Pierce's stolen computer, the man used his gun to point at the computer.

"You see this, Mr. Cross?" he snarled. "This is what we're both after. We're after the same thing, you know? And I must say you are either extremely smart or extremely lucky to have made it this far in the game."

He paused and studied the computer. Matt could see the LanCaster program downloading numbers.

The man's gaze turned back to Matt. "No, I think it's just luck but either way, this is where your luck ends."

Matt pursed his lips as anger and hatred for this man burst forward, just as it had when he found out what he'd done to Newt and Rose. This was the man that Matt hated with all of his being.

He'd destroyed the science labs.

He'd violated Rose.

He'd murdered Newt.

He'd been the cause of Jesse's accident.

Now, he was stealing millions of dollars right in front of his next victim.

This was the image of a lunatic.

Of all the different thoughts and questions that raced inside him, there was one blinding question he had to know the answer to before he died.

"Why would you do this?"

He grinned at Matt through his mask. "I've often asked myself that same question and I've come up with two answers of which both are equal in truth. It's the rush. Here I am stealing over three million dollars in taxes and no one cares – except you that is. It was so simple.

I come in, punch in a few numbers and bam, I'm rich. Now there's a thrill."

"Do you think you can do all this without punishment?" Matt exclaimed. "Just walk in and walk out untouched? One of these days, they'll catch you. You've got no idea what's going to happen to you."

Dark eyes glared at Matt. "You think I've walked in and out untouched? I paid my price."

He knelt to the ground, rolled up his right pant leg and extended his leg for Matt to see the two-inch pink scar that rose up his calf.

"I took a bullet for all this money, all this glory. That's quite a punishment, wouldn't you say?"

He unrolled his pant leg and stood. "And that leads me to my second reason – the money. Where else can you get three million dollars by just pushing a couple buttons? You don't think I could make this kind of money working at the school, do you?"

"What about all the innocent people?" Matt questioned.

"What people?"

"You killed my dog," Matt said through clenched teeth.

Hatred again flared as he thought of Newt lying dead in the hay.

"I had to have some way to show you that I meant business, Mr. Cross. I figured you would get my point. Apparently, you didn't. Besides, your dog is not a person. I have never murdered anyone. Yes, I killed your dog but it was only an animal, one I figured you cared about."

Matt yanked on his handcuffs until his wrists turned red. Ignoring the pain, he continued to jerk and twist. He wanted to lash out and strangle this man and a little pain wasn't going to keep him from doing so.

"What about Jesse?" Matt managed as he struggled.

"What about him?" he asked as he lazily sat on a stack of crates.

"He's in a coma and it's your fault."

"No, no," he said. "That's where our stories part ways."

"Yeah, right. You –"

"Ah, ah, ah …" the figure interrupted and held up his gun. "I talk and then you talk. If I don't want you to talk, you don't talk. If you talk out of turn, you won't talk again. Understand?"

Matt went still.

"Good, now where was I?"

He stood.

"Oh yes, the Jesse thing. I had nothing to do with Jesse's accident. I'll admit that I killed your dog. I'll even admit that I beckoned him to the barn and beat him with a shovel until there was no longer any life in him. I'll also admit that I threatened you afterward and said that you'd look like your dog if you tried to stop me. However, none of that has anything to do with Jesse."

"*Liar!*"

Matt yanked and pulled hard on the cuffs until blood dripped down his hand in small beads.

"You killed Newt and Jesse's gone because of you. What about Rose? Remember what you did to her?"

"Rose?" The man stopped. "What did I do to Rose?"

"When you grabbed her in the office," Matt hollered. "She said you were kissing her and touching her. That's what you did to her, you sick pervert."

The man paused and frowned. "I've never once laid my hands on Rose. I have no idea what you're talking about."

"More *lies*!" Matt roared as the handcuffs tore into his flesh. "I'll *kill* you. I swear I will. *I'll kill you!*"

Sitting back down on a stack of milk crates, the man laid his gun on the table and spun it like a top.

"I'd like to see you try," he said. "Your hands and feet are handcuffed to a pipe that goes down at least fifteen feet. Not to mention, through a concrete floor that's three feet thick. And …" He stopped his gun from spinning. "I have the gun."

"I *hate* you!"

He no longer cared about living or dying. He knew he was going to die. There was no hope. He'd been too naive to see it before. This monster, Fears, was going to kill him and nothing could change that fact.

"You're crazy," Matt cried. "You don't deserve any of this."

The man stood again. "Now there's where you're wrong. You see, Mr. Cross, there are two kinds of people in this world – people who want power and those who take it. I live in a world full of people who casually go to work, come home, exchange a few pleasantries with their kids, pray, eat dinner, make love occasionally and do it all over again the next day. They proclaim they are living happy and fulfilling lives. Ha! That's the biggest lie this world can ever impose on you.

"There's only way you can be truly happy and that's by taking the best thing this world has to offer you – power. In the society we live in, money is power. Let's just say, I'm seizing my opportunity. This is my defining moment. My glorious achievement is at hand and I'm not going to let *anyone* get in the way."

Matt continued to struggle.

The dark figure went on, "Haven't you dreamed of possessing power, Mr. Cross? Having things beyond your wildest imagination? You've been the big man in control during this ploy to catch me, haven't you? You wanted to catch me so bad that it became more about you than your stupid dog, didn't it? It may have originally started about me but the more power you gained, the more power you wanted. You wanted people to look up to you and wish that they had done what you did, didn't you?"

Matt stopped. He realized it was true. He had imagined his name in the paper and seeing himself on television. He wanted people to look up to him in awe. However, he pushed that thought away. He would never admit to it.

"You know you've had these thoughts, Mr. Cross, but you never acted on them. That's why I am greater than you, Mr. Cross. That's why I deserve this. That's why I will win and you … you will die."

"You're wrong," Matt hollered kicking at the pipe. "You're totally wrong. You're stealing from innocent people."

Matt could see another evil grin through the man's mask.

"Am I? Or are you too brainwashed to see the truth? Has society stuffed your brain so full of lies that you believe stealing is wrong? Okay, I'll give you that, so is cursing. So is lust. So is hatred. So is greed. Every other person on this earth has felt these feelings of want and power but how many act on them?

"You and I are exactly alike in almost every way. We both have dreams of wealth and power. The difference between you and me is one simple thing. I'm unafraid to take what I want."

Tears streamed down Matt's cheeks as he fought through the pain in his wrists. If only he could break free, he would show Fears who deserved it more. Matt imagined the look on Fears's face if he got out of his handcuffs.

"Take that stupid mask off, you coward," he demanded. "Face me like a real man, Fears."

The man burst out laughing.

"Ah, yes. Right, right, the whole 'Fears' thing. You never did quite figure that one out, did you?"

And with one yank, the mask was gone.

Shock ran through Matt and rendered him motionless.

The figure grinned. "Looks can be deceiving, can they not?"

Abby tried to remain absolutely still underneath the squad car. The officer's boots shuffled from one side of the car to the other as he contemplated his repair. She could hear him messing with something underneath the hood. He muttered something about how he wasn't supposed to have to fix his own car. Abby snickered under her breath and then Mo's voice spoke in her ear.

"Abby. Abby, are you there?"

She couldn't respond.

"Matt's in big trouble. Fears is inside the school. He's got Matt. You've got to try and help."

Abby glanced toward the officer's feet. They had stopped moving. Abby allowed only her eyes to move. Maybe the officer hadn't heard anything. He was probably –

"Well, hello, there." The officer's head appeared beneath the car.

His flashlight shining on her face caused Abby to blink and throw her arm up to protect her eyes.

"Man, is it my lucky day or what?" the officer asked himself. "Come on out."

Abby reluctantly obeyed. Glancing in the back window, she could see Rose's expression of dismay. Abby stood and the officer put a second pair of handcuffs on her.

"Sir, please," Abby said. "A friend of mine is still in the school. Mr. Fears is in there with him."

"Mr. Fears?" The officer asked as he opened the back door and threw her in alongside Rose. "There isn't anything left in that school, Miss. I've been scanning every hall in there all night. Trust me."

Abby began to speak but the officer slammed the door in her face. Abby hung her head.

"What's wrong?" Rose asked.

"Matt's in trouble," Abby replied. "Fears has him inside the school."

Rose's eyes went wide at the news. "Fears . . ?"

She felt like crying. Now, there was nothing that anyone could do.

Zeke glanced at the speeding train, then through his side mirror at Andrew behind him and then, finally, back at the train again. With eyes full of fear and a deathly pale face, Zeke felt the cold sweat run down his brow. If not glued to the steering wheel, his fingers would be shaking.

Lily sat on the passenger side, frozen stiff, her knees and elbows locked. Back straight against the seat, her eyes darted from the train and then back to the tracks every other second or so.

The crossing was less than a one hundred feet away. Zeke could see the two red and yellow crossing bars blocking the tracks ahead. He had no choice but to race across and hope he and Lily made it out okay. Andrew's truck tailgated Zeke's bumper.

Bringing up the rear, Andrew was in a much worse position than Zeke. Zeke knew that if he made it across the track, the train would then be right on top of Andrew.

The train sounded again as Zeke, Andrew and the police cars charged toward the crossing. Zeke felt the roar of Andrew's truck on top of him. He didn't even want to think about the possibility of not making it across the tracks. There was no way the train could stop in time.

A large crash outside his window caused Zeke and Lily to snap their heads toward the train. Without slowing, the train had smashed into Andrew's fake wooden train. Pieces of wood exploded and the headlight on top of the contraption was crushed beneath the train. Sparks erupted from the stereo as if thrown from the top of a building. Zeke's heart skipped a beat, hoping his fate wouldn't be the same as Andrew's train.

HILLS

    Hands aching from squeezing the wheel, Zeke clenched his teeth as though they would pop out of his head. His leg locked in place, the accelerator solid against the floor, the crossing bars came into full view. From no more than thirty feet away, the monstrous train bore down on them as it barreled into the crossing.
    Zeke's heart pounded, sweat rolled, sirens blared and engines roared and Zeke heard a deafening yell burst from somewhere inside him as he pressed the accelerated through the floor.
    Nineteen feet.
    Lily shrieked. She covered her face.
    Twelve feet.
    The train thundered down the tracks.
    Eight feet.
    Someone screamed. Another cried.
    Three feet.
    Stretching his mouth wider, Zeke bellowed as the car crashed through the first crossing bar, snapping it like a twig. His windshield cracked. Over the tracks he flew, through the second bar. Glass from his windshield shattered in all directions.
    Zeke cleared the tracks, stomped the brakes and twisted in his seat to see Andrew's truck go airborne and soar right overt the tracks. The giant train howled as it snagged the swinging angel ornament from the hitch of Andrew's back bumper.
    Andrew's tires reached the cement and Zeke watched him bounce inside the truck. Andrew slammed on the brakes, slowed and then stopped next to Zeke on the highway.
    Over the roar of the train, Zeke could hear the squeal of the officers' tires as they screeched to a stop on the other side of the train. Sirens echoed through the night sky.
    Andrew and Zeke leaned back in their seats, chests heaving while Lily continued to weep with her hands covering her face.
    Looking out his window, Zeke saw Andrew thanking God for His miraculous intervention. Zeke silently thanked Him for not letting the three of them become one with the train track.
    A grin emerged on Andrew's face as he rolled down his window.
    "Angels?" Andrew asked.

"Yeah." Zeke nodded as he leaned his head back on his seat. "Angels."

They breathed hard as the train rolled on past them.

"Hey, Zeke?" Andrew called.

"Yeah, man?"

"Do ya' want to do it all over again so we can feel this rush when we're done?"

Zeke shook his head with a hint of a smile.

"I'd have to kill you."

On the other side of the train, Officer Dave jumped out of his squad car and threw his hat on the ground. He imagined the drivers speeding away thinking they'd beat the cops. The idea infuriated him. He sat back in his car.

Then Frank said, "Hey, Dave, didn't two of our guys get a call to go assist an accident or something before that Nissan showed up?"

"Yeah," Dave replied. "Yeah, that's right. Weren't they heading down this highway?"

Frank thought a moment. "Yeah, they were headed for Fate's Crossing."

"Call 'em up."

Frank grabbed his radio and made the call.

Looking for the accident, the two officers had traveled seven miles past the train tracks, each of them in different squad cars.

Officer Patterson was a middle-aged man. He ran his hand through his short brown hair with an expression of determination. His partner, Officer Taylor, younger by three years and trying to prove he was as capable as any experienced officer, had no trouble keeping up with Patterson.

The two had searched Highway Sixty-six for at least half an hour, traveling to Fate's Crossing and back again with no sign of an accident. Taylor grabbed the radio and called Patterson.

"Do you think it could have been a prank? Over."

"No," Patterson replied, "It couldn't have been. We had two different reports of it."

"Well accidents like that don't just disappear," Taylor gripped.

Patterson didn't respond and a few minutes later, the radio blared in the silence of the vehicle. "Four-sixteen to four-twenty-five. Do you copy? Over."

Taylor grabbed the radio.

"This is Four-twenty-five. Go ahead."

"There is a black 1980 Nissan and a red '98 Chevrolet heading your way. We have reason to believe that they're the ones who've been breaking into the high school. We were in hot pursuit but the train passed and separated us. They're headed down Highway Sixty-six. We need you to intercept them immediately. Over."

"Yes, sir," Taylor replied.

Patterson hit the brakes, pulled a quick U-turn and headed in the opposite direction towards the train tracks with Taylor close behind.

"We'll get them."

29

Matt was speechless. Any sliver of hope Matt had, vanished when the man pulled off his mask. He and his friends had made so many preparations for this one night. His friends were risking their lives so they could expose the school's most hated faculty member. Now, all of this effort would come crashing down like a glass tower.

All hope was lost.

Matt could no longer recall being happy. Every feeling evaporated from his mind. Only loneliness swept over him as Rose's father, Mr. Hudson, laughed in his face.

"You seem surprised to see me."

Matt couldn't reply.

"Well, I'd probably be surprised, too. I mean, after all you did think I was Fears."

It couldn't be true. Fears had done it. Fears was the intruder. Matt forced himself to speak.

"I – I saw Fears in Dr. Pierce's office. He was stealing the tax money."

Hudson smirked. "You probably saw that fool trying to find out what I had done to the system. He knew I'd made some changes and was trying to change it back."

"But he entered an account number from his wallet …" Matt murmured as thoughts bounced in his head. "I saw Fears in Dr. Pierce's office at the festival."

"Ah, yes," Hudson said, "the account numbers. You *thought* you saw Fears putting tax money into his own account, right? Well, what you failed to see was he was putting in one of the school's account numbers. Don't ever assume anything. You know what they say about people who assume too much."

Matt wasn't listening. "Fears was trying to stop you? What about Newt?"

"Ah, as I said before," the man replied. "I lured him into the barn and beat the life out of him with a shovel."

"… but you were working the night Newt was killed, over in Hills East."

"Yes, I 'got called to work'," Hudson said. "I beeped myself, just as I did all the other times. That was my excuse to get away. Do you really think that my job would require me to be out as much as I was?"

Betrayal burned Matt's heart like hot coals.

He wanted to crawl into a hole and die. Never in any of his plans had he ever expected something like this.

"You were my friend," Matt hollered as tears began to form. "I *trusted* you."

"Trust is a valuable thing, Mr. Cross." Hudson picked his gun up off the table. "You should never fully trust anyone. That's the first rule of life I'm giving to you before your life ends."

Matt eyed Hudson's gun. "You won't kill me. You can't. Not after all we've talked about and been through."

Hudson sneered. "Rule number two: Don't form quick attachments."

Matt shook his head as disbelief began to fade. Hudson was the intruder all this time. It didn't seem possible.

"How did you know I was coming tonight?" Matt questioned.

"Hello?" Hudson replied. "You told me face to face at my house, remember?"

Matt bit his lip and jerked on his cuffs again, sending a shooting pain through his arm.

"What about Rose?" Matt asked. "Fears abused her. He was grabbing her and kissing her. She told me."

Hudson jumped up and raised the gun to Matt's head. Matt leaned back against the wall as much as he could and eyed the barrel between his eyes. Holding his breath, he watched Hudson's finger as it rested on the trigger.

"Stop lying to me, you *worthless* little —"

"I'm not lying," Matt yelled over him.

"She would have told me," Hudson continued. "I would never let that happen."

"She wouldn't have told you," Matt shouted back. "You were never around to listen to her."

"She loves me. I'm the only one that's ever been there for her."

Matt looked over the barrel of the gun and met Hudson's demented eyes. "I think you'll find that Rose will need a little persuading."

In a flash, Hudson's fist struck Matt's jaw causing his head to whip back and strike the concrete wall. Sharp pains pulsated through his head, and the taste of blood spilled into his mouth.

"She loves me," he said. "She *will* be happy."

Matt spat blood in Hudson's face. He was going to die anyway, he might as well go down hard. Hudson turned away and wiped the blood away with his mask, then turned and slammed his fist into Matt's abdomen.

The air escaped from his lungs and both legs collapsed from under him. The cuffs above his head caught his weight and he gave a short cry as they dug deeper into his wrists. Matt sputtered and coughed, through clenched eyes.

"Don't fight me, Mr. Cross," Hudson said. "I can make your death quick and easy or we can have some fun. What's it going to be?"

Matt tried to catch his breath, but Hudson smacked Matt's face on the injured cheek and sent another agonizing flash of pain through his face.

Matt had to take it. He'd signed up for it. When he stayed up making the plan … When he and Zeke practiced the stunt in the deserted parking lot … When he sat with the others strategizing … He knew this outcome was an option but he had hoped it would never become reality.

Somehow, Matt found the strength to straighten his legs and stand up, releasing some of the pressure from his wrists. He coughed as blood ran down his throat.

"Oh, so you're the brave one, huh?" Hudson asked. "You really want me to beat the life out of you before I end it?"

Hudson motioned to the numbers that were transferring. "Do you see that?"

The monitor showed the download was thirty-three percent complete.

"At one hundred percent, I pull the trigger," Hudson said. "Until then, let's see how brave you really are. I would like to have something to do while I wait."

He hit Matt on the side of his head with the butt of his gun and Matt's cries of agony echoed through the empty hallways.

Bruce flew through the high school drive to find an officer leaning over his engine tampering with something under his hood.

The officer spun around, adjusted his large framed glasses and shined his flashlight at the truck. He motioned for Bruce to stop. Bruce obeyed and jumped out of his truck.

"What seems to be the problem, officer?"

"Please, sir," the officer began, "get back in your truck. There is nothing here for you to see."

Bruce glanced through the back window of the car and saw the silhouette of Rose and Abby in the dim lighting.

"What are these girls doing here?"

"I'm not at liberty to —"

"I know them," Bruce exclaimed. "I came here for them."

He paused as he realized that he hadn't come for the girls but he'd take as many people as he could get. "Tell me what they did."

The officer sighed. "These girls are suspects in the break-ins that have been occurring at the school."

"I'm sorry, officer but I'm afraid ya' have the wrong people. I can't let ya' arrest them."

"Well, sir, this is a police matter and it's none your business to tell me who and who not to arrest."

Bruce straightened his shoulders. "I'm makin' it my business."

"Listen, pal, you wanna get rough with me?" Crawford asked as he pulled his nightstick from his belt. "I don't think it's in your best interest to get involved. I suggest you leave. *Now.*"

He motioned to Bruce's truck with his stick.

Bruce stood still. "I'm not goin' anywhere."

Crawford stepped forward and took a swing which Bruce ducked. Crawford swung again and Bruce stepped aside easily avoiding him. Officer Crawford pushed his glasses up on his face and swung once more.

This time, as Bruce stepped aside, he stuck his foot out tripping the officer and as Crawford started to fall, his precious glasses slipped from his face.

Crawford felt his face and cried out, "My glasses, I gotta have my glasses. Where did they go? I'm blind without them."

Bruce snatched Crawford's glasses from the pavement and watched as the officer kneeled, feeling the surrounding area. Peering through the lenses, he commented, "Man, you are blind."

"Did you find them?" Crawford asked as he stood.

Bruce turned away and slipped them into his pocket. "Nope."

Crawford tripped, fell on his knees and continued his search.

"Don't worry. I'll get you a new pair," Bruce said as he walked over and grabbed the keys from Crawford's belt.

"Hey, what are you –?" Crawford began as he felt his sidearm disappear from its holster as well.

"You can't do that!"

Going to the squad car, Bruce released Abby and Rose. Unlocking their handcuffs, he switched off the radio.

"Watch the officer," he told the girls. "We wouldn't want him getting into any more trouble tonight."

"You're under arrest," Crawford yelled from the pavement. "You're all under arrest!"

Bruce tucked the gun under his belt, turned and headed toward the school.

"We'll see."

Jake waited on the shoulder of Highway Sixty-six in the U-Haul truck, his blue cap pulled low over his eyes. He didn't mind waiting. Heck, he'd wait all night for this kind of payday.

Suddenly, Mo was in his earpiece.

"Jake? Zeke and Lily are almost there. Be ready for them."

Jake immediately jumped out of the U-Haul, went to the back and raised the door. He pulled a metallic ramp from inside and lowered it to the ground. Climbing back in the truck, he waited.

Soon from his side mirror, Jake saw Zeke approach with another car following behind him. Both cars pulled to the shoulder and Jake went to help. He hadn't expected Andrew to be with him. Since the events of the night had unfolded differently than expected, Zeke, Jake and Andrew discussed a new plan

Traveling down the road a bit, Andrew found a small darkened house. Andrew slowly drove his truck onto their property and hid it behind the house so it couldn't be seen from the highway. He figured he'd come back later and get it. Running back to the U-Haul truck, he jumped in the passenger seat.

Lily rode with Zeke as he drove his Nissan up the ramp and into the back of the U-Haul. Returning the ramp to the back of the truck, Jake closed the door, made a U-turn and headed back to the shop.

It wasn't long before Jake saw flashing lights in his side mirror as two squad cars raced up behind them. Jake's eyes darted from one mirror to the next and Andrew ducked down in the passenger seat. For an instant, Jake was worried but he snuffed out the feeling and pulled onto the shoulder of the road as the squad cars flew past. Jake waved to the officers as they flew by and on down the highway.

Andrew sat up again. "Too bad they're looking for a Nissan and a Chevy and all they can find is a U-Haul."

Jake looked at Andrew and the two laughed all the way back to the shop.

Hudson repeatedly punched Matt in the stomach then in his face, causing his eyebrow to split open. He kicked Matt's shins and smacked his face.

In between blows, Hudson laughed. It had become a sick game.

Matt's lips busted open, eyes were swollen shut and his legs were bruised and beaten making it difficult to stand. Pressure increased on his wrists from the handcuffs and blood trickled down his arm from the weight. Every time he took a breath, he felt a sharp pain in his side. He felt certain his ribs were broken.

When he tried to move his body to avoid a hit, it only hurt worse. He was too weak to fight and too weak to express his pain. Tears dripped down his face and fear dug in deep. He was going to die.

The computer screen flashed. The transfer was complete. Hudson looked at the computer, pulled out the jump drive out and viciously snickered.

"I know the time we spent together was short-lived, Mr. Cross, but I have what I came for. I'm sure you'd like to continue our little chat but I'm afraid that's not possible. It's time for me to go and your time as well."

He waved the jump drive in front of Matt's face and tapped it on top of his head.

"Look at this, Mr. Cross."

Matt head dangled aimlessly from his neck. He could no longer lift it.

"*Look* at this," Hudson snapped, grabbing Matt's head and slamming it back against the wall and holding it there. Unseeing, Matt peered through his swollen eyes.

"Do you see this jump drive, Mr. Cross?" Hudson asked. "This is what your death looks like. All this chaos for this little thing. If only you had this …"

Hudson put the jump drive in his pocket.

"Has Jesus saved you, Mr. Cross?" He let Matt's head drop again and clicked the safety off the gun.

Matt was silent.

"I hope so," Hudson went on, "because it would be quite a sight to see you in hell."

Jesus? Matt thought. If anyone could help him, it would have to be Jesus.

Jesus, please help …

He looked into the barrel of the 9mm and into the sick mind of his former friend.

Jesus, please. I'm sorry …

Hudson grinned as he placed his finger on the trigger.

Jesus, please. Help me …

"I'm afraid in the end, you are the one who loses," Hudson said. "Goodbye, Mr. Cross."

Matt opened his eyes, determined to face death and, instead, saw a shadow emerge from the sliver of light beneath the door. Matt blinked his swollen eyes and stared. Hudson started to turn.

"What are you –?" he began when the door flew open and collided with a stack of crates.

"Drop the gun," a familiar voice yelled. "Drop it, or I swear I'll blow you away."

Hudson grinned an awful grin and then, lowering his gun to the floor, he turned and faced the man.

"Put your hands behind your head," the man at the door said.

Matt recognized Bruce's voice.

Hudson casually lifted his arms like he didn't have a care in the world.

"Hudson?" Bruce asked in disbelief as though he hadn't seen him in years. "What are ya' doing here? What in the world do ya' think you're doing?"

Hudson spoke. "Well, well, if it isn't Bruce Cross. You two are related? Hmm ... interesting work of fate, is it not?"

He turned back toward Matt, "If only we had your father with us, we'd all be back together again."

He gave Matt a small wink and Matt frowned but there was little time to dwell on the comment.

"Time to go," Hudson whispered and, in a blink of an eye, he was on the floor with the gun in his hand.

A shot erupted from Bruce's gun but Hudson rolled behind a stack of crates. Before Bruce could react Hudson was on his feet firing at Bruce.

Bruce hit the floor hard and Matt heard the wind leave his body.

He lay motionless.

"Bruce ..." Matt muttered as he tugged on his cuffs again.

Hudson turned the barrel from Bruce and pointed it at Matt's head.

"This *is* the end of your story, Mr. Cross."

Matt watched Hudson's finger tighten on the trigger. Matt closed his eyes and ... heard a gunshot.

There was no pain.

Matt opened his eyes. Hudson grabbed him. His eyes stared into nothingness as he slid down Matt and onto the floor, blood spilling from a hole in his lower back.

Matt looked at Bruce, lying flat, arm outstretched with the smoking barrel still pointed at Hudson. He dropped the gun and it clattered on the floor.

In another minute, Bruce found the strength to stand, grab the keys from Hudson's belt and free Matt of the handcuffs.

Blood saturated Matt's body while Bruce, fighting the pain in his shoulder, held Matt and asked, "Are you all right?"

"Rose … Rose …" Matt whispered.

Bruce's lip trembled. "Matt … stay with me. Matt, you're gonna be all right. I promise."

Laying him on the cold floor, Bruce painfully removed his jacket and rested Matt's head on it. Crawling to Hudson, he pulled his arms behind his back and used Matt's handcuffs to hold them.

With what breath he had left, Matt tried to speak. "Bruce … jump drive … pocket"

Rolling Hudson over, Bruce grabbed the jump drive from Hudson's pocket.

"Bruce …" Matt whispered again.

Bruce knelt by his side.

"Yeah, bud?" He stroked Matt's head.

"Radio … the table."

Bruce stood and grabbed Matt's earpiece off the table.

"Here you go, bud."

Matt took it in his hands and depressed the button.

"Mo … You there?"

"Yeah, Matt," Mo exclaimed. "Where are you? What's going on?"

"I've got the proof," Matt's said allowing his head to fall back on Bruce's jacket. "We did it."

30

Within minutes, two ambulances had arrived and Matt and Hudson were lifted onto stretchers, both conscious but weak. Hudson didn't speak. He winced every now and then but was otherwise silent.

"Make sure … you get … Rose and Abby," Matt said from his stretcher.

Bruce nodded. "Don't worry. I've taken care of them."

As the paramedics opened the front door and carried the stretchers outside, the girls rushed over to help.

Abby was the first to arrive. "Are they okay?"

Bruce looked away and was silent. Hudson turned his face away from the girls.

"Wait …" Abby said. "That's … that's not Fears."

Abby tried to get a good look at the man's face. As it all became clear, she gasped throwing her hand over her mouth.

"What?" Rose asked as she approached.

"It's —" Abby began but didn't finish.

Rose stopped. Her face blanched as she realized who lay there. "Dad?"

As Bruce explained what had happened in the school, Rose shook her head and backed up, her hand to her mouth.

Then her emotion exploded out of her like a rocket. Rushing to his stretcher, she shouted, "Tell me it's not true, Dad!"

Tears rolled down her face. "It's not true, is it?"

Hudson didn't make eye contact at first and then, at last, he raised his eyes. Rose jumped back in fear. This man was not her father. Her father had a caring, loving spirit. This man had a wicked fire burning in his eyes. His cheeks sunk into his skull making him look as though he'd been on a hunger strike for weeks. Blood had dried on his hands, face and chest.

"It can't be," she cried. "It can't be!"

She jumped at her father, preparing to smack him. Wincing in pain, Bruce managed to stop her.

"Rose, don't," Bruce cried but she never heard him.

"Tell me it's not true, Dad," she howled in anguish. "*Tell* me!"

The paramedics continued to wheel both Matt and Hudson toward the ambulance.

Rose screamed through tears of pain as she followed behind the stretchers. Bruce motioned for Abby to come and comfort her while he went to get checked for any serious injuries before the paramedics started for the hospital. He also needed to speak with Officer Crawford.

Bruce found Crawford standing next to the building, looking bewildered. He pulled the officer's glasses out of his pocket and placed them in Crawford's hands.

"I found your glasses," he said.

"Yes, there they are," Crawford exclaimed. "Thanks."

Officer Crawford placed his glasses back on his nose and Bruce pointed at Hudson.

"If you want the real intruder who's been stealing taxes from the school, it's him. Come on. I'll prove it."

Together, they went to find Matt.

As Matt barely managed to explain what had happened in the school, he could hear Rose sobbing in the distance. He longed to hold and comfort her but now was not the time.

"Well, I've still got a lot of questions," Crawford said. "But, we can take care of that later. We need to get your medical attention taken care of first."

Crawford stepped back and Matt asked if Rose could ride with him.

She was all alone now.

The paramedics and Bruce agreed and the ambulance finally pulled out of the parking lot.

At the Emergency Room, the doctors tended to Matt and Bruce's injuries while Crawford questioned the two of them again. One of the nurses was sewing up Bruce's flesh wound on his left arm and he flinched in pain.

"Hey, easy does it with the fingertips there, sweetheart. I'm gonna need this arm again someday."

"I'm sorry, sir," she replied. "I hope you know how lucky you are. If the bullet had entered your arm half an inch lower, you'd be in surgery. I'll be right back." She smiled and left the room.

Bruce rolled his eyes and looked at Matt. "I get shot and she thinks I should feel lucky."

Matt smiled as though he'd never smiled before in his life.

Just then Mary frantically dashed into the room. "Oh, dear God. Matthew! Look at your face. What on earth happened?"

"It's not as bad as it looks, Mom. Really."

"I've taken way too many trips to the hospital in one month," Mary continued. "I don't like this. I don't like this at all."

"Mom, I'm really am –" Matt began.

"How did this happen?" Mary interrupted. "You told me you had homework and needed to stay home tonight. This didn't happen at home, did it? I knew I should have made you come to the hospital with me."

"No, Mom. It's kind of a long story."

Matt felt exhausted. He didn't want to relive the night again.

"So," Crawford prompted, "after you knocked the power out, you went to the office. Then you went from the office to the furnace room? Why?"

Matt reluctantly continued, "The computer was –"

"You were at *school*?" Mary asked. "What in the –"

Sheriff Stronson stormed into the room with Dr. Pierce close behind him. "Would someone please tell me what the heck happened here?"

Crawford stood a bit straighter and stepped forward. "Uh, sir … I think I should be the first to take full responsibility for –"

"Savin' us," Bruce interrupted.

Stronson turned to Bruce. "What? Saving you?"

"Yeah, Officer Crawford here saved us. If it weren't for him, we might not have made it out alive."

Mary looked from Matt to Bruce to Sheriff Stronson and back to Matt in utter confusion.

A look of surprise crossed Stronson's face as he turned to Crawford. "Really?"

"Yeah," Matt added. "He saved me when Hudson was about to shoot me. He shot Hudson with his own gun and everything."

"Gun?" Mary asked.

Bruce pointed to his bandaged arm. "What do ya' think did this, babe? An arrow?"

"Bruce," Mary exclaimed. "You've been shot."

"Oh man," Bruce replied. "Is that what that pain is?"

Mary gave him a slap on his other arm.

"There goes my pity for you," she said with a smirk on her face.

Stronson put his hand on Crawford's shoulder. "Well, Crawford," he said, "It looks like we're going to have to talk promotion, doesn't it?"

Crawford's jaw dropped unable to speak.

"Crawford?" Stronson said again.

Crawford's eyes jerked open as he came back to reality. He looked from Bruce to Stronson.

"Ye – yes, sir. Uh – thank you, sir."

"Well, come on, Crawford," Stronson said. "I've got a couple officers with me who can keep on eye on these guys. How about we head down to the station and discuss that promotion?"

Stronson turned and led the way out of the room. Crawford followed as far the door then turned, stepped back into the room and mouthed, "Thank you" to Matt and Bruce.

"We can just forget that little incident in the school parking lot, right?" Bruce asked.

"What incident?" Crawford smiled as he trailed off after Stronson.

"Yeah, what incident?" Mary inquired.

Bruce shook his head and taking Mary by the arm led her into the hall to tell her what had happened.

HILLS

Dr. Pierce came in, sat down next to Matt and eyed his injuries. Matt's face was severely beaten and bruised. Both of his eyes were nearly swollen shut. His left eyebrow, lips and wrists had all required stitches. The nurses had wrapped his ribs, which fortunately, were not broken. He was under strict orders to refrain from strenuous activity for quite a while.

"My gosh …" Dr. Pierce said. "Why did you do all this, Matt?"

He sighed. "It's complicated."

"You are a bright student. Why did you feel the need to get involved in all this? You threw your life away."

"I wasn't throwing my life away," Matt replied.

"What were you doing, then?"

"A really smart guy told me once that 'no matter how good we think we are, we can always get better'."

Dr. Pierce's face flushed.

Matt went on, "Hills West is a great school but there were a few little things that needed to be fixed, actually, a few *major* things. Now they're fixed. Now Hills West can be all it is supposed to be. You don't have to worry about intruders and guards anymore. The school is better now."

Dr. Pierce's took a deep breath. "You're right. And it's getting better as we speak."

"What do you mean?"

Dr. Pierce ran his fingers through his hair. "I just got a call from Scott Fears, the assistant principal. He's resigning."

Matt's eyes stared at Dr. Pierce for a moment in shock.

"Wow … wha – did he say why?"

"No, but he did say he was going to leave as soon as possible. I figured his decision had something to do with all of this mess. Do you know if he was involved with the break-ins at the school?"

"Well, he –" Matt stopped himself and thought a moment.

If he told Dr. Pierce, what Fears had done to Rose then the school would remove Fears, whereas if Fears resigned free and clear then Matt wouldn't have to tell Dr. Pierce about Rose and Fears would still be gone. It would have to be Rose's decision as to whether or not to report Fears.

"No," Matt said. "Fears didn't do anything to the school."

"Are you sure? How do you know that?"

"Hudson worked alone. He told me."

"Okay. Enough said," Dr. Pierce nodded. "I want to thank you again for what you did. You are right, the school is a better place now and you have no idea how grateful I am for that. Now the punishment for breaking –"

Matt's jaw dropped. Punishment? After that nice, little speech?

Dr. Pierce's expression turned to a smile. "I wouldn't worry about it, Matt."

Matt's shoulders relaxed and he sighed with relief.

Dr. Pierce rose. "Okay, enough discussion, then. I gotta go now and let you get some rest. I'll get back to you when the board decides what to do. Take care kid, you did well."

Matt gave a small wave as Dr. Pierce left the room.

Mary and Bruce had returned from the hall waiting for Dr. Pierce to leave.

Mary sat next to Matt with a sorrowful look on her face. "Matthew …" Her voice trailed into silence. Finally, she looked at him with the bare beginnings of a twinkle in her eyes. "I'm not sure what to do with – you're punishment I mean."

"A car would be nice."

"I was thinking more in the realm of being grounded."

"What? Mom … for how long?"

"I don't know. I don't really care but as a Mom, I'm supposed to say things like that. What you did was dangerous. You could have been killed. However, I do think you've taken enough abuse for one night, so surely, you don't want any more from me."

Matt sighed and leaned back. "Thank God. I don't know how much more of this I could take."

About an hour later, the police allowed everyone to leave.

Dr. Pierce soon informed Matt and the team that expulsion was not to be part of their punishment. However, it was made clear they would have to do some kind of community service.

Hudson was a different story. The officers had taken the jump drive down to the station and the evidence was clear. Hudson had broken into the school and had attempted to steal over three million dollars, not counting how much he'd taken already. Hudson would recover from the gunshot wound and be charged with breaking and entering, attempted theft and attempted murder. When released from the hospital, he would go to jail to await trial.

What Rose had discovered about her dad seemed to make her crazy.

For several long hours, she'd sat in the truck alone refusing to speak with anyone. Bruce told the police he and Mary would keep Rose until they contacted her grandmother in Hills East and got things squared away. Eventually, Bruce and Mary talked to her and helped her to realize that she had good friends to help her through this.

With everyone patched up, Bruce took Matt, Rose and Abby all back to Zeke's shop. Arriving at the shop, the group bombarded Matt and Abby with the same questions they had just answered at the hospital. Rose again huddled in her shell and refused to get out of Bruce's truck. Matt was happy that they'd actually pulled off the heist and discovered the truth, but he couldn't feel the happiness that the others expressed. He wished it'd had a different outcome. Everyone talked in a group for a few minutes relaying their adventures to one another.

"So tell us, Matt," Andrew said. "What did Hudson say when you were in the school with him?"

Matt stopped. Whatever happened in that room would stay in that room for the rest of his life. He wasn't about to relive that nightmare.

Matt shook his head. "We didn't talk."

Matt needed rest. He was tired of all this, tired of life in general. He needed a moment to breathe. He imagined it was only he and Rose that weren't excited about the outcome of the chain of events.

His grief for Rose was great. Her life would never be the same.

Matt shook his head.

"No, we didn't talk at all."

No one argued.

After a long talk, they all decided to part ways and go home. On the way home, Rose fell asleep on Matt's shoulder.

Matt leaned back in the seat and smiled for the first time in what seemed ages when he saw the beautiful sunrise stretch across the horizon. The whites and greens radiating off the purples and blues created a beautiful masterpiece in the sky.

Matt hadn't forgotten what Jesus did for him back in that furnace room. He didn't think he could ever forget.

Matt opened his eyes from a deep sleep.

His mother sat on the bed watching him. She smiled. "Hey there, tough guy."

Matt blinked and sat up a little. "Hey."

"How do you feel?"

"Tired. Sore …" He tried to come up with other words to describe what he felt. "Yeah, tired and sore pretty much sums it up."

"Well, with some rest, I'm sure you'll be okay. Is there anything I can get you?"

"Where's Rose?"

"She's sleeping."

"How's she doing?"

"She's …" Mary struggled to find the right word to describe her. "She's *managing*. This is going to be very hard for her. We've got to support her through this."

"Where's she going to go?"

"I tried calling her grandmother."

"And?"

"I didn't get an answer."

"Is that a problem?"

"Well, I guess not. She can stay here as long as she needs to but she can't stay forever."

"You took Jesse in."

"Yes, but that's because he had no one else."

"His parents are –"

"Matt," she interrupted. "You don't have to lie for him. I know that he probably won't be leaving here for a while."

Matt nodded.

Silence.

"Plus," his mom went on, "it's probably not a good idea to have you and Rose living in such close quarters."

"Mom …" Matt sighed and shook his head.

"Well, it's true. You're still a couple. I've got to keep an eye on you two. Don't think that I wasn't your age once."

"It doesn't matter now anyway," Matt said.

"What do you mean?"

"I don't think things will ever be quite the same between us. I think she might be upset with me. I mean, I caught her father and now he's going to jail. It's my fault."

"This in no way is your fault, Matthew Cross. Mr. Hudson is a grown man. He made his own choices. You did the right thing."

"You think so?"

"Well … sort of, no, not really. It was just so dangerous. You should have told me or something."

Matt smiled. "I love you, Mom."

"I love you, too, sweetheart. Now go back to sleep. When you wake up, I'll make you some something."

Mary stood and closed the door quietly behind her.

Matt sighed. He was awake now. It would be difficult to get back to sleep. He reached for his father's leather journal resting on his nightstand and opened it.

> *February 12, 1984*
>
> *Dear Journal,*
>
> *After six months of being without women, I met someone. We went out on our first date last week, and I was unsure if I wanted to remember it. So I left it out of this journal. Now I realize that I really like her, and she likes me. I definitely want to remember her.*
>
> *Her name is Mary Cole. We met last week at the soda machine after lunch.*

I was walking down the hall, and I saw her put her money in but her soda wouldn't come, so she shook and kicked the machine. She was becoming very aggravated by all this. I could tell that she desperately wanted a soda by the way she was beating the machine. So I went behind her and put my hands on her shoulders. She stopped and turned toward me.

I said, "Settle down. You're doing it wrong."

Then I went to the side of the machine and tipped it slightly, and her soda fell to the bottom. She smiled as she took it.

"I'm Brian, by the way," I said.

"Mary."

Then for whatever reason, I decided to be bold. "So what are you doing?"

"Drinking a soda," she replied and turned to walk away.

I caught up with her, and we continued walking. "I mean tonight."

"Are you ... are you asking me out on a date?"

"Well, do you have a boyfriend?"

"Well, no. Actually, I just broke up with my boyfriend a few days ago. I'm really not looking for a relationship right now."

"Good. Neither am I, but I've got this feeling that I'm going to be thirsty as heck tonight. I'll probably be at Fiddles tonight around eight. If you happen to have an unquenchable thirst about that time, I'll be there."

She smiled. "I'll think about it."

"You do that. Enjoy your soda."

Later that night, I waited by myself in a booth at Fiddles. It was five after eight and I was beginning to think she wasn't coming. I'd already had two sodas brought to the table.

Then Mary walked in with her long, dark hair. She truly is beautiful. It's a wonder I'd never noticed her before.

She sat down and thanked me for the soda. We didn't get anything to eat. We simply ordered more and more soda. By the end of the conversation, it was nearly ten o'clock, and we'd had eight sodas between us.

She began talking about her ex-boyfriend, Scott. I didn't want to talk about him, but she brought him up. I was a little uneasy about the whole situation, because I didn't know the guy. I talked with her about him anyway. She said she broke up with him because he was crazy. I thought that was a little odd, but maybe it's just me.

"What exactly are you looking for in a guy?" I asked her.

"I want someone who I can talk to and have fun with. I want someone who can support me and our kids."

"You want kids?"

"Oh, yeah, I love kids."

"How many kids do you want?" I asked.

"Three. I want a boy first, though."

"Any reason?"

"Not really. I just think I need to start out with a boy."

"What else do you look for in a guy?"

"He has to make me laugh. He has to have handsome eyes. I'm a sucker for the eyes. He needs to be skilled in whatever he does. I don't want to marry an idiot."

"There's a lot of people who'd fit that description," I said.

"Well, I'm having a hard time trying to find someone."

"What if you did?" I asked.

"What?"

"What if you found someone who fit that description?"

"Then, I'd be with that person."

"Really?"

"Yes," she said.

"It's that simple?"

"Yes. Why wouldn't it be?"

"Just asking."

According to Mary's requirements, I am a good guy for her. I don't know much about her, I'm learning more and more every time we get together. I think if we end up together, I'll be happy. I'm thinking that she'll be happy, too. That's really all I want for her. That's what keeps me going. I want her to be happy.

Brian Cross

Matt looked up from the journal. That's what Dad wanted. He wanted Mom to be happy. He read the entry again and said to himself, "That's what keeps him going."

Matt started down the stairs but stopped when he heard voices. He peeked around the corner and could see his mom reading on the couch while Bruce sat on the leather chair reading the paper, his arm in a sling.

Matt sat down on the stairs, out of sight, and listened to them talk.

"Matt didn't make today's paper." Paper rustled as Bruce laid it on the table. "I guess news doesn't travel that fast."

"It will," Mary replied.

"Will that be a good thing though?" Bruce asked. "Does Matt want everyone to know exactly what happened last night? I mean it was pretty personal and intense."

"They can only print what he tells them," Mary responded.

"Yeah, I guess you're right but still, I'm lookin' forward to seein' the headlines. You should've heard the stories those kids were tellin' about this whole thing. They were crawlin' through vents and racin' trains ..."

"All the more reason to keep a closer eye on Matt and his friends," Mary said.

"Yeah, you're right," Bruce admitted. "But you've gotta admit, it was kinda cool."

Matt smirked on the stairs. He heard Bruce rise from the chair.

"I'm gonna make some lunch," Bruce said. "Do ya' want anythin'?"

"I'll get it," she said.

Matt heard her rise from the couch as well.

"You're hurt," she said. "Why would you –?"

"No, no," Bruce interrupted. "I'm already up. Do ya' want something?"

"It's almost five o' clock," Mary said,

"Yeah, so? You can have lunch anytime ya' want. Ya' want somethin'?"

There was silence and then Matt heard Bruce head for the kitchen. Without a word, Matt descended down the stairs and sat beside his mother.

Mary put her book down, removed her reading glasses and looked at her son. His lips were still swollen and purple and his right eye was a deep red, even though the swelling had gone down some. Mary reached up and ran her fingers through his shaggy hair.

"Oh, sweetie …" She gave him a gentle kiss on the forehead. "I'm so glad you're okay."

Matt rested a moment in her arms until he got the nerve to ask her a question he'd been wondering about for some time. "Mom," he said. "Do you like Bruce?"

Mary paused and looked at her son. "Do I what?"

"Do you like Bruce?"

She thought a moment.

"Well, he's a great guy. He's sociable and fun to –"

"You know what I mean, Mom," he said. "Do you *like* him?"

"So what if I did?" she asked. "What if I did, you know … like him?"

"You guys went out on a date, didn't you?" Matt asked. "You said you had a good time, didn't you?"

Mary smiled. "Yeah."

"Why don't you go out with him again?"

Mary raised her eyebrows in surprise. "What?"

"You should go out with him again," Matt said. "If it doesn't work, you'll know you tried. If it does, you'll have someone."

"Why does it matter?"

"Because, Mom, it's been a long time since I've seen you really happy. Since Dad died, you've tried so hard to carry the load of both parents. What if you had someone you loved and someone who cared for the both of us? Think how much happier you would be."

A lump swelled in her throat. Mary had dreamed of such a life but she'd never thought it would become a reality.

"Do you think Bruce is a good guy for me?" she asked.

"What do you think, Mom?" he replied. "*Is* he a good guy for you?"

She thought a moment. "We'll have to see, won't we?"

Matt nodded and he leaned into his mother's arms.

A few moments later he heard her ask, "Why have you taken to Bruce so well all of the sudden?"

Matt sat up. "There's just something about someone who can come in when you have no hope left and save your life. He did it for me. He deserves to be happy. If that means that he can date you then …"

"Okay," she said. "Go upstairs and wake Rose. We're going to go see Jesse. He's out of his coma, did you know?"

Matt's spirits lifted. "He is?"

"Yeah," she replied. "Go get dressed and we'll go see him in a little bit. I'll tell you all about it on the way."

Matt quickly jumped off the couch, stopped and winced in pain.

"I'm okay," he breathed. "I'll just be …" He pointed upstairs and carefully made his way to his room.

Mary shook her head and went into the kitchen. When she turned the corner, she found Bruce spreading mayonnaise on his sandwich. He looked at her and grinned.

"Oh, hey," he said. "Did you change your mind? I've got some more salami and some —"

Mary softly put her finger on his lips. "Shh."

She stepped in close, put her hands on his hips and looked up into his eyes.

"I wanted to thank you for what you did today," she said. "You really did save him."

She eyed his sling. "You're a tough guy to be in the kitchen fixing a sandwich after getting shot."

"Ah," he brushed it off. "It just skimmed the surface. I was just —"

She hushed him by giving him a long, soft kiss.

When their kissing slowed to a stop, Bruce raised his eyebrows and asked, "Would ya' like to go out again sometime?"

Mary smiled and kissed him again.

Bruce grinned. "You're not sure. That's fine. I understand."

Mary blushed and gently smacked his hurt arm.

He winced in pain.

"Oh, I'm so sorry!" she cried as she reached for his arm.

A brilliant white light radiated in from Jesse's window in his hospital room. Jesse was reading the Bible when he heard a gentle knock at the door. When Matt, Rose, Mary and Bruce walked in, Jesse's face brightened.

"Hey." Jesse shut the book. "How are you guys? You're — oh …"

He hadn't expected to see Matt in such bad shape. Matt sat down beside Jesse's bed.

"I'm better now that you're awake," Matt said.

"Wow, Matt …" Jesse mumbled. "Gosh … What did you do to yourself? I leave you for three days and you tear yourself apart?"

Jesse pushed himself up his bed and extended his hand. Matt reached out and took his hand. A cold tingle passed through his body.

"You have to tell me everything," Jesse said.

Matt sighed and he spent the next hour retelling the entire story, answering Jesse's questions as he went along. Mary and Bruce listened to the story but Rose excused herself to the bathroom. She didn't come back for a long time.

"I felt terrible when you ran away, Jesse," Matt said. "I'm *really* sorry."

"I forgive you," Jesse replied. "I guess we understand each other now. You barely made it through and there were people that got hurt in the process." He motioned toward the bathroom door.

Matt knew he was talking about Rose. "You're right," he said.

There was a moment of silence then Jesse looked at Mary. "Can I come home now?"

That night, Matt and Rose relaxed in the living room, each with a bowl of ice cream. Matt was flipping through the channels to see if anyone had covered the story of his break-in.

"What are you doing?" Rose asked.

"What? Nothing."

"You're looking for the news channels, aren't you?"

"Maybe."

"You want to see us on TV, don't you?"

"I don't know."

Rose set her bowl down. "Who cares? Gimme that remote."

She jumped on him and reached for the remote.

"Wait!" Matt exclaimed, thinking that it would hurt to wrestle. However, surprisingly it didn't hurt at all. "Well, never mind."

Before long, the two of them were wrestling on the couch over the remote, which had fallen to the floor and out of sight.

The phone rang.

Mary answered it. "Hello? … One moment, please."

Mary interrupted Matt and Rose's feud and handed Matt the phone.

Rose leapt onto the floor, grabbed the remote and dashed back to the couch on the other side of the living room. She changed channels while Matt took the call.

"Hello?" he said.

"Is this Matthew Cross?"

"Yes."

"My name is Angelina Williams. You might have heard of my husband, Clarence Williams, who was a teacher at Hills West and passed away two years ago."

Matt sat up in his seat. "Uh, yes, ma'am."

"Clarence left much of his money to the school. Unfortunately his efforts to improve the school were destroyed by the intruder. I've heard that you and your friends have managed to apprehend this intruder. Is that true?"

"Yeah, uh – yes!" Matt stammered. "That is correct!"

"Well, I wanted to thank you for your efforts. I will meet you at the trial and I can personally thank you there. However, I wanted to discuss the reward that was issued for this intruder's conviction. Are you aware of this award?"

"Uh – yes! Yes, I am!"

"Did you hear the reward reached the sum of one hundred thousand dollars?" Mrs. Williams asked.

"Yes, I did."

"Well, I'm sure you and your friends could use a little extra cash, so I have decided to add twenty thousand dollars to the reward I had previously stated."

Matt couldn't believe his ears. "Well, th – thank you! That's very, uh, kind of you!" He pulled out a pen and quickly did the math. Each of them would make fifteen thousand dollars!

"I will give you your check after the hearing if this man is convicted." She lowered her voice a bit. "But judging from the evidence, convicting him shouldn't be a problem."

Matt beamed. "Yes, ma'am. I understand."

"Well, you have a good evening now," Mrs. Williams said. "I'll see you at the trial."

"I'll see you then. Goodbye."

When Matt hung up, he threw his arms into the air and whooped. He stopped and reached back to his ribs expecting a sharp pain but, there wasn't one. There was only the dull pain that he'd had all along.

Matt brushed these thoughts aside when Rose looked up and asked, "What? What is it?"

"Mrs. Williams increased the reward. She added twenty thousand to the total! Can you believe it?" Matt exclaimed. "One hundred and twenty thousand!"

He gave her a fat kiss and was again surprised when his lips didn't throb with pain.

"Mom! Bruce!" he excitedly hollered throughout the house. "We can keep the house! Mom!"

Rose managed a weak smile as Matt dashed into the next room. She turned away from him and wiped away another tear. She ran her fingers through her long hair, collapsed back down on the couch, and gave a long sigh. She didn't know what would come of her future. She didn't think she wanted to find out.

The next day, Matt went to see Mr. Parish. He knocked on his doorframe and Mr. Parish looked up.

"Matthew. Come in, come in," he ushered. "Have a seat. You're right on time. I'm nearly finished with this puzzle and I could use some help with it."

Matt sat down and began scanning the puzzle. He'd noticed that his puzzling skills had gotten better after his many visits with Mr. Parish.

Mr. Parish pushed the newspaper across the table. "I saw that you made the front page, Matthew. You must be very proud of yourself."

Matt shrugged. "Yeah, I suppose." He reached over, picked up the paper and read the article.

After Matt finished, Mr. Parish asked, "Do you want to tell me about it?"

Matt then proceeded to tell Mr. Parish everything that had happened on Sunday night. Mr. Parish listened as he worked his puzzle.

"... and I ended up not getting expelled and that's pretty much it."

"Are you okay?"

"I got stitches on my lips, eyebrow and both wrists. I got some bruised ribs, but otherwise I'm okay."

Mr. Parish glanced at Matt's face. "Your face sure looks fine to me."

Matt paused. "What?"

"Your face. It looks fine. I don't see any stitches or a busted lip or anything like what you're talking about."

"Oh, ha, ha, very funny," Matt said. "Like my face doesn't look beaten up or anything. Yeah, right."

"Your face is fine, really," Mr. Parish replied. "Go look in the mirror."

Matt stood and went into the bathroom. To his complete surprise, the scratches on his face were gone. Everything was gone. He grabbed his bottom lip, squeezed it and waited for the pain.

Nothing.

He stretched his arms over his head and cautiously hopped in the air. His ribs felt fine. Mr. Parish was right. He not only looked fine but felt that way too.

"Mr. Parish," Matt exclaimed as he came back into the room. "I look great."

"I told you," he said.

"No, no. You don't understand, I looked *terrible* yesterday."

Mr. Parish looked up at him from the table.

"Well, thank the Lord Almighty. Miracles still happen."

Matt sat down. He couldn't believe it. He'd healed almost as fast as —

"So did you have a punishment for all the stuff you did?" Mr. Parish asked interrupting Matt's thoughts. "Or did you get off totally clean?"

"Well, they say I'm probably going to have to do some community service."

Mr. Parish grinned without looking from the puzzle.

"That means you'll have to come and visit me some more, right?"

Matt smiled. "Yeah, and that's hardly a punishment."

After a few moments of concentrating on the puzzle, Matt asked, "Mr. Parish?"

"Hmm?"

"Hudson spoke of getting saved. Just before he was going to shoot me, he said 'I hope Jesus saved you' or something like that. And I prayed to Jesus, well, I think I prayed anyway. I hadn't really prayed by myself before so I wasn't sure how it went but after I did, my uncle came in and saved me."

Mr. Parish smiled and looked up from his puzzle. He looked Matt directly in the eyes. "You want to know what it means to be saved?"

Matt nodded and stuck another piece in the puzzle.

"You see?" Mr. Parish said. "It was just as I said before. This was all part of an elaborate wake up call for you. If this hadn't happened, we wouldn't be here right now discussing this. It's like Romans Eight Twenty-eight, '… All things work together for the good of those who love God and are called according to his purpose.'"

Matt smiled. He had prayed with Mr. Parish for Jesus to forgive him. He knew he shouldn't have taken matters into his own hands, gotten involved and gotten into trouble. But maybe everything did happen for a reason. Even though things didn't quite work out the way he had planned, maybe it had worked out according to God's plan.

"But that isn't all there is to it, is it?" Matt reached over and put the last piece in the puzzle.

Mr. Parish smiled.

"No, it doesn't have to end there, it's only the beginning. With that said, would you like to know more about Jesus?"

"Many are the plans in a man's heart,

but it is the LORD's purpose that prevails."

– Proverbs 19:21
NIV

ACKNOWLEDGEMENTS

God has had such a profound impact on this book and on my life. Without His endurance, I would have never been able to complete this novel in the time allotted. It wasn't until the summer of 2005 that I really felt called to finish *Hills*. It was God that opened every door for me. I give all my thanks to Him.

My parents and sister, Rich, Darla, and Andrea Statler were always there when I needed them.

Thanks Dad for all of your great ideas whenever I got stuck in my own story. You helped to inspire Zeke, Andrew, and Lily's race across the train tracks and Neil's sermon. Without your ideas, these parts of the story wouldn't have made it to print.

Mom, I'd like to thank you for stepping up to the plate when I told you that *Hills* was nearing completion. You immediately began researching publishers and marketing strategies to get this book moving. I really appreciate you and everything you do.

To Andrea, my younger sister. Even though I kicked you out of the office on numerous occasions (and still do), I want you to know I still love you. Please continue with your writing, singing, dancing, and acting. I believe in you and know that with God you will one day be all that you can be.

To my grandparents – Lola and Clarence Hamman and Velma Statler. To my aunts and uncles – Al and Cindy Callahan, Ron and Phyllis James, and Nick and Donna Statler. To my cousins – Alissa Callahan and Jay Stienbroner, Chris, Amy and Felix James, Phillip James, and Sarah and Scott Statler. To my godparents – Skip and Lisa Gerstner. All of you have been encouraging and enthusiastic about my writing. Thank you all for your continued support and prayers. I know I would not be where I am today without your constant support. I love you guys.

To my best friend, Michael "Eugene" Stone, who was beside me through every chapter. Thank you for making the countless trips to my house to talk about the words on these pages even when at times we felt there was no way to pull off this type of heist. I'm going to miss you when run off to become a Marine. "Fare ye well, Michael."

I'd like to also thank my previous youth pastor, Andy McFarland. I remember how we would sit outside after church and discuss the moral dilemma of breaking into a school to stop someone else from breaking into a school. I know your schedule was pretty tight sometimes. Much of your wisdom was put into Mr. Parish's character. Thank you, Andy, for making time for me and always being supportive.

To my friend Katy King who for many months took most of the heat from this book. I know your patience may have run thin when I couldn't peel myself from my computer. You have been a great supporter of mine. Thank you for your help and constant encouragement.

Jackie Burress also had a significant impact on this book. Thank you, Jackie, for reading through the many chapters. You inspired many different stories in this book and books to come. Thank you for being there for me when I needed you most. I enjoyed the balance and the company. I pray this encouragement will continue into the future.

I'd like to thank my editors, Michael Huskey, Debbie Wilson, Sharon Tricamo, and Dorry Pease each in turn.

My special thanks go out to Michael Huskey, my English teacher, which I had the pleasure of learning from for five semesters. Thank you for putting up with me and supporting me throughout our time together. You taught me that, "Crickets don't chirp in January" among many other things. You are an amazing teacher, Mr. Huskey. You have no idea what kind of impact you have had on my life.

Thank you, Debbie, for reading *Hills* with such enthusiasm. Your smile and encouraging ideas really helped inspire Brian's journal entries. It was your excitement that really motivated me to keep pressing on through the long editing process. I really appreciate everything you did for me.

Sharon, on numerous occasions you sat with me to discuss the book and to help with our marketing strategies. I enjoyed our conversations and will remember your kind words and thoughts about the issues involving the timeline of the story. Thank you, your comments were very helpful.

Dorry, you have read this book almost as many times as I have. Thank you for the demanding work and sleepless nights you've put into this work. Your wisdom and writing techniques have helped to make *Hills* everything I hoped it would be. There is no way I can express my gratitude.

I'd like to thank the Thebeau family – Chris, Tina, Christina, and Jake. You were all very supportive from the beginning. Mrs. Thebeau was actually the sole person that inspired this whole project. I'd like to thank Mrs. Thebeau and Christina for meeting with me to take pictures for the cover and the web site. I really appreciate everything you all have done.

Thank you Matt Redman and Billy Barton for helping me make chadstatler.com. I know that without your expertise in this matter, I would be without a brilliant web page. You guys are great. Keep up the good work.

My church family at Farmington, MO has always been supportive. A very special thanks goes out to them for being there for me. Much of Matt's youth pastor, Neil, was inspired by my youth director Dave Shepard. You really are a great guy, Dave. Keep smiling.

The Writer's Society of Jefferson County helped me in many ways and I pray that the members of that group will continue to be as supportive as they have been these past few months.

How could I forget all of those in my "little, black book?" The little, black book almost became a competition or game among my friends. People would constantly say something interesting, funny, or thought provoking with hopes that their quote would be added to the little black book.

In *Hills*, numerous quotes were used from people all around me. Some quotes are attributed to Michael Huskey, Rich Statler, Jackie Burress, and Holly Pfeiffer. I already have great ideas for my next installment of this story, titled *"Found."* Some of the new story line has been spurred from the quotes sitting in the pages of my "little, black book." For all those who were quoted in *Hills* and who may be quoted in subsequent writings, I thank you. Please keep those creative juices flowing.

Once again, I thank God. I know this is just the beginning of what He has in store for my life. I can't wait to write the next book and hopefully impact someone's life that may be lost or confused. If I have touched just one lost soul, then I have done my job and am honored to be part of God's masterful plan.

Thank you, Jesus.

Order Chad's Personal Story Today …

"BETWEEN THE LINES"

BETWEEN THE LINES is Chad's personal story on how at age five he began writing for fun never knowing God would one day turn his Ninja Turtle doodles into a passion for writing and ultimately a Christian novel for the world to enjoy.

In great detail Chad shares how he accepted this challenge and stayed motivated through the years in order to see it to completion.

Learn what obstacles he overcame and how he persevered to make this dream a reality before High School graduation in May 2006.

Full of lively stories and moving motivation, **BETWEEN THE LINES** is a wonderful addition to HILLS. A must read for all ages who wish to be encouraged and inspired by this young Christian author.

Available Only Through Chad's Web Site

A final note: Learn today how you can schedule Chad to speak at your group. Don't miss this opportunity to meet Chad and hear him share how God continues to use him and how God wants to use you too. Log onto his web site to learn more.

www.chadstatler.com

Printed in the United States
46509LVS00004B/88-255